Praise for Kara Isaac's *C*

"A fabulous debut. Well-written, clever, and warmhearted, this love story with the backdrop of *Lord of the Rings* will delight romance readers everywhere. Add Isaac to your favorites list."

—Rachel Hauck, *USA Today* bestselling author of *The Wedding Chapel*

"Kara Isaac is a fresh new voice in inspirational contemporary romance! *Close to You* is well-crafted, funny, unique, and endearing. A delight!"

—Becky Wade, author of *A Love Like Ours*

"Well-written and fun, *Close to You* made me laugh out loud and fall in love. An enchanting romantic escape into the land of Frodo and Aragorn."

—Susan May Warren, award-winning, bestselling author of the Christiansen Family series

"I can't remember the last time I enjoyed a debut novel so much. *Close to You* is filled with warmth, wit, and more than a few laugh-out-loud moments! Kara Isaac has proven herself to be an exciting addition to the world of Christian romance."

—Carla Laureano, RITA Award–winning author of *Five Days in Skye* and *Under Scottish Stars*

"*Close to You* is a tasty blend of unlikely romance, lovably flawed characters, and dialogue just snarky enough to make me want to pull up a chair and watch. Kara's unique voice and fresh premise combine to create a compelling story that lingers like your favorite dessert long after the last page."

—Betsy St. Amant, author of *All's Fair in Love and Cupcakes* and *Love Arrives in Pieces*

"Kara Isaac is a fresh new voice in the world of inspirational contemporary romance . . . and I can't even decide what I love most about her debut novel. The setting, the romance, the wit, I love it all! I especially loved the undercurrent of hope and redeemed dreams. Definitely an author to watch and characters to love!"

—Melissa Tagg, author of *From the Start* and *Like Never Before*

KARA ISAAC

New York Nashville London Toronto Sydney New Delhi

Howard Books
An Imprint of Simon & Schuster, Inc.
1230 Avenue of the Americas
New York, NY 10020

This book is a work of fiction. Any references to historical events, real people, or real places are used fictitiously. Other names, characters, places, and events are products of the author's imagination, and any resemblance to actual events or places or persons, living or dead, is entirely coincidental.

First Howard Books trade paperback edition October 2016

For information about special discounts for bulk purchases, please contact Simon & Schuster Special Sales at 1-866-506-1949 or business@simonandschuster.com.

The Simon & Schuster Speakers Bureau can bring authors to your live event. For more information or to book an event contact the Simon & Schuster Speakers Bureau at 1-866-248-3049 or visit our website at www.simonspeakers.com.

Manufactured in the United States of America

10 9 8 7 6 5 4 3 2 1

Library of Congress Cataloging-in-Publication Data

Names: Isaac, Kara, author.
Title: Can't Help Falling : a novel / Kara Isaac.
Description: First edition. | Nashville : Howard Books, 2016.
Identifiers: LCCN 2016008985|
Subjects: | BISAC: FICTION / Christian / Romance. | FICTION / Romance / Contemporary. | GSAFD: Love stories.
Classification: LCC PR9639.4.I83 C36 2016 | DDC 823/.92—dc23 LC record available at https://lccn.loc.gov/2016008985

ISBN 978-1-5011-1734-3
ISBN 978-1-5011-1735-0 (ebook)

For Melody

World's greatest sister, longest suffering reader, most honest critic, and loudest cheerleader. Thank you.

One

It was like being in jail. But worse, because Emelia Mason had paid for it. Nonrefundable. Nontransferable. Not that she hated anyone on the planet enough to try transferring this epic disaster in online booking to them.

Emelia turned around, taking in the full three hundred sixty degrees of the small, dark, cold room. Her breath wafted in front of her. Inside. At four in the afternoon. The space was pretty much bare, save for a rickety desk, an ancient minifridge, a few hangers on a metal stand, and a bed. She suppressed a shudder at the sight of the sagging mattress in the corner. Even from a good six feet away, Emelia could tell it would light up like the Rockefeller Center Christmas tree if a UV light ever came within a block of it.

Well, she'd wanted to reinvent herself. She'd certainly done that. Even if being one step up from homeless hadn't exactly been in the game plan. Though, after what she'd done, it was about what she deserved.

Stupid, stupid. Emelia still had no idea how she'd managed to book three weeks at the euphemistically named Magnolia Manor, instead of the Magnolia Inn. A mistake she'd discovered when she'd shown up at the latter, only to be told they had no record of her. A review of her furiously waved booking confirmation revealed her error.

Emelia stretched her arms above her head and lifted herself onto her toes. Her fingers scraped the ceiling, dust brushing against their tips.

Brilliant. No doubt in a few minutes she'd be sneezing like Earth's rotation depended on it.

"Do you need anything else?" The voice coming from behind her clearly said there was only one acceptable answer. Emelia turned around. She hadn't realized the dour manager had stayed in the doorway. Was watching her with gray, beady eyes.

"No." Emelia couldn't bring herself to say thank you. She felt ill just thinking about how much she'd paid to stay in this hole. She had no job. Minimal savings. And when she'd come through the front door, its paint flaking, the greasy-haired woman who had opened it had taken one look at her and pointed at the NO REFUNDS, NO EXCEPTIONS sign that hung on the wall.

Emelia bit the inside of her cheek to stop the tears she could feel welling. It was a room. With a roof. There were worse things in life. That's why she was here. Squaring her shoulders, she moved to the door and put her hand on the handle, clearly signaling her desire for the woman to leave her alone.

"I finish serving breakfast at eight on the dot." Even the woman's English accent was unappealing. Guttural and harsh.

If the room was any indication of the quality of the food, Emelia planned on never ever eating anything served under this roof for as long as she was stuck there. "Okay, thanks."

The woman finally got the hint and shuffled off down the

dim corridor decorated with peeling wallpaper and brown shag carpet that had probably been passé in the seventies.

Emelia had to put her shoulder into getting the door to close properly. The wood finally smashed into the swollen frame.

She dropped her purse on the decrepit desk. The scarred top was graffitied with years' worth of contributions, most of which were R-rated. Emelia reached inside her bag for her gloves so she could strip the bed without risking contact with her skin. Tonight, she'd sleep in her clothes.

As she pulled out the leather set, a pale pink slip of paper fell out onto the desktop. Her stepmother's cursive handwriting swirled up at her. An envelope had arrived the day Emelia had left for Oxford. She'd been foolish enough to hope it contained something useful, like cash. But no, all it held was pages of Carolina's deluded social aspirations.

I really don't understand your reluctance about Harry. All the benefits of royalty without the responsibility of the crown. And Kate would be your sister-in-law. Just imagine!

Emelia suppressed a shudder as she crumpled the lavender-scented note and tossed it at the trash can in the corner of the room. The pink ball hit the rim and bounced to the floor, rolling across the worn carpet.

No offense to the duchess, who, from all appearances, seemed like a thoroughly decent human being. But given the events that had resulted in Emelia's transatlantic relocation, her stepmother's obsession with getting a foot in the door of the House of Windsor was about as appealing as the contents of Emelia's inherited minifridge. And she hadn't even opened it yet.

She took a swig from her water bottle as she assessed the disconcerting situation she'd found herself in.

This wasn't exactly the arrival at Oxford she'd imagined.

But then, her childhood dreams had also included visions of a full academic scholarship to study her literary idols. Living at one of the university colleges. Lectures and tutorials and being someplace where everyone spoke the same language as she did.

This. Was. Not. That.

Wiping her hands against her travel-worn jeans, she suddenly couldn't take the silence anymore.

She needed to get out of this grubby room.

She needed to find a wardrobe.

Two

Peter Carlisle had spent ten years hunting for the perfect birthday present for his mother. A saner man would have given up by now and settled for a sweater. But no. He had to go and develop an obsession with a teacup that was more elusive than the White Witch's sense of humor in *The Lion, the Witch and the Wardrobe*.

His feet slipped on the icy cobblestones of Oxford's Turl Street. He zipped his jacket up until it covered his chin and tugged his hat down to minimize exposure to the icy February sleet.

Dodging a slow taxi, he cut across the road, one of the few pedestrians crazy enough to be out on a night like this. He checked his watch. Quarter to six. He should make it just in time, even though it was a total long shot that Oxford Antiques would have the prized piece of bone china he was seeking. But he'd spent the last two hours scouring every antiques shop in town, hoping a miracle would happen at the last second. This was the final store.

It had seemed like a fun challenge ten years ago. He'd decided, at his mother's fiftieth birthday party, that by her sixtieth, he would have found the last four teacups for her vintage floral

Aynsley collection. He'd thought it would be easy. And he'd succeeded with the first three for her fifty-first, fifty-fourth, and fifty-seventh birthdays respectively. But the last one, a 1950s corset-shaped teacup with large pink roses, had proved determinedly elusive. Not even the disturbing development of an eBay obsession that saw him losing hours of his life on the site had come through.

So here he was. The day before his self-imposed deadline expired. About to fail. Which pretty much summed up the last twelve months of his life. At least this time only he would know about it. Wouldn't be subjected to the sympathetic inquiries of family and friends asking how he was doing.

Steeling himself against the inevitable disappointment he was about to be dealt, he turned the knob to the door of the antiques store, the bell above announcing his entrance.

The shop was almost the same temperature as the street. Reginald, the proprietor, didn't believe in heating. He proclaimed it better for his wares if customers shivered while they browsed. It certainly had the effect of weeding out anyone who wasn't a serious buyer.

Peter gave a nod to the elderly owner at his usual perch behind the cash register. And he meant *cash* register. The man must have been one of the only retailers still left who dealt in cash and only cash.

Peter ducked into the corner where Reginald stacked his mismatched assortment of vintage crockery. For the second before he saw what sat there, a hit of anticipation buzzed inside him. And left just as quickly. His gaze scanned the five teacups that sat arranged on a sideboard. All familiar. Only one Aynsley, already in his mother's collection.

His phone vibrated deep in his pocket. Probably one of the team wanting his take on how they'd done at training. The famous Oxford vs. Cambridge Boat Race was less than two months away and the provisional rowing crew for Oxford's Blue Boat had been selected. But the men who'd just missed out on the lineup and been consigned to a reserve boat were still putting up a fight. As the brutal sets of five-hundred-meter sprints earlier in the day on Dorney Lake had shown.

He pulled the phone out and glanced at the screen. *Victor* flashed up at him. He would've welcomed talking to anyone else. In the background, the bell rang above the door, signaling someone else doing some last-minute antiquing. He answered the call.

"Hi." His tone was curt.

"Bunny." His brother's voice held a familiar cadence. The one that indicated he was a few beers down but not yet obliterated. When Peter had left Victor a few hours before, he'd been drinking beer out of a fellow rower's shoe in the back of the team van. All class, his big brother. "So, whatcha doing?"

Peter almost didn't tell him. An uncharitable part of him hoped his brother had forgotten what the following day was. "Shopping for Mum's birthday present."

A pause was followed by a muffled curse. "Was it today?"

"Tomorrow." February 21. Same date every year, strangely enough.

"What are you getting her? Want to go in together?"

Ha. Not likely. "Don't know yet, so probably best if you sort yourself out." He stepped back to allow a girl with brown, wavy hair and a focused expression to brush past him, heading for the adjoining room. There was something in the tilt of her head, the determined stride of her legs, that pulled his gaze to follow her as she walked.

"Do you mind if I crash at your place for a couple of nights? Marissa's kicked me out." His brother's voice jerked his attention away from the woman and back to their conversation.

"Again?" Peter couldn't think of anything he'd like less. He already saw way more of his brother than he had any desire to.

"Says the guy who's had all of, what? One girlfriend in his entire life? How about we talk when you have some experience under your belt, little bro." Peter couldn't have been less interested in the kind of experience Victor referred to, but his brother's jab still hurt.

Didn't matter what Peter said; his brother would have taken up residence on his foldout by the time Peter got home. "Two nights. Max."

"Gotcha."

No doubt Victor would be on the charm offensive tomorrow, wooing his way back into his on-again, off-again girlfriend's forgiveness for whatever his latest transgression was. And she'd relent, as she always did. For a smart girl, Marissa was mighty dumb when it came to his brother. Peter would have put money on Afghanistan's winning an Olympic rowing gold over his brother's backing up the promises that slipped off his lips like honey but always delivered vinegar.

"And pick up some milk and cereal on your way over. We're out." He ended the call before his brother could reply. If Victor managed one out of the two, Peter would count it as a win.

He'd spent his entire life covering his older brother's backside, and it had reached new heights in the last year. He was over it. Over being hauled out of bed at crazy hours to get him out of trouble. Over his flat being treated like a halfway house whenever it suited. Over helping Victor achieve the very dream that Peter had been robbed of. Over trying to help cover up the gaping crevices in his brother's character. Yet he kept doing it because the alternative was worse.

He scanned the teacups one last time. As if one might have miraculously transformed in the last thirty seconds. Nope. Still nothing.

Jamming his phone back into his pocket, he turned to head back to the front door, then paused. Might as well keep looking around. Maybe the teacup was a bust, but something else might grab his eye. It wasn't like he'd been smart enough to come up with a Plan B on the present front.

Turning back, he pulled his hat off his head as he ducked under the archway into the next room, partly intrigued to see what it was the girl with the wavy hair had been so intent on reaching.

Stopping, he blinked, trying to work out what he was seeing. Or wasn't. There were no exits from the room except the one he was standing in. But the girl had disappeared.

Once Emelia had located the town center, it had been easy to find an antiques shop. Now she just hoped it held the one thing she was looking for. It had to. This was England. The first room hadn't yielded anything apart from a gentleman manning the register who looked like he predated most of his shop's contents and a tall guy on a phone.

Ducking through an archway, she stepped into another room packed with furniture. It was almost impossible to move between tables, chairs, side tables, and desks to get farther into the space.

But there it was, in the far corner: a tall, wide wardrobe flush against the wall. How she didn't see it as soon as she walked in, she had no idea. Imposing. Majestic. In the crowded room, there was space around it, a gap between it and the other pieces of furniture. As if even inanimate objects instinctively knew that this was something deserving of deference. Not to be crowded around like baked beans packed into a can.

Moving furniture out of the way as quietly as possible so as not to attract any attention, Emelia drew closer. Until she was close enough to touch it, to see her breath fog up the varnished mahogany.

Of course, the real one was made of apple-tree wood, but who really knew what that looked like?

It was deep, one of the deepest she'd ever seen. And tall. Towering above her, not even an inch between its top and the ceiling.

Lifting her left hand, she brushed the wood with her fingertips, then placed her palm flat against the cool surface.

Looking over her shoulder, she scanned the space. No one. The only sound was the low, muffled voice of the guy on the phone in the other room.

Biting her bottom lip, she let her fingers run along the side of the door. The wardrobe tugged at her, the way all wardrobes like this had since she was a little girl.

Wherever you are, Emmy, you will always find safety in here. And one day, one day, you and me? We'll find the wardrobe.

The words her mom had whispered to her tiptoed through her mind. Whispers of the past that haunted her every step.

The door swung open without even a squeak. Smoothly, on hinges that felt like they'd been oiled seconds ago, even though the cobwebs in the top corner told a different story.

She stuck her head in. Darkness met her like a warm embrace. For all the unfulfilled promises her mother had made, for some reason the one about always feeling safe in wardrobes had stuck. Along with the compulsion to continue her mother's lifelong mission to find *the one*.

There were rules, of course. No feeling for the back until you were inside. No playing it safe, keeping your feet on the outside and reaching out. You had to commit. Narnia would never be found by those who were uncertain or ambivalent.

Sitting on the bottom, she swung her legs inside, tucked them toward her chest, and pulled the door closed behind her until just a sliver of light remained. Her hand hit something small. In the darkness she couldn't see what. Picking it up, she held it right in front of her face. A floral teacup and saucer set. What was a teacup doing in a wardrobe? Though, to be fair, it was probably thinking the same thing about her. Her hand relocated it under her tented knees so she wouldn't accidentally break it.

She sat for a second. Felt her shoulders relax against the wood. Then realized she wasn't alone in this space. Something soft brushed against her head. Reaching up, she grasped a sleeve. Her pulse drummed in her throat. Maybe . . . She'd never really allowed herself to hope it might be true. Even though she couldn't deny her compulsion to climb inside every antique-looking, wooden wardrobe. The deep-seated kind that wouldn't allow her to walk away until she knew *for sure* it wasn't a portal.

But there had never been one filled with coats before.

Well, if this was it, she wasn't going to discover the mystical land sitting on her backside. Pushing herself up to standing, she faced the back of the wardrobe and reached out a hand in front, preparing for disappointment, yet half expecting to feel the soft whisper of a snowflake against her fingers.

Her hand hit wood. Solid, unmoving wood. Her whole body sagged. There was no portal here. She was crazy. Just like her mother.

Emelia battled the urge to sink to the floor. To curl herself up into a ball and cry. What was she doing here? In Oxford. In an antiques shop. In a wardrobe. It would have been funny, if it weren't so pathetic.

Turning around, she leaned her forehead against the frame of the door, trying to settle her thundering pulse and soothe the unreasonable disappointment that had blossomed inside.

Suddenly, light flooded in. Everything shifted and her body jolted, discombobulated by the sudden change.

"Argh . . ." Arms flailing, she plunged headlong into the space where the door had vanished faster than a Turkish delight within Edmund's reach.

"Oomph." The sound of air bursting from lungs registered about the same time as the sensation of arms grasping her waist, preventing her from hitting the floor.

A blur of navy blue and the scent of cinnamon were all she managed to distinguish from the chaos as her feet found the ground.

One thing she knew for sure: there was no chance this was the octogenarian who'd been holding down the fort when she'd walked in. A good thing, since she would have squashed him flat. Instead, she found herself staring up into the very surprised face of a green-eyed male with an unruly thatch of what could only be described as flaming ginger hair.

Relinquishing his hold, he grinned down at her. "So . . ." The accent told her he was as English as mushy peas and warm beer. "Are you a Susan or a Lucy?"

A Susan or a Lucy? Where did that come from? Victor was always the one with the lines, not him. Never him. Peter was the guy who could practice a line for days and be left dry mouthed and mute when it came time to deliver it. Let alone when someone who looked like a Narnian wood nymph fell on top of him.

The missing girl stared up at him. All wide blue-gray eyes and wavy hair the color of Cadbury milk chocolate. She was tall too, reaching his nose when most girls barely made it to his shoulders.

She was clearly a Lucy. Susan, ever the older sister, was way too practical to go climbing into wardrobes on a whim.

"Let me guess. You're Peter." Both her tone and her face were inscrutable. The only thing that gave anything away was the American accent.

He frowned, searching her face for anything that could trigger a memory of her. "Do I know you?"

Now she looked confused as she shook her head, hair bouncing across her shoulders. "No. Why?"

"Then how do you know my name?"

"Your name?"

This was the weirdest conversation ever. Not that, he supposed, much more could be expected when it began with someone falling out of a wardrobe onto you. "How did you know my name was Peter?"

Now she gave him the kind of look one gave someone extraordinarily thick. "I was being sarcastic. Peter. As in Peter and Edmund. Lucy and Susan's brothers. And no one ever wants to be Edmund, do they?"

Good one, clever clogs. For once in your life, you come up with a good line and you manage to blow it.

"Are you trying to say your name is actually Peter?"

"Guilty."

Awkward silence. She stared up at him, her face unreadable. "It's a bad line. It gives you away."

"As what?"

"That you're not a real Narnia fan."

"I'm not a real Narnia fan?" He almost laughed aloud at how wrong she was.

"A true Narnia fan would never ask a girl if they were a Susan or a Lucy."

And with that cryptic remark she somehow managed to cut past him, weave her way through the furniture-filled room, and disappear. Leaving Peter to stare after her with her final statement resounding in his ears. The sound of the bell ringing and then the front door slamming shut shook him from his daze. What had just happened?

He turned back to the wardrobe and its open door. He'd seen it in here before but never really paid it much attention. He stepped toward it. It looked deep. A few coats hung on old metal hangers. Reaching in, his fingers traversed past the rough woolen material before grazing the wooden back and then traveling down.

His hand brushed against something cool and smooth sitting on the floor as he leaned back. Crouching down, he looked into the depths, his breath snagging at what peered back at him. He blinked, then rubbed his eyes to check he wasn't dreaming.

A teacup. Slowly he reached for it, pinching the saucer between his fingers and pulling it toward him, not even daring to breathe.

Not just any teacup.

The elusive Aynsley 1950s corset-shaped teacup with pink roses he'd spent the last ten years looking for.

Three

"FIVE, FOUR, THREE, TWO, ONE." PETER COUNTED DOWN THE sprint as Max's seat on the rowing machine moved like a blur. At Peter's last count, the tall, muscular athlete let go of the handles and collapsed over his knees, shuddering and gulping in air.

"Good work." Peter uttered the useless words as he dropped to one knee. Max didn't even acknowledge them. It didn't matter what he said. The only thing that mattered was the numbers.

The athlete didn't even flinch when Peter drew blood. A tiny prick was nothing compared to the abuse every muscle in his body was giving to him.

Peter tagged the sample and read the numbered sticker out to Grant, so the cox could note it on the clipboard he held. The Boat Race may have been considered an amateur rowing race, but the teams had access to all the same training support as the professionals. The lactate levels in his blood would tell the coaching team far more about how Max's body was responding to the ever-increasing training load than anything else.

Peter looked at the time on the screen. Grant would note that too. Not incredible, but not bad, keeping him squarely in the middle of the pack. It was going to be a close call who the last oarsman would be for the Blue Boat. Peter was glad he was just the assistant coach—a token one at that—and the decision wasn't on him.

It had looked pretty cut-and-dried after the winter training in Spain, and then James had gone and gotten pneumonia, taking him out of the running and opening the field up again. The news had just come this morning that he wasn't going to be fit to return anytime soon. The guys contending for the now-open seat were throwing everything they had at the opportunity.

Peter clapped Max's sweat-covered shoulder as he stumbled away to cool down. A year ago, he'd been that guy. Body sagging over his knees, lungs trying to grab oxygen with rapid short breaths. Now he was standing in a gym in Oxford, drawing blood and cross-checking paperwork. He'd only gotten the job because Sean had taken pity on him, scrounging up enough hours between working here and teaching some beginners' rowing courses at the Oxford Academicals Rowing Club to pay what he needed to barely scrape by.

"Ethan, you're up next." The big American ambled forward and set himself up on the erg. He'd lost a lot of the cockiness he'd rolled in with in September, used to being the big man on campus at Harvard with a string of impressive victories behind him.

It happened every year with the internationals, accustomed to being rowing superstars back home. They showed up at Oxford expecting to be a shoo-in for a seat in the coveted Blue Boat. Then the reality that there was a world of mind-breaking pain between the standard race distance of two thousand meters and the Boat Race distance of six thousand eight hundred set in.

Ethan rolled his shoulders and swung his arms a couple of times before gripping the handles.

"Whenever you're ready." Peter stepped away before the muscular rower could even start. The machine would do all the counting he needed.

Exiting the gym, he walked down the hall to drop the blood off with all the other samples that had been taken that morning.

He let his mind drift back to the excitement on his mum's face the night before when he'd presented her with her present. It had been more than worth the price tag, which would have him pretty much living on rice and cereal for the next few weeks.

Not even Victor, who had gone easy but expensive with some kind of day spa experience, had come close. And his brother's glower showed he knew it too. It was nice to be one up on the golden boy for once. Especially when said golden boy lied through his teeth to their parents about pretty much everything and dragged Peter along as an unwilling accomplice.

His mind flipped over to the girl, a thought not far from his mind during the last couple of days. It still all seemed like a surreal dream. Her falling out of the wardrobe onto him. The teacup being left behind. It was about as crazy as anything that had happened in Narnia. If he'd heard it from one of the guys, he'd have assumed someone had been consuming something that was definitely not approved by UK Anti-Doping.

"Who is she?"

"What?" He turned to where the burly president of the club was leaning against the doorframe. He hadn't even heard Tim approach.

"You have a weird smile on your face. You have a hot date last night?"

"If by 'hot date' you mean my mother's birthday, then yes."

"Huh." Tim didn't look convinced but let it drop. "How are the guys doing?"

Peter looked down at the clipboard Grant had handed to him. "Pretty good considering the brutal row yesterday. Max and Hayden are pretty much neck and neck, time-wise. Will be interesting to see what their bloods show."

Tim rubbed a hand across his forehead. "I hate this part. One of them is going to have his dreams come true, the other will miss out by the slimmest margin. And he'll know it."

"Yes, well. Anything can happen still." As he well knew. One second a rower on the Great Britain national team, a sure thing for Olympic selection, the next a has-been before he'd managed the has.

"Victor's been throwing some crazy-big numbers. Cambridge would stroke out if they could see them." Tim made the observation casually.

"Good for him." Peter managed to keep most of the bitterness out of his voice. It had been easy to excuse himself from any role in Victor's selection for the Blue Boat, not so much to try to hide the animosity that existed between the two of them.

His brother hadn't rowed a day in his life until Peter had gotten injured. Peter had almost lost his breakfast the day Victor had shown up at trials. There was a glint in his eye as he said he'd decided to "give it a go." Just his luck his brother had proven to be freakishly good at it. Like he was at pretty much everything he tried.

Tim's eyes narrowed. "How's the physio going?"

"Okay." He wasn't ready to admit aloud that his improvement had plateaued a month ago. That even Kevin, one of the country's best sports physiotherapists, seemed to be less optimistic with every session.

Peter rotated his left shoulder, checking for any pain or tension. Plateauing wasn't an option. The only option was total recovery. He had not come all this way to be permanently out of the game now. He was going to make a comeback if it killed him. He owed it to Anita.

"You'll get there." Tim gave him the same shoulder clap Peter had given Max a few minutes before. "You've got time until Tokyo."

It wasn't supposed to be Tokyo, it was supposed to be Rio, he wanted to shout. His entire life since he was fourteen had been oriented around being in the Team Great Britain boat in 2016. And he'd almost made it too. Then he'd had to try to be the good guy. And paid for it by losing the only thing he'd ever really wanted.

Four

Emelia sucked in a breath. Forced one out. Curling her fingers around the bottom of her rickety chair, she stared straight ahead at the notice board on the wall opposite. The flyers and pamphlets sat at all angles, pinned seemingly at random. Some proclaiming dates months old. Emelia's fingers itched to go over there and restore order to the poor overladen board. But no. She, more than anyone, knew the importance of first impressions.

Everything rested on now. She'd cut ties with LA. Changed her appearance. Booked a one-way ticket to England. Spent four nights in a hovel that deserved to be condemned. All for this. There was no Plan B.

For some reason, the green eyes and red hair of a certain Englishman floated into her mind. *"Are you a Susan or a Lucy?"* His half-laughing question had echoed there since he'd asked it. It was a great pickup line. She had to give him that. If she'd been a girl who had only seen the movies. Unfortunately for him, she was a true Narnia fan. She knew what had happened to Susan. Worse, she knew she *was* a Susan.

"Emelia Mason?" The words came from her right. Emelia loosened her death grip on the chair and stood. Next to her was a woman with an immaculate gray bob and a weary face. Her voice sounded tentative, even though Emelia was the only one there. She could only hope that meant there were few contenders for this job.

She pressed her palms to her skirt for a second, then held out her hand. "Hello, I'm Emelia."

The woman gave her a quick handshake but didn't quite look Emelia in the eye. Not a promising start. "Elizabeth Bradman. Thanks for coming in." The woman gestured toward a hallway and then led her through a door that sat ajar a short distance away.

They entered a cramped, utilitarian room. Along one wall stood a row of filing cabinets, in the middle a battered wooden desk. Facing the desk was one worn chair, stuffing poking through a couple of cracks in the brown leather cover. No one was ever going to accuse the charity of wasting donors' money on aesthetics, that was for sure.

The one incongruous thing was the top of the desk. Precisely positioned folders and papers surrounded a green blotter, on which sat one piece of paper at a ninety-degree angle to the edge of the blotter. A fountain pen sat to the side, parallel with the edge of the paper. Perfect order. It made Emelia feel happy just looking at it. A woman after her own heart.

"Take a seat." Elizabeth gestured to the chair positioned facing the desk, again, right in the center.

Emelia's feet moved across the worn carpet, her breath shallow in case it happened to dislodge any of the papers.

She placed her purse on the floor and perched on the chair as the woman moved behind the desk and sat. Her posture remained as straight as a broomstick. "I'm the acting executive officer for SpringBoard. Please tell me, succinctly, why you applied for this job."

Clearly this was not a woman who believed in small talk. Or making potential employees comfortable, for that matter. Fortunately, Emelia had prepared for this question. "I have recently moved to Oxford. As you'll see from my résumé I've had a range of involvement with charities in Los Angeles. I've spent the last few years working as a journalist but am looking for a career change. This seemed like a role that would be a good fit for my skills."

Ms. Bradman tapped a tapered finger on the sheet of paper in front of her. "You have an American accent, yet your application states you have the right to work in the UK. Is that correct?"

"I'm a British citizen. My mother was British." The only thing her mom had left her that turned out to be any use. "I have my passport with me if you'd like to see it." She reached for her purse, but Ms. Bradman waved her hand.

"Why the sudden desire for a change from journalism?"

Because I was the type who made headlines out of other people's misery. Because somewhere in the last five years, I lost myself in pursuit of scandal. Because someone is dead because of me. Because this job is my one chance to make some kind of atonement.

The thoughts flashed through her mind, robbing her of breath for a second. She forced herself to push them back, to focus on the task at hand. Emelia framed her response carefully. "I enjoyed the work that I did with charities back home and when I read this job description it looked like a great fit for me."

SpringBoard focused on getting books to kids at poor schools. Not unlike thousands of other charities around the world. But their point of difference was they then connected every book they provided with experts who came in and talked to the classes, made them real. Academics, historians, archaeologists, even a few of the authors themselves were listed on the honor roll on the charity's website.

"I see." Ms. Bradman looked her up and down. Emelia was thankful she'd worn the most conservative outfit she owned. Black skirt and jacket, blue shirt. Finally, a sigh escaped. "I'm not going to lie. We are not in good shape here. The last executive officer quit without notice a few months ago. I'm filling in temporarily as a favor. The board has given us until the end of the year to turn things around. You seem like a perfectly nice young woman but I can't afford to make a hiring mistake. And the truth is that Americans and the English are very different. I'm not sure I can trust our one chance to someone who doesn't even know the English way." She started to push her chair back as if to signal the end of an interview that hadn't ever really begun.

A streak of desperation surged through Emelia. She was in Oxford for this job. She had burned her bridges, had nothing to go back to. It could not already be over after less than ten minutes in a closet-sized office. "I knew Anita." She just blurted out the words from between her lips, causing her chest to constrict.

Something crossed Ms. Bradman's face. She didn't say anything but paused, seeming to really look at Emelia for the first time.

Emelia scrambled to explain without lying. "We weren't close but I promise you, I will do everything in my power to get her charity back on its feet."

The woman's face softened at the mention of SpringBoard's founder. "So this is personal."

It couldn't get any more personal. "Very much so."

Ms. Bradman pursed her lips, tapped her capped fountain pen on the blotter in front of her. "You've seen the salary?"

Emelia could understand her hesitation. "Salary" was a generous term for the pittance they were offering. If she were still in LA it wouldn't have even covered her mortgage payments. "Yes, ma'am."

"When are you available from?"

"I just moved to Oxford. I can start as soon as you want." The desperation practically leached out of her pores.

"Okay." Ms. Bradman scribbled something on the piece of paper in front of her. "Tell me about your references."

"Ava Brownley is the event co-coordinator for LA Lit, which is a charity for inner-city children in LA. It has a number of similarities with SpringBoard's work. I worked on a number of fund-raising events for her. Kevin Wright is the chair of Outside the Box, which is a foundation that assists people with mental illness. I did some communications and PR work for them."

Not for the first time, she gave thanks that she'd kept her charity work and her real job completely separate. Neither Ava nor Kevin knew anything about Mia Caldwell, so there was no chance of their inadvertently dropping the name that would ruin everything.

"Okay. Assuming your references check out, let's go with starting on Monday. I'll take a copy of your passport and I'll be in touch tomorrow with what further information we require."

What? That was it? Emelia couldn't have been more surprised if the woman had offered to fly her to the moon. "Um, yes. That would be fine. Thank you." The woman didn't even look up from what she was writing. Right. Dismissed then.

Emelia crept out of the room, hardly daring to breathe until she was out the door lest the woman inside change her mind.

Once in the hallway, she sagged against the wall. She'd done it. Gotten the job that she'd thrown her whole life in for. Now she just had to work out how on earth to do the impossible.

Five

Peter walked in his front door and stifled a groan. Not again. From his entryway, he could see his brother's feet hanging off the end of his couch.

He was cold. He was soaked through from two hours in the freezing February rain. It had not been a good rowing session. The team had spent most of the time struggling to get into a good rhythm on the lake, all of them growing more frustrated when they failed. And now he knew, without a doubt, he would get into the shower and discover Victor had used up all the hot water.

He'd just seen Victor all of an hour ago at training. Funny how his brother hadn't thought to mention then he was planning to take up residency on his couch. Again. It had only been three days since his last stint. But then, Victor had always lived by the motto that it was easier to ask forgiveness than permission. Not that he ever bothered with the former either.

Stomping into his living room, Peter found his brother balancing a bag of potato crisps on his torso and a beer in his hand. Both of them Peter's. Because that was what his brother specialized in: taking.

And he was done.

"What did you do this time?" Peter picked up his brother's keys off the coffee table and started flipping through them. Finding his house key, he started twisting it off the ring.

"I— Hey! What are you doing?" Victor lifted his head to watch Peter extract his key and stuff it in his pocket.

"We're done with this being a halfway house. I have an actual flatmate. And both of us like having hot showers and not having our food eaten. So I don't care what kind of girlfriend troubles you have, I'm no longer your alternate for when she kicks you out."

"Wow, look at you, little bro. Gone and grown a backbone and everything." Victor cast him a sardonic smile as he reached for another handful of crisps. "And here I was just enjoying some of your moments of glory."

Peter looked toward the TV to find some kind of sports highlights show on and saw his team, faces taut with agony, pulling back against the oars. The yellow Team Great Britain boat chasing Germany's green one.

In a split second, he was back in the previous June. Out on the water in Varese, Italy. With his guys. Lungs burning. Body screaming. Sun beating down. The longest five minutes and twenty-seven seconds of his life as they'd fought to take the lead and then hold it against the powerful Germans, who took the fight right to the end. A third of a second was all that separated them at the finish line.

It was one of his biggest victories. It was also the last time he'd raced. Little did that guy in the boat know he was only hours away from losing everything.

He steeled his face before he turned back to Victor, refusing to let him see how much it hurt. His brother would only go out of his way to pour more salt in the wound if he knew.

"I might need to stay a few days. Marissa and I, we're proper done this time."

Peter couldn't say he was sorry. The truth was Marissa was better off without his brother. The guy treated women like they were disposable. He just hoped she'd been the one to work it out and end things. There were already too many girls bearing the scars of Victor's charm-them-and-leave-them approach to life. Once he donned the blue jacket, the sign of having reached the highest sporting level at Oxford, he would be unbearable.

"You've got two days. I've got a friend crashing this week-end." Jackson was actually going to sleep in Tony's room, since his flatmate was going to be away, but there was no need for Victor to know that.

Victor took another slurp of his beer. "Okay, fine. Relax. I guess I can always go home. Tell Mum you kicked me out."

He'd forgotten for a few brave moments his parents thought he and Victor lived together. Victor had spun that tale a while back, and Peter had never found a way to break his mother's heart and tell her the truth—that her eldest son was actually shacked up with some girl she'd never met.

"Sure. Go for it."

They stared at each other. Despite all his brother's character flaws—and they made a long list—Victor did actually seem to care about their parents. As much as he cared about anyone.

Peter had long since stopped praying that they would ever be friends. There was too much between them. Had been since the day he dared to be born. The gap had just grown exponentially over the years. Something he was reminded of every time he looked at the scar marring his brother's face.

About the only thing that still held them together was their uneasy truce to keep the depths of their antagonism from their parents. So Peter was going to take his chances that Victor wouldn't go out of his way to upset their mother.

"So, little brother, how much does it suck knowing you've already lived the greatest moment of your life?" Victor pointed at the TV screen as the two boats crossed the finish line, Team Great Britain just ahead. Peter's eyes locked on the sheer joy and exhilaration that radiated from his face. From the faces of his entire team.

Victor's taunting question was one that dogged his every waking moment. It was the reason that, no matter what the experts said, he couldn't accept he would never experience that again. He had to. There was no other option.

Emelia stepped into the small office she'd been assigned at SpringBoard, dropping her bag on the top of her pristine desk. She didn't officially start for another forty-five minutes, but her latest strategy was to spend as little time in the hovel as possible.

Hopefully the alerts she'd put on roommate-search websites would yield something. So far she hadn't been able to find anything that fit her criteria. She didn't think she was being too picky. Her standards had started off pretty high but slipped by the day as her desperation mounted. Now she was down to affordable, within cycling distance of the city center, not with weirdos, and in a building that didn't deserve to be condemned.

Sitting in her chair, Emelia ran her hand over the wooden desk. Four days since she'd started and there was no hint of anything personal. Nothing that would tell a passerby anything about her. Just stacks of paper and a plastic tray that held her stationery. The way she liked it. It was a habit she'd gained as a tabloid hack where the competition was as fierce between colleagues as it was between outlets. Anything personal hinted at a potential weakness. You didn't get to be the best in the cutthroat world of tabloid journalism by displaying your vulnerabilities.

Emelia logged in to her computer, pulling up all the websites she'd been searching, hoping that maybe, in the last twelve hours, someone had listed her dream situation. But as the minutes ticked by, her hopes deflated. She was paid up at the so-called Manor until next Wednesday. She would not be staying there for one night more. If she didn't have somewhere new to live by then, she'd dig into her meager savings. Stay in a hotel for a couple of nights. If even just to remind herself what it was like to be able to shower in bare feet again.

Closing down the sites, she pulled up the to-do list that Elizabeth had emailed her the previous afternoon. With the staff down to a bare skeleton crew, everyone was pitching in to cover basic administration. She scanned the columns. Photocopying, envelope stuffing, a few phone calls to the few remaining donors to take their pulse. Not exactly a heavy intellectual load.

Picking up the stack of photocopying that had been left on top of the filing cabinet, she double-checked the instructions. Eighty copies each. That should keep the photocopier humming for a while.

Walking down the hall, she stepped into the photocopier/stationery cupboard. As she crossed the threshold she was met by a loud bang. Emelia jumped, a small scream slipping from her lips.

Startled, the petite redhead standing at the photocopier also let out a shriek.

They stared at each other for a second.

"Sorry. I didn't know anyone else was here." They spoke in unison, then paused.

Emelia glanced at the red flashing lights on the copier. "Do you need some help?"

The other girl looked at her with an expression of defeat. "Could you? It just keeps jamming and I can't work out why." She gestured to the floor by the machine, which was strewn with a collection of rumpled, half-torn pieces of paper. "I think it just hates me." The accent wasn't English. Australian, maybe?

Emelia placed her papers on a shelf and walked over. "We've had a few battles this week. I make no guarantees, but I'll see what I can do."

She started opening doors and flicking knobs, pulling out crinkled pieces of paper as she went.

"I'm Allie, by the way."

Emelia glanced at the friendly green eyes and smattering of freckles. The woman's auburn hair was pulled back in a messy ponytail. She could have been anywhere between her midtwenties and midthirties. That was a contrast to the norm at the charity. All the other volunteers she'd met had decades on her.

"Emelia."

Reaching deep into the bowels of the machine, she reached for one of the last places she'd discovered paper could get caught and felt her fingers brush against the edge of a sheet.

"Are you new here?"

"Yes. I started on Monday. I'm the new fund-raising coordinator." She said it with far more confidence than she felt. What did she know about fund-raising? Yes, she'd helped Ava with some event-related stuff for LA Lit but the woman had been a seasoned veteran of the LA charity scene and made it all look easy.

"Thank goodness. I've only been volunteering here a few

weeks but even I know we need you badly." There was no hint of a joke in Allie's expression. "Where are you from?"

"Boston." She didn't really think of herself as from anywhere. But Boston was where she'd been happiest. When she'd had dreams of being an investigative reporter working for the *Post* or the *Times*. So that was what she claimed. "You?" Her fingers managed to grasp the corner of the paper and pull it free. She crumpled it up and dropped it to the floor to join its comrades.

"New Zealand. Have you been in England long?"

Emelia flicked knobs and switches, closing the copier doors as she went. "Almost a couple of weeks." Standing, she closed the final door. "That should hopefully do it. Let's give it a shot."

Allie loaded the feeder again, tapped "20" into the keypad, and hit the green button. They both watched as the machine whirred and then started spitting out copies.

"Fund-raising coordinator and photocopier miracle worker." Allie smiled. "Don't you dare go leaving anytime soon."

Emelia flushed. Why, she had no idea. Of all the praise she'd had in her life, it wasn't exactly near the top of the list. Fortunately, the sound of the machine spitting out sheets of paper covered the potentially awkward silence. "Glad I could help. It's the last turny thing. The one right at the back. Where the paper gets stuck. People don't usually think to look there." Now she was just blabbering like an idiot. She pivoted to collect her copying from the shelf.

"Emelia?"

She turned back. Allie was gathering up her set of papers. "If you're new in town, you probably haven't met many people yet. Our age, I mean. This place isn't exactly brimming with youth."

"Um, no. Not really. I've been trying to get settled."

"I'm having a house party on Saturday night. Just a small gathering. You should come. I mean, you don't have to. Obviously. But if you don't have anything better to do."

What did she say to a party invite from someone she'd known all of two minutes? This didn't happen in LA, where the people she crossed paths with specialized in the superficial.

Allie grabbed a pen and scribbled something on a Post-it. "Look. No pressure. But I just moved here in September so I know what it's like to be in a new city." She handed her the piece of paper. "This is my address. Anytime from seven thirty."

Emelia took the paper, folded it, and put it in her pocket. As far as things that she hated most, going to a party where she didn't know a single soul rated up there, but it might just beat any other option she had. Really, she only had one: another night hanging out in a used book shop she'd found that stayed open late. "Thanks."

Allie's machine spat out its last copy and stopped whirring. She gathered up the papers, placing them perpendicularly across the first. "Anyway, thanks so much for the help. I would've been stuck here all day if it wasn't for you." She made a face. "Showing up at my first school visit without the handouts wouldn't be great. I might see you Saturday?"

"Yeah, maybe." Emelia watched as Allie disappeared in a flurry of papers and swishing trench coat, a warm feeling expanding in her chest. For the first time since she'd arrived in Oxford, she felt like she wasn't alone.

Seven

THE NOISE PRACTICALLY BURST OUT OF THE SMALL HOUSE, SOUNDS of laughter and music. Through the windows, Emelia could see people already packed in and talking. What was she doing coming to a party hosted by someone she'd met for all of three minutes? She didn't even know Allie's last name.

Her fingers gripped tighter to the paper bag that contained the fancy-looking soda she'd brought. Maybe she could just walk in, put it down somewhere, and walk right out the back door.

Emelia didn't know what she was even doing here. A small gathering, Allie had said. If this was what they called a small gathering in New Zealand, she would have hated to see a large one.

She was bad with people. Especially strangers. The old her had been great with strangers. With anyone. But she wasn't professional schmoozer Mia Caldwell anymore, with her blond hair and sassy smile. She didn't know who she was, but it wasn't her.

Emelia stopped on the front stoop. Frozen. Not able to knock on the door, but her feet refused to obey her instructions to turn around.

C'mon, Emelia.

Nothing could be worse than another night staring at the walls of her freezing room, listening to *Coronation Street* at full blast in the lounge directly below. The only other option she had was hiding out in the used book shop. That was where she'd spent the last few evenings, smuggling in a sandwich and hunkering down between the stacks. But the owner had started giving her looks of sympathy. Being the object of a stranger's pity grated. So here she was.

It's just people. They don't know you. That's why you're here. To reinvent yourself. To start again. To atone.

Blowing out a breath of icy air, she raised her hand, only for the door to fly open before she'd even touched the wood.

"Thank goodness. For a second there I thought you were going to turn around and leave." Allie greeted her with a cheery smile, like Emelia wasn't basically a stranger.

"I, uh . . ." Struggling for words, Emelia half shoved her brown paper bag at Allie. Like she was six years old and trying to bribe someone to be friends with her by giving them cookies.

"Oh, thanks. Come in. Come in." Allie said the right words but didn't move at all. The only way Emelia was going anywhere would be if she shoved her out of the way. "I'm so glad you came."

"You going to actually let the poor girl in, hon?" a voice said from behind Allie.

"Yes, of course. Sorry." Allie stepped back into the entryway, allowing Emelia to step across the threshold. "This is Jackson." Allie gestured behind her to a tall guy with piercing blue eyes and a warm grin.

He reached around Allie and held out his hand. "You'll

have to excuse her. This is the first house party she's hosted. She's a bit excited." Never had Emelia thought she'd be so glad to see another American. The familiarity of his accent was like a balm to her nerves.

"Emelia."

His hand enveloped hers as she shook it. A good firm handshake. "Nice to meet you." He planted a kiss on Allie's cheek. "I'll just go refill the snacks."

Allie closed the door and put the bottle Emelia had handed her on a table nearby. "Let me take your coat."

Emelia scanned the entryway quickly before she started unbuttoning it. She'd had no idea what to wear to something like this. Hadn't even thought to ask in the surprise of the invitation. So she'd played it safe with black pants and a tunic top. Not that she had much to work with given the minimal clothing she'd brought across the Atlantic with her. It was the first time since she'd left that she'd hankered for the extensive collection she'd had back home.

"Can I get you a drink?"

"Just a soda—um, fizzy drink, would be great." She was still trying to come to terms with what the English called things. Thankfully, with a large international student population in Oxford, when she fumbled and asked where to find a drugstore, people knew she meant a chemist, not a place to acquire illicit substances.

"Great. I'll just go grab you something." Allie gestured down the entryway to a room filled with people. "Go mingle. They're all friendly. There's a couple of other volunteers here. Lindsay. April. Elizabeth said she might drop by. I'll come find you."

And with that, she was gone.

The floorboards creaked as Emelia walked. Peering into the room, which turned out to be a combined kitchen and living area, she looked for Lindsay, a serious girl whom she'd met once. A PhD student, if she recalled correctly. They may not exactly have been kindred spirits, but she would take whatever she could get over walking into a room full of complete strangers.

No sign of the studious blonde.

"Excuse us." A couple of guys stood behind her, wanting to get past.

"Sorry." She stepped back, but even then she ended up pressed into the wall, personal space nonexistent.

What was she even doing here?

Everything whirled around her. All the conversations near her were academic debates. Dante and Hobbes. Something about quantum physics. People stood shoulder to shoulder in intense discussion. All of them way over her head. No room for a newcomer. She hadn't felt so out of place since her first day interning at the *Washington Herald*. The place that had taught her connections mattered more than talent.

Her hands were clammy, her face hot. She didn't belong here. Turning around, she almost fell into a table filled with presents running along the entryway. A card on top of one seared her vision. *Happy Birthday.*

She had made a mistake coming. That much had been obvious before she'd even realized she'd crashed a birthday party. *Coronation Street* at full trumpet blast was definitely better than this.

"Here you go." Allie had appeared beside her like a mirage,

a glass of light pink soda in her hand. "Hope you like pink grapefruit."

"Great, thanks." Her voice wavered a bit at the last word. Emelia tried to force her face into a neutral expression, but it was too late.

Allie peered up at her. "Are you okay?"

"I'm . . . I'm so sorry. I had no idea I was crashing your birthday party." She gestured at the table.

Allie looked around, as if surprised to see the presents. "Oh, you're not. You're totally not. It's not. My birthday was ages ago, I just never had a party and some crazy friends decided to use this as an excuse. Knowing them, they're probably all empty boxes." Allie tapped one with her knuckles. Sure enough, it sounded hollow. "You're new to the snowy spires of Oxford, right? You said you'd just arrived? Do you have family here?"

"Yes. Week before last. And no. No family." No anyone. Which had been part of the appeal, but now that she was here, she was realizing a life of splendid isolation wasn't all it was cracked up to be.

She'd expected to miss Lacey, her cousin, the only family member she was still close to. What she hadn't anticipated was that in the last few days, there'd even been the odd instance she'd have welcomed a conversation with Carolina. Which was saying a lot, given that the few times she'd seen her stepmother in the last couple of years, her social climbing and simpering had almost had Emelia reaching for the nearest blunt object.

Allie gave her a sympathetic look. "I get how crazy moving to a new country can be. I've only been here five months too. But please, don't go. If you need some space, head on upstairs. Bathroom's up there. Take a few minutes. I have to go rescue some food in the oven, but I promise, when I'm done I'll introduce you to some great people. And if you're still not having fun in an hour, I will personally call you a cab. Deal?"

Emelia didn't have the heart to disappoint the hopeful face looking at her. She could always just hide in the bathroom for the next half an hour. She could hardly count on the party hostess to coddle her for the evening. "Deal."

As Allie disappeared back into the crowd, Emelia took a deep breath and wound her way to the staircase at the end of the hall. Climbing up it, she felt immediately calmer as she rose above the noise and crowd.

There were four doors leading off the upper landing. All closed. Turning to the one to her right, she knocked and pressed her ear to the door. Silence. Turning the handle, she pushed the door open and peered into the room.

Not a bathroom. A bedroom. Allie's, judging by the large photo of her and her boyfriend on the dresser. Emelia was about to retreat when her gaze drifted past the dresser and stopped on a large wardrobe nearly covering one wall.

Another Narnia wardrobe. Was Oxford full of them?

She turned, ready to pull the door closed behind her, but spun back around before she could.

Don't be crazy, Emelia.

You can't.

Her feet stepped into the room as her mind argued.

But she hadn't been able to resist the pull of finding Narnia her whole life. No matter the consequences.

Just like her mother. And for her the consequences had been fatal.

Peter wasn't a party guy. Especially when he had a training session early the next morning. Never when he had a session the next morning. Not even for Jackson and Allie, who seemed to have made friends with the entire city in the months they'd been in England.

So why was he breaking his rule tonight? There was zero explanation beyond the internal tugging he'd felt that he needed to be here. He could only hope the reason would become apparent sooner rather than later so he could go home to bed.

"Peter!"

Peter almost dropped the wrapped present cradled in his arm thanks to the trumpeting shout that erupted beside his left eardrum.

He looked down at the firecracker hostess standing beside him. "Thanks, Allie. I didn't need to hear out of that ear."

"Sorry." She didn't look sorry in the least.

"Happy not-birthday." He held out the large gift.

She looked with horror at the box. "Seriously? What am I supposed to do with all this stuff? You remember my contract is up in six months, right? No job, no England."

He seriously doubted there was any chance of that. From what he'd heard, Allie's Tolkien classes were so popular, there had almost been a few brawls between students trying to get seats.

She took the box, a smile quirking up at his amateur wrapping attempt before she placed it on a stack of other presents.

His eyes widened at the height of the pile, and he suppressed a grin. When someone had suggested that everyone put their presents into the biggest boxes they could find, just to wind Allie up, he hadn't expected they'd do so well.

"I'm glad you're here. There's someone I want you to meet."

He sighed. "C'mon, Al. I know you're all flush with love, but I thought we'd agreed no more setups after the last one." Most excruciating blind date ever.

"How was I supposed to know she'd go all fan girl on you?"

It had been the longest two hours of his life, starting with the girl wanting to take selfies of them and then spending half the time tweeting or Instagramming or whatevering them to her friends. "Awkward" didn't even begin to describe it.

"I don't need to be set up, okay? Especially not with only weeks to go until the Boat Race. That's all I'm going to have time for." And after that, all he'd have time for was his coaching commitments to the local rowing club and training for his own comeback. Doing everything in his power to keep his promise.

Allie pulled a face. "Don't try and use that excuse with me. Do you forget some of your guys are in my classes? I've got plenty to keep them occupied the hours they're not rowing. It's not a setup, anyway. She's new in town. I just met her at church on Sunday."

Well, she'd come to the right place. Allie had the amazing ability to make people feel like they'd been friends since they were missing front teeth and drinking out of juice boxes.

"She's a rower too, so I'm sure she's not going to go all gaga on you like the last one." Allie studied him through critical eyes. "Though I'm not sure if I want her to meet you like this. You look like a total dork. What is with that sweater?"

He looked down at his green-, blue-, and red-covered torso. "Don't go knocking the jumper. My grandmother knitted this." And he was only wearing it because, between training, the horrible weather, and not having a dryer, he hadn't done laundry in weeks. It was the ugly jumper that only came out in times of desperation. Not that he'd ever admit it to Allie now.

"Is your grandmother coming to this party?" Allie made a show of looking around. "Because that is the only acceptable reason I can think of on God's green earth for you to be wearing that monstrosity."

He couldn't hold in his laugh. Jackson was never going to have a boring life with this girl, that was for sure.

"There she is." Allie waved at someone over his shoulder. "Stay right there, don't move." She ducked around him. Peter stayed where he was, as ordered. The room was so packed that even if he'd wanted to make an escape he wouldn't have been able to before Allie caught him.

She appeared beside him, a petite blonde trailing behind her. Peter's whole body tensed. It couldn't be. Surely not—

"Peter, this is Sabine. Sabine, this is Peter."

It was. His ex-girlfriend's blond hair hung around her face like a golden sheet, her blue eyes big. This was about to get as awkward as the blind date Allie had set him up on. "Sabine."

"Hi, Peter." She looked as weirded out as he felt. No surprises there. Months of no contact and the first time they saw each other was like this. "Look, I had no idea it was you. That you'd be here."

"You two already know each other?" Allie tucked a piece of hair behind her ear as she directed the question to Peter.

Peter fidgeted. Shoved his hands in his pockets. "Sabine and I used to date."

Allie raised her eyebrows while Sabine gave him a look he couldn't quite interpret. Then she turned to Allie. "For three years. Right, Seven?" She used his old nickname, after his rowing position. He hadn't heard it in months.

Allie glanced between the two of them as Peter tried to beg her with his gaze to save him somehow. Of all the things he'd come prepared for tonight, the second face-to-face post-breakup conversation with his ex was not one of them.

Allie either didn't see his plea or ignored it. "So, um, I'm just going to go and top up the snacks." Traitor. The girl moved faster than a speeding snowball as she turned and disappeared into the crowd.

The two of them studied each other for a second, both trying to find their bearings.

"Seriously, what are you doing here, Bine?" He switched to her nickname. As far as he knew, since their breakup, she'd stayed ensconced in London or wherever the women's rowing team was training. Both of them staying out of each other's turf. Her presence now in the middle of his was a clear breach of the unofficial settlement they'd drawn up. After three years together, a decent geographical distance between them seemed sensible.

Sabine shrugged a slender shoulder. "The team is on break for a couple of weeks so I came down to visit. Annabelle was coming to this and suggested I tag along."

He studied her feigned nonchalance, letting his eyes linger on her perfectly coiffed blond hair, immaculate makeup, and clothes that made the most of her figure without being ostentatious. He checked his emotions. Tried to work out what was tangled there. Was relieved to see that it didn't seem to be dormant attraction.

Certainly nothing compared to the girl who'd fallen out of the wardrobe, which was insane considering he had a long and complicated history with the girl standing in front of him and absolutely none with the one he'd met in the most unorthodox of ways.

"Since I ran into you, can we talk?" Sabine placed a hand on his arm.

"Bine, I don't think we have anything to talk about." He tried to say the words gently. It had been six months since their relationship had ended. It had been hard enough at the time, pain filling her face the day he'd broken it off. He didn't see what good could come from revisiting it.

"Peter, please." She looked up at him, hurt on her face. "Don't I deserve more than that after three years?"

Was he being too hasty? Was the reason he was here tonight to mend some kind of bridge with Sabine? He ran a hand through his hair. "You're right. I'm sorry. How are you?"

"I'm good." She looked up with the limpid gaze that had caused many a male rower twice her size to turn to jelly in her presence. "I've heard you're trying to save SpringBoard."

He was momentarily speechless. That wasn't what he'd expected her to say. "Yeah."

"I want to help."

"Sabine, I don't think that's a good idea." Working with his ex-girlfriend trying to save his dead cousin's charity? That had all sorts of shades of disaster painted around it.

"Anita was my friend too. This isn't about you. I can help."

She was right. He wasn't being fair. He still forgot he wasn't the only one who had loved Anita. He sighed. "Okay. I'll let you know—"

"Sorry to interrupt." Jackson didn't look sorry at all. Peter might've hugged the guy if his arms hadn't been laden with coats. "Do you mind taking these upstairs? We're out of room here. Al says there should be some space in her wardrobe. Otherwise just leave them on her bed. Her room's first on the right."

Peter took them. "Sure thing."

"I don't think we've met. Jackson Gregory." Jackson poured on the charm as he held out his hand to Sabine. At which point Peter knew he'd been sent over by Allie with orders to extricate him. The guy was so besotted with his fiancée, he didn't give strange girls the time of day unless there was a good reason.

Sabine held out her hand. "Sabine Montclair."

"Not the Sabine Montclair nominated for sportswoman of the year?"

Peter did a double take halfway into his exit. He hadn't known about that. It had been one of her dreams for as long as he could remember. He tamped down the urge to give his ex-girlfriend a hug, but she deserved the accolade as much as anyone he knew. Sabine may not have been the girl for him, but he still wanted great things for her.

Sabine's eyes widened, and her jaw dropped a little. She clearly hadn't expected it either. Then a radiant smile spread across her face. "Yes. It was a huge surprise." Peter gave it about thirty seconds before Allie returned to stake her claim. It was now or never if he wanted to escape.

Stepping back, he squeezed through the crowd and headed for the stairs. Lifting the coats so they didn't drag on the floor and trip him up, he turned on the landing and walked to where the first door on the right stood open.

He dropped the coats on the bed, grabbed one of the hangers that Allie had left on the cover, and hooked a red wool coat over it.

Turning, he paused at the sight of a large, ornately carved wardrobe. A smile played on his lips. The last time he'd seen one of these, it had been under far more interesting conditions.

No doubt he'd never see the girl again. A pity since she'd intrigued him far more than he'd have liked to admit. Who climbed into a wardrobe in an antiques shop? And, the question that bugged him most, what had she meant with her comment about his not being a Narnia fan? And how did the teacup he'd been looking for for a decade fit into it all?

He'd almost prayed that they'd cross paths again but had stopped himself. It felt too trivial, too crazy. God had better things to be doing with His time than that. If He was going to do Peter any favors, he'd prefer it involved fixing his shoulder.

Swinging open the wardrobe door, Peter pushed a few hangers aside to make room for the coat, then shoved it in. It was a squeeze, but there might be room for a couple more.

He turned and walked back to the bed and picked up a designer-looking beige trench coat to go next. Settling it on a hanger, he turned. *"Argh!"*

The garment slipped from his hands and fell onto the floor like a sandcastle collapsing under a wave. He blinked. Once. Twice. Just to make sure he wasn't hallucinating.

There she sat. The Narnian wood nymph. Perched on the edge of the wardrobe, boot-clad feet on the floor, clothing swinging around her head, like it was the most natural thing in the world.

THE POOR GUY LOOKED LIKE HE'D SEEN A GHOST. NOT THAT Emelia could blame him. Having someone fall out of a wardrobe once was strange. Finding them in a second one was just lunacy.

She'd held her breath when someone had first opened the door. Almost choked on it when she'd gotten a glimpse of his profile. The only reason Peter hadn't seen her was because he hadn't looked down. She'd hoped with all the desperation of Lucy trying to find Narnia a second time that there was only one coat. But when he hadn't closed the door, she'd known he'd be back and there was no chance he was going to miss a person folded into the bottom of the wardrobe again.

So she'd made a split-second decision to salvage what little dignity she had left and make herself known before she was found.

And so, here they were. She half in and half out of the wardrobe. And he staring at her, opening and closing his mouth like he'd lost the ability to speak.

Emelia took the advantage of surprise to study him a bit more. His hair was as flaming ginger as she remembered, his eyes as green, and his height still as imposing. So she cataloged the smattering of freckles across his face, his wide mouth, his athletic build, and his ugly sweater. Oh, his so-ugly sweater. Green with blue and red diamonds. It had better have some serious sentimental value, because there was no reason anyone should have been wearing it otherwise.

He had a nice face. Not one that would be called up for a *GQ* advertisement anytime soon, unlike Allie's guy, whose name she'd forgotten, but it was nice.

He still hadn't said anything. Instead, he'd kind of sagged onto the bed, still just staring.

Wow. Now this really was getting awkward. It looked as if the ball was in her court. "Hi. Um, sorry if I scared you." She pushed herself up as she spoke. Tried to subtly stretch her legs out.

"You're real." There was a kind of childlike wonder in his voice that wrapped around her heart. "I mean, of course you're real, I just . . ." He flapped one hand around. "Sorry. I'm just not used to finding cute girls in wardrobes."

She laughed as he pinched the bridge of his nose. "If it helps, I'm not used to being found in wardrobes either."

He seemed to regather himself at her words. Rising to his feet, he stood just under a head taller than her in her flat boots. Which would put him at about six foot three to her five foot nine. "I have a model of the *Dawn Treader*. I built it with my grandfather."

What? "Um, that's nice?"

He slid a smile at her that made her feel like she needed to sit back down for a few seconds. "It took us six months. It was like a gazillion pieces. You can't tell a guy who spent six months of his childhood building the *Dawn Treader* that he's not a Narnia fan."

Oh, that. "So you're practically Drinian." She threw out the name of the captain of the ship to test him. If he was such a fan, what was with the Susan/Lucy question? Only those whose knowledge of Narnia began at *The Lion, the Witch and the Wardrobe* and ended at *Prince Caspian* would ever want to be a Susan.

"I like to think I'm slightly less cynical than he was, but just as loyal." Peter tilted his head. "So, do I at least get to know the name of the girl who's almost given me two heart attacks?"

She wanted to offer her name, but something held her back. Once she gave him her name, it would be personal. She'd be more than the crazy wardrobe girl. She wasn't here to do personal. Well, not this kind of personal. She was here for atonement. That couldn't be derailed by some cute English guy, especially not one who had already been exposed to her particular brand of crazy twice and didn't seem to think she belonged in the closest psych ward.

The moment stalled.

"Great, you've found Emelia." Allie bustled into the room with another coat slung over her arm. She looked at Emelia. "Please don't judge him by the sweater. I promise he's cooler than he looks."

Emelia couldn't stop the grin that spread up her cheeks. "It would be hard not to be."

Peter looked back and forth between her and Allie. "She was lost?" She spent every day surrounded by accents, but for some reason, his tugged at something in her every time.

Allie shook her head. "Not lost. Just new. Emelia's recently moved to Oxford. I promised I'd introduce her to a few people."

He gave her a wink and held out his hand. "Well, I guess we should meet officially then. Peter Carlisle."

She held out her hand, aware of Allie watching their every move. "Emelia Mason."

His hand enveloped hers, and his gaze captured hers. Warm, secure. "Nice to meet you, Emelia Mason." Something about the way he smiled sent her heart beating in a way that a host of A-list celebrities with their million-watt grins hadn't managed.

It was nice to meet him too. Which made it a very big problem.

"Did he really spend six months building a model of the *Dawn Treader*?" Emelia directed her question to Allie, giving Peter a second to try to get some air. He had a name. And for some reason, his heart pounded like he'd just sprinted a mile.

"Oh, is that how long that took?" Allie didn't look in the slightest bit put out by the weird question as she grabbed a hanger out of the wardrobe and hooked the coat over it. "I don't know if that's true. But I can tell you he certainly has a model of the boat that he gets very anxious about if someone as much as breathes heavily near it."

"Hey now." That was an overexaggeration if there ever was one. Between the digs at his attire, the Sabine situation, and this, he was beginning to think Allie was more foe than friend.

"Who's your favorite character in the book?" Emelia was still studying him as if she was setting a test and waiting for him to fail.

"*There was a boy called Eustace Clarence Scrubb, and he almost deserved it.*" Peter quoted the first line of *The Voyage of the Dawn Treader* without even thinking about it. Admittedly, the boy was a certified pain in the backside at the beginning, but he was also the character who underwent the biggest transformation over its pages.

"Huh. Interesting." Emelia pulled some kind of upside-down fish-mouth thing as she turned his answer over in her mind. Peter waited for an indication as to whether he had passed or failed whatever the test was, but she gave away nothing. Instead, she plucked another hanger out of the wardrobe and picked another coat off the bed, mirroring Allie's smooth movements.

"Who's yours?"

Emelia thought for a second, her head tilted. *"To defeat the darkness out there, you must defeat the darkness inside yourself."* She took a couple of steps and shoved the final coat into the already full wardrobe.

The words came from the magician Coriakin. Peter tucked away the knowledge that Emelia felt a kinship with the magician who had once been a star but had fallen from grace.

Allie turned from closing the wardrobe doors. "Okay, you two. Are we done trading lines or do we need a few more minutes to hide in here? Want me to bring up snacks and some drinks to tide you over a bit longer?"

Emelia looked startled. As he was sure he did too.

Allie looked at Emelia. "You're hiding from having to try to infiltrate a room full of strangers. Which is fair enough because I hate those as much as the next person, but that's going to change because I'm going to introduce you around now." Allie pointed her finger at Peter. "And he's hiding from his ex-girlfriend. Who I tried to set him up with. My bad. But I can't help him with that short of tying my sheets together so he can shimmy out my window. Which could be quite fun."

Peter blinked as Allie threw him under the bus. Hold on, she was the one who'd sent him up here with the coats . . .

"I'm quite good with tying knots," Emelia offered.

The three of them all stilled for a second as they processed her words.

"I mean . . ." The girl blushed to the tips of her hair as her words trailed off.

Peter's phone buzzed in his pocket. He pulled it out and looked at the screen. *Victor* flashed up at him. Silencing the call, he slid the phone back in his pocket. He was done being his brother's keeper for tonight. Victor would be turning twenty-nine this year. Time for him to get it together. He was the oldest in the rowing squad and still acted like some eighteen-year-old kid getting his first taste of freedom.

His phone started vibrating again.

"Looks like someone really wants to talk to you." Emelia tilted her head at him.

His finger itched to just turn his phone off, but he couldn't do it. He huffed out a breath. "I'm sorry. I should probably take it." Swiping to answer, he walked out into the hallway as he put his phone to his ear. "This had better be good."

"It'shh always good, little bro." His brother's slurred voice came over the line. Charming. Drunk before nine. "I just wanted to let you know, I took your carsh. But I'll bring it back tonight."

"You took my car?"

"Just for a couple of hours. I'll drive it back shoon. No problem."

Uh, yes problem. Very big problem. "Victor, you can't drive."

"I'm fine. Right as rain."

"Where are you?"

"Mazza's place."

Had they all lost their minds? They had training most of the day tomorrow. Starting at six. Not to mention a big five-kilometer erg test first thing on Monday.

Peter heard the sound of shuffling, then someone else on the line. "Coach?"

"Mitchell?" "Mazza" was what the rowing boys called him, but Peter stayed away from nicknames as much as he could. Tried to keep some sort of boundary between coach and team. Even if his brother made it his mission to make it almost impossible.

"Victor's pretty hammered, Coach." The seasoned international didn't sound impressed. Not that Peter could blame him. The guys took their rowing seriously. It probably killed them as much as it killed him that Victor had the superhuman ability to drink until he was completely trollied and still somehow pull phenomenal times on the rowing machine the next morning.

"I'd let him stay here but honestly last time he did, he made a bit of a mess and my flatmates weren't very happy."

It was about a twenty-minute walk from Allie's to Mitchell's flat. As much as he'd have liked to tell the guy just to tip Victor out into the gutter and let him sleep it off, he couldn't. Especially since the sod had nicked his car, and Peter needed it in the morning to get to Wallingford for training. No doubt with his brother half passed out in the passenger seat. "Okay, I'll be there in about half an hour."

Turning, he walked back into Allie's room. "I'm sorry, I have to go." He tried to keep his gaze from Emelia. If he even looked at her, it would probably be written all over his face how much he didn't want to leave.

Allie gave him the stink eye but didn't say anything. She didn't need to. Her view that he should just leave Victor to fend for himself in situations like this was already well established.

"It was nice to meet you, Emelia." In trying to not give himself away, he came off disinterested. It was probably better that way. Meeting a girl who intrigued him was not in the cards for this year. There was no time to be distracted. The only thing that mattered was getting back in the game. He could never make up for how he'd failed Anita, but he was going to do everything he could not to break the final promise he'd made to her.

Nine

Week two. At the job that, if Emelia got it right, would be her atonement. Or some of it at least.

She'd spent the previous week learning about the charity and her way around the system. Now she was on her own. Emelia straightened the pad of paper on her desktop and picked up a ballpoint pen. Across the top of the page she scrawled *HOW TO SAVE SPRINGBOARD?* in large block letters and stared at the four words.

In nine months she'd have either answered that question or not. If it was the former, she could return to LA with some sense of closure. If not, Anita's legacy would be consigned to the same scrap heap as the many other charities that had tried and failed.

Peter did not feel very brave; indeed, he felt he was going to be sick. But that made no difference to what he had to do. The quote from *The Lion, the Witch and the Wardrobe* flashed through her head. That was basically how she felt about the rest of the year.

"Emelia?" Elizabeth stuck her head in the door. "Great, you're here. Can you drop by my office at nine thirty? I need to introduce you to the board member who's been given oversight of fund-raising this year."

Great. Just what she needed. Some pompous middle-aged man breathing down her neck. Emelia summoned up a smile about as fake as the color of Pink's hair. "Sure. Who will I be meeting?"

"Of course, his—" The phone in Elizabeth's hand buzzed and she looked down at the screen. "Sorry, I need to take this." She put her phone to her ear and her gray head disappeared from view.

Oh, well, it couldn't be that hard to figure out. Emelia had done her research on the board before she'd interviewed for the role. There were three men on it. Pulling up the homepage, she refreshed herself on their details. One was a retired lawyer, one a semiretired teacher, and the last a has-been children's author from the nineties. Calling any of them middle-aged would have been generous. She sighed as she closed out of the page.

She doodled on her paper. No point trying to dream up any grand fund-raising plans until she had the measure of what she was going to have to work with. Or, more likely, work around.

Her phone buzzed in her purse. Picking the purse up off the floor, she placed it on the top of her desk and started rifling through it. Unable to locate her phone, she tipped the contents of her bag onto the surface, everything falling out into a messy pile. Her cousin's name lit up the screen of her phone.

"Hey, Lace." She wedged the phone between her ear and shoulder as she returned her wallet, change, and a handful of pens. A copy of *The Silver Chair* teetered on the edge of her desk. She reached for it but only succeeded in tipping it over the edge. It landed with a slap on the floor. She'd salvage it later.

"I still can't believe you managed to talk them into it." Though Lacey's opening line didn't show it, her cousin was a professional schmoozer who excelled at small talk. She just only used it when she had to.

"Clearly a case of desperate times, desperate measures." Emelia didn't mention that she'd gone out of her way to hide her connection to Mia Caldwell. She already knew what her cousin would think of that.

"So what's it like?"

Emelia cast her gaze over the industrial metal filing cabinet in the corner of her office, the old desk in front of her, and the faded wallpaper. "Let's just say no one is ever going to accuse them of wasting money on high-class office space." In her mind's eye she imagined Lacey's LA office with its large windows and sprawling view of the city. Her cousin's idea of slumming it would be Starbucks running out of hazelnut syrup for her latte.

"So what's up on today's agenda?"

Emelia let a groan rumble out of her throat. "Apparently I've got some board member who is going to be overseeing my work. I'm meeting him in"—she glanced at the clock—"seven minutes."

"Oooooooh." Her cousin was the type who saw romantic possibilities around every corner. Which was also part of the reason she went through men like water.

"You wouldn't be saying that if you'd seen the three options. Go have a look at the website." She waited a few seconds for her cousin to do just that. Lacey was perma-attached to multiple devices. For her, a high-speed Internet connection was a close second to oxygen.

She knew the instant her cousin had seen the page by the sound of the snort coming from the other end of the line, one Lacey tried to smother by clearing her throat. "Okay, maybe not. But you never know. New city, new possibilities."

"I'm not here for new possibilities, I'm here to save Anita's charity. That's it. The last thing I need is some British guy complicating things." She forced her mind away from a very specific British guy in particular. There was no way she could ever mention Peter to Lacey. What Emelia planned to write off as nothing more than a set of random and meaningless coincidences, Lacey would see as some kind of crazy cosmic intervention.

Whatever the phone call Saturday night was about, it had made him leave the party at full speed. She'd lasted another hour, the time simply a blur of names and faces as Allie had been on a mission to introduce her to people. Stupidly, she'd stayed that long hoping Peter would come back. Which was about as crazy as climbing into strangers' wardrobes.

"Are you sure you want to be doing this?" Her cousin's question jolted her back to the present.

"I have to do this."

"I worry about you, Meels. I worry about what will happen if this doesn't work out."

"Don't. It's going to work." It had to. She didn't know how she'd live with herself if it didn't. The clock on her screen changed to 9:27. Time to find out if she was being paired up with googly eyes, bad teeth, or rampant facial hair. "Gotta go, Lace. I'll talk to you later."

Closing out the call, she stood and smoothed down her navy knee-length wool skirt. *You can do this, Emelia.* She gave herself a pep talk as she exited her office and headed down the hall. *You have charmed the world's crankiest misogynistic men to get a story. And this is more important than any of those stories ever were.*

She approached Elizabeth's door, which stood ajar. From inside the office, a male voice came. Clipped, frustrated. Emelia's hand froze just before it knocked, as she registered what he was saying.

". . . an American? You know what they are like. Loud. In your face. Treading over everyone's toes. They offend people even when they don't mean to."

Loud? Offensive? Emelia felt her face flush.

"Well, it wasn't like I had much choice." Elizabeth's voice came back low and terse. "For what we were offering we're lucky we got any applicants at all. I grant you, it's not ideal, but at least she had some charity experience in LA. The one other applicant may have had the right accent but she was so witless she couldn't have organized a drink in a brewery. Anyway, it's done. She's been hired and will be here any minute now."

Googly eyes, or whichever he was, heaved a sigh. "I think we're making a big mistake. Americans seem to think everything can be solved with a GoFundMe page. Putting someone in charge of saving SpringBoard who doesn't even know how the English do things? I agreed to help out with supervising, not babysitting."

Babysitting? At that Emelia lost all sense of self-preservation and pushed the door open. Her gaze first landed on Elizabeth's startled face, before she pivoted to face her self-christened "babysitter." "I can promise you, I don't need any—"

Then she registered the agape mouth and green eyes staring at her. Oh. No. It couldn't be. "Peter?"

There was no way. There was absolutely no way. Except there was. The American he'd just been so vehemently deriding, who'd overheard presumably every word he'd spoken, was the same one he hadn't been able to stop thinking about since their first meeting.

"Do you two know each other?" Elizabeth tilted her head, scrutinizing him.

"Um, yes. We've met." Peter managed to force the words around a chest that felt like he'd just rowed 5K at full stroke.

Elizabeth's gaze bounced between the two of them. Peter had no doubt he'd turned as white as the snowflakes drifting from the sky outside. Emelia's blue-gray eyes were so large they dominated her face.

The only person in the room who was taking things in her stride was the calm executive officer. "I see. Is this going to be a problem?"

Peter opened his mouth to say no, but no matter how much he tried, he was unable to force the word out. Emelia seemed to be waiting for him to take the lead.

After a couple of seconds of silence, Elizabeth took control of the situation. "Emelia, can you give us a few minutes? I'll come and find you when we're done."

Emelia didn't say a word as she stepped backward and closed the door firmly behind her.

Elizabeth waited for the door to click before crossing her arms over her red cardigan as she leaned against her desk.

"Care to tell me what that was about?" Even though he had a good foot and forty kilos on her, Peter felt like a six-year-old boy summoned into the headmistress's office to be told off.

Peter looked down at the résumé he held in his hand. Emelia's résumé. He hadn't even opened it. All he'd heard Elizabeth say was that she'd hired an American and he'd gone off. For no good reason. At least none that was related to the matter at hand.

"Do you mind if I sit down?" Without waiting for an answer he sagged into the seat behind him. It creaked under his weight, the arms pressing his legs together.

He sucked in a breath. *Pull it together, Peter.* Emelia, *Emelia*, of all people, was SpringBoard's new fund-raising coordinator.

"It's nothing, Elizabeth. Really." It still felt weird calling her Elizabeth. Since he'd been ten he'd known her as Greg's mum. "Mrs. Bradman" or "ma'am" whenever a designation beyond that was required.

She snorted. Loudly. He couldn't have been more surprised if the ladylike, conservative Elizabeth Bradman had started dancing a jig. "Peter, whatever that was, it was not nothing. And I need to know exactly what it was. Is she an ex? A one-night stand? Some rowing groupie you took home once and now there's a voodoo doll with your face on it stabbed with a hundred pins sitting on her dresser?"

"What? *No!*"

"Well, then *what*?" Her fingernails tapped on the desk beside her.

"We just met at a party on Saturday night, that's all."

"Really."

What was he supposed to do? Tell Emelia's boss they'd

met when she'd fallen out of a wardrobe onto him? That at the party she'd been hiding in another one? Mrs. Bradman had always seemed like a good sort but who knew how she'd take that. "Look, I think we were both surprised to see each other here. That's all."

Mrs. Bradman—Elizabeth—sighed. Gave him a look that said loud and clear she knew there was far more to it than that. "Peter, you aren't getting this. I have an employment issue here. I've hired Emelia. On her second week she has just overheard one of the board members openly doubting her ability to do her role. And not just any board member, the one whom she is meant to be working with. Putting aside the fact that she's an American, do you have any kind of knowledge, or evidence, that Emelia is not fit for this position?"

"No."

"Well then." She said the two words with a sense of finality.

Well then?

"You're going to be the one to step down."

Step down? His shock must have shown on his face because she quickly added, "Not from the board. But you can't be the member in charge of fund-raising. We'll have to ask one of the others to do it."

Peter cast his mind across the remaining three board members. All well-meaning, perfectly nice people, but totally ill suited to the task at hand. That was the whole reason he'd joined the board. Because even from a distance it was obvious that the status quo was going to lead to Anita's dreams for the charity going up in smoke. And that couldn't happen.

He tried to speak calmly, rationally. "Elizabeth, you and I both know that none of them are up to the task." He attempted to ignore the little voice in his head suggesting that wasn't the only reason he didn't want to give the role up.

"What I know is that I can't have the two key people we need to give us a chance at saving this place at odds with each other. Or with some kind of unresolved tension, whatever that's about. That's a recipe for failure right from the beginning." She leaned forward and touched him briefly on the shoulder. The same lilac scent she'd had for years wafted with her. "Peter, I know this is personal. But you know I'm right. If this isn't going to be a viable partnership then we need to change it now."

"Let me go and talk to her." He put his hands on the chair's arms and stood, managing to unwedge his legs from their grip.

"I don't know if that's a good idea."

"Please. And, after that, if she says that she would prefer to work with another board member, I'll step down. No questions asked."

Elizabeth leaned back against her desk, considering for a few seconds. "Okay, but don't let me regret it."

He could only hope he wouldn't either.

Emelia sat ramrod straight in her chair. Hands clasped in her lap. Waiting for Elizabeth to walk in and try to fire her. "Try" being an important word because there was no way Emelia was letting this job go without a fight. Not when she'd crossed an ocean for it. She'd left her door open. Figured she might as well see it coming.

Peter Carlisle. The whole crazy scenario made working with googly eyes or bad teeth or rampant facial hair look like a costarring role with Brad Pitt in comparison.

Her fingers ached to pull up Google. All she would need to do is type in his name and a few key words, and in seconds she'd at least have a clue what she was dealing with. Some kind of idea as to why, of all the charities in the world, he was on the board of this small, unglamorous, almost bankrupt one that couldn't even keep its website up to date.

She'd even typed in his first name before she'd remembered her vow to no longer snoop about people online and closed the browser, pried her fingers off the keyboard.

She'd almost called Lacey, but then she would've had to fill her cousin in on the whole backstory, and that really wasn't worth it with a girl whose guilty hobby was churning through Fabio-covered romance novels like they were Diet Coke.

So instead she sat, still as a statue, counting the seconds and waiting for the sound of Elizabeth's door opening.

Five hundred and eleven. That was how many she counted before the sound came, accompanied by heavy footsteps in the hall. Peter. She waited for his footsteps to head toward the exit, but instead they came toward her office.

For some insane reason she held her breath. Like it would—what? Cast some kind of invisible cloak around her?

The sound of his approach stalled as he got closer to her door. Emelia pictured him standing there, just out of sight. Well, she wasn't going to sit there like some kind of piece of prey. "So, are you planning to come in or just stay out there all day?"

Her voice was clipped, no-nonsense, betraying none of the breakdancing her insides were performing.

After a second or two, Peter's head came around the corner, followed by the rest of him. Between his impressive height and muscular build, he took up the entire doorway. She took the opportunity to notice what she hadn't in her shocked stupor. The ugly sweater was gone, replaced by a dark jacket, V-neck T, and worn jeans. "I was wondering if you were going to throw something at me."

Tempting. And not just the throwing part. Emelia gestured around her empty desk and sparse office. "That would have been a distinct possibility, but as you can see, I don't actually have anything suitable."

Peter took a step into her office, his presence dwarfing her. She had to tilt her chin up just to see his face. "I, um, owe you an apology."

"Are you sorry that you said it or just that I overheard it?"

His green eyes widened. What? Had he expected her to go easy on him? Brush it under the carpet? Pretend it hadn't happened? If they were going to have to work together it wasn't going to start out with her acting like a doormat. Even if it was all very *American* of her.

"I just—" Peter pulled out the chair opposite her desk and squished his frame into it. Leaning forward, he placed his elbows on his knees and clasped his hands. He gave her a wry smile. "I'm definitely sorry that you overheard it. Elizabeth has just read me the riot act."

Emelia said nothing. Just looked at him. That was his apology? His red hair stuck up at all angles. It hadn't been like that in Elizabeth's office. She could almost see him running his hands through it in agitation as if she'd been there.

"Look, I'm sorry. I was rude. I'm sorry for how I said what I did."

Yeah, still not a real apology. "But you meant it."

Peter looked trapped. She waited. She could already tell he was a terrible liar, so it would be interesting to see if he tried to bluff his way through. He huffed out a breath, shoulders dropping. "Look, I'm sorry that I was rude, I'm sorry that you heard it, but I can't pretend that I don't have concerns about whether an American can do this job. English and Americans, we're just . . . different. And, as I'm sure you've worked out, Spring-Board is in trouble. We can't afford to make any mistakes." At least he had the guts to look her straight in the face as he said it. She had to give him that.

"You're new. On the board." He could read whatever he wanted into her leaving his half apology on the table.

He gave her a look of grudging respect. "Yes. Just a couple of months."

"How bad is it?" Her number one job for the week had been to try to put an exact dollar figure on what she needed to accomplish. She might as well take advantage of having a board member in her office to get the intel. And one who owed her. "How much do we need to raise between now and the end of the year to make it viable again?"

"One point one, give or take."

A million pounds was roughly 1.5 million US dollars. It was worse than she'd thought. Emelia schooled her expression into neutral. Unlike the guy sitting opposite her, she was a great poker player. If worst came to worst she might well need it to supplement her paltry wage from this place. "Okay."

"Okay?"

"I guess we've got our work cut out for us."

"So you'll work with me? Even after what I said." Peter ran his hand through his hair, sending the tufts in a different direction.

"If it's not you, then it's one of the other board members, right?"

Peter eased back in the chair. "Yup."

"Well then, I choose you." For some reason, when the words came out, it felt like they had a lot more meaning than she'd intended them to.

She was here for atonement, not for anything else. And definitely not with some guy who was practically her boss.

Ten

Emelia walked into work on Wednesday morning, her brain hazy and body aching. This week was it. No matter what, she was getting out of the ghetto B and B with the cray-cray landlady.

The night before had been the final straw. The TV in the room below had blared infomercials until after four. Then this morning a new boarder had eyed her up and down like he'd just done a ten-year stretch and she was the first woman he'd seen on the outside. She was done. She had two days to come up with a plan that would let her prove herself to Peter and she couldn't do that when she was so tired she could barely think coherently.

"You okay?" Elizabeth looked over at her from where she sat at the front desk, sorting the mail. Her boss spent most of her time in that spot since SpringBoard could no longer afford a receptionist.

"I . . ." Emelia rubbed the back of her neck. She didn't really want to admit how bad her living situation was, but it was her own naivety that had gotten her into it. Maybe she'd have better luck if she got some local help. "I need a new place to live. The one I'm in isn't working out so well."

"Where are you at the moment?" Elizabeth took a sip from the porcelain teacup that always sat wherever she was working and was never empty. Its pretty floral pattern reminded Emelia of the one she'd found in the wardrobe the night she'd met Peter.

Emelia sighed. "The Magnolia Manor."

Phswew. Tea sprayed back into Elizabeth's cup. She looked like Emelia had just told her she was sleeping under a park bench.

Reaching for her linen napkin—yes, she kept one of those on hand too—Elizabeth dabbed at a tiny spot of tea that had landed on her gray skirt. "I think that would be a good idea. I've heard it's not the most salubrious of establishments."

The British. The epitome of understated.

"Any ideas?"

"I have to admit that I'm not exactly tapped into where the young folk find flatmates these days, but I'll ask around." Her boss ran the napkin over the sides of her cup.

"I've been keeping my eyes on a few websites, but nothing I'm interested in is available for a few more weeks, and I'd like to find a new place sooner rather than later." There was no chance she'd survive in the B and B for much longer without committing a felony.

Elizabeth scrunched her face up, then brightened. "Oh, I know. There's a bulletin board in the staff room. Occasionally, there's accommodation listings on that."

Emelia checked the clock. Still six minutes before she officially started work. "I think I'll go and take a quick look." Yes, she was that desperate.

Dropping her bag and coat in her office as she walked past, she made her way to the staff room. Which was a generous term to describe the small kitchenette with a sink, microwave, and minifridge. Above the counter hung a corkboard, a hodgepodge of notices stuck to it. Some were so faded and curled, Emelia was sure they'd been there since the last millennium.

Housemate wanted. Female. Town house within 30 minutes' walk of university. 150 pounds a week + expenses. Available immediately. See Dr. Allison Shire.

Emelia looked at the date in the right-hand corner. It had been posted a couple of weeks ago. She was probably already too late. And one fifty a week would take a hefty chunk out of her paycheck. But she'd happily pay it for a room where she could sleep at night. Even if it was with a seventy-year-old spinster academic.

She pulled the stiff card off the bulletin board and walked back to the front desk, the edges of the card poking into her hands. *Available immediately.* The magic words.

"Anything?" Elizabeth's gray bob swung as she looked up when Emelia returned.

"Maybe. A Dr. Shire is looking for a female housemate. Or was, anyway. Do you know if she still is?" Emelia held up the card in front of her.

"No. I haven't had much to do with her. She's a recent volunteer but seems lovely. Rave reviews from the first school we sent her to. The kids adored her. Unfortunately, she's just here until September. She's a guest lecturer at the university. Specialty is Tolkien."

Emelia almost choked. Was this some kind of joke? "Dr. Shire's specialty is Tolkien." She didn't quite manage to keep the incredulity out of her voice.

A smile tugged at Elizabeth's peach-colored lips. "I know."

"She's also kind of hobbit-sized." Emelia froze as a familiar female voice came from behind her along with a gust of cold air. She glanced over to Elizabeth to find she was studiously staring at her screen like it contained the solution to world peace.

Emelia turned to see Allie's green eyes and freckles. In a stylish beige overcoat and high-heeled brown leather boots, she looked about ten years older than she had battling the copier. Allie. Allie. Allison. *Oh.*

"Morning." Allie smiled as she pulled a gray knit cap off her head, shaking her copper hair free.

"Hi." Emelia's mind was still trying to wrap around the fact that the pretty young girl she'd taken for a student was actually a lecturer. Who'd just heard her mocking her name. Who'd been her one hope of escaping the ghetto anytime soon.

Oh, this was bad. She didn't need to feel the heat creeping up her cheeks to know she was turning as red as a blood moon.

Allie—Dr. Shire—shifted the pile of books she was holding in one arm. "Anyway, the answer is yes."

"Yes?"

"Yes, I'm still looking for a housemate. Are you interested?"

In living in Allie's cute town house. Was she serious? "Yes."

"The lease is only through September because that's when my contract currently finishes up. And you can hassle my name all you want as long as you don't make the mistake of calling me Australian. We New Zealanders are a bit precious about that."

"Have you been to Hobbiton?" The question was out before Emelia could stop it. Ever since she'd seen the movies, she'd wanted to visit. Allie probably got asked that all the time. Way to be original. She could've kicked herself.

"Many, many times. So rent is one fifty a week and power,

Internet, stuff like that usually adds up to another thirty. Excluding food. I hadn't really thought too much about that. I figure we can just buy our own breakfast and lunch stuff and see how we go for dinners."

Under two hundred pounds a week. She'd gladly have paid double that and lived on noodles. More so with every passing second. "Sounds fine."

"Um, what else . . ." Allie tilted her head and looked into space. "Oh, I should tell you about Jackson."

The name rang a bell.

"He's my fiancé. He's at Cambridge doing an MBA, so I'm up there every second weekend and he comes down here every other weekend."

Of course. The good-looking guy from the party who had stared at Allie with besotted eyes whenever they were in the same room. Responsible for the very large diamond on Allie's finger, which Emelia had just noticed. "I think I met him on Saturday."

Allie's face brightened. "Of course you did."

So she'd be the third wheel for three days out of every fourteen. And probably need to buy some earplugs. Sounded like a bargain price to pay. "When are you getting married?"

"We, uh, haven't set a date yet." Something in Allie's countenance shifted. Huh. Interesting. From what she'd observed they were practically the world's most smitten couple, yet they hadn't set a wedding date. Her journalistic radar pinged with the scent of a story but she ignored it.

Allie hurried on. "So, what do you think?"

Emelia's face must have been blank because Allie expanded on her question. "About moving in?"

That was it? A ninety-second quasi-interview? "Don't you

want to know anything more about me?" Emelia regretted the question as soon as she'd asked it. What was wrong with her, inviting questions she might not be able to answer? She liked Allie. Didn't want to lie to her. But there was no chance Allie would have her as a roommate if she had any idea what Emelia had done. The pain she'd caused.

Allie scrunched up her forehead, then shook her head. "Not really. Peter likes you and Elizabeth hired you." Emelia looked to where her boss was watching the whole exchange with an amused look. "Between those two things, I know pretty much the most important stuff. And if you end up being one of those flatmates urban legends are made of, my name is the one on the lease, so I can just change the locks and leave your stuff on the stoop." She grinned.

Emelia's heart rate had escalated at the mention of Peter, but Allie moved on before she could dwell on the words "Peter likes you."

"When do you want to move in?"

It almost killed her to say it, but she didn't want to appear too eager. "How about this weekend?" Two more nights wouldn't kill her.

"Sure. Where are you staying at the moment?"

"The Magnolia Manor."

Allie's mouth almost dropped off her face at the same time as the top book slid off her pile and hit the floor with a bang. "The grotty place they parole inmates to?" She ignored the tome at her feet.

"They do?" Well, that explained a lot.

"I have a car. How about tonight?"

Eleven

PETER OPENED THE DOOR TO SPRINGBOARD'S OFFICE AND stepped inside, a blast of sleet accompanying him. Someone had forgotten to tell nature it was spring already. Slamming the inclement weather out, he pulled his hat off and ran his fingers through his damp hair.

After an hour standing on the riverbank, watching guys out on the water, frozen to the bone, bodies straining against the wind and rain, not even a shower with the hot water on full blast could get the chill out of his bones.

"Morning." Elizabeth looked up from her perch at the front desk.

"Morning. How's everything looking?" She was probably doing month-end. There was a board meeting coming up where Elizabeth would be giving the latest financial update.

She pulled her glasses off and pinched the bridge of her nose.

"That bad, huh?"

"We're going to need a miracle. You here to meet with Emelia?"

"Yeah." His pulse thrummed in his neck. It had been five days since she'd managed to see a way through his behaving like a donkey's behind and not replace him with another board member.

Elizabeth gave him a piercing look. "Emelia told me she's willing to work with you, but don't forget what I said. If there are any issues . . ."

He would be the one to go. "I know." There wouldn't be. He wouldn't allow it. Saving SpringBoard was way too important. He could do cordial-but-distant. Lord knew he'd had enough experience with some of the rowing groupies over the years. "We'll come up with a plan, Elizabeth. A good one." At least the board had given them until the April meeting to come back with some formal fund-raising proposals.

"Just do your best, that's all any of us can do." He hated that there was an air of defeat about the way that she said it as she turned her attention back to her computer screen. But then she was the one taking the calls from donors with every excuse under the sun as to why they were pulling their support.

Shrugging out of his coat, he hung it on the rack in the corner, adding his hat to another hook. Stalling for time. The twisting in his gut was a sensation from the past. It was reserved for the starting lines of big races. He hadn't been on one of those in nine months. It didn't belong in this dingy office, about to start a meeting with a girl he had to maintain a professional distance from.

He strode down the hall, the sound of his feet announcing his approach. Emelia looked up as he rounded her door. Her wavy hair was pulled back into a thick braid and she wore a fitted red sweater that did nothing to downplay her curves.

His confident stride stalled at the distinctly unprofessional, non-distant thought.

"Morning." She tilted her head. "Are you planning to come in?"

"Yes. Sorry." He took a couple of steps forward, sat down in the chair opposite her desk. It was different from the one he'd sat in last time.

"I traded it out. It looked pretty uncomfortable. Being wedged in the last one." She answered his question before he could even think it, the hint of a smile on her full lips.

"Thanks." Interesting. Emelia was very observant. He filed the piece of information away.

They sat in silence for a couple of seconds.

"So—" they both said at once.

"You go first—" And again. Then silence.

"How are you finding Oxford?" Peter grasped at the first thing that came to mind. Good one. That wasn't lame at all.

Emelia leaned back in her chair. "Pretty good." She cast a glance up to her small window, where the sound of wind whipping around outside seeped through. "Can't say this is what I imagined when I pictured an English spring."

"Are you staying with family?" He tried to sound only politely interested. Hopefully she'd say she was living with her boyfriend. Some nerdy Harvard alumnus doing his PhD in biophysics. He was busy hibernating in a lab somewhere, which was why he hadn't been at the party. That would kill whatever this distracting chemistry was between them. Force him to focus on the task at hand. The one that mattered.

"I've, um, moved in with Allie."

Peter just stared at her. Had she just said she'd moved in with Allie? His Allie? Well, not *his* Allie, but . . .

"If it's going to create problems, I can find somewhere else."

Emelia rushed in, seeming to take his silence as discontent. "I'm sorry. I didn't think about this. Us." Her hand gestured between the two of them. "I mean not us us. Obviously. I mean they're your friends. I get that it might be awkward. Or weird. Of course it is. I fall out of a wardrobe onto you. Then you find me in another one at a party. Then I'm working here. Now I've moved in with your friend. Wow. Now that I've said it aloud it's very weird. I'll find somewhere else." Her words kind of tumbled out, falling over each other.

"No." He held his hand up to try to slow the tirade. "It's not weird."

Her brow rumpled. "It's not?"

"I mean, it's certainly an interesting lineup of events. I was just surprised." *In the kind of good way that should have alarm bells flashing.* "Look, Allie is great. And I know Jackson will be happy she's got a roommate. He worries about her living alone since he's in Cambridge." He flashed her a grin. "The *Lord of the Rings* and Narnia nerds together under one roof. Tolkien and Lewis would be thrilled."

Emelia laughed. "I'm pretty sure I have a long way to go before I'll come even close to Allie's level."

The sound of her laughter resonated inside him, resulting in a lighthearted feeling that he hadn't felt since Anita died. If his cousin were here right now, she'd probably have been giving him eyes, mouthing "I like her" at him.

But she wasn't. And it was all his fault.

If Lacey were here right now, she'd have been mentally designing her couture bridesmaid's dress. And part of Emelia wouldn't have blamed her. She hadn't had this kind of chemistry with anyone since . . . well, ever, if truth be told.

She'd walked in here this morning knowing exactly what she was doing. Guarded. After two nights of real sleep and hot showers she was back on her game. Playbook prepared and memorized. Two minutes of small talk, then down to business. Cordial but professional. Everything had changed now that Peter was her sort-of boss.

Then it had all unraveled the instant she had connected that moving in with Allie put them in not only the same professional circle but also the same personal one.

"So, um . . ." Peter cleared his throat. "We should probably talk about how we want to approach this. Working together."

Emelia tried to divert her gaze from the way his sweater stretched across his sculpted shoulders. Allie had mentioned he coached the Oxford rowing team and he was clearly a rower as well. Or had been. Even though she'd managed to find him a larger chair his powerful physique still dwarfed it like it was a piece of doll's furniture.

"Emelia?" Peter tilted his head and gave her a bemused look.

"Yes, of course." *Focus, Emelia. Guard up.* Her self-imposed Google exile still stood, so she couldn't research him online, but there was only one reason she could think of why a guy like Peter would be involved in a failing charity. There had to be some kind of personal connection. Which meant that if he knew who she really was, he would hate her. Rightfully so. "I've drawn up a draft proposal for your consideration. Very high level." Picking up two copies of the plan she'd spent the day before sweating over, she pushed one copy across her desk toward him.

He reached forward, the movement doing absolutely nothing to hide his muscular physique. She forced her gaze to the page in front of her. The words swam out of focus but it didn't matter. She knew the whole thing back to front.

There were only three things that mattered: Saving Anita's charity. No one here finding out who she was. And keeping her wildly inappropriate attraction when it came to the man sitting opposite her firmly in check.

Peter scanned the pages. Emelia pretended to be looking over hers, while reading into every tap of his fingertips, twitch of his cheek, and furrow of his brow.

He hated it. Oh, he hated it. Maybe he was right. She didn't have any business being here. Her little stints of charity involvement back home had nothing on this.

Finally, he lowered the pages and leaned forward, looking directly at her. "Tell me about these three big events."

Emelia leaked out a breath. He hadn't shot her down outright. That was a start. "Given our size and resources"—*or lack thereof*—"I think that we're better placed to focus on three major fund-raising events. We can fit in smaller ones around them if it works but one of the big mistakes charities often make is spreading themselves too thinly across too many small activities that just don't offer a good return on investment."

Something flickered in his green eyes. Not quite approval, but maybe grudging acceptance. "What kind of things could they be?"

"It could be anything. Sporting. Cultural. Intellectual. We are in Oxford after all. I have a couple of ideas but I was hoping you could maybe give me some guidance." As much as it pained her to admit it, he was right. She did need someone who knew the "English way."

"You're thinking summer, autumn, and winter?"

"Yes, since we're already into spring. I was thinking everything should culminate in a big event toward the end of the year. That also gives us some time to . . ." She trailed off, not sure how to say what she needed to. But it had to be said if they were going to make any headway. Or they'd just be spitting into the wind.

"To?"

"Work on reputation repair." She said the words quietly, gaze focused at a spot just over his shoulder.

"You're referring to Anita." His shoulders tensed a little, but his gaze, his tone, remained neutral. Nothing to give her any hint as to how close their personal relationship was. Or even if they had one.

"Yes. I'm assuming that's part of why you've been losing donors."

Peter leaned back, looped his hands around his propped-up knee. "It would be fair to say that a number have given that as their reason for reconsidering their involvement with SpringBoard, yes. She was also our biggest fund-raising weapon. The board are well-meaning and dedicated to the cause but none of us have the hobnobbing skills that she did. SpringBoard's success was all down to her."

"I'm sorry." Emelia struggled to keep a hitch from her voice. She'd seen Anita out on the LA social circuit a few times. The girl was beautiful, vivacious, and intelligent. The type who could sell sand to Saudi Arabia. If it wasn't for who Anita had been engaged to, she'd still have been alive and Emelia would still have been in LA making a career off destroying people's lives. She couldn't change it. The one thing left was to ensure Anita's legacy didn't die along with her.

Peter turned his attention back to her as he finished the document. "So, tell me, what's your great idea?"

Under the intensity of his gaze she suddenly doubted herself. What if it wasn't a good idea at all? Not that she'd even claimed it was. "So Cambridge and Oxford are quite big rivals, right?"

Peter's mouth twitched. "Very."

"Could we use that somehow? Have some kind of Oxford-versus-Cambridge event? Or even a couple of them?"

"Go on."

"I was thinking you obviously have an in with the rowing team. What if after the Boat Race we set up some other kind of contest between the two teams? It wouldn't have to be rowing. It could be something more friendly." The famous annual rowing fixture between the two universities was only a few weeks away. The opportunity to leverage off it was too good not to explore.

Peter barked out a laugh. "You could have a knitting contest between the Oxford and Cambridge rowing teams and it wouldn't be friendly." He bit the bottom of his lip, thinking. "We'd have to get the go-ahead pretty fast. Once the Boat Race is over the guys are generally pretty jammed catching up with their studies and preparing for exams. Then they all disappear in July. And it wouldn't be an official Oxford-versus-Cambridge fixture."

"But even if it was something unofficial? With only some of the guys voluntarily participating? Would it still be enough to get people interested?"

She held her breath as he pondered her question across from her.

After a few seconds he grinned, a dimple she hadn't noticed before appearing on his left cheek. "Probably. The rowing competition is so intense people would pay to watch them play tiddlywinks against each other. You might just have cracked something. I'm embarrassed I didn't think of it myself."

She couldn't stop herself from grinning back.

"I'll just need to talk to a few people. I'm sure I could get some of the Oxford guys on board easy enough. Give me a few days to sound out my Cambridge connections. I'll work out if it will be better to formally raise it before the race or after."

His moss-green gaze connected with hers across her desk and for a second neither of them looked away. "Right, so . . ." She trailed off, not having a plan for either his unbridled enthusiasm for her idea or whatever it was that was bouncing between them.

"The team leaves for London tomorrow. We train there the last few weeks before the race. Is it better for me to call or email when I've talked to a few people?" He quirked up a smile. "Actually, we'll be keeping some pretty weird hours, I'll just email."

"No!" They both jumped a little as she practically yelled. Why didn't she just write *call me* across her forehead? "I mean, phone is fine—"

A ringtone saved her from herself. Not hers. Peter fumbled for a second, then pulled his iPhone out of his pocket.

"Sorry. I need to take this." Swiping the screen, he put it to his ear. "Hi." The other person spoke for a couple of seconds. "You're joking." A few more words. "Okay, I'll be there as soon as I can." Stabbing the screen, Peter shoved the phone back into his pocket and blew out a huff of air. "I'm really sorry. I've got to go."

"Right. Sure." The sudden sense of loss left her disconcerted.

Peter was already out of his chair and halfway through her door. Then he paused and turned back. "Are you coming? To the Boat Race?"

"I, um . . ." She floundered. For all the hype around the city about the big annual showdown between the two universities, it hadn't occurred to her to go.

"You should. Jackson and Allie are coming. It's pretty amazing." He tilted his head, flashing the dimple. "I think you'd like it, Emelia Mason."

She couldn't have said no if she tried. "Okay."

"Okay, I'll see you there." And with that he was gone, leaving her as flushed and flustered as a dorky mathlete who'd just been invited to the prom by the star quarterback.

Emelia Mason. She replayed the way he'd said her name in her head. It had sounded nice. Respectable. Maybe even a little bit girl-next-door.

Everything she wasn't.

Twelve

Peter tried to clamp down on the churning inside of him as he ran, cutting across lanes and streets, almost slipping a few times on cobblestones. Puffing, he pulled up in front of his destination, sweat trickling between his shoulder blades despite the cold. He wished he could say it was the first time, but it wasn't. Far from it. The Saint Aldates police station sat in front of him, three imposing stories of beige stone. At least it was barely a couple of kilometers from the SpringBoard offices.

What had his brother done now? Peter trudged through the main door, pausing to let out a man who smelled like he hadn't taken a shower this side of Christmas. Walking inside, his feet tramped their way across the familiar peeling linoleum to the front desk. The bobby tending it offered up a flicker of recognition. "Can I help?"

"Peter Carlisle. I've had a call from Sergeant Grant."

The flicker of recognition turned into a mental connection. "Ah, you're the brother. I'll just get the sarge for you."

Peter drummed his fingers on the front desk as the constable disappeared through the door behind him. In a few seconds, he returned with Sergeant Mark Grant behind him. His friend opened the partition off to the side and let him through. Mark looked weary, annoyed, which was to be expected.

No point wasting any time. "What was it this time?"

Mark strode ahead of him through the bowels of the station. "The usual. Drunk and disorderly. Urinating in a public place as a bonus."

Classy, his brother. Peter glanced at his watch. "It's barely lunchtime." He'd only last seen Victor a few hours ago at training. They still had the second session of the day this evening. What on earth was wrong with him?

"We picked him up at ten. I gave him a couple of hours to dry out before I even called."

A sigh escaped him. "Thanks, Mark. I really appreciate it."

His friend studied him with a somber face. "He's got to sort it out, Pete. And I mean soon. This is the third time this month. At this rate, it's only a matter of time before he's going to get charged with something. And when that happens, there's no special favors. He'll get exactly the same as anyone else."

Peter pinched the bridge of his nose. "I'll talk to him." Like Victor would listen. But what else could he do? His brother's wild ways were already breaking his parents' hearts, and they didn't even know the half of it.

"You ever think that you might be making it worse by constantly rescuing him?"

Well, it clearly wasn't making it any better. "What happens if I don't? If you call me and I don't come, then what?"

Mark shrugged. "Depends on the situation. But maybe it's time to let him find out."

And take the risk that the papers would get wind of the fact that the future Viscount Downley spent half his life sobering up in the slammer? No thanks.

Victor would be off the squad for sure if Sean had any

idea what he got up to. Even if the race was only weeks away. The head coach had no tolerance for stuff like this and there were plenty of reserve rowers desperate for Victor's spot. Who wanted it more, deserved it more. Which would be a relief for Peter. Not having his brother rub it in his face every day that he was living his dream. So why did he keep on saving him? Most of the time he didn't even know.

"Think about it, okay?" Without waiting for Peter's response, Mark nodded to the copper at the entry to the cells and pulled out his keys as they went in. The stench of urine, vomit, and body odor hit Peter like a wall. Why anyone would put themselves on a path that led to getting locked in here more than once was beyond him.

In the end cell, his brother lay on the rudimentary bed, hands tucked under his head, staring up at the ceiling. He looked as relaxed as if he were enjoying an afternoon on a lounge chair in the Bahamas.

Mark gave the bars a shake. "Time to go, sunshine."

Victor rolled over, his expression revealing nothing when he saw the two of them. Pushing himself up, he stood and waited for Mark to unlock the door and swing it open. "Excellent hospitality as always, Sergeant. See you next time."

"There isn't going to be a next time." Peter quashed the desire to push his brother behind the bars and tell Mark to lock him back up.

Victor cocked an eyebrow at Peter. "Says who? The fun police?"

"You are such a pillock."

"Look, little brother. No one made you come here to get me. Lord knows I certainly didn't ask to see your smug, sanctimonious mug. If you want me to grovel with gratitude for your liberating me again, then like I've already told you, you're going to be waiting a long time."

"You've got five seconds to get out of my cells or I'll arrest you myself." Mark intervened before Peter lost his cool and did something that would put him where Victor had just been.

"Sorry, officer." Victor gave Mark a mock salute.

Striding out of the cells, past the station traffic, Mark led them back out into the main entryway. And closed the gate behind them

"No lecture this time?" Victor tossed the question at Mark.

The bobby crossed his arms over his broad chest. "I'm done lecturing. I've got better things to do with my time. Let's be clear, Victor. I don't care what our family connections are. I will arrest you if you keep on this track. That will give our mothers something to talk about at bridge."

For a second, Peter saw something flicker across Victor's face that cut through his insolent, smug expression. But then it was gone, and the usual mask fell back into place before he could work out what that expression even was.

"Oh, look at that." Victor checked his watch. "Perfect timing. I've got to check in with the professor at two. She's always happy to see me."

Only Victor could manage to be a full-time drunkard, genius scholar, and top-level rower. Peter should've just left him in jail. Let him see what it felt like to be on the losing side for once.

Thirteen

The day of the Boat Race. You'd have had to be deaf, dumb, and blind if you were within five miles of the Thames and didn't know about the famous rowing race.

Emelia tugged her Oxford-dark-blue sweater down and peered at her fitted jeans tucked into her brown leather boots. She'd spent a decent chunk of the morning trying to work out what one wore to a rowing race. In London. And had landed on this. Only to show up at the river's edge and discover that it really didn't matter. The entire spectrum was there, from men in suits to women in yoga gear.

"You cannot be serious!" Emelia turned to where Allie was pointing a finger at Jackson. Who, at some point, without either of them noticing, had draped his neck with a scarf in Cambridge light blue.

Jackson smirked at his fiancée as she tugged at her opposing dark blue scarf. "It's a win-win. No matter what happens, at least one of us will be victorious."

"If Cambridge wins, I'll choke you with it." Emelia raised an eyebrow. For someone who had been at Oxford all of six months, Allie had certainly drunk the Kool-Aid.

So much, in fact, that they had been there hours early to

stake out a prime spot on the Thames bank by the finish line. At least England had finally gotten into the swing of spring and the skies were blue and the sun shining.

Emelia patted her phone in her pocket, confirming it was still there. Over the last couple of weeks she'd exchanged a few sporadic emails and phone calls with Peter about the fund-raising idea. All very professional and aboveboard. He was clearly very busy with the team and absorbed with race preparation. The distance had her half-convinced that she'd overblown the attraction that she'd felt between them.

Though not even that had prevented her stomach knotting itself up when she'd texted him an hour ago, wishing him luck, despite the talk she'd given herself about how he probably wasn't even near his phone. She probably wouldn't even see him today. He had much more important things to be doing than responding to her lame message, but she still couldn't help but check her screen every time a phone went off. Which was often, since she was surrounded by a crowd of people.

Emelia glanced over her shoulder to see that Allie had her grip on Jackson's scarf, holding on to its ends as she tugged him down for a kiss. That was what she got for agreeing to be the third wheel.

A helicopter buzzed overhead. The hum of the crowd seemed to get louder as the minutes counted down to the start. The women's race had already happened, followed by the men's reserve crews.

The banks of the river were awash with people in the two shades of blue. According to the news reports, they were expecting over two hundred and fifty thousand in the crowd along the course. Another fifteen million would be watching it on TV. It was like the British version of the Rose Bowl. She'd had no idea this would be so huge. And to think that Peter was in the middle of it all.

Her phone buzzed in her pocket, and she pulled it out, her breath stalling as she saw his name on the screen.

Thanks. Thanks for being here.

She read the message once, twice.

"What are you smiling at?" Allie had curiosity written all over her face.

"Oh, nothing." She tried to slide her phone back into her pocket subtly, but her roommate's eyes missed nothing.

"If that was nothing, I'd love to see something."

Thankfully Emelia was saved from having to reply by another helicopter roaring right overhead.

It was stupid, whatever it was. She'd come to England to reinvent herself, to make amends for what she'd done. The last thing she needed was a relationship. Not with Peter. Especially not with Peter. Instinct told her that he wasn't a guy who went into something lightly. The idea of dating someone just for a bit of fun wouldn't even be on his radar.

Not that it was on hers, but it was all she had to offer.

Which made a text that made her wistful a big problem. As big as the strapping guy who'd sent it.

"They're coming down." Emelia craned her neck to look at one of the big screens nearby. They'd been erected along the river's banks especially for the race. Sure enough, the cameras panned across the cox of the Oxford team leading the dark blues down to the water.

Emelia's heart thumped against her rib cage. She didn't

know a single guy on either side, with the exception of one ginger-headed assistant coach, but suddenly she felt like she was as invested as anyone.

She craned her neck back up at the screen again. It showed the two teams maneuvering at the start line, both coxes' hands in the air to show the umpire they weren't ready to start.

The commentators droned on about each athlete in each boat, reeling off height, weight, and rowing lineage. Emelia stopped listening and focused on the boats bobbing in the current. The race was meant to start when both coxes' hands were down, signaling their boat was ready. But the two seemed to be playing some kind of game of rowing Ping-Pong, one dropping his hand, only for the other to shoot his up. A few more seconds passed, the crowds growing silent as they waited for the two boats to finally be ready.

The Cambridge cox dropped his hand but the Oxford one remained upright.

Finally, his hand dropped.

"Attention, go!" The umpire wasn't wasting any time.

Both boats surged forward, all sixteen men pulling their oars in perfect unison. Forward and back, forward and back. The boats leapt, accelerating swiftly.

Emelia was peering through her fingers without even realizing it. How was she going to survive this for another sixteen or so minutes? Oxford had a nose in front, then Cambridge. The slight coxes yelled instructions through their headsets, hands on the rudders. Oxford managed to get maybe a quarter of a boat length ahead.

"C'mon, Oxford!" Allie's yell ripped through Emelia's right eardrum. She sure had a lot of volume for such a small person.

Emelia watched, her heart trying to break out of her sternum, as the Cambridge crew drew back even. Then Oxford managed to get a slight lead back in the first bend.

She kept her eyes glued on the screen as the crews approached Hammersmith Bridge. The perfect synchronization of the oars, the bodies in motion. The crowd roared as the boats swept along the course, coxes screaming, the rowers' bodies flexing and straining. She'd never seen anything like it before.

The boys almost tumbled out of the boat as it pulled up to the riverbank. The buzz of adrenaline and euphoria saturated the air.

"Good work." Peter hugged crew member after crew member, clapping backs, shaking hands, rubbing heads.

He should have been as euphoric as everyone else but it all felt a bit hollow. He pasted on a broad smile, forcing himself to pretend he wouldn't have given anything to be one of the guys in the boat, stroking their way to victory, instead of just a bystander, a glorified water boy.

It killed him even more that his brother had been in the boat. And he hated himself for having the fleeting thought, more than once, that if they lost it would be good that Victor would know what it felt like, for once, to taste defeat. Never mind the other seven rowers and cox in the boat, who would be utterly heartbroken.

"Great work, Grant." He clasped hands with their slight cox, towering over him.

"You too, Coach."

He hadn't done anything. This day had no more to do with him than if he'd been standing on the banks of the Thames as an average-joe spectator.

"Bunny!" His brother's voice boomed in his ear, one of his hands slapping him on his bad shoulder. Peter tried to cover up a grimace as pain radiated out from his brother's palm print.

Peter turned his head and braced himself for his brother's usual smug smirk. Victor's hair was wet from the combination of the Thames and the magnum of champagne that had already been sprayed over the team. His brother grinned at him, for once no hint of cynicism or loathing in his expression. Just unrestrained joy. Even his scar seemed to fade into the background.

"Congratulations. It was a great race. You earned it." Peter found himself actually meaning the words. Maybe this could be a turning point. Maybe they could finally leave the animosity between them in the past.

"Tough luck you'll never know what it feels like again." His brother gave him another whack on his shoulder, as if to underscore his point, and just like that the magic was gone.

Before Peter could even conjure up a response, some curvy brunette was hanging off his brother's arm, and Victor's attention had shifted.

Whatever joy he'd had in the win evaporated, and Peter left the boys to their celebrations. Busying himself supervising the removal of the boat from the water, he tried to ignore the press pack still swarming around, snapping photos from every conceivable angle.

He stayed as far away from them as possible. More than

a few requests for interviews with him and Victor had come in since the Blue Boat lineup was named. All of them framing their story as some variation of a human-interest piece on "passing the torch" from the tragic injured Olympic hopeful to the rowing-prodigy brother who hadn't so much as picked up an oar in his life until he'd decided to try out for the team. Uncharacteristically, Victor had been no more interested in the attention than Peter. Declining every single overture was the first and last thing they'd agreed on in years.

Exhaustion seeped through him. The Boat Race was over. The thing that had driven him to get out of bed every morning for the last six months was done. Tomorrow morning he'd wake up and there'd be no training to go to. No drills to oversee. No tactics to strategize. The boys would go back to what they were ostensibly here for—academics, prepping for exams—and he would be left with a few beginning rowing courses that he could teach with both hands tied behind his back. At least he still had the fund-raising for SpringBoard to keep him going while he waited to hear back on the latest scans of his shoulder.

"Did no one tell you you won?" Emelia's voice came from behind him. He turned to see her standing about six feet away. One of her hands held her hair off her face. She wore a navy sweater for Oxford.

"The boys won. Not me."

Emelia sized him up with a long look. "I may not know much about rowing, but even I know that Sean Bowden doesn't have anyone on his team out of charity."

How did she . . . ?

Emelia smiled at his look of confusion. "Allie loaned me

Blood over Water when I said I was coming. I've only just started though, so don't expect too much."

Peter tried not to read anything into the fact that she was reading his favorite book, about two brothers who rowed on opposing teams in the Boat Race one year. She probably wouldn't even finish it now that the race was over.

Emelia pulled her hair into a pile on top of her head, took a hair tie from her wrist, and twisted it around the knot as she crossed the distance between them. "If you're this sad over their win, I would hate to see you if they lost."

He would never confess that there had been moments where he'd hoped for just that. So he wouldn't be the puddle of failure in a sea of victory.

He tried to summon a smile. "I was just thinking it's going to be weird waking up tomorrow. Without this." The beginners' courses he had lined up would keep the bills paid, but they weren't exactly all-consuming like the Boat Race had been.

But then the plan had been that by now his shoulder would be ready to get back into some serious training. So much for that.

"Well, you don't need to worry about that. I have plenty to keep you occupied."

"Is that right?"

"While you've been busy in London, I've been busy with the spreadsheets and planning. How do you feel about origami swans? One of the schools SpringBoard works in is having an origami contest. Could get us a good profile. Now that you've got some time on your hands I thought we could put them to good use folding."

Peter flexed his large hands, trying to imagine them transforming pieces of paper into birds. "Are you serious?"

She looked at him straight-faced, her head tilted, her hands tucked into the back pockets of her jeans. "It's not a real contest without origami swans."

He waited for her to give him some clue that she was joking, but she gave him nothing beyond big blue eyes and a Mona Lisa smile. It didn't even matter. There was something about this girl that made him want to learn to fold ridiculous shapes out of pieces of paper if it would make her happy.

"Peter!" One of the staff gestured at him. Almost time to go and claim the trophy.

"I've got to go. I'll see you tonight. To talk about the swans?"

Emelia sent him a smile that made him feel like he was trying to breathe underwater. "Wouldn't miss it for anything."

Fourteen

THE ROOMS AT THE HURLINGHAM CLUB BUZZED WITH A STRANGE mix of euphoria and simmering disappointment. Emelia ran her palms down the front of the cocktail-length navy blue dress she'd picked up on sale the day before. As if smoothing her dress would somehow calm the butterflies flurrying up a hurricane in her stomach. It was only because Allie had somehow sourced a last-minute spare ticket that she was even there at all.

The rowers, rowing alumni, and other guests had been seated in two separate rooms for the meal, but now that dinner was over and the music had started, people were crossing between the rooms.

She sucked in a breath, trying to convince herself she'd dreamed up the chemistry that had arched between them on the riverbank. But the way her nerves were contorting themselves insisted differently.

"Go dance, you guys." She gave Allie and Jackson full props for not making her feel like the third wheel for most of the day, but the two of them didn't get enough time together as it was. She certainly didn't want them wasting any more of it babysitting her.

Allie laughed as she put her water glass down on the tabletop. "I'm not sure my toes are up to being mangled quite yet." She slid a teasing look at Jackson.

"I'm pretty sure I specifically mentioned my lack of skill the first time we danced." Jackson's arm rested around his fiancée's shoulder, his fingers twisting a lock of hair that had fallen out of her chignon. The strands shimmered like spun copper under the lights.

"But not with enough conviction to make me realize it was really true." Allie giggled as Jackson nuzzled her hair. Right, time to leave.

Emelia pushed back her chair as the music changed to something slow. "I'm going to get another drink. Either of you want anything?" They both shook their heads. Despite Allie's protestations, Emelia was certain by the time she returned they'd be dancing, lead feet or not. You didn't put your fiancé in a tux, bring him to an event like this, and not get in at least one slow dance.

Dodging the limbs and elbows of people who had already imbibed a bit too much, she threaded her way to the bar. The lights had dimmed, turning people into moving shadows.

The crowd parted for a second, and her breath stuttered as she thought she saw a familiar profile. It wasn't possible. He couldn't be here. She stood on her tiptoes, scanning the room, heart threatening to break out of her rib cage.

She was seeing things. The room was filled with plenty of tall blond men in their twenties who thought they were God's gift to mankind. There was no reason for *him* to be here. Last time they'd crossed paths, he'd been well entrenched in the LA party scene, using his title to cultivate a harem of socialites and C-list TV stars. The entitled son of the Viscount Downley belonged here about as much as she did.

She forced herself to let her breath out as another scan of the room yielded a number of blond men but not him. Then, in the middle of the crowd, she felt her hand being grasped and tugged.

It was over. She'd been found out. Somehow she'd always known it was going to happen. It had been a nice time while it lasted.

Preparing herself for the worst, she turned, ready to see the person she had one horrible thing in common with: the same person's blood on their hands.

Peter.

If it hadn't been for the crowd, she might have hit the floor as a wave of relief weakened her legs.

Peter's brow furrowed. "You okay?"

Emelia placed her palm on her chest. "You scared me."

"Sorry." He bent down low, close to her ear. "Didn't want to risk losing you in the crowd."

The guy was like six foot three, and she stood a good half a head above most of the women. There was no chance he would lose her in the crowd. Her insides warmed like the hand he was still holding.

"How was dinner?" It was the best she could manage as she processed that she still had her boring, normal English life. Her cover hadn't been blown.

He shrugged. "Fine. The boys are in great form. But considering I've spent the last six months with them, I'm glad to be done."

"So, how can I help?" She had to half yell the question to be heard over the background noise. The guy was easy on the eyes, she couldn't deny it, but for her own good she needed to maintain distance with her quasi-boss. Especially when just looking at him made her think inappropriately of slow dances against a certain broad chest.

"Do you have a second? I've had an idea."

"Sure."

He placed a hand on the small of her back. "Let's go outside, where we can hear ourselves think."

Cutting through the crowd, it took them a couple of minutes to work their way outside, where a few ball-goers stood around smoking and one ardent couple pressed up against a wall seemed to have forgotten they were still in public.

The sudden change from hot packed ballroom to cool spring night had Emelia suppressing a shiver. But Peter's eyes didn't miss anything. "Here, take this." He shrugged out of his jacket and draped it around her shoulders before she could protest.

"Thanks." Emelia tucked it around her torso and tried to ignore the scents of cedar and sandalwood enveloping her.

Of course he had good taste in cologne.

"So, tell me about this idea."

"We need something big for our final event, right? Something to make lots of money. Put the charity back in the black but also something high-profile."

"Yes. All of the above."

Peter gestured around him. "What about this?"

"This?"

"A ball. A big black-tie charity ball."

He looked so excited she didn't have the heart to tell him that she'd already considered it and nixed the idea. Balls cost a bomb. You could just as easily come out of them in the red as make lots of money. And there was no way the charity had the money to pay a lot of the up-front costs that would be required before tickets even went on sale.

She gripped the silky inside of his jacket. "Peter, balls are really, *really* expensive to put on. There would be a huge risk we wouldn't even make back what it cost to do one well."

"Look, I know that SpringBoard doesn't have any money. But the one thing we do have is some connections. Between the board members we would know enough people to be able to make a real go of this."

How could she phrase this nicely? She didn't want to kill the guy's enthusiasm. Especially not when she was going to be stuck with him for the next eight months on whatever they did end up going with. "Look, I'm not doubting that the board knows a lot of people, but for a charity ball to be a success it's not enough to know people, you have to know *people*." She put the emphasis on the last word, hoping he would not ask her to spell out what she meant.

"I know." He studied her face, the moonlight making his freckles stand out. "You think I don't know what you mean?"

"Why don't you tell me who you're thinking of?" She hoped she was about to be surprised. She wasn't sure what she would do if he said he knew the local ancient county squire or something. Was that even still a thing in England?

He crossed his arms, stretching his white dress shirt across his chest. "Well, before I injured my shoulder, I was on the Great Britain rowing team so I know quite a few Olympians."

Emelia knew that her mouth had sagged but she couldn't do anything to lift it. Peter was on the national team? How did she not know this? How had no one mentioned it? She stared at him, her mind spinning at warp speed through the Rolodex of opportunities she'd just been presented with. He was still talking but she'd missed the last couple of sentences until a name cut through.

"Anita had quite a few celebrity friends with good connections I'm sure we could tap as well."

"Okay, great." She tried to sound nonchalant. This changed everything.

Just then a couple of Oxford boys, easily identifiable in their blue jackets, stumbled toward them.

"Oh, brother." Peter muttered the words under his breath. "Sorry, those are mine. I need to make sure they get away okay. Should we pick this up next week? At the office."

"Sure. Great. Yes." She watched as Peter strode away, catching up to the boys in a few steps.

She turned, adrenaline suddenly buzzing through her system. She needed to go and tell Allie she was leaving, get back to the hotel they were staying at, and start working on some spreadsheets. She had a ball to start planning.

She half ran back toward the entrance. Coming around the front door, she barreled straight into someone with the height and width of a large tree.

"S—" Looking up, her apology cut out as the slate gray eyes of her worst nightmare drilled into her. *Speak, Emelia. Then move!* "Sorry, entirely my fault."

The heir to the Viscount Downley unraveled one of the smiles that had taken many a simpering starlet out at the knees. The jagged scar that ran down one cheek twitched. "My fault. I insist." Then he tilted his head and gave her a quizzical look. "You look familiar. Have we met?"

She shook her head, too fast, too desperate. "I don't think so." He couldn't. Her hair was a different color and style, her eyes no longer enhanced by colored contacts. She stepped to the side, trying to go around him, but was blocked by some people coming the other way.

"Excuse me." Someone brushed past her but she didn't even look at them.

He narrowed his gray eyes at her, then they widened and he dropped an expletive. "What are *you* doing *here*?"

Think fast, Emelia, think fast. Show no fear. Pulling herself up to her full height, which was not much compared to his, admittedly, she stared Victor straight in the eye. "I could ask you the same question. Daddy recall you back home after our last meeting?" She forced the words out in a cavalier way. If she gave any hint that he had the power to ruin her, everything she was here for would be destroyed.

He averted his gaze for a second. Good. It showed he had something to lose. Maybe not as much as she did, but something. And she'd grasp at any straw, no matter how thin. She took her chance. "Look. I don't know what you're doing here and I don't really care. London's a big city. So how about we just stay out of each other's way and let the past stay there?"

Victor was silent for a few seconds. Obviously weighing having no idea what she was doing in London and whether he had any leverage over her versus what she knew about him and what evidence might or might not exist to back it up. "I never saw you."

She tilted her head at him and shrugged, as if it didn't matter to her one way or the other. An Oscar-worthy farce if there ever was one. "Right back at you."

It was only after he'd stormed past her that she realized she was still shrouded in Peter's coat. And had wrapped it around herself so tightly it was practically a straitjacket.

Peter walked back toward the ball, having tipped his two drunken rowers into a taxi and dispatched them back to the house the team was staying in. He passed the spot where he'd spoken to Emelia and a smile tugged at his lips. A charity ball. He was sure they could pull it off. Between his connections and Emelia's tenacity—something about her made him think that when she decided to do something she was all in—it was the one real shot they had.

Victor stood outside, leaning against the wall, bow tie hanging askew.

"You all right?" The guy looked like he'd seen a ghost.

"Fine." His brother shook his head, his expression haunted. "Big day. Think I'm going to head back to base."

Hmmm . . . that wasn't like Victor at all. Usually he was the last one to leave a party. If he left at all, rather than being found the next day passed out somewhere.

"Okay." Peter didn't push it, too relieved that he wasn't going to have to spend the rest of his night trying to keep Victor out of trouble. "See you in the morning."

Striding back into the ball, he scanned the room. He was off the clock. All of the team were over eighteen and could look after themselves. Or not, as the morning might reveal, but none of them were his official responsibility. Not that it stopped him from keeping an eye out for them. He'd experienced what they were living. Could well remember what could happen when you were heady with victory and felt ten feet tall and bulletproof. His shoulder twinged and he rotated it, checking for pain. He wouldn't wish what he was going through on his worst enemy.

He smiled as he remembered Emelia's shocked expression when he'd told her he'd been on the GB rowing team. Her full, rosy lips making the kind of O he'd thought only happened in cartoons. It had been all he could do not to run his thumb across the lower one, to see if it was as soft as it looked.

He shook his head. He couldn't allow himself to think like that when he had to spend the next eight months working with her. He didn't know anything about Emelia. Not why she was in Oxford, her background, or, most importantly, her beliefs. And after having a front-row seat to his parents' difficult marriage, he had promised himself he would never make the same mistake. A couple of meetings that belonged in a rom-com movie did not happily-ever-after make.

"Fancy a dance, stranger?" It was a familiar woman's voice, but definitely not the one he'd been thinking of.

"Um, sure." Sabine's hand already rested on his arm, and he mechanically took her other hand, his movements awkward and stilted.

At five foot four, Sabine barely reached the top of his chest. Which made her perfect for the talented cox that she was, but not perfect for him. A thought he'd never had until meeting a certain brunette.

"For a guy whose team just won the Boat Race, you sure look glum."

He turned his attention to the intelligent eyes staring up at him. "What are you doing, Sabine?"

She moved smoothly through the crowded dance floor, ignoring the fact that he was doing a lousy job at leading her. "I just wanted to say congratulations. Or is that not allowed?"

He sighed. "Of course it's allowed. Sorry. Thanks."

Sabine was a great girl. Any guy would have been lucky to have her. It wasn't like they had parted ways badly. It had just become obvious, after his injury, that their shared obsession with rowing had allowed them to ignore all the other problems in their relationship. Ones that became as obvious as the neon signs at Piccadilly Circus once it became clear it would be a long time before he rowed competitively again.

"I hear you're back in the boat." She leaned up on tiptoes and had to practically shout the words to be heard above the music and crowd.

Where had she heard that? He'd been keeping his occasional forays on the river in his scull pretty quiet. He shrugged and leaned down so she could hear his response. "Barely. Just for a bit of exercise. Nothing serious. The last set of scans, well, they weren't great." It felt good to be honest about it with someone. Sabine got what the dream meant.

She tilted her head, staring straight into his eyes. "I'm really sorry, Peter. But I know you can come back from this. You are a great rower. You're going to stand on that podium one day."

That was one of the best things about Sabine. She'd always believed in him. Even more than he believed in himself. Even still. After everything.

"By the way, what's happening with SpringBoard? How can I help?"

Peter blinked at the abrupt change in subject. "Actually,

we're looking at setting up some kind of friendly between the Oxford and Cambridge rowing teams. I'm sure we could use you with that somehow." She would be perfect. If he failed at convincing some of the guys, there wouldn't be a rower on either team who would be able to turn her down.

Sabine laughed. "Like there would be anything friendly about that. Sounds like fun. Just let me know what I can do."

He shuffled them between a couple of pairs. "How about you? How are you doing?"

She shrugged a slender shoulder against his chest. "I'm thinking it might be time for me to retire soon."

"What are you talking about?" He could no more imagine Sabine voluntarily giving up rowing than he could the queen giving up the throne. She'd coxed her women's eight to the final in the London Olympics. There had been scuttlebutt about her maybe even coxing the men's team one day. She still had years left on her career. He might have had the potential to be great, but she actually was.

Sabine tilted her head so that she was looking right at him. "Maybe I need to move on. Look at what rowing's cost me."

"Like what?"

"Like you."

He stepped back, tried to subtly put a little more space between them. "Rowing didn't cost you me. If anything, it held us together for far longer than we would've lasted otherwise. You know that."

She stared up at him, her blue eyes full of consternation. "No, Peter. I don't know that. What I know is that after you got injured, you were angry, and frustrated, and hurt. You wanted an excuse to push me away and you used that.

When I think the truth was that it hurt too much to see me still doing what you loved, and I don't blame you. You can't pretend there wasn't still something there that night we had coffee."

She was right. There had been a night soon after they'd split up that they'd run into each other at Paddington station. Both the victims of delayed trains. They'd had a drink. And there had been something still there. But he'd told himself that was natural after three years. And then Anita had died and everything changed. "We were together for a long time, Bine. Feelings don't die just because something didn't work out."

She shook her head, adamant. "It was more than that."

"What are you saying?"

She looked up at him, all big blue eyes and pleading expression. "I'm saying I think you made a big mistake breaking up with me, and I think I made one letting you. I'm saying being here, with you, feels like everything is finally right again after it being all wrong for months."

They'd stopped any attempt at dancing. Instead, they just shuffled along the edge of the dance floor as he stared at her.

What on earth was going on tonight? One second he'd been thinking about kissing Emelia, which would have been unwise at best. The next Sabine was making some kind of case . . . for what?

"Sabine, this is crazy talk. All of it. You don't have any time for a relationship right now. You are at the peak of your career. We both know that's all you have capacity for." Just like it was all he'd have had capacity for if his shoulder hadn't been shredded in a barroom brawl.

From the hope that sparked in her eyes, Peter saw he'd said the wrong thing. He should've just said a straight no instead of trying to soften the blow.

"I know. I'm not asking you to wait. I'm just asking you not to . . ." She trailed off, looked down for a second.

"Not to what?"

"Not to choose someone else." She scrutinized him. "Or am I too late already?"

"I don't know." *Emelia.* The luxurious wavy hair. The enigmatic smile. The intensity behind her gaze. The way that when she laughed it made him feel lighter. But when her heady presence left, all the reasons as to why pursuing something between them was crazy remained.

"Look, I don't want to be the villain ex-girlfriend here. I'm not jealous that you might have moved on. Well, maybe I am a little, but that isn't what this is about. I've been trying to get the nerve up for months and I'm kicking myself. I should've said something at Allie's party that night but you just disappeared."

The same night he'd properly met Emelia. In the second wardrobe. What might have happened if he'd never gone up those stairs? If Sabine had snagged him there for this conversation?

"If you can look me in the eye and tell me that it's her, not me, then I will walk away. I will. I don't want to make your life harder. In fact, I want you to be happy. I just believe that I can give you more than she can." She cast a sad smile. "Whoever she is."

His mouth opened, but nothing came out. Just the sound of silent panic.

"You don't have to decide right now. You just have to not decide." And with that, she stood on her tiptoes and dropped a kiss onto his left cheek while sliding her other hand down his right. "See you 'round, Seven." And with that, she turned and disappeared into the crowd, leaving him an island on the dance floor.

Fifteen

Emelia was early. Like an hour early. Between the ſund-raising ideas bouncing around inside her head and her excitement over getting to see where C. S. Lewis and the Inklings used to meet, the afternoon had dragged on agonizingly slowly.

She'd suggested they meet somewhere other than the office given that you couldn't swing a cat in any of the rooms there, let alone spread papers out and plan. She'd meant the library or something similar but when Peter had suggested the Eagle and Child, Emelia hadn't been able to say yes fast enough.

She looked around the room, trying her best not to look like some wide-eyed tourist. The historic pub looked just like she'd imagined it would. Wood paneling, rich tones. The kind of decor that was somehow both ancient and timeless. It didn't take much imagination to see Lewis, Tolkien, and the other Inklings gathered around a table somewhere, engaged in debate or critiquing each other's work.

"What can I get for you?" A bored-sounding waitress materialized beside her.

"Um, can I just have a Coke, please?" She didn't even like

Coke that much, but it was one of the few drinks that she didn't have to struggle to remember the British translation for.

"Would you like a menu?"

"Yes, please." The buzz of the busy room didn't bother her. She could happily sit here until Peter arrived and lose herself in Lewis. *The Magician's Nephew* perched inside her bag for this exact occasion. "Actually, no need. I'll have the fish and chips, please." She'd been intending to try some ever since she'd arrived.

"Garden peas or mushy?"

"Mushy." When in England, do as the English do. At least once. And she hadn't tried them yet.

Pulling out her battered paperback copy of the book that chronologically started Narnia, she flipped it open and reread the words that were engraved in her brain: *"This is a story about something that happened long ago . . ."*

Within a couple of sentences she was back with Digory, Polly, and crazy Uncle Andrew.

"Fish and chips are generally best hot." His voice cut into her world just as Digory struck the bell that awoke the slumbering world of Charn and brought about the White Witch's first appearance. It was one of her favorite parts in the whole series.

Slipping her bookmark between the pages, Emelia closed the paperback and placed it down on the tabletop. Craning her neck, she let her gaze travel up, landing on Peter's freckled face. "You're early."

He smiled as he slid across from her. "Not as early as you."

Touché. Along with Peter, her early supper had also arrived at some point and been placed in front of her.

"Sorry for interrupting. You looked very absorbed. But, honestly, cold fish and chips are nasty."

"This is the first time I've had them." For some reason, the presence of the muscular rower made her forget all notions she'd had of being happy sitting here reading alone.

Guard up, Emelia.

His face registered shock. "Really? How can you have never had fish and chips?"

She shrugged her shoulders. "They're just not really a thing where I come from."

He gestured to the plate. "Well, please don't let me stop you."

Now that she was looking at the food, the smell of its greasy goodness wafting up at her, she registered the hole her stomach had gnawed in her insides.

"You sure?" She didn't give him a chance to answer before she picked up a fry—which wasn't really a fry; it was much fatter—and popped it into her mouth. Grease and salt and potato all exploded into a hot bite of bliss. Two more followed in quick succession. "Want some?" She nudged the plate toward him, and he helped himself.

"Thanks."

She managed to find her manners long enough to use her cutlery to get a bite of fish. But she almost forgot about them when she bit into the flaky goodness. "Oh, wow."

"Good, huh?"

She nodded, her mouth too full with the next bite to reply.

The peas were next. She loaded her fork up with a pile of the bright green lumpy sludge that looked like baby food. Popping it into her mouth, she prepared herself to be overwhelmed by the new experience.

Which she was. In the worst way. Wrong, wrong, wrong. It was all wrong. The consistency. The taste. The . . . all of it. If she'd been by herself, she would've spat it into her napkin. Instead she forced herself to swallow the nasty things down.

"Not a fan, huh?" Peter's eyes crinkled as he smiled.

"What did those poor peas ever do to you? To this country?" She picked up another pile of the green sludge on her fork and studied it, trying to work out how it could taste so nasty. "Why would you do that to them?"

He laughed. "Ease up. They're a national treasure."

"If these are a national treasure, I'll—" She'd always been the kind of person who gestured when she talked. Which the poor guy discovered when the fork suddenly jumped in her hand and catapulted the pile of green at him.

It was like something from a slow-motion sequence. She watched the sludge fly through the air. At the last second, she closed her eyes, unable to bear seeing where it landed.

Knowing her luck it would be . . . she slid one eye open. Yup. It'd hit him right on the side of his face and was already starting to slide down his cheek. An avalanche of green.

Peter blinked and pointed at her napkin, which lay on the table. "May I?"

Only the British would be so polite after someone had just assaulted them with a vegetable. "Of course."

Picking it up, he swiped at the mess and caught a decent amount before it dropped off his jawline onto his sweater. Folding the napkin, he gave it a second attempt, leaving only a green smear across part of his cheek. "Got it all?"

Emelia shook her head. "There's just a little bit left about halfway down." He wiped. Missed. "Here." Plucking the napkin from his hand, she leaned over and blotted away the last bit. His moss-colored gaze caught hers as she did it, and he gave her the kind of smile that almost made her forget where she was, what she was doing.

"Well, Emelia Mason." The accent got her every time. The guy could have been about to insult her five ways to Christmas and she would have listened happily. "I have to say, it's never boring when I see you."

She stared at him. At a loss for words.

He didn't seem to notice. "Think I might order something as well. I won't have time to go home and eat before church."

She blinked at him. Replayed the sentence. Yes, he had definitely said "church." Huh. Apart from the occasional door-to-door types back home, she didn't know a single person her age who was religious. Though, now that she thought about it, she wouldn't have been surprised if that was where Allie went on Sunday mornings. She was always gone by the time Emelia woke up. She'd just assumed she and Jackson went out for brunch every time he was in town.

Peter smiled at her. "That bad, huh? You look like I just said I was on my way to rob a retirement village."

"No—I mean—"

"Would you like anything, sir?"

Thank goodness she was saved from herself by the waitress. She tuned out Peter ordering while she filed away this new piece of information about him, unsure what to make of it. Who even still went to church these days? And on a *Monday night*?

"How did you enjoy the rest of the ball?" Peter asked the question around one of her fries.

"Um, I left pretty soon after we spoke. I wanted to get back to the hotel to start planning."

"Planning?" He looked puzzled.

"The ball."

He stared at her for a couple of seconds, then started laughing, shoulders jumping like crickets.

She held up her hands. "I know, I know, I'm a total nerd."

He finally stopped laughing and swiped another fry, dragging it through the disgusting pea sludge. "Well, you certainly get points for commitment to the cause."

"Thanks. I think." She picked up another fry and crunched down.

"Why don't we talk about the other two. We should get started on planning those first since they'll be sooner. What do you think of a row-off and a cricket match?"

"You're going to have to explain the terminology."

"Well, a row-off is pretty much as it sounds. We'd hire a gym or some other similar large space. Chuck a few ergs on the floor and have all the rowers race over a set distance. I was thinking we could pair up the Oxford and Cambridge rowers by position. That will make it really competitive."

She was going to guess that "erg" was another name for a rowing machine. Didn't want to look dumb as a hammer asking. Especially not when she now knew an Olympic-level rower sat across from her.

Emelia pulled out her planner from the bag beside her and made a show of reading her notes. She knew them all by heart but it was a helpful distraction from the unwavering gaze sitting across from her. "When we last talked about dates, we were thinking about the end of May for the first one, assuming the board approves it next week. Will that still work or is it getting too close to exams?"

"We might want to make it mid-May. I think exams are early June but I'll check with a few of the guys and get back to you. If we were going to try a second event it would probably need to be straight after exams end, before everyone leaves for summer." Peter snagged another fry.

Which would give them a month to get this row-off approved by the board, organized, and done, and then another month to arrange the cricket thing. Whatever that was. Hard but not impossible. Especially if they started soon and could capitalize on the post–Boat Race fever. "Have you got anyone willing to do it yet?"

"I've asked a few and have had good responses—depending on that date, of course. But if anyone says no to me they definitely won't say no to Sabine."

"Sabine?" Emelia tried to ask the question lightly, disconcerted at the spurt of jealousy that had shot through her at just the sound of his mentioning another girl's name.

"She used to row with Anita back in school and wants to help out. She's now the cox of the women's Olympic eights team. No guy rower will be able to turn her down." Including him, Emelia would have guessed by the way his gaze flickered as he talked about her. Peter drummed his fingers on the table, evading her gaze slightly. "In the interest of full disclosure, we used to date. We broke up about eight months ago. Is that okay?"

Emelia tried to untangle the question. Was what okay? That they broke up? That they used to date?

"That she helps, I mean." Peter's food had arrived and he speared a piece of fish.

"She's your ex-girlfriend. If it's okay with you, then it is more than okay with me. Sounds like she'll be a great asset." Emelia did her best to keep her tone neutral, hiding her expression by jotting some meaningless notes down on her pad.

Sabine was probably blond and gorgeous. To be a cox she was definitely going to be as petite as they came. And as far as Emelia was concerned there were only two reasons you offered to help out your ex-boyfriend with something like this. Sabine was either the nicest person on the face of the earth or she was on a mission to take the "ex" out of "ex-boyfriend."

Emelia would have placed some good money on which one it was.

Sixteen

"Someone has told you we're planning a ball, not a war, right?" A week later, Peter paused in the doorway of Allie's—Emelia's—living room and scanned it for somewhere to put down the pizza he was carrying. Every flat surface was stacked with reams of paper, magazines, brochures, or her computer.

"You're right. War would be way easier." Emelia barely even glanced up at him from where she sat hunched over her laptop and didn't seem the slightest bit surprised at his appearance. He'd happened to arrive just as Allie was heading out and let him in. Emelia's hair was bunched up in a bun on top of her head, a pencil shoved through the middle. She wore a baggy gray sweatshirt and black track pants. He felt overdressed in his jeans and jumper.

In the last seven days they'd gotten approval from the board for the row-off and the cricket match and agreement for Peter and Emelia to work up a more detailed proposal for a winter ball. He'd gone into the office to run a few things past her, only for Elizabeth to give a knowing smile at his clothes and say Emelia was working from home for most of the week.

"Can I get you a drink while I'm up?"

Emelia rolled her head across her shoulders. "A soda, please. There should be some in the fridge."

Walking into the kitchen, he grabbed a couple of chilled cans and headed back toward the bunker. "What are you working on?" He sat down on the couch next to her, maintaining appropriate distance.

"Our plan of attack. Look." Emelia turned her screen to face him, and he was hit by a haze of boxes and bright colors.

Had he stepped into some kind of time warp or something? Been frozen like a Narnian statue and brought back to life a few months later? How on earth had she managed to achieve all this in the few days since the board meeting? He blinked, the colors spinning in front of his eyes. "So, I got a phone call on the way here."

Emelia tilted her head. "About?"

"It was the eighties. They want their fluoro back."

"Oh, you're a comedian now, Drinian?" But she was unable to stop a grin from spreading across her face. It filled his chest with the kind of feeling usually reserved for winning big races.

"You make it too easy." Peter grinned back at her and something jumped between them that he'd never experienced in his life. He cleared his throat, turned his attention back to the spreadsheet. Right across the bottom there were even more marked tabs. Venues. Caterers. Florists. Rental places. The list went on.

Emelia clicked on the one marked *Venues*. Another color-coded screen. "So, I created a matrix listing all the material characteristics. Most important of which, obviously, is availability, but you can't get that off websites. But then I added in scoring based on criteria including location, cost, capacity, in-house catering or whether you can bring your own, indoor and outdoor options, those sorts of things. And I'm thinking we should probably talk to Elizabeth to run the weightings past her. I mean, availability is obviously critical, but after that would she rather be somewhere farther out but cheaper? Somewhere that you can bring your own caterers or somewhere that has a superior layout? Once they're all weighted and we've scored them, then the formula will practically make the choice for us."

Emelia leaned closer into him as she pointed at the screen. "We could also further distill the variables. And we'd probably have to allow a category for gut reaction as well. There's a lot to be said for instinct, don't you think?"

She blinked up at him, eyes shining, cheeks rosy.

Marry me. The words flashed through his head. That was the instinct that he had when faced with a woman who could probably have made organizing the Normandy invasion look easy. Except that when he mentioned going to church she'd looked at him like he'd sprouted an antenna and started talking in Klingon. He swallowed it back down. "Yes. Definitely. A lot to be said for instinct." His words came out husky and a little stilted. But she didn't seem to notice.

"I've done some short-listing."

"Of course you have."

Emelia raised an eyebrow at him. "Anyway, using the very rudimentary criteria I've already drawn up, I've got us fifteen places to go visit."

Peter almost choked on the gulp of soda he'd just taken. "I'm sorry. Did you say fifteen? As in one-five?"

"What were you thinking?"

Peter shrugged. "I don't know. Three." Seemed like a good number. More than two, less than five.

Emelia skewered him with her gaze. "*Three*. You have got

to be joking. This is saving SpringBoard we're talking about here. We can't leave any stone unturned. Twelve. And that's me being generous."

"Ten." Peter uttered the word in desperation.

"Twelve." Emelia smiled with satisfaction, as if she knew she had him.

"We can't do twelve. When are we going to look at twelve venues?"

"This weekend. We need to get it done before it gets busy with the row-off. They're all scheduled." She flipped to another screen and there he saw it, his entire weekend laid out in Technicolor glory.

"Seven? We're seeing the first one at seven in the morning?"

"They have two weddings. It was the only time I could get. Besides . . ." She smiled sweetly. "Seven is luxuriously late for you, isn't it, rower boy?"

He couldn't have stopped himself from grinning if he tried. Lord help him, he liked this girl. More than was smart. Why? Why did she have to be so perfect in every way except the one that mattered most? More importantly, how on earth was he going to hold on to his self-control while spending the next seven months planning a ball with the one person he desperately wanted but couldn't have?

Seventeen

"Coffee?" Peter asked the question as they got back in the car after viewing venue possibility number four.

"You just had one before the last place."

He quirked an eyebrow at her. "Don't judge me. I thought all you Americans would consume the stuff intravenously if you could."

"I'm not judging you. I'm just . . ." Emelia trailed off before she could ask the guy if he had a bladder the size of a planet. When he'd arrived to pick her up at six forty, he had been clasping a venti-size coffee cup like it was his firstborn. Plus one for her, which she'd made it about a quarter of the way through.

Since then, he'd had another two. And no bathroom break. And not a single hint that he might need one in the future. She might've suspected he'd decided to answer the call of nature somewhere if not for the fact that the only time she'd left his side, for her own bathroom trip, he'd been in the care of the venue's events coordinator, who had been flirting up a storm with him.

It was totally ridiculous, since Peter had a good foot on the girl, so most of her eye-batting was directed straight at his armpit. Not to mention, the man himself was completely oblivious.

"Fine. I guess coffee can wait until after this one."

Emelia started, realizing she'd left the conversation hanging and he thought she was still thinking about his caffeine habit.

"Where to next?"

Emelia consulted her color-coded list. "Rhodes House."

Peter let out a low whistle. "Nice."

"Have you been?"

"Not personally, but I've heard of it. Didn't realize we had that kind of budget."

Emelia consulted her spreadsheet. Rental cost was eight hundred and forty pounds including tax, which put it midrange of all the places on her list. "It's pretty reasonable, actually."

Peter glanced at her but didn't say anything as he pulled out into the road. Emelia tried to look anywhere except out the windshield. Even after a couple of months, driving on the left still caused her blood pressure to climb like one of those never-ending stair climbers at the gym.

Time to find something to talk about. Anything. "So, is the team ready?" She blurted out the first safe thing that came to mind. Between all the ball organizing, she couldn't lose sight of the "friendly" row-off that was taking place in a few weeks' time. Its head-to-head nature was getting more press than she'd imagined. She could only hope the money would follow.

Peter kept his eyes on the road. "More than. They're all still feeling pretty cocky from the big win."

"Is it weird? Being on the other side?" She regretted the question almost as soon as she asked it. *Good one, Emelia. Nothing like reminding the guy of what he can't do.*

His fingers tightened as he changed down a gear. "Very."

She waited for more but realized after a few seconds it wasn't coming.

"How's your shoulder doing?"

"Not great." Another two-syllable answer. She'd interviewed rocks more talkative than this guy.

"I'm sorry."

Peter pulled in front of the gray mansion she'd seen in the website photos. In real life, it was even more impressive. And enormous. Four huge stone columns lined the front of the verandah, with another four behind them, guarding the black front door. The entryway of the house, covered with a dome-shaped roof, connected onto a Colonial-style building.

"Oh. Wow." For a second, Emelia was speechless and glad they'd both dressed up for the day in smart casual clothing, instead of the pair of jeans she'd been tempted to put on. But even in her knit dress, the towering building made her feel like she should apologize for not wearing designer cocktail attire.

Getting out of the car, they crossed the sidewalk and approached the doors, stepping up to the porch, whose ceiling was so high she had to tilt her head back to see the top.

"Good morning." A thickset man with slicked-back gray hair and fierce eyebrows opened the door before she had even knocked.

Emelia stared at him for a second. If Carson from *Downton Abbey* had a brother, this guy was it. "Good morning, I'm Emelia Mason. We have an appointment at ten o'clock to tour the venue." She pulled out her snootiest voice. The one she'd always used to get herself into parties she had no business being at.

The man inclined his head. "Miss Mason. My name is Stuart Goldfinch. I will be showing you around Rhodes House today."

"Nice to meet you. This is Peter Carlisle."

The man's ramrod posture grew even straighter. "Mr. Carlisle. Of course." He was practically fawning as he held out his hand to Peter. "Welcome to Rhodes House. May I say, I was so sorry to hear about your retirement? But of course, such great luck for the Blue Boat to have you with them."

"Thank you for seeing us on such short notice."

Emelia stared at him. Apparently she wasn't the only one who could put on the posh accent. Peter suddenly sounded like he lived in a palace and regularly took tea with the Queen.

"It is our pleasure. Now please . . ." The portly man gestured into the mansion.

Emelia tried to take in the soaring walls of oak and stone, the huge windows giving a glimpse of extensive gardens. It had looked gorgeous on the website, but that didn't even come close to doing its grandeur justice. She barely listened as the man rattled off the selling points of the venue. Room sizes, layout options, they all flowed over her head. She hoped Peter was taking it in, because she was ready to sign on the dotted line.

This was it. She could feel it in her bones. She could see men in tuxes and women in gowns dancing. Tables set with silverware and huge arrangements. Waiters in white gloves with silver trays.

Before she got her hopes up, she knew she should double-check . . . "Now, as I said on the phone, the ball is going to be in early December. Is it correct you've still got a weekend available?"

"Yes. Generally, our weekend dates are booked far in advance. But it has just so happened that this weekend we've had a cancellation for the first Saturday. Fate, may I suggest?"

"Maybe."

"Now, you'll see in our brochure we have a number of excellent catering firms we partner with. I can guarantee you they all serve exquisite cuisine. Fit for royalty, one might even say, should any be joining you."

"I'm sure," Peter said evenly.

Emelia half listened to the exchange as she flipped open the brochure she'd been handed. A set of numbers seared her retinas. Oh. Wow. Oh. No. She read them again, hoping that maybe she was seeing things wrong. But no, that had been the first time. This venue wasn't the reasonable eight hundred and forty pounds she'd thought it was. Try adding a zero. Try eight thousand four hundred pounds.

"Emelia?" The way Peter was looking at her suggested it wasn't the first time he'd said her name.

"Yes?"

"Would you like to see the gardens?"

"Yes." Her voice sounded weak. "Some air would be excellent."

Emelia had realized her mistake. Peter had seen it the instant her pupils had dilated as she'd read the brochure and her face had gone a shade paler. He'd known there had to be an error the moment she'd called Rhodes House "reasonable." Sure, if she was secretly a multimillionaire heiress.

Maybe he should've asked more questions. But he couldn't bring himself to ruin the satisfaction she derived from her perfectly coded and mapped spreadsheet. And, he had to admit, there was a certain amount of fun in watching her discover something was ten times more expensive than she'd thought when she was making him suffer through twelve potential locations.

"You okay?" He bent his head toward hers, lowering his voice so their escort couldn't hear.

Emelia licked her lips. "There's . . . I seem to have . . ." She must have seen something in his expression because she promptly whacked him on the arm. "You knew!" She hissed the words under her breath.

"Ow." He rubbed the spot above his elbow. The girl packed some power.

"You've been having a great time, haven't you, Smirky McSmirkster. Watching me fall in love with a place, thinking I'd found the venue bargain of the century." Her words were sharp, but a touch of a smile hovered at the edge of her lips.

"I can neither confirm nor deny."

"As is no doubt evident, the gardens are award winning." Their tour guide spread his arms and gestured around him. Peter had to admit the garden was impressive. If he had almost ten grand to spare, they would've won him over.

"They have entertained many a distinguished guest." The man waggled his caterpillar eyebrows at Peter meaningfully. Peter wished he would stop. Emelia wasn't stupid. He didn't want to rouse her suspicions. Didn't want her knowing who he was until she needed to. Emelia was one of the few people he didn't have to worry about being a groupie. A rowing one or a peerage one. He preferred to keep it that way for as long as humanly possible.

"Well, that's that, then." Emelia slumped into the passenger seat after they left the twelfth, and final, venue for the day.

"What was wrong with that one?"

Never before had Peter imagined how hard it could possibly be to find a ball venue. Over the last twelve hours, Emelia had knocked off every place they'd visited. For reasons Peter would have never even thought to consider. This was why guys had as little as possible to do with planning things like this.

"I thought it was fine." It had been nice enough. A ballroom at one of the big hotels. Maybe not exactly unique, but nice, with staff who clearly did the big-event thing all the time.

"Fine isn't enough. To save SpringBoard we need spectacular." Emelia blinked rapidly.

Wait, was she . . . Peter stepped a bit closer. She was close to tears.

"Hey." He rested his hand lightly on hers. "It's okay. We'll find something."

Emelia blinked some more and swiped her hands across her eyes. "I know we will. I just thought . . . I just wish . . ."

"What?"

She was silent for a second, then she sucked in a breath.

"I just wish I'd never seen Rhodes House."

It was like a kick to his solar plexus. "I'm sorry. That was all my fault. I shouldn't have let us go there. I just didn't want to be the one to tell you your perfect spreadsheet had a critical error."

That got half a smile out of her. "No, it was mine. I don't know why I thought something so great would cost so little. I guess I just thought that maybe, if there was a God, this was His way of making some magic happen."

He'd thought it wasn't possible but at that, he felt even worse.

"I just saw it there, you know. We walked in and I could imagine a huge ball. The kind that would get people writing the huge checks we need. I just felt like it was it. And I know I'm being super picky about all the other ones we've seen. It's just that once I saw that one, nothing else has measured up since."

Which pretty much summed up how he felt about her.

"I'm sorry." She ran her hands through her hair. "You have more important things to do than this. Look at you. You've been slammed with Boat Race stuff the last few months and now you've spent the day driving me around ball venues. Plus everything you've been doing for the row-off." She sucked in a breath and straightened her shoulders. "It's okay. We'll find something even better than Rhodes House. I just need to broaden the parameters. We can reconvene after the row-off. I need to focus on that now anyway."

The combination of disappointment and determination did him in. If he'd had eight and a half grand, he would have handed it over there and then.

So he offered up the only thing he did have. The one thing that was going to force him to reveal to her what he'd been avoiding. "I might know somewhere else we can look at."

Eighteen

"And Cambridge takes this one by four point seven seconds!" Emelia could barely hear the announcer's words over the sound of people yelling, clapping, and stomping. An hour into the row-off and her ears were ringing. Apparently the passing of the Boat Race had done nothing to dull the competitive spirit between the Oxford and Cambridge crews.

Peter had really been the one who had pulled off the event. Somehow between him and Sabine they'd managed to get almost every single crew member to agree to be part of the fund-raiser, as well as the two coxes. All Emelia had to do was organize ticketing and logistics.

Like Peter had suggested, the crew members from the same seat in the Boat Race were pitted against each other in a head-to-head battle over one mile. Not only had it meant all they'd had to do was relocate four ergs—two for racing and two for warm-up—onto the gymnasium floor, but with the big screens they'd put up, the place was packed full of spectators. Family members, friends, rowing groupies—they'd all somehow been convinced to part with twenty pounds each to watch.

And that was before Sabine had pulled a rabbit out of her hat. She'd somehow gotten some BBC sports commentator—

whom Emelia didn't know from a piece of pine but everyone else was giddy over—to commentate the event, with highlights screening on some sports show later in the week.

It still wouldn't be close to the kind of money they needed to be pulling in, but hopefully it would create momentum. And that was what the first event was about.

"This next one is going to be a dead heat. John and James are pretty much identical in height and weight." Sabine made the observation from where she stood a few feet away on the sidelines. Emelia had been exactly right about Peter's ex-girlfriend. Blond, petite, and gorgeous. She'd walked into the gym at six a.m. and immediately taken charge of all the things Emelia had no clue about and Peter hadn't thought of. The only thing she couldn't get her head around was whether Sabine was the coolest ex-girlfriend in the world or making a play to get her man back. If it was the second, she was one of the best players Emelia had ever seen. Not so much as a hint of neediness or desperation.

Even in a pair of jeans and T-shirt, there was no hiding Sabine was a top-class athlete. From her perfect posture, to the muscles that rippled under the denim, to the determined set of her jaw, it oozed from her. It wasn't difficult to see why she was an elite-level cox. Or why Peter had once dated her. Or that pretty much any other guy in the room would have jumped at the chance. Emelia felt like a pudgy Amazon next to her. "I understand you're a cox for the Olympic team. That's impressive."

"Thanks." Sabine kept her eyes on the two rowers next up as they finished their warm-up. The roar in the room had dulled to the buzz of conversation as people waited for the next race.

"Thanks so much for your help. I'm sure it's obvious I'm

way out of my depth when it comes to anything to do with rowing." For some reason Emelia felt the need to fill the conversational void.

"If you don't know rowing, you can never know Peter. Not really." Sabine didn't so much as glance Emelia's way.

Her pointed delivery hit Emelia like a barb in the side. Left her breathless for a moment. "I think you underestimate him. He's more than rowing." She delivered her own sting back.

Sabine swung around, ponytail bouncing. "Of course he is. But what have the last ten years of his life been about? Rowing. It's what he ate, slept, and breathed. It was what he dreamed about. It was why he trained twelve times a week for years. It's what he would still be doing if he hadn't been sidelined by injury. The fact that he can't is what breaks him every day. Have you even Googled him? Do you have the faintest clue how great he was? How far he could've gone?"

Emelia just stared at her.

"No. Well, let me enlighten you. He was a shoo-in Team GB for the eight. He would've been competing at Rio. And I would have bet everything I had that the question wasn't if he got his team to the podium, it was just where. He was *that* good."

"But he's not." Emelia wasn't even sure what she was doing. It wasn't like she and Peter were dating. It wasn't like they were *anything*. So what was she fighting for exactly? "I may not know much about his injury, but I'm guessing that it's bad to have taken him out of rowing this long. Maybe he will never row at that level again. That's reality. No matter how much any of us may want it to be different, it's just not. So you're right. I haven't lived in your little rowing bubble. I don't get it all. But he doesn't live there anymore either."

Sabine jammed her hands in her pockets and sucked in a breath. "Look, I'm sure you're very nice. You have a cute accent and you seem smart enough. I'm sure you're very refreshing with your naivety about rowing because he's hurting. At some point, when he starts his comeback, the fact that you don't know anything about what he loves isn't going to be cute, it's going to be irritating. The fact that you have no insight into what drives someone to train that brutally for so long will mean you can never really get him. So I have nothing against you, but you are not right for him."

Emelia tried to keep her face impassive, not let Sabine see how much her words were shaking her. "And you are?"

Sabine summoned up a regret-filled smile. "I was."

They watched as the next two rowers slid their feet into the footplates on the ergs and adjusted the straps.

"Look, I made a mistake when he was injured. I let him push me away. I thought that maybe space was what he needed. It was the wrong move. And I'm sorry that I'm the inconvenient ex-girlfriend showing up and throwing a spanner in your little fledgling romance, or whatever it is. But I've never quit on something I've wanted in my entire life, and until the day he can look me in the eyes and tell me there's no hope for us, I'm not going to quit on him."

"Sounds like you already did."

Sabine flinched like Emelia had struck her.

"I'm sorry. I . . ." Emelia floundered for words. "Look, we're not even dating. So it's not like I'm in your way. He's free for the taking."

Sabine studied her for a second, her gaze softening. "I know competition when I see it. I'm not sneaky. I fight fair. I just want you to know that I'm in this."

In what? Emelia ran her hands through her hair. This was an insane conversation. "Fine. Thanks for the heads-up. Notice received."

Someone called Sabine's name from across the room and she gave them a wave as she turned toward them. Allie appeared on Emelia's other side, watching Sabine as she stalked away. "She doesn't look happy. What was that about?"

"I think it was the English version of throwing down the gauntlet."

Allie raised her eyebrows. "For Peter?"

"For Peter."

Allie gave her a look that Emelia couldn't quite decipher. "I didn't know there was a gauntlet for Peter."

"You and me both." Emelia had only spoken to the guy in passing all day. She had no idea what it was Sabine had seen that had made her think they were in some kind of competition for him. Time to change the subject. "Speaking of gauntlets, have you guys set a date yet?" Emelia regretted the question as soon as she asked it. Something crossed Allie's face that wasn't the smile most brides-to-be seemed unable to restrain. Which made no sense given Emelia's observation that their relationship was one of the most functional she'd ever seen.

"No."

Hadn't they been engaged for like seven months? Not that she could talk. She avoided relationships like someone with a peanut allergy avoided a Snickers. "I'm sorry. It's none of my business."

Her roommate let out a sigh. "It's complicated." Allie dropped to the bench behind them, pulled her legs up to her chest, and wrapped her arms around them.

"Visa stuff?" Emelia settled in beside her, keeping her

gaze on the guys in front of them taking a few warm-up rows. Through the windows tree leaves were a lush green. Summer was definitely in the air.

"Sort of. I'm from New Zealand. He's from America. We live in England. But only temporarily. I might get an offer to stay at Oxford. I might not. It's all just uncertain."

Emelia shifted her focus to her roommate. "Is that the real reason?" It was only a guess, but Emelia had a strong suspicion that there had to be more than that to it. The couple she knew wouldn't let something like a little uncertainty stop them from getting hitched. People from different countries faced the same thing all the time.

"Yes . . . no." Allie ran her hands through her hair and blinked rapidly. Allie sucked in a breath, looking like she was trying to get her emotions under control. "I guess I thought the fear would go away. I'm thirty-two years old and I foolishly believed when we got engaged that everything would magically be okay. How stupid is that?"

This was definitely a side of her bubbly, confident friend she hadn't met. "What are you afraid of?"

"Getting married."

"As in . . ." Emelia was clearly missing a connection here, but she wasn't sure what it was.

"The wedding." Allie's fingers were twisting over themselves. Again and again. Emelia wanted to reach out and make them stop. "Every time I think about it, I freak out. I walk into a dress shop and start hyperventilating just looking at them. We start talking about where and when and I just feel this vise in my chest. The last time I got married was the worst day of my life. I just didn't know it. And now when I think about getting married that's all I remember. I don't get excited. I want to throw up."

Wow. Emelia never would have guessed that underneath Allie's bubbly exterior sat all this angst. Or that she'd been married before. "So elope. Go stand in front of a judge, or whatever it is here, and just get married." Emelia shoved aside the selfish thought that Allie's marriage would leave her homeless. No way was she living with newlyweds.

Allie looked at her, eyes wet. "I can't do that to Jackson. He wants the real wedding. He deserves a proper one. His family, they're amazing, and he's the only son. I can't take that away from them. Not because of my stupid mistakes. I know that once I'm walking down the aisle and he's waiting for me, I'll be fine. I just don't know how to get there."

"Does Jackson know this?" She raised her voice as the announcer started counting down to the beginning of the next race.

"Some of it. I don't want to hurt him. And every time I mention Derek, he gets this set in his jaw like he wants to go and hunt him down and beat him." A wry smile played on Allie's lips as she traced something on the wooden bench with her pointer finger.

"Have you tried . . ." Emelia couldn't believe the words that were about to come out of her mouth. "Praying about it?" That was what church people did, right? Prayed about stuff? If there was a God, surely He would listen to Allie. She studied the big screen for a few seconds. The guys had started rowing; the crowd's roar was low but it would grow exponentially over the next few minutes.

"All the time." Allie shrugged. "But God's not like a magical fairy up there waving a magical wand that will—poof!—make everything all better. I need to take responsibility for dealing with my own stuff. And it's hard. And it wrecks me that Jackson has to deal with it too. That he has a fiancée who turns into a mess every time we try to talk about what should be one of the best days of our lives. That I'm dreading it, instead of excited about it." She heaved a sigh and ran her hands through her hair. "Maybe we should actually have an engagement party first. See if that helps."

Emelia turned to her. "You haven't had an engagement party?"

Allie shrugged. "When we got engaged, I'd only been in England a couple of months and Jackson even less. We hadn't made a lot of friends, and with him in Cambridge and me here and our families on two different continents, it just hasn't happened."

"Okay. So have an engagement party. Start with that."

Allie sighed. "The only problem is even that will probably be over my mother's dead body."

Two hours later, Emelia closed the gym door behind her and breathed in a lungful of fresh air. It had come down to the two coxes, Cambridge winning with five rowers winning to Oxford's three and a margin of three seconds. The way they'd whooped and danced you would've thought it was the real thing. The part of her that cheered for the underdog had smiled on the inside, careful not to let any of the Oxford team see.

Allie unlocked her car and they both opened their doors. Emelia's backside had almost hit the seat when she remembered. "I left my water bottle in there."

They'd been almost the last to leave too. Knowing her luck, the facilities manager had locked the door behind her.

Allie stuck the key in the ignition. "Run back. I'm sure someone will still be there. I'll wait."

Emelia climbed out of the car and jogged toward the gym. She could picture exactly where she'd left it. Against the wall behind the ergometer she'd tried out rowing before the crowds had showed up. And after a thousand meters of feeling like she was about to pass out, she'd decided it was definitely not the sport for her.

The door swung open easily, and she took the stairs two at a time. Allie had some kind of guest-lecture thing tonight. She didn't want to make her late.

Turning the corner at the top, she could hear the whirring of an erg. The rowing club was going to collect them the following morning. She rounded the corner, then stopped. Peter sat on one of the rowing machines, his back to her. Even from meters away, she could see the sweat beads rolling down his neck, his shoulders and arms rippling as he pulled the handle with such power, it wouldn't have surprised her if the tether broke.

His left shoulder had some strapping tape across it. One large strip came out from under his sleeveless top. Not that from the way his arms and quads rippled as he rowed you'd have had any idea he'd been injured.

She inched forward, trying to get a glimpse of the numbers on the display screen. Her jaw almost unhinged as she caught sight of them flashing up over his shoulder. Her average split of two minutes ten over five hundred meters had made her feel like she was about to lose everything she'd eaten in the last week. Peter was pulling a minute thirty-five and, judging by the determined set of his profile, had no intention of slowing down anytime soon. And this was him injured.

This guy wasn't good—he was superhuman. Her confrontation with his ex still rang in her ears. Sabine was right, Emelia was never going to be able to understand what this sport meant to him.

Her gaze shifted from Peter to her water bottle, sitting right where she'd left it. Tiptoeing over, she picked it up silently and moved back toward the exit, allowing herself one last glimpse at the pure athleticism in motion. What had happened to him? Maybe it was time to break her self-imposed Google exile to find out. It wouldn't be prying, exactly. It wasn't like it wouldn't be public knowledge.

So why don't you just ask him yourself then? The question followed her as she walked away. Emelia was almost at the top of the stairs when a roar followed by a smacking sound made her spin and sprint back into the room.

Peter was on the mat beside his erg, knees curled up to his chest, one hand gripping the opposite shoulder. By his head, the seat still slid up and down on the rail, the fan still spinning.

Emelia sprang over the three ergs that were between them and dropped to her knees beside him. His eyes were clenched shut, face tinged with gray under the sheen of sweat.

"Peter. Peter!"

His eyes opened enough to become slits. "Emelia?"

"What do you need?"

"My bag. Pills." He huffed the words out as though it took extreme effort to speak. Closed his eyes again. Turning, she saw a black backpack by the far wall. Jumping over his erg, she ran to it, ripped the zipper open, and emptied the contents onto the floor. Thermal top, water bottle, muesli bars, and then the hollow sound of a circular medicine container, then another. She grabbed them both, along with the water bottle, and scrambled back.

"Which one?" She tried to read the labels, but they blurred in front of her eyes.

"OxyContin. The green one." Oh boy. She was no doctor, but she knew from her days as a fill-in sports reporter that was only prescribed for serious pain.

She opened the first container; the round green pills were inside. Pulling one out, she held it between her fingertips. "Open your mouth."

His mouth cracked open enough for her to poke it through his lips. "Water coming." She angled the water bottle carefully to control the flow. Last thing the guy needed right now was her drowning him. He lifted his head up a little to gulp the water, then dropped it back to the mat.

The whole time his eyes didn't crack open. "Thanks."

She stepped back over the erg and put all his stuff back in his backpack, carrying it over to him in case he needed anything else.

"I'm fine. Just give me a few minutes."

Typical English stiff upper lip. "Don't be stupid." She assessed the way he was holding his upper arm against the side of his chest. "Dislocated shoulder or rotator cuff?"

He opened his eyes and stared at her. "Rotator."

Oh boy. That was bad. Not that it took a genius to figure that out when he was in the fetal position and the color of ash.

"Do you have a car here?" He couldn't drive, that was for sure. But he needed to be home. Resting.

"Yup. I'll be fine. Honestly." All of a sudden, Emelia remembered Allie. Sitting in the car. No doubt wondering what the heck had happened to her.

Right on cue, she heard someone approaching. "Emelia?" her roommate called out. "Everything okay?"

Emelia stood just as Allie rounded the corner. "I'm fine." She gestured to the man at her feet. "He is not."

At that, Peter somehow managed to roll himself into a sitting position, face contorted in pain. "I'll be fine. I just need a few minutes for the Oxy to kick in."

Allie skirted around the machines as Peter stumbled to his feet, his right hand now supporting his left elbow.

Allie stopped in front of him, her neck craning so she could look up at his face. "What have you done? You said you were going easy on it." She sounded like a bossy older sister.

"I was."

Emelia bit the inside of her cheek as she observed the way Peter avoided Allie's gaze. Whatever it was that she had seen, "going easy" wasn't it.

From the expression on her face, Allie didn't believe him either. She let out a sigh and ran a hand through her copper hair as she shook her head.

Emelia stepped forward. "You have a lecture. You should go. I'll make sure he gets home okay."

Allie glanced between the two of them, obviously torn.

"She's right, Allie. You need to go. I'll call you later." Peter's sweaty T-shirt stuck to him like cling wrap outlining his muscular physique. Emelia forced her gaze away and onto her roommate, who still looked a little uncertain. There wasn't even any decision to be made. This wasn't community college. You didn't just not show up for a lecture at Oxford.

"Can you walk okay?" Emelia directed the question to Peter. "I'll take your backpack, but I'm just going to need to grab my stuff out of Allie's car."

Peter nodded, managing something that was more shuffle than walk, but at least it was forward movement.

"I'll go get your stuff. You come with him." Allie finally accepted that she was going to have to leave this to Emelia.

A few minutes later, Emelia was holding her gear and watching Allie drive away. It was only as the ashen-faced guy leaned against the passenger door of his car that she realized her rescue plan had one significant flaw.

She had never driven on the wrong side of the road before.

Nineteen

PETER TRIED TO BITE BACK A GROAN, BUT ONE ESCAPED ANYWAY as he settled himself into the passenger seat and gritted his teeth against the feeling of someone taking an ice pick to his shoulder.

His arm lay useless against his side like a broken wing. Any attempt to move it sent shards of pain through his shoulder.

The last time it had felt this bad, he'd been on a bar floor in Verona, not knowing what had happened but knowing it was bad. His next clear memory was of the white ceiling of the local hospital, the buzz of serious pain meds, and the grim face of the head coach. No words were necessary to tell him the dream was over before it had really begun.

"Can you pass me your seat belt or do you need me to get it?" Emelia's voice broke through his ramble down bad-memory lane. Peter slowly moved his right hand from where it was supporting his left elbow and reached up until his fingers hooked around the belt and pulled it forward.

He squashed down a yelp as even the small movement sent fire down his side.

"I've got it." Emelia took it, and he heard a whir as she pulled it around his body. Then a click as it tightened across his torso.

He anchored his hand back under his elbow and forced himself to breathe against the fireworks display taking place on the back of his eyelids. He'd lost track of how much time had passed since the shredding pain had sent him off the erg and onto the floor, but it couldn't be long before the Oxy kicked in.

Kevin was going to kill him. Peter had promised his physio he was taking it slow and steady. That was the condition that had gotten him the okay to get back on the water. A pace that would have had a disabled pensioner passing him. And he had been. But after weeks of good easy rows out on the water and only the occasional twinge from his shoulder, he'd thought it was time to push it a little.

How could he have been so stupid? He had years until Tokyo. Enough time to rebuild his strength and fitness to be a contender in all the lead-up races that mattered. But no, he'd had to go and be the big man. And now he'd put himself back what, months?

It was the email that had caused Peter to be reckless. The weekly newsfeed from America that helped him keep tabs on the journalist who'd been responsible for Anita's death. He should quit it. Just the sight of her byline was enough to have him seeing red. This week she'd been stalking some poor celebrity who had checked into rehab. Degrading them. Smearing their character with allegations and insinuations that could never be undone. That was what he'd been thinking of as he'd pulled on the handle of the erg so hard the numbers on the display could hardly keep up.

He registered that the engine had started, but the car wasn't moving. Cracking open his eyelids, he turned his head slightly to see what was going on. Emelia sat in the driver's seat, staring out the windshield, fingers grasping the steering wheel.

"You okay?" Then he realized she was missing a key piece of information. "Sorry. You don't even know where I live."

Emelia shook her head. "Allie told me where you live. It's . . ." He watched something flicker across her profile. For a second, he didn't think she was going to tell him whatever it was. "So, I've never driven in England before."

It took him a second to work out what the problem was. "You'll be fine. Just make sure you stay left." He tried to smile, lighten up the mood. "I'll just keep my eyes shut." At least that way he wouldn't have to see if she turned him in front of oncoming traffic or something. Though even that didn't sound too bad.

Right now, death would almost have been preferable to reality.

Emelia spent the fifteen-minute drive to Peter's place hunched over the steering wheel, peering out the windshield like an old lady, and going an average of maybe ten miles an hour. Just trying to translate the speedometer from kilometers an hour stressed her out, so she just didn't look at it. The drive was a lesson in what was required to break the renowned English reserve, as drivers behind her honked and passed her, offering gestures that didn't exactly say "Welcome to England."

She didn't care. Every corner felt like it would be her last, every oncoming vehicle had her sucking in air through her pursed lips like she was breathing through a straw.

Peter offered directions but his eyes stayed shut for the journey. The meds must have been kicking in though, because he was starting to look more white-gray than the gray-gray of the gym floor.

She directed compliments to the speed junkies under her breath as yet another driver tailgated her and sat on his horn.

"I'm pretty sure I've run this route faster." Peter didn't open his eyes but did turn his head slightly to make the helpful observation.

"I am not going that slowly." She looked in the rearview mirror. Thank goodness the guy couldn't turn around to see she was being abused by a man who had to be at least seventy.

"My grandmother drives faster than you and she's blind."

She finally relaxed her death grip on the steering wheel when she knew they had to be getting close.

She chanced a glance over at him. Even when he was in excruciating pain, there was something about his presence that made her feel safe. The way she'd always imagined Peter Pevensie would. "You okay?"

"I'll be fine." His pinched voice said the opposite.

Emelia knew the voice. Knew the words. They were the same ones she'd used the day she'd lost out on her dream job as reporter for the *Boston Globe* to a congressman's daughter who couldn't have told an adverb from an adjective if her vapid existence depended on it. Apparently none of that mattered when you had a daddy with a Rolodex full of prestigious contacts you could go simpering to when you needed a story.

She knew what broken dreams looked like, so she wasn't about to offer perky motivational lines that weren't worth the air they traveled on.

She turned the wipers on instead of the blinker, and then

made a left into a small, narrow street. Then realized Peter had said to take the next right.

"Um, Peter? I just turned left instead of right."

Peter opened his eyes and peered out the windshield. "So you did. Know what else?"

"What?"

A smile flickered on his lips. "This is a one-way street and it's not this way."

Emelia stomped on the brakes, leaving Peter sucking in a sharp breath as his shoulder tilted forward.

"Sorry. Sorry!" She managed to reverse the car into a tiny driveway and turn it around.

"*Girls aren't very good at keeping maps in their brains.*" Peter uttered Edmund's well-known line with a twisted smile.

"That's because we've got something in them." Emelia threw Lucy's responding line back as she turned onto the original road. Driving a little farther down, she took the next right. "Did you say you're number thirty-six?"

She looked sideways when Peter didn't answer to find him staring at her. "What? Did I get that wrong too?"

"You quoted right back. The line. You didn't even have to think about it. Who can do that?"

She came to a stop at the curb. "Someone who's read Narnia more than a few times." Avoiding the intent look in his gaze that made her feel like he was peering into her soul, she reached over, released Peter's seat belt, and watched as it traveled over his torso. His sweat-soaked T-shirt stuck to his chest, leaving little to the imagination.

Reaching across to open his door, Peter got out of the car, slamming it shut behind him. Scrambling after him, Emelia grabbed his backpack from the backseat and followed him up the path. What had just happened? One second it felt like they were having some kind of moment, the next he was stomping away like an adolescent boy losing Xbox privileges.

He turned around at the front door. His face was still contorted, but every step didn't make him look like he might be about to keel over. At least that was something. "Thanks for bringing me home. I've got it."

She raised an eyebrow at him. "You've got what, exactly?"

"I'm good."

Emelia suddenly realized she hadn't thought past this point. How was she going to get home from here? It wasn't like she could drive his car. It was a miracle someone hadn't reported her to the cops on the way here.

She returned her attention to the stubborn guy in front of her. "Tell you what. I'll make you a deal. If you can open your front door, then I'll leave you alone." There must be a bus route or something nearby. She dropped his backpack near his feet.

Leaning over, he picked it up, wedged it between his knees, and used the hand on his uninjured arm to lever the zipper open enough for him to get his hand through. It reappeared with a bunch of keys dangling off his fingers.

Giving her a smug look, Peter inserted a gold key into the lock and twisted it. A small click rewarded him. He turned the knob and went to open the door, but it didn't move. Still held fast by the dead bolt located just above.

Muttering something under his breath, he pulled the key out, flipped the ring around, and picked out a silver one. He shoved it into the dead bolt, twisted that one, and then looked at the lower doorknob as if willing it to move with the power of his mind.

He moved closer to the door and reached for the lower handle with his injured arm. But even that small movement made him wince and clench his jaw.

Short of being strung out on enough opiates to take down a horse, there was no way it was going to happen. Emelia wasn't going to stand here all day watching him try.

Without warning, he pulled the key from the dead bolt and threw the set to the ground with such force they bounced.

Emelia stepped forward and swiped the keys off the ground. "Easy. I know it hasn't been a good day but—"

"A good day?" Peter turned toward her, pain etched across his face. "I probably just tore my rotator cuff again. It was meant to be better. After eleven months—*eleven*. 'Not a good day' doesn't even come close to it."

"I'm sorry. I'm sure it's just a minor setback." And there she went, offering up a pointless platitude when she knew nothing of the sort. Exactly the kind of words that she'd hated. The ones she'd wanted to throw back in people's faces when she lost out on serious journalism jobs to people who had better connections, or had rich daddies to pave their career path, or were better looking. Never mind that the only way they could have found a story was if it was handed to them on a diamond-encrusted spoon. An apology formed on her lips but didn't make it out before Peter rounded on her, clutching his shoulder, green eyes flashing.

"You have no idea what you're talking about. You know where I'm meant to be right now? Training. With my team. I trained for ten years to get there. Ten years. Of early mornings. Hundreds of thousands of kilometers of rowing. Half the year in sleet, until my hands bled and I could taste the blood in my mouth. What would you know about that? What would you know about having a crazy, audacious dream and then getting it ripped away from you when it was finally within reach? You're just a glorified admin assistant."

Emelia stepped back as if she'd been slapped. "Excuse me?" He had not just gone there. Peter's mouth opened but she didn't even give him a chance to get out a syllable. "You have *no* idea what you're talking about. You don't know anything about me. Not really. Oh, you probably think you do. Maybe you think it's funny that I hide in wardrobes. Whatever. You probably think it's cute that I can quote Narnia off the top of my head. None of that means you know anything that matters about me." She shoved the key in the dead bolt, twisted it, turned the door handle below, and threw the door open with such force it slammed against the wall.

"Sabine is welcome to you."

Twenty

The following Thursday, Peter approached Emelia's office doorway like it framed gallows. In his hand he held a box of Cadbury chocolates. After his appalling behavior, he was hoping they'd buy him enough time to explain himself before she threw him out.

The last time he'd put his foot in his mouth so badly he'd ended up doing a similar walk to penance. Thankfully, this time Elizabeth wasn't around to give him the third degree. Her eagle eyes missed nothing.

He paused, peering around the side of the door. Emelia sat at her decrepit desk, intent on some documents. Her wavy hair was in a ponytail, a few loose strands spilling over her bare shoulders, the dark purple sleeveless, filmy top she was wearing skimming her curves in all the right ways.

As she jotted something down on the paper in front of her, a small smile lifted at one end of her lips. She turned to her keyboard and typed out a few words, then tugged a piece of hair behind her ear.

Peter could have watched her all day, except any second now she would look up and find him peering at her like some kind of Peeping Tom. And that would go down so well after everything else.

He tapped on the doorframe, holding the box of chocolates up to his chest like a shield. Maybe she'd take pity on a guy with a sling.

Her gaze landed on him. "Hi." Her face was a study in neutrality.

"Hi." He walked in. "Chocolates?"

Emelia tilted her head. "As in, do I like them? Would I like one? Or you've come armed with a large box as an attempt at a truce?"

"All of the above?" He still lurked awkwardly in her doorway, not sure whether he should enter.

"Yes, but only because I'm a sucker for Cadbury." She stood up, walked around the desk, and plucked the box from his hand. "Come in. We need to talk."

Peter braced himself for her to tell him that she'd talked to Elizabeth and told her that they couldn't work together anymore.

He had to see this through. For Anita. "All the other board members would be pants at this!" The words fell out of his mouth as Emelia was using her scissors to slice open the cellophane wrapping.

She stopped and looked at him like he was talking gibberish. "I'm sorry. Did you just say something about the board members' pants?"

He'd forgotten Americans didn't use the saying. "Pants. Rubbish. No good. I know that I've been a total jerk but replacing me with one of the other board members . . . none of them would be any good." The truth was that, from what he'd seen, Emelia didn't need a board member at all. She could get all the guidance that she needed off Elizabeth. But he was hardly going to point that out. Since the Boat Race was over and his stupid rush of blood to the head after the row-off had put his shoulder back months in rehabilitation—this, helping save Anita's charity, was the only thing that gave his life meaning.

He tried to ignore the fact that working with Emelia was also a distinct bonus.

"Chocolate?" Emelia offered him the box and he grabbed a caramel one. Dropping the box on the desk, she walked back around it and sat down. She offered him that same half smile as he stood there awkwardly. He wasn't sure if her offering of chocolate was Emelia's version of an olive branch. "You can sit." Reaching over, she picked out a circular one and popped it into her mouth.

Peter chomped his chocolate as he lowered himself into the same chair he'd groveled from last time, careful not to jar his shoulder. "I'm sorry I was such a plonker to you."

"What happened to your shoulder?" It didn't pass his notice that, once again, she didn't explicitly accept his apology. "The first time." Emelia leaned forward in her chair, grabbed another chocolate. It made a nice change from Sabine, who had pedantically tracked every calorie that passed her lips, determined to hover just on the minimum weight allowed for coxes.

Peter's body stiffened. He hated talking about that night. But she was right, he owed her an explanation. "Bar brawl."

"Wow. I wouldn't have guessed that."

He blew out a breath. Him neither. "We were at the world champs in Verona. We'd won a big race that day. So the team decided to go out for drinks to celebrate." As usual, he'd only had one beer, left the real celebratory drinking up to a few of the other guys. "We decided to go to a club. Not my thing but we had some younger guys on the squad who could get a bit cocky once they had a few drinks in them and I wanted to make sure they kept their noses clean.

"Anyway, one of them ended up hitting on some guy's girlfriend. He took exception to it and the next thing I knew fists were swinging. I waded in to try and break it up. One of the guy's friends cracked me with a bottle across the back of my head and the next thing I really remember is waking up in hospital. Tore my rotator cuff up pretty bad." That was an understatement. "The worst I've ever operated on" were the words the surgeon had used.

According to his teammates who'd seen it, he'd gone down like a tree, arm outstretched like a branch. To this day he couldn't work out how he'd fallen like that.

"I'm sorry." Emelia leaned over and picked another chocolate. "I know I'm only a glorified admin assistant now, but I know what it's like to have big dreams that don't come true."

He flinched at the words he'd used to describe her. "Emelia, I was mad at myself for being so stupid. You're far more than that." He stopped himself before he could say anything else. Things that he didn't even really understand himself and would just make things awkward for both of them. "What was your crazy dream?"

She studied him for a moment, as if deciding whether he was worthy of being trusted with it. More than anything else he wanted to be, even though he knew he had a track record with her of the absolute opposite.

"I wanted to be a journalist. A real one. Like Christiane Amanpour. Reporting from war zones, natural disasters, the world's hot spots."

"What happened?"

She shrugged. "Didn't have the right connections, I guess." From the look in her eyes, he could see there was far more to it than that. For a second it looked like she might say more, but then a guard sprang up and she turned her attention to the papers on her desk. "Anyway, we should talk about the row-off. It did better than we expected. I'm just finalizing the report to the board for you to review. And we also need to talk about this cricket match and the mystery ball venue you have up your sleeve."

He didn't care about the board, or some report to review, or even, in that second, about saving Anita's legacy. All he cared about was knowing the story of the girl sitting in front of him.

Twenty-One

"How can you even be asking that of me?" The words hit Emelia as she closed the front door. Jackson sounded frustrated and hurt. The golden couple having a disagreement. That was a first. When Emelia had left to run a few errands they'd been snuggled up on the couch, so cozy you would've struggled to fit a paper clip between them.

Allie responded, but Emelia couldn't quite make out the words.

Sliding her bag off her shoulder, she dropped it to the floor so she could take off her lightweight trench coat and hang it up.

Her stomach let out a low rumble, and she pressed her hand against it. Her dinner, leftovers waiting in the fridge, was going to have to wait. There was no way she wanted to walk in on whatever was going down in the living area. At least she still had half a box of Peter's chocolates up in her room.

Grabbing her bag, she placed a foot on the stairs, only to jump when the door to the living area suddenly flew open and Jackson marched out, face set. "I need some air."

Emelia wasn't sure if his words were directed at Allie, himself, or her. He yanked his coat off one of the hooks and didn't even take the time to shrug it on before he wrenched open the front door and marched into the night.

Emelia stood frozen on the step. What was she supposed to do? She'd never been good at the whole girl-talk thing. And, as much as she liked Allie, they'd only known each other a few months. Would it be better or worse for her to know Emelia was home?

A sob made up her mind for her. She couldn't leave Allie alone. Not after everything she'd done for her. Padding down the hall, Emelia paused in the doorway. Allie sat on one of the couches, leaning forward, her head in her hands and her fingers pressed into her auburn hair.

On the coffee table in front of her sat a set of papers. Official-looking ones on letterhead.

"Is everything okay?" Emelia flinched at the stupidity of her question. Everything clearly wasn't.

Allie raised her head, eyes red rimmed. "Hey. Did you just get home?"

"Yeah. Just as Jackson was, um, leaving." No point pretending she hadn't heard or seen anything.

"How angry did he look?"

"Not angry. More . . ." Emelia shrugged, grimacing a little. "Frustrated? Ticked off?"

Allie heaved out a sigh. "I don't blame him."

Emelia inched into the room, uncertain what she was meant to do or say.

Allie poked at the pile of papers in front of her. "My parents want him to sign a prenup."

"Ah." Emelia sat down on the armchair, perching on the edge. "Why? I mean . . . sorry . . . it's really none of my business."

"It's okay." Allie swiped her hands across her cheeks, wiping away the remains of tears. "It's a long story. Let's just say my family has money and some of my relationship choices in the past haven't exactly been stellar. They're just trying to protect me the way they think is best."

"And Jackson doesn't see it that way?"

Allie grimaced. "It's hardly a good sign, is it? Planning to get married while drawing up contracts for who gets what if it doesn't work out."

Emelia didn't know how to respond. She could hardly say a prenup epitomized certainty that their love would last forever.

"Jackson thinks it means I don't trust him. The truth is I don't care. It hadn't even crossed my mind before these papers from my dad's lawyer showed up, but my family dynamics are challenging, to say the least. Jackson signing them would make things a bit easier on that end."

"Did you explain that to him?"

"I tried. Didn't do a good job of it."

"I'm sure he'll be back in the morning. He probably just needs a bit of time to calm down. To process it rationally." For reasons Emelia hadn't been able to work out, Jackson never stayed over when he was in town for the weekend. Instead, he seemed to rotate around the couches and spare rooms of various friends.

"You think?" Hope glowed from Allie's large green eyes.

Emelia had no idea. She hadn't had anything approaching a serious relationship in years, and she'd certainly never had anything close to what Jackson and Allie had. "He may be a little mad at the moment, but he's even madder about you."

"I should text him. Tell him it doesn't matter." Allie reached for her phone.

"Would it be true?"

"What?"

"That it doesn't matter."

Allie bit her bottom lip for a second. "Yes . . . no . . . I don't know."

Emelia had never seen her roommate look so uncertain. "Well then, what are the pros and cons of him signing?"

"It would make my parents happy."

"And?"

"And . . ." Allie hesitated. There was clearly something there, but she didn't want to verbalize it.

"Does part of you worry Jackson is attracted to your money?"

"No!" The word erupted out of Allie. The maiden doth protest too much. Allie's shoulders slumped. "The last guy I married was after my money. I guess I still carry more baggage about that than I realized. I know Jackson isn't after me for that . . . but then I guess a small part of me reminds me that at one time I would've sworn the same thing about Derek too."

Yep, Emelia could see how that would play mind games with a girl. "Did he clean you out when you got divorced? Is that why your parents are worried?"

Allie shook her head. "We didn't get divorced. The marriage was annulled. He got nothing. Well, nothing more."

Emelia's journalistic radar was practically in cardiac arrest. She'd have bet everything she had that there was one mighty big story crammed into those four short sentences. But now wasn't the time. "Jackson knows all about Derek though?"

"Jackson knows everything." Allie wrung her hands. "We've never fought like this."

Jealousy snuck up on Emelia. Did Allie know how lucky she was that she could say that? No one knew everything about her. There was no one she'd ever been able to imagine trusting with her messy, mistake-ridden life.

An image of Peter slipped into her mind. The only person she'd ever met who made her want to indulge in the fantasy of what it would be like to have someone truly know you. She shook it loose. That was crazy thinking. She barely knew the guy, and, as she'd so emphatically told him, he definitely didn't know the first thing about her.

"Not that I'm exactly one to be giving relationship advice, but if I were you, I wouldn't worry about the prenup."

"Why's that?" Allie looked up from staring at the papers.

"That guy is head-over-heels insane about you. He would sooner lose a limb than ever leave you. If you guys can't make it, no one can."

Peter leaned back in his La-Z-Boy, his one piece of decent furniture; settled his family-sized bag of crisps on his lap; cracked open his one Saturday-night beer; and flicked on some sports highlights. His finger was poised on the remote to change channels if there was any sign of rowing coverage. Almost a year on, it still hurt too much to see his old teammates living his dream to be able to watch without something fierce and ugly twisting up his gut. So it was better that he didn't.

He heard, then felt, the front door slam. He checked his watch. Not even eight. His flatmate, Tony, was on an evening shift at the hospital. And when Jackson was staying with them, he was never back before eleven. Occasionally he'd sneak in after midnight with a slightly sheepish look on his face, like he had a curfew or something.

But Peter's couch guest stormed into the room, pulling up short when he saw Peter sitting there, staring at him.

"Sorry, didn't think you'd be home."

From the guy who was constantly giving him stick about his lack of a social life.

Jackson stomped to the fridge, reached in, and pulled out a bottle of beer. "Mind?" He was already twisting it open as he asked.

"Be my guest."

"Thanks." Jackson stomped back over, slumped onto the couch, placed his shoe-clad feet on the coffee table, and took a slug. Clearly not the right moment to remind him of the "no shoes on the furniture" rule.

"Highlights, huh?"

"Yup." Peter aimed for nonchalant.

"Anything on the rowing?"

Peter didn't bother to answer, just picked up the remote and turned the commentary on the diving down a couple of notches. "So, what's up in paradise?"

"What do you mean?" Jackson did nonchalant badly.

"It's not even eight."

Jackson shrugged, faked being glued to some whippet-sized Chinese girl performing a double pike. "Maybe I just felt like an early night."

Peter snorted. In all the months that Jackson had been spending weekends on his couch, Jackson and Allie had only separated themselves to get the bare minimum hours of functional sleep. The pair didn't know what an "early night" was when they were in the same place. "Is this your first barney?" He'd have put money on it. He'd never seen the two of them really disagree. Which was odd, considering they were two quite strong personalities.

"First what?"

"Big fight."

Jackson didn't say anything. Just toed one shoe off and then another, leaving them to lie where they fell on the floor. Peter forced himself to take a casual sip of his beer, like it didn't bother him. The guy may have come with model looks, but he certainly hadn't come with model housekeeping habits.

They sat in silence for a few seconds, watching an Australian girl cram in a lot of somersaults between leaving the diving board and hitting the water.

Peter held out his bowl of crisps, shoulder twinging, and offered them to Jackson. He waved them away.

"She wants me to sign a prenup." Jackson's eyes didn't leave the screen.

"Allie?"

"No, my other fiancée. Yes, Allie."

"Huh." Peter snagged a couple of crisps and palmed them into his mouth. Thought while he chewed. "And you don't want to."

"Would you?"

Peter shrugged. "Can't say I've ever thought about it. I don't think there's a blanket right or wrong answer; I think it depends on the situation. I can imagine Mum and Dad would want Victor to if the estate wasn't already in an ironclad trust." Not that there was any chance of his brother making a commitment to any woman for longer than a night.

"You don't see anything wrong with signing some contract before you get married about how you're going to divvy up your assets if you split up?"

"Well, I can't say it's the most romantic thing I've ever heard of."

"It doesn't feel right. It's like having a Plan B. Like 'Oh well, hopefully this works out but if not we already know what everyone's getting out of it.'"

Peter grabbed a handful of crisps and chomped down on them as Jackson continued.

"It's insulting. It's humiliating. Like they'd better cover the bases in case I'm after her for her money."

"Who's they?"

"Her family. Her family has money. The prenup came from her father's lawyer."

"So it wasn't Allie's idea."

Jackson shook his head. "The papers just showed up today."

"So, let me get this straight. It wasn't Allie's idea, it was her father's. Her family has a lot of money. Plus, they barely know you. It's not like the two of you spent the last five years dating so you can convince them you're the guy for her. Given all that, I'd be stunned if they didn't want one."

"Guess I didn't think of it like that."

"Do you care about her money? Their money?" Peter took another sip of his beer.

"Of course not!" One of Jackson's hands curled into a fist.

"Then what does it even matter? Just sign the thing if it makes her parents happy. It's never going to be needed. Anyone who has to spend more than thirty seconds witnessing how nauseatingly perfect you guys are for each other knows that."

Jackson groaned. "I was such a jerk."

Peter didn't say anything. If he'd had any girl look at him the way Allie looked at Jackson, he would've signed the thing with his own blood if she'd asked it.

Jackson got to his feet. "I need to fix this."

Peter turned back to the TV screen just in time to see the camera panning over a lake and a lineup of boats. He didn't even wait to see who was racing before his finger hit the off button on the remote. "Want a ride?"

Twenty-Two

Emelia and Allie made hot chocolates and settled into the comfy chairs to watch *Notting Hill*. There were some situations that just needed a floppy-haired Hugh Grant from the nineties.

Emelia was immersed in Hugh interviewing Julia when the door flew open. They both jumped and turned as Jackson strode back into the room.

Emelia looked at her watch. An hour and forty minutes since he'd left. That was fast. She'd cooked meals that took longer than this fight.

Without even glancing Emelia's way, he strode up to Allie, who'd risen from her chair. "Hi."

"Hi." Allie looked a little wary. Not that Emelia could blame her, given how he'd stormed out, but it was a different guy who was back.

Wrapping his arms around her, Jackson tugged Allie to him. "I'm sorry."

Allie's lip wobbled. "I'm sorry too. You're right. I never should have asked it of you."

"No. You should've. It's okay. Your family hardly knows me. I don't blame them for being wary. And I don't care. I don't care about any of it. I will sign whatever you want me to. Your father can have all of my stuff too if he wants it. All I care about is marrying you."

Allie reached up and fisted her hands around his sweater, tugging him down to her. "And all I care about is marrying you. I don't want a prenup. I'm so sorry that between Derek and my family I'm making this all so hard. Way harder than it should be."

Emelia really needed to get out of here before it got awkward. Allie had clearly forgotten that she was in there, and she wasn't sure if Jackson had even noticed.

She backed out of the room at a quiet shuffle, eyes to the ground. She moved the door enough for her to slip through, and she got out and breathed a sigh of relief in the hallway.

She sent a silent prayer of thanks up for their old-fashioned no-sleepovers thing. At least she wouldn't have to deal with loud make-up sex on top of everything else.

"What's the everything else?"

Pure reflexes kicked in and she spun around, her leg lashing out and sweeping the person behind her off their feet.

They went down with an oomph. A streak of orange streamed across her vision, confirming the voice she'd identified a split second after she'd kicked him. Peter hit the recycling bin Emelia had put down earlier, halfway through taking it outside. Cans and bottles rolled everywhere.

"Are you an actual ninja?" Peter offered up his question from where he lay splayed on the wooden floor.

"Oh my gosh." Emelia put her palm to her thundering chest and sucked in a couple of gulps of air. "Do you want to give me a heart attack?" Oh, wow. This was not good. "Your shoulder! Did you land on it? Is it okay?

She was going to be the girl who'd destroyed whatever big

comeback dreams he still had. She had to remember Oxford wasn't LA. And she was just a charity fund-raiser. Not a tabloid reporter who regularly received death threats.

"It's fine." He sucked in a breath as he rotated it. "Well, no worse than it was before you floored me anyway."

Well, at least there was that. To buy herself a few seconds, Emelia crouched down. Righting the bin, she picked up a couple of cans and bottles, tossing them back in.

"I'm sorry." He at least had the decency to look sheepish. He pushed his torso up off the floor, then levered himself onto his feet so he was crouching. "Jackson left his wallet in my car. I was going to just put it on the table and text him, but then you came out . . . well, more like backed out . . . and I didn't want you to turn around and just find me standing here."

"Yeah, because that would've been so much less terrifying than what you did." She reached for a bottle just as he did, both of their hands grasping it. She let go, her gaze moving up his broad chest.

"Sorry." His mouth quirked, like he was struggling to contain laughter, which made her review the last few minutes.

She felt the burn starting at the end of her feet and working up her body. "I said my last thought aloud, didn't I?" She must've. Because she distinctly recalled his asking what the everything else was.

The quirk broke into a grin as he stood. "You did."

Wow. That wasn't embarrassing at all. And now they were both staring at each other thinking about make-up sex. Awkward.

"So . . ." She cleared her throat. She tried to work out where to go from here. Then busied herself trying to pick up the nearest pieces of trash.

"What happened?" Emelia glanced over her shoulder to see that the commotion had even jolted the lovebirds out of their canoodling.

Peter stood. "I made the mistake of giving Emelia a fright. Didn't realize she was a ninja."

Emelia put her hands up. "Just a few self-defense classes." She preferred to keep her martial arts abilities to herself.

Jackson let out a low whistle as Allie picked up the last couple of bottles by her feet and added them to the bin. "Those must've been some classes."

Peter held out Jackson's wallet. "Don't say I've never put my body on the line for you. You forgot this."

Jackson took it and stuffed it in his jeans pocket. "Thanks. We were just going to head out and grab something to eat. We'll see you guys later." The front door opened, then shut, and they were gone, leaving her and Peter alone.

Emelia went for the first thing she thought of to fill the silence. "Would you like coffee? Or tea?" She had no idea what it was with the British and their tea. Almost everyone she'd met drank so much of the stuff, it might as well have been in an IV line.

Then she blinked, realizing she'd just asked a guy she was crazy attracted to to stay. Late at night. With no one else there. She never would have done that back home. Not in a second. "So, um, how about we talk about the cricket?"

One second he'd been mesmerized by the sight of Emelia backing out of the living area muttering under her breath. The next he'd been on his back, winded. Thank goodness he'd managed to instinctively twist himself to cushion his shoulder from the worst of the blow. He'd only just liberated it from the sling.

Put on his butt by a girl. Not that he necessarily had an issue with that. Rowing, he'd met a lot of girls who could beat most guys arm wrestling just using their pinkies. But it was like she hadn't even tried. The words were barely out of his mouth before he'd been staring at the ceiling. And he wasn't a small guy.

He watched the ninja out of the corner of his eye as she put something in the microwave, then turned and poured tea into one cup and hot water into a second. Self-defense classes. Huh. There was no chance she'd learned that move from a course at the Y.

There was more to this girl than met the eye. And his eyes already liked what they saw. A lot. Peter blew out a puff of air. What was he thinking?

"Milk?" From the way Emelia said it, it wasn't the first time she'd asked.

"Um, yes, thanks. Just a little."

"Sugar?"

Did he take sugar? With her staring expectantly at him like that, he couldn't remember. "No. Thanks."

She doctored his cup and then carried them over. "Sorry if it's no good. I know how seriously your country takes your tea." She placed her cup on the coffee table, leaned over and put his in front of him, then stepped back and settled into the other end of the couch. If he reached out and moved over slightly, he could run his fingers through her gorgeous wavy hair. It was loose, spilling over her shoulders. The last few times he'd seen her, it had been in a ponytail. He liked it this way a whole lot more.

He reined himself in, kept his hands busy picking up his cup and taking a sip. It was bad. Too weak. How long had she steeped it for, like thirty seconds? And not enough milk.

"Okay?" Emelia was watching him over the rim of her cup.

"Great. Thanks." He put the cup down. Hoped he could avoid having to drink all of it. "So, how would next Sunday work for you to go and look at this potential ball venue? We could go around lunchtime. I've got church in the morning." He watched her closely to see what her reaction was to his use of the C-word again. A small foolish part of him hoped that she might want to join him.

"Okay. Sounds good. What time does church finish?" There wasn't any interest, but it also wasn't the allergic reaction he'd gotten the first time, so he'd take it.

"About eleven. I'll pick you up at twelve." He lifted his tea up again, gave it another try. Still horrid.

"Why doesn't Jackson stay over?" Emelia took a tentative sip of her drink.

Tea sloshed over the rim of his cup, searing the top side of his finger. He'd expected the question about as much as he'd anticipated her sweeping kick. "Um, I think they're waiting until they're married."

"To . . . ?"

Was she really going to make him say it?

Then it connected. "Oh. Wow. Really? That's, um, different." Her mouth said "different." Her face said "weird." "Crazy." "Unbelievable." "But they're so . . . so . . ."

"All over each other."

She grinned. "Understatement of the year." He watched thoughts shift her expression as she pondered it. "But they're so . . . he's so . . . okay, sorry, this is a weird conversation. I just didn't realize people like them existed. Especially . . ."

He could practically see what she was thinking. People who were smart. Normal. Ridiculously good-looking. In her world, the only people who saved themselves for marriage were probably losers who didn't have any other choice.

"Are you like them too?" Her hand flew to her mouth. "Sorry. Don't answer that. Right. I'm going to stop talking now." She leaned over and took a huge gulp of her drink.

Peter started laughing. He couldn't help it. The girl looked like a paleontologist who'd just stumbled over a living dinosaur. Then the scent of singed air made him pause. Something was burning. He put his drink down and stood up. "What's that smell?"

"Smell?" Emelia looked around, then wrinkled her nose as well. Her hand flew to her mouth. "The popcorn!"

Slamming her cup onto the coffee table, she jumped off the couch and sprinted toward the kitchen. Peter strode after her, almost colliding into her when she stopped in front of the microwave. "Fire!"

Sure enough, inside the microwave a fireball rotated, the flames devouring what had once been a popcorn bag. Wow. The little boy inside who had once aspired to work in pyrotechnics was momentarily entranced.

The black smoke coming out the side was a bit concerning though.

The next thing he knew, Emelia had thrown the back door open, ripped the microwave's cord out of the socket, and picked it up off the counter.

"Wait . . . no—" But he was too late, she was already running with it out the back door. He ran after her, just in time to see her somehow launch the white box so it flew through the air before landing with a loud crack on the cobblestones outside, flipping over once and coming to rest on its back.

They both just stood there, watching the remaining flames flicker behind the now-cracked door.

Emelia peeked up at him from under long lashes, a nearby streetlight casting a dim halo over her. "So, um, maybe a little overdramatic?"

Peter couldn't help but grin back. "Well, I was just going to turn it off so the fan stopped feeding the fire, but that worked too. How long did you put it on for, Smoky?"

Emelia wrinkled her nose. "I meant to set it for three minutes but I must've set it for thirty by mistake. Guess I'm going to have to go buy Allie a new microwave."

In the sad, rectangular box, the last of the flames had dimmed to embers. Even outside in the almost dark, it was clear there was no resuscitating it. The smell of smoke still lingered in the air. "At least it went out in style. Not many microwaves can claim an ending like that." He walked toward it and started to pick it up, but the moment he attempted to lift it off the ground, his shoulder told him to think again.

"What's the prognosis?"

Emelia spoke from behind him as he let it go and stood back up.

"Unclear. No more rowing for a while, that's for sure." When he'd been forced to confess to Kevin what he'd done he'd thought his physio was going to clock him. And he didn't blame him. Months of rehab work out the window. He wanted to clock himself.

"Well, for what it's worth, the few seconds I did see of you on that erg were pretty impressive." Emelia stepped around him and scooped the appliance off the ground. Turning around, she carried it a few feet and set it against the side of the house next to the rubbish bin. He felt so useless not being able to even perform a simple task like that.

He blew out a breath. Not wanting to remember how, for a few minutes, it had felt like somehow the miraculous had happened. Maybe his shoulder had completely healed. A blissful few hundred seconds of feeling the burn again in his legs, lungs, and arms.

"Sabine mentioned you want to make a comeback." It wasn't a question.

Peter started at the unexpected mention of his ex. "Yes."

"Is it possible? With your shoulder?" The question was tentative, as if she knew how much just hearing the words hurt.

"It has to be." He rubbed his hand along the bristles that covered his jawline. His shoulder couldn't even manage a decent shave at the moment. "I need to do it for my cousin. She was my biggest cheerleader. Even on the worst day, she never stopped believing that I would be able to row again at an elite level."

"What happened to her?" Emelia dusted her hands off as she approached him. Somehow she'd gotten a smudge of dirt across her cheekbone.

"What do you mean?" Peter shuffled on his feet.

"You said 'never stopped.' Past tense."

Nothing got past this girl. "She died. Last year."

"I'm sorry."

Peter tried to shove the guilt down. He hadn't been there for Anita, but maybe he could be there for this feisty, independent girl with professional deflection skills. Something in his gut told him she'd spent a lot of her life having to fend for herself. "What about you? What brought you to Oxford?"

Emelia shrugged and wrapped her arms around herself. "I'm not nearly as interesting as you. No Olympic aspirations for me." She gestured to the door. "It's cold out here. We should go back inside."

Peter reached out, catching her elbow as she started to move past him. "Any girl who can put me on my backside when I don't even see it coming is pretty much the most interesting one I've ever met. Besides, you were right. I don't know much about you that matters. And I would really like to." Even in the darkness, he could see the wariness in her eyes. "Please."

She studied him for a second, as if weighing something. "Starting over."

What? "Sorry?"

"That's what brought me to Oxford. I made a huge mistake. I came here to try to start over. But then that's never really possible, is it? Because wherever you go, you're still there. You can never escape yourself."

Her voice was tinged with resignation and hurt. She looked at him as if hoping he would be able to tell her she was wrong, but knowing he couldn't. Especially not when that pretty much captured how he'd felt ever since Anita died.

Some days it took everything he had not to just knock back

another Oxy to try to escape the condemnation ringing in his own head. And that was while clinging to the knowledge that God still had a plan. Even if he couldn't see any of it. Emelia didn't even have that to hang on to.

He didn't know what to say, but he had to say something. He could already see her expression starting to close, as if she'd realized she'd said too much. "Em—"

"What's the worst-case scenario?" She cut him off. Changed the subject.

"For what?"

"So best-case scenario is you make a blazing comeback and win gold in Tokyo. What's the worst case? If you put yourself back into training and it happens all over again?"

"That I do permanent irreversible damage."

"Which means?"

"Lifelong weakness. Pain." Or as his consultant so bluntly put it, not being able to ever lift his arm again. The next fifty years on hard-core opiates.

"And which is more likely? The best or the worst?"

"The worst." By a long mile.

"And it's still worth it to you? The minute chance of winning an Olympic medal versus the very real chance that you could become permanently disabled?"

He'd never really had to have this conversation before. Sabine got it. His teammates got it. His parents didn't but trusted him to make his own decision. How did you explain the drive to beat all the odds? No matter what the risk? To be the best? To stand on a podium and hear your country's national anthem playing? "Yes."

She shook her head. "That's crazy."

He bristled. "Aren't you the girl who once wanted to be the next Christiane Amanpour? To be a war correspondent? Do you have any idea how many journalists and photographers come back in body bags? Or without limbs? Or, at the least, with post-traumatic stress disorder? My dream doesn't involve the real risk of me dying."

"Seventy-one." She said the words as she walked past him toward the door.

"Sorry?"

Emelia looked right at him. "Seventy-one journalists were killed last year."

"Want to know how many Olympic rowers were shot? Or executed? Or thrown in prison? None." He wasn't even sure what the point was that he was trying to make.

"But at least they were doing something worth—" She cut her own words off but not before he knew exactly what she was about to say.

"Worthwhile? Worthy? Whereas my dream is just, what? Selfish? All about my ego? Pride? Ambition?"

Emelia didn't say anything.

He blew out a breath. Well, that was a great kick of reality. Nothing quite like finding out the girl you have a crush on thinks your biggest dream is self-absorbed stupidity.

"What are you guys doing out here?" Allie saved Emelia from being forced to confirm that was exactly what she thought. She stood in the doorway, a brown paper bag in her hand, the local burger place's branding on the side. Allie didn't even wait for an answer before she launched into her next thing. "Guess what? Jackson and I have talked and we're going to have an engagement party." She looked at them with expectation. What did she want? A medal? They'd been engaged for like eight months already.

"Great. Took you long enough."

"Congratulations."

Peter and Emelia spoke over each other.

Allie scrunched her nose. "Why does it smell like smoke?"

Twenty-Three

Emelia watched the English countryside pass by the car window. All lush and green with flowers poking up their bright heads. There were cobbled stone fences and pastures filled with cattle. Quaint villages with looming church spires reaching toward the heavens. The scenery was outstanding, but everything else about the drive to visit Peter's potential venue had been very mysterious so far. When she'd tried to dig, all she'd managed to get out of him was that there was a "family connection." Words that made her realize she knew pretty much nothing about his family.

She still had no idea how that had morphed into her coming with him to his parents' house for lunch, except that it seemed to make sense at the time. Something about its being near the potential location. And she needed to apologize for basically saying his dream was stupid.

"You okay?" Peter flicked on the blinker and turned a corner.

"Fine." Emelia returned her gaze to the road. Her pulse increased for a second as she instinctively reacted to being on the wrong side. "Just a bit nervous, I guess."

The silence from his side wasn't exactly comforting.

Suck it up, Emelia. Just say sorry. "I'm sorry about last weekend. About your shoulder. My opinion doesn't matter. But permanent damage to a rotator is bad. You want a medal so much you'd be willing to live a life of excruciating pain? Risk never being able to throw a ball with your kids?" She stopped herself from saying any more. She'd already said more than enough.

"You're wrong."

Maybe she was. She was dredging her memory of what she knew about sports players who had suffered a similar injury.

"Your opinion does matter." He looked over at her and captured her with his gaze.

Oh. She forced herself to break the connection. "Can you tell me about your family?" She didn't care that she'd changed the subject with all the subtlety of a Miley Cyrus music video. Staring into eyes like that as he told her that she mattered was just asking for trouble.

"What would you like to know?"

She turned her face toward him. "Um, their names?"

He looked directly across at her. "I haven't even told you their names?"

"No."

"Sorry." His fingers tightened around the steering wheel. He cast a half smile her way. "I guess I'm a bit nervous too. It's been a long time since I brought a girl home."

Brought a girl home. The words twisted inside her. Both terrifying and exciting, the emotions fighting for dominance. She'd never been the girl anyone brought home. Not ever.

"My father is William. Bill. My mother is Margaret; everyone calls her Maggie. My brother is Victor."

She winced at his brother's name. Even though she was sure Peter's brother was nothing like her nemesis.

"What are they like?"

His fingers relaxed slightly. "My dad is tall, big. Played rugby. Almost made the English team when he was young. Apparently was pretty much a steamroller on the field. He has the kind of booming laugh that you can hear for miles. He works hard. He doesn't really care about what we do, all that matters to him is who we are. My mum is the sweetest woman you'll ever meet. The glue that holds our family together. She was diagnosed with multiple sclerosis a couple of years ago but you'd never know it. Never complains, always looking for opportunities to help everyone else. You'll love her . . . she'll love you." He added the last sentence almost as an afterthought. She didn't know if it was to make her feel better or if his mom was just the type to love everyone.

"What about your brother?"

Something twinged in his jaw as he stared at the road, face set, seeming to ponder her question. Finally, he lifted one hand and pushed it through his hair. "Look, I wish that I could say that we're best mates but the truth is we have a . . ." He paused, searching for the right word. "Challenging relationship. He's older by three years but we've never been close. He wasn't too crazy about me from the day I arrived."

"I'm sorry."

"How about your family?"

"My dad remarried a few years ago, someone closer to my age than his. I've got two half brothers and a half sister. He's pretty busy with them. Though my stepmother was excited about me coming here. She has high hopes of me snagging Harry. Or at least a member of the aristocracy with a large estate so she can come and play *Downton*." Maybe if she distracted him with tales of her social climbing stepmother he wouldn't ask about her mother.

Peter suddenly started coughing. "Excuse me. How old are your siblings? Half siblings? Sorry. I'm not sure of the terminology."

"It's okay." She wasn't sure how to refer to them most of the time herself. They were young enough to be her nieces and nephews. "Um . . ." She had to pause for a second to calculate. "Charles is six, George is three, and Katherine-Elizabeth is almost two."

He couldn't hold back his grin. "Wow. You weren't kidding about your stepmother being a royal fan."

"Unfortunately not."

He glanced across at her. Opened his mouth as if to ask another question, but then closed it without saying anything.

Time to steer things onto a more neutral topic. "So who will be at lunch?"

"Probably just be the four of us. Victor doesn't often show up for family lunches." He turned off the main road onto a smaller side road with tall hedges lining both sides. "So there's something I need to tell you." Peter stared straight ahead as he said it.

Emelia's stomach clenched at something foreboding in his tone. "What?"

"So, um, our house isn't so much a house. And when I said my parents lived near the potential location, it would have been more accurate to say they are the location."

"I don't understand."

"Well, it's more of an estate."

She still wasn't getting what he was saying. "Are you trying to tell me your parents are rich?"

He laughed. "Definitely not with money, but there is quite a bit of land."

"How much land?"

They'd turned onto a smaller road again, one lined with picturesque stone walls and lush fields on either side. He gestured around them. "We're almost there. This is some of it."

Shadows covered the car as it passed through a stand of trees and across a small bridge. They came around a bend, and in front of them, in the distance, loomed a huge house. A mansion. And not just any mansion. One that twisted knots of dread in her stomach until she thought she might choke.

She stared at it, trying to process what her eyes were telling her. Finally words started forming in her head. "Highbridge Manor is your house?" Too late she realized her slip. Why would an average American know the name of this estate?

He grimaced. "It is."

"Stop!" She hadn't meant to shout, the outburst filling the small space.

Peter hit the brakes. Hard. The car slammed to a stop in the middle of the road. Her seat belt cut across her as it held her in her seat. Her head bounced back against the headrest. She was going to be feeling the effects of that at some point but the realization flooding her mind had nothing on the impact her body had just taken.

She turned her entire body sideways as much as she could and asked the question she already knew the horrible answer to. "Who exactly are you?"

Peter had no idea what to make of the expression on her face. It could have been anything from horror to excitement. Oh, he hoped she wasn't one of those liberal anti-aristocracy types. Probably should've thought to subtly check for that before he brought her home.

"I'm Peter Carlisle." He refused to be defined by his father's title. Especially when they'd only come into it by a combination of tragedy and rotten luck.

"Don't be obtuse."

"I'm not." It was his turn to get a bit short, which wasn't entirely fair. He probably should've given her some warning of all this. "You asked who I was. I told you."

Emelia gave a half roll of her eyes. "Fine. Who is your father?"

"William Carlisle. Also known as Viscount Downley."

With a click, she'd undone her seat belt and had her head between her knees. Of all the reactions he'd anticipated, this was not one of them.

"You okay?" His shoulder ached from the abrupt stop.

"Give me a minute." Her words were muffled, directed at the passenger's foot well.

A horn sounded behind them, and he realized the car had stalled when they'd slammed to a stop.

He restarted the engine and pulled the car over to the side of the road. Fortunately, no one he knew was behind the steering wheel. Emelia's head remained wedged between her knees, the back of it almost clipping the glove box as he bumped over the grass verge.

Finally, he couldn't take the silence anymore. "Do you hate the peerage, is that it?"

At that Emelia levered herself up and leaned back against her seat. "No. I don't hate the peerage. What is a viscount, anyway?"

"It sits between a baron and an earl. Small potatoes in the hierarchy."

Emelia made a show of looking all around them, finishing with the house. "Call this what you will. But it is not small potatoes."

"Touché."

She pressed fingers to both temples. "Sorry for my reaction. I just . . . I was nervous enough meeting everyone. Then you suddenly spring this on me. It's a bit overwhelming. Why didn't you tell me?"

Peter shrugged. Why hadn't he? It wasn't that he was ashamed of his lineage. Quite the opposite. But he just liked being an ordinary guy. When people found out his background, it always changed how they saw him. As per Exhibit A, sitting right beside him. "We weren't born into this. It was never meant to be ours. It landed on us through a combination of early deaths and titleholders without children. Dad inherited the title from his cousin when I was ten."

Emelia heaved out a breath, gathered her hair in a pile behind her head, and then let it fall. "So, what do I call your parents? Am I supposed to curtsy?" A panicked look crossed her face. "I don't even know how to curtsy. You could've at least given me a warning to learn!"

He laughed. "No, definitely no curtsies. If it makes you feel better, feel free to call them Viscount and Viscountess when you meet them, but they'll tell you to call them Bill and Maggie. They're even less into titles than I am." Unlike his brother, who threw "the Honorable" around like it was cheap currency. "If it's really that overwhelming, we can turn around and I'll take you home." He meant it as a lame joke, but she seemed to actually consider it for a few seconds. His heart thumped against his ribs. What if she said yes?

What was he even hoping for? Emelia didn't share his faith. He'd always told himself that was one line he wouldn't cross. He'd watched the reality of how that played out his whole life. His parents had a good marriage. But there was no missing the wistfulness in his mother's eyes when she left for church on Sundays, leaving his father behind. Or her hopefulness every Easter and Christmas when he deigned to attend. Or her attempt to conceal her hurt when his father made it clear saying grace was an impediment to be suffered through to get to his meal. And those were only the things he saw.

He wanted more than that. But he wanted the girl sitting beside him too. And for the first time in his life, he understood how what looked black and white could be so easily blurred into gray.

"Peter?" She was staring at him quizzically. She'd obviously answered his question while he'd been lost in what-ifs.

"Sorry, what?"

"I said I'm good. Let's go."

Twenty-Four

THE MINUTE PETER HAD SAID "VISCOUNT DOWNLEY" OUT LOUD, Emelia had thought she was going to have a stroke. It wasn't possible. Except it was. Of all the guys she had to meet. The only time she'd ever been taken home to meet the family, it had to be this one.

This guy, who made her feel like maybe an ordinary, boring life could be possible, was also intimately linked to the web of her past. A past that managed to still reach out with its sticky threads and wrap them around her in a different country, a different life.

Stupid peerages, with their differing names and titles. If Peter's last name had been Downley, she would've broken her stupid vow and been researching him in a second. Would've made the connection in two. Would've known to never set foot in his life ever again.

But nooooo, she had to go and put herself on a Google fast to kill her old reporter's habit of prying into other people's lives.

Peter started driving again, the wheels crunching over the stones on the narrow road. The huge redbrick house loomed closer and closer.

Before they got there, she needed to confirm one final nail

in the coffin of their non-relationship. She couldn't believe she hadn't worked it out when he'd talked about his cousin who had died last year. Yet again, another flamingly obvious answer staring her right in the face that she didn't see. She cleared her throat. "So is your brother a rower too?"

If Peter thought it was a strange question, he didn't show it. "Yes. He was in the Oxford Blue Boat crew."

A tingling feeling started between her eyes. How had she not seen him in the line-up of rowers in the boat? How had she missed his face all over TV screens?

Act normal, Emelia. Your only chance of getting through this is to pretend Victor is a stranger to you, if he's there, and to hope he plays along.

"He goes to Oxford?" Was his title just as handy for charming his way into one of the world's most prestigious universities as into the beds of LA party girls?

"He's in his first year of a PhD in philosophy."

Peter couldn't have shocked her more if he'd said Victor was studying midwifery. Emelia barely managed to keep her jaw from unhinging. She forced herself to focus on the imposing house. "Wow."

She forced herself to breathe. What was she going to do? She'd come to Oxford because she couldn't stay in LA after Anita's death. Couldn't live with the person she'd become. Oxford was meant to be a fresh start and the Fates had sent her headlong into the girl's cousin.

The whole situation was so insane she had to squash the hysterical laughter rising up inside as Peter drove around the circular drive in front of the house and parked near the front door.

And the poor guy next to her thought she was overwhelmed because his father had a title and owned some land.

"Well, here we are. You'll be great." Peter sent her the kind of smile that ordinarily would've raised her pulse. The car shifted as he got out and strode around to open her door.

Peter was right about one thing though: he and his brother were nothing alike.

Her door opened, and Peter held out his hand. Like she hadn't been getting out of a car by herself for the best part of three decades. It was horribly old-fashioned. It was totally adorable. And, for one second, it distracted her from the mission at hand.

"Thanks." She stepped out, her wedges sinking into the gravel. *Game face, Emelia.* It wasn't like she hadn't spent years perfecting a poker face facade as Mia. But when she'd left the US, she'd planned to leave that behind.

But plans changed.

"Peter!" The front door opened, and a petite blonde came half tumbling down the steps. "You're late! I was beginning to worry."

Peter laughed. "We're not late. I said one-ish and it's like twenty past."

His mother reached him. He dwarfed her. Emelia dwarfed her. Mother and son looked nothing alike. She had blond hair and the same gray-blue eyes as her eldest son, which meant Peter had to have gotten his looks from . . . yep, the man who appeared at the top of the stairs. Same ginger hair, same towering height, same honest-looking face.

"Mother, this is Emelia."

Oh, drat, what was she supposed to do again? "It's lovely to meet you, Viscountess." She bobbed into something that was a peculiar mix of curtsy, bow, and poppet-on-a-string.

She looked up to see Peter smothering a grin. Oh, right. No curtsy.

His mother appeared startled. "Please, just call me Maggie. Whenever someone says 'Viscountess,' I have no idea who on earth they're talking to. Surely Peter told you we're purely accidental blue bloods."

Peter's father came off the bottom step with a broad smile and twinkling green eyes. She liked him already. "And I'm Bill." He shook her hand. A good, strong handshake. "Lovely to meet you, Emelia. Welcome to Highbridge Manor."

Emelia's response was cut off by crunching footsteps behind them. "Bunny, you made it."

Emelia flinched. Out of the corner of her eye, she observed Peter doing the same. Interesting. And *Bunny*?

She shaped her face into an expression of polite interest.

Remember, Emelia, you have never met this man before in your life. He's merely the brother of the guy you're not dating. He was drinking at the ball. Maybe he doesn't even remember you were there.

"Bunny?" She murmured the question under her breath at Peter. A pathetic attempt at delaying the inevitable.

He glanced down at her. "Don't ask." His voice was all resignation, no humor.

Peter turned around, forcing Emelia to follow.

"Of course I made it. I was hardly going to miss Mum's cooking, was I?" Was she the only one who caught the forced cheer in his voice?

Victor stopped still at the sight of her, a strange look across his face. Her heart stopped too. Was this it? The moment that her whole crazy plan blew up in her face?

"Well." He dropped an expletive. "Bunny brought a girl home. Who would've thought?"

"Victor!" It was impressive how much censure Maggie could fit into six letters.

Emelia waited for an apology, even a token "Sorry, Mother." But none was forthcoming. Awkward silence reigned, accented only by the sound of birds chirping and tree branches bending in the wind.

Victor was the same in broad daylight as he had been in the shadows. Same blond mop, flinty gray-blue eyes, strong jaw, and sardonic smile. None of which could distract from the angry red scar that wound its way up one cheek.

Finally, Peter cleared his throat. "Victor, this is Emelia. Emelia, my brother, Victor." His voice was strained.

"Hi." She nodded. She certainly wasn't going to shake his hand.

He gave her a nod back. His gaze piercing, a smirk playing on his lips. He knew exactly who she was. "Emelia. Interesting name. Had it for long?"

She forced a clueless smile. "Just my whole life."

"Right. So, let's go inside. Get a cup of tea, shall we?" Bill's words softened the tension, but nothing could soften the dark looks the brothers were giving each other.

This was going to be an interesting afternoon. The perfect family Emelia had conjured up was not so perfect. At all.

The only reason Peter hadn't bundled Emelia right back into the car and driven away was because of the hurt it would have caused his mum.

It was like being sucker punched twice in quick succession. First with the mocking childhood nickname he'd always hated.

Then with the caustic reminder of what a failure he was when it came to relationships. Like it hadn't been obvious their entire lives that he was neither as smart nor as good-looking as his brother.

Fortunately Victor, having achieved his goal of total humiliation, had lost interest and taken off in his car, promising he'd be back for lunch. Watching him careen down the drive even made the air smell sweeter.

"Peter tells me the two of you are hoping to plan a charity ball? To help SpringBoard?" His mother addressed her question to Emelia as they entered the house's main door.

"We are. It will be our one big event of the year."

"We haven't been having much luck with venues." Peter draped his arm around his mother's shoulder. "Any chance the house is free the first Saturday in December?"

"I'll have a look at the booking schedule, but I can't think of anything off the top of my head."

"On that note, want a tour?" He turned to Emelia, who looked remarkably composed considering what he'd landed on her in the last half hour.

"Sure." Emelia looked around the atrium they'd entered, her gaze trailing over the many doors and large staircase leading up to the next level.

"Do you want to come?" He directed the question at his parents. Out of courtesy, not desire, though it was fifty-fifty whether they'd pick up on that.

His mother shook her head. "Oh no. I'll go check the calendar, and I need to finish the pudding."

"I can—" His father got cut off by an obvious elbow to the torso from his mum. "I just need to do a few things and, um, stuff."

"So, we'll leave you two to it." His mother smiled sweetly.

"Okay then. We won't be too long."

His father disappeared back out the front door while his mother headed toward the kitchen with a rustle of trousers, in a cloud of floral perfume. Peter touched Emelia's elbow to steer her into the front parlor.

"How long have you lived here?"

"Not long, in the grand scheme of things. Like I said, we never dreamt in a million years Dad would inherit the title, but as life would have it, his uncle died without having any children, so it passed to his brother, then Dad's cousin inherited it. He was the only son and only had daughters. So when he died in a car accident when I was ten, the title came to Dad. He was an army man. In fact, when he inherited, he was serving in Iraq. So things were a bit crazy until he finished his tour and got discharged."

Emelia spun around, taking in the bookcase-lined wall, the large oriental rugs covering hardwood floors, and the gleaming windows overlooking part of the garden. "I can't believe you had us checking out all those venues when you had the perfect thing right here."

"I wouldn't call it perfect. It's a decent drive from Oxford and we still don't know it's available." And if it hadn't been for her heartbreak over Rhodes House, he never would have said anything about it. Not having to wonder if someone was his friend because of his sporting accomplishments or his aristocratic connections was liberating. "We should go look at the ballroom." He steered her out of the parlor and across the main hall toward the double doors.

"Still, you owe me."

"What?"

"Hmmmm." She pursed her lips, pretending to ponder, but

she didn't even need to think about it. "I want the story behind Bunny."

He groaned. "Seriously? How about something else?" Anything else.

She grinned. "Nope. Bunny."

"It's actually not very exciting." Far from being exciting, it laid bare the animosity that had existed between his brother and him since before he'd even been born. She was a smart girl. She'd be able to read between the lines of even the most concise version.

He sighed. "Victor was two when they found out they were having me. He wasn't thrilled at the idea of having a sibling, so, as a way to placate him, they told him he could help name me." Clearly his normally conservative, predictable parents had been drunk or something that day. They still couldn't explain what had possessed them to offer up naming the baby to their two-year-old as some kind of sibling consolation prize.

"Peter Rabbit was his favorite story at the time, so he decided to name me Peter. But from the day I was born, he called me Bunny."

They would never know if the nickname had started as one of endearment, but for as long as Peter could remember, it had only been used to mock and torment him. And mockery had turned to outright disdain on the day that had changed everything.

Emelia studied him for a second, probably seeing on his face everything he hadn't put into words.

"This is the ballroom through here." Turning the cool brass handle, he opened the door and stepped back so Emelia could enter first.

"Wrrrreeeeoooow." The sound registered as something flew through the air and landed on Emelia's head. She screamed. Her hands flapped in the air as she reached up to her head, only to jerk away when an angry hiss resounded.

Oh, dear. He'd completely forgotten about Reepicheep.

Twenty-Five

One second Peter was explaining how he'd come to be named after a rabbit and the next something sharp had landed on top of her head and latched there.

Emelia spun in a circle, screaming and trying to dislodge whatever type of creature it was while it gripped her hair and hissed.

"Stop moving!" Peter's authoritative tone cut through her hysteria, and she stopped midspin.

"Is it a rat?" *Please don't let it be a rat.* If there was a rat in her hair, she'd probably puke.

"It's okay, Reep." Peter's voice was soft and soothing. And it wasn't directed at her. He stepped closer and reached out toward her head. "Come to me." Her head got lighter, but the feeling of her hair being pulled with it caused her to cry out.

"Shhhhh."

He had so better not be directing that at her.

She could feel him trying to untangle her hair from something. He was so close, she could smell his woodsy cologne.

"There we go. Good boy." The weight lifted from her head as Peter stepped back, taking the thing with him. "Emelia, meet Reepicheep."

In his hands was the ugliest runt of a cat she had seen in her entire life. "Cat" was almost too kind a description. His fur was calico. Where one ear should have been was a half-jagged edge. He was fat, but with stumpy little limbs. If there was ever a contest for the world's ugliest cat, he would be a sure winner.

He glared at her with evil little cat eyes. He clearly rated her about as highly as she rated him.

"Reepicheep after the mouse in *Prince Caspian*?" He couldn't be serious. This insult to cats around the world couldn't be named after one of Lewis's best creations.

"Do you know of another?" Peter flipped the cat around so he faced him. "The most valiant cat in the land, aren't we, boy?"

If he kissed him, she was gone. "Try psychotic."

"You just gave him a fright."

"I just walked into the room!"

"He likes to sleep on top of the table sometimes." He gestured to a table near the door. Presumably the launchpad for his stealth attack. "He's usually very friendly. Here, give him a pat." He held up the evil spawn toward her.

"You have got to be joking. He tried to scalp me." Emelia put a hand up to her head, which was still throbbing. She had never been a cat person, and this little ball of spite only confirmed her perception of the species. "Why did you name him Reepicheep?" She may have hated the bearer of the name, but she was curious about the rationale.

Peter rubbed a hand down the cat's back. "He was abandoned in a ditch down the road. I found him a couple of years ago. In a sack. There were other kittens in it too. They had all drowned, but somehow he'd managed to get out of the sack and crawl up the side away from the water. When I found him he was half-dead. The vet said he wasn't going to make it, but he fought hard and pulled through. He's been mine ever since. The name just seemed to fit."

The connection between a feisty talking mouse with a sword and a psycho cat was clear only to Peter.

"And he's yours?"

"Usually he lives with me, but I brought him up here in the lead-up to the Boat Race since I was away so much. He prefers the country life. But I'll bring him home with us."

In the same car as her? They'd be building snowmen in the Bahamas before that happened.

Peter ran his hand over the cat and the little sociopath purred under his fingers while giving Emelia dagger eyes. "See? You two will be friends in no time."

She'd known Peter was too perfect. She'd just never guessed his biggest flaw was going to come in the form of a feline terrorist. While hers was that she'd killed his cousin.

The gravel crunched under Emelia's feet as they said farewell to Peter's parents and started walking back to his car.

She'd survived lunch. Survived Victor sitting there, staring at her, throwing in verbal jabs every now and then that only she understood. Survived touring the house and gardens with Maggie. Forced herself to concentrate on why they were there. The ball.

Tried desperately to come up with something, anything, that would mean they couldn't have it there. But there was nothing. Especially not when Maggie had returned with the information that the first Saturday in December was free and she and Bill would donate the use of the house for the event.

She was tied firmly in a noose of her own making.

She let her glance move sideways. Striding next to her, Peter appeared equally deep in thought. Hands shoved in his jeans pockets, gaze downward.

"Peter!" The call came from behind them. His father. "You forgot your cat." From the tone of his voice he couldn't wait to see the back of the thing.

Gah. She'd forgotten about the rabid feline. From the surprised look on his face, so had Peter. "You go get him. I'll just wait out here." She wasn't going near that cat again as long as she could help it. Named after a Narnia character or not.

"Okay, I'll just be a couple of minutes." He pulled the car keys out of his pocket and clicked open the trunk. Pulling a cat carrier out, he slammed it shut, tossed her the keys, and strode back to the house. Emelia shook her head at this optimism. There was about as much chance of it only taking a couple of minutes to get that cat contained as there was that she was going to be the next president.

Leaning against the car, she sucked in a lungful of early summer air and looked over the house. For all the hideous personal complications it posed to her, it was the perfect venue. The stately home of a viscount. Her mind churned with the possibilities. She wondered if it had been in any movies or TV shows. Country manors might have been a dime a dozen to the English but if she could get an in with the—

"So, which is it? Emelia Mason or Mia Caldwell? Or something else altogether?" Victor's sarcastic query cut through her thoughts.

He'd snuck up on her, coming from who knew where. Now he walked around the back of the car, coming to lean casually against the roof a couple of feet from her.

The one good thing about years spent as a tabloid journalist was her well-honed ability to bluff. Emelia took her time, letting her gaze sweep Victor from head to toe. "What does it matter to you?"

Victor shrugged. "It doesn't. But it certainly will to my brother."

It took all her skills not to flinch. "I thought we had a deal."

"We did. To stay out of each other's way. I don't think showing up at my parents' house with my brother could exactly be considered you keeping your side of it."

Touché.

"Look. I had no idea Peter was your brother or this was your parents' place." She tried to assume a nonchalant air. "As far as I'm concerned this doesn't need to change anything." She kept an eye on the front door. The last thing she could afford was Peter overhearing this.

Victor barked out a laugh. "You cannot be serious. The same tabloid hack who is responsible for my cousin's death is now working for her charity trying to save it? Under another name? I'd say that changes everything."

It did. And they both knew it. Her palm itched to wipe the gloating look off Victor's face but instead she reached for the only weapon she had left in her arsenal. "Look." The word came out icy. "Expose me if you want. Go right ahead. But we both know what happens if you do. I'm not the only one with a lot to lose here."

"Careful not to overplay your hand, Miss Caldwell. I'm not sure if you've noticed, but I'm the black sheep of this particular family." His voice held a lot of bravado but something flickered in his face that told her she'd gained a foothold.

"Well, I guess that remains to be seen." Movement drew her attention back to the house, where Peter had just emerged out of the front door with a squalling cat carrier.

When he saw Victor standing next to her, his speed increased across the gravel. "Everything okay here?" His gaze jumped between the two of them. Emelia almost couldn't hear his words for the sound of her heart trying to break out of her rib cage.

This was it. Thirty seconds from now it might all be over. She didn't have any words. Had never planned what she was going to say if her secret was revealed without any warning. Which was stupid on her part. As soon as she'd seen Victor at that ball she should've prepared for exactly this kind of thing.

Victor casually pushed himself off the roof. "Simmer down, Bunny. We were just talking about the cricket game. I'm looking forward to it."

Peter looked confused. "You said you weren't going to play."

"Well, Emelia here has helped me see the error of my ways. It is for Anita, after all."

"Okay." Peter looked like he didn't buy a word of it. "If you want in now you need to talk to Max. He's captaining."

"Consider it done, Captain Bunny." Victor gave him a mock salute.

"Great." Peter unlocked the doors and gave his brother a pointed look. "Do you mind? I need to put Reep in the car."

Victor stepped out of the way. "You're way too wound up, little brother. You need to get laid more often."

Emelia almost choked. The guy's jerkdom really knew no bounds. Peter just ignored him as he put the carrier in the backseat and slammed the door shut.

Victor threw her a wink. "So nice to meet you, Emelia. Look forward to seeing you around. Peter's very lucky to have someone with your experience on this."

He may not have given up her secret but she was under no illusions; his silence would be coming with a high price tag. The only question was whether it would be one she'd be prepared to pay.

Twenty-Six

"I still don't understand why we couldn't just get a DJ." Since they now had a date and a venue, apparently the entertainment was the next big thing on the spreadsheet. Which was proving to be more of a challenge than he'd anticipated, given their meager budget. Most of which Emelia had already allocated to a string quartet for the first half of the evening.

"Because this is a high-class fund-raising ball, not a school disco. Because a live band is so much cooler. Besides, that DJ you came up with, remind me again, he wasn't available on our day because of . . . ?" Emelia cocked an eyebrow at him.

Peter mumbled the answer under his breath. She was never going to let him live it down.

"Say again?"

"He's due to have his hip replaced."

"So I say no to the octogenarian DJ."

"You hate all my ideas." He tried to get a smile out of Emelia. Since the trip home, she'd been guarded. Excruciatingly polite, but the easy camaraderie and chemistry had disappeared like it never existed.

She crossed off something in her notebook, all business.

"No, I only hate the really bad ones. Unfortunately your track record so far has pretty much only been bad ones."

"Edible table arrangements are going to be the next big thing. It's not my fault if I'm a visionary ahead of the trend." He finally got the hint of a smile playing at the side of her mouth. He'd take it. "So, who are we seeing tonight?"

Emelia checked her list. "They're called the Groovestars."

Peter smirked. This could be entertaining.

"What? They had a flyer up at Tesco's and they have a Facebook page."

"You'll have to excuse me if I'm not brimming with excitement about seeing a band who advertise by the fruit and veg aisle."

"Oh, don't be such a spoilsport."

"And this is where they're playing tonight?" They were standing outside a run-down pub. Flakes of paint peeled off the outside. Peter thought he knew Oxford rather well. Lord knew he'd hauled his brother out of almost every pub in town. But not even Victor had stooped to this one.

Emelia double-checked the address and nodded. "Don't judge a book by its cover. They're probably young. Just starting out. Playing whatever gigs they can get. And, most importantly, we can afford them."

They stepped inside. The dim room smelled like the carpet hadn't been cleaned since the Beatles were big. Along one side ran a bar, behind it rows of the cheapest, nastiest liquor you'd find anywhere in the country. A few peeling signs displayed advertising that had to be pre-millennium. There wasn't a bartender to be seen.

Four very senior citizens sat around one square Formica table. In the corner sat a tattooed couple hunched over beers.

Emelia looked around, not even bothering to hide her dismay.

One of the old men stood up. "You right, luv?"

"We're, um, here to see the Groovestars. They were supposed to be playing here tonight?"

The old man's face brightened. "That's us!"

Peter tried to restrain the smile he felt taking over his face but failed miserably. So miserably you could probably have seen it from space.

"Boys. Look! We have gropies!"

A guy who had to be going on ninety and was wearing a gray cardigan spoke up. "I think, George, you'll find the word is 'groupies.'"

George ignored the guy. "I told you having a page on that face thingy would work!"

"I'm going to take a wild guess that someone's great-grandchild is responsible for these young startups being on the face thingy." Peter murmured the words to Emelia, who looked like she wasn't sure whether to punch him or laugh.

George turned back to them. "Sorry, we're a bit delayed. Harold needs to take his medication and he can't have it on an empty stomach, so we're just waiting for him to finish his snack." George gestured to where an old man with an impressive white mullet was eating a bag of crisps. On the table in front of him sat a pair of drumsticks, and lined up along them was a row of pills of varying sizes and colors.

Peter couldn't see. The tears of laughter he was trying to restrain had blurred his sight. His chest hurt from trying to contain it.

"We're looking for a band for a fund-raising ball."

"There's going to be a squall? Why would that be? Winter's long finished," Harold barked from the table as he popped two pills in his mouth and took a slug of water.

Peter's shoulders jumped up and down like a demented grasshopper with the effort of trying to contain his mirth.

"Don't worry. We're better than we look. Not that that's saying much. I'm Norm, by the way." It was the guy with the cardigan who spoke, eyes twinkling.

Peter scanned the room and realized he had previously missed a drum kit the size of a postage stamp, a lone bass plugged into a small amp, and a microphone.

"Help yourself to a drink." George gestured toward the bar. "We operate on an honor system while the band is playing. Just leave what you think is right on the bar."

"Thanks." Peter managed to get the word out before he walked toward the bar, Emelia trailing after him.

"Would you like something?"

Emelia cast her gaze to a brown stain on the ceiling. "Only if it comes in a sealed container."

Peter ducked behind the bar and grabbed two cans of Coke from the fridge, setting a handful of change on the bar as the twang of a guitar came over the amp. He took the drinks back to Emelia and made a show of snapping hers open in front of her. Handing it over, he did the same with his and took a long sip.

Next came the sound of something hitting the drums followed by the squeal of . . . no, surely not. But there was no mistaking the distinctive sound. Bagpipes.

"Hello, everyone." It was Norm at the microphone. "Welcome to our gig tonight. We're the Groovestars." The couple in the corner didn't even make any sign they'd heard him. The band launched into "Walking on Sunshine." Every single band member had a hearing aid. Probably turned off, going by the bumpy first few lines.

It was unlike any music Peter had ever heard before. Norm half crooning, half barking like an aged Elvis. George powering it along on the bagpipes. Harold tapping away on the drums, and the guy they hadn't been introduced to barely managing to keep up with the rest of them on the bass.

"Would you like to dance?" He turned to Emelia.

"What?"

"You heard the man. We're his gropies, Smoky. We can't let him down."

"Try groping anything and you'll lose your hand. Just remember that." The quiver of Emelia's lips finally gave her away.

"Oh, c'mon. I'd be making my move chaperoned by four octogenarians. It doesn't get any better than that. It would be the most excitement they've had at one of their gigs since Harold's last heart attack."

Emelia looked at the band, shook her head, and smiled. Ha! Got her. "Why not?"

Taking her Coke and putting it down on a table with his, Peter grabbed her hand and tugged her between the two tables separating them from the band. He put his hand on Emelia's waist and started spinning her across the 1970s-era brown and orange carpet until she was breathless and smiling.

It was no ball, but for some reason, it was even more fun.

As he turned her around on the nonexistent dance floor, he saw George's eyes twinkling at them, and the old man gave him a wink.

He lowered Emelia into a dip with his good arm, and she clasped her hands around his neck, grinning up at him. Their gazes caught and something in her expression softened. For a second, the final note of the bagpipes, the worn carpet, and the dingy pub all faded away and there was only her. Wavy hair falling out behind her, the ends touching the floor, her eyes sparkling, her smile carefree.

Friends, just friends. She thought he was crazy for wanting to make a comeback. He forced the thoughts through his brain before he did something stupid. Were there any more torturous words in the English language?

She should never have said yes to dancing with Peter. Emelia's heart started pounding again under the intensity of his gaze. Not knowing what to do or say, she tucked her chin into his shoulder as he pulled her back to her feet.

He let her go into one final spin as the song ended, and she immediately missed the feeling of being cradled against his chest.

Her gaze lingered on him for a second at the other end of his outstretched arm, then she let go of his hand and turned toward the band, clapping.

The four old men grinned and offered little bows.

Shoot. She so wanted to hire them for the ball. High society or not. What they lacked in talent, they more than made up for with chutzpah.

"Let's slow it down, gentlemen."

The opening notes of "It Had to Be You" drifted out and Peter held out his hand.

Emelia studied it for a second, then moved toward him, captivated by some weird magic. Tucking her against his chest, Peter waltzed her across the floor, the top of her head against his chin, the feel of his breath wafting down the side of her face, tormenting all her senses.

I wandered around, and finally found . . . The words drifted across the room.

The heat of his hand warmed through the back of her top, and she gasped as he lowered her into another graceful dip, his hold strong and steady underneath her. "Don't worry. I'm not going to drop you."

"I know." She looked into his face and suddenly wasn't sure if they were talking about dancing anymore. Time to change the subject. Fast. "What are your plans until Boat Race training for next year starts? Besides babysitting me, of course." She tried to keep her tone light, teasing.

He pulled her back onto her feet. "Summer is busy for beginners' courses and I've still got a couple of coaching jobs."

"How's your shoulder?" Emelia focused on keeping some distance between them, despite the almost overwhelming urge to tuck her head into the curve of his neck and rest against his chest.

"Not horrible. Not great. I'm due to have some more scans soon. That will tell us more about when I can get back into training."

She noted his use of "when." But she kept her mouth closed. The guy was an elite athlete. He had to have some of the best sports doctors in the country giving him advice. He didn't need to hear any more of hers.

"Enough about me. Let's talk about you, Miss Mason. Starting with, what were you called back home?"

"Sorry?" She was thrown by the sudden change in topic.

"Emelia. It's beautiful, but at four syllables, I can't believe it didn't get shortened."

She drew a deep breath. "Mia. Most of the time I was called Mia."

He studied her, but nothing in his gaze made her think he was connecting the dots. "You don't like it?"

The urge came over her to pour out her entire gritty past right there in a decrepit pub in Oxford, but she tamped it down. She'd tell him one day, but not tonight. After the ball. She wasn't going to ruin this.

"I never felt like Mia." That was as close as she could get to telling him the truth. And it was true. There was a reason she'd picked Mia Caldwell as her byline. Because then, in some way, she could separate herself from her alter ego.

"What about Emmy?"

She actually jolted that time. It would have been easier to dodge the question, but she was tired of doing that. She wanted to give him something. A piece of her that was true. That mattered. Emelia sucked in a breath. "My mom used to call me Emmy. I haven't let anyone else call me that since she . . ." She choked up, unable to get the final word out. Emmy had died the day her mom did. She hadn't let anyone call her it since. "My mom died when I was six."

Peter's hand tightened around her waist, and she found herself cradled between his arm and his chest. He didn't say anything, his breath whispering across her cheek.

Slowly, she relaxed into the music, his strength, and their steady steps across the worn carpet. After a few more seconds, she lifted her head to find his green eyes focused on her. "Thank you."

"For what?"

"For not trying to make it okay."

"Thank you for telling me."

Whatever her response was going to be, it faded as she realized that at some point in the last few minutes her fingers had slid up his shoulders and were tracing the nape of his neck.

"I concede defeat. You win." Peter leaned down and whispered the words in Emelia's ear. She leaned back, tilting her head and peering up at him from under her lashes.

"I win what?"

"The band. We should hire them. We'll just have to make sure we get everyone's donations first." He gave her a grin.

For a second disappointment flooded through her but she masked it. She looked at the four pensioners, a smile coming to her lips.

"You're probably right. It is a ball about second chances, after all."

"Is that what you're in Oxford looking for? A second chance?" Peter gazed at her like he could see all her secrets and didn't hate her. Which was how she knew it was just a fantasy.

Emelia shook her head. "I don't believe in looking for something I don't deserve." She pushed off from his chest and stepped away. "We should go. We've got what we came here for."

Twenty-Seven

Cricket. Possibly the most boring game in the world. Peter hadn't mentioned that at any point. As far as Emelia could work out, a guy ran up and threw a ball, and a guy at the other end hit the ball. Other players in the field tried to catch it or pick it up and throw it at some sticks that were behind the batter. And so it went on. For hours. Occasionally punctuated by players throwing their hands up in the air and yelling something indecipherable.

Emelia stifled a yawn as she surveyed the grounds at Oxford's historic University Parks. She could now add this game to her list of things that only the English understood. They'd sold out of tickets weeks ago, even though the setting meant that people could just wander up and watch for free if they so desired. Apparently the appetite in this town for anything that featured the historical Oxford–Cambridge rivalry was pretty much insatiable.

She breathed in the warm summer air. Somehow, every member of both squads had committed to play. Along with a few of the coaching staff to make up numbers. Even though some of the guys had already finished their exams and had left their respective universities for summer, they'd come back for this.

As much as Emelia hated to admit it, it was all thanks to Sabine again. The two of them had given each other a wide berth but she'd seen her talking to Peter a few times. They'd certainly looked more friendly than most exes she knew.

"You look like you'd rather be watching paint dry."

She looked up to see Peter walking toward her. His blue fitted T-shirt highlighted his muscular physique, the strapping tape poking out from underneath one of the sleeves displaying the reason he wasn't on the field for Oxford.

He lowered himself down beside her on the grass. After doing her last set of rounds to check on refreshments for the teams, she'd found herself a spot at the far end of the field, where spectators were sparse.

"Do you wish you were out there?" She nodded toward the pitch.

Peter shook his head. "Nah. Cricket's not really my thing."

"Oh, thank goodness." The words burst out of her. "I don't think I've seen such a boring game in all my life."

Peter let out a snort of laughter. "I wouldn't go saying that too loudly. We English are quite protective of our national sport." He grinned at her and the air crackled between them. They hadn't really seen each other since the evening at the pub. Emelia had been busy with final details for the match—thank goodness that had required zero knowledge of the game—and Peter had, well, apart from the rowing beginners' courses he'd mentioned teaching, she actually had no clue what he did with most of his time now that the Boat Race was over.

Not that it mattered. Not that he could matter. Knowing he was Anita's cousin. Knowing that at any second Victor could decide to renege on their deal. That day had been a game changer. Any foolish fantasies she might have harbored that there could ever be something between them were well and truly destroyed. The dancing at the pub had been a mistake. She'd let herself get carried away and now was taunted by the memory of being in his arms when it couldn't be allowed to ever happen again.

She searched for something neutral to say. "Oh. I finally finished the book about the brothers who rowed in the Boat Race."

If he was surprised by her abrupt change in topic, he didn't show it. "What did you think?" Peter leaned back on his good arm.

What did she think? She thought it was the craziest thing she'd ever read. Ever heard of. "In the first bit. That guy. Seb. Is that true? Did he really pass out?"

"He did indeed. Cost Cambridge the race."

"He was unconscious!" Emelia was offended on the guy's behalf. Even if it had been over a decade ago. She'd reread the first chapter over and over, trying to understand what it was that would make someone not even stop rowing when they were passing out.

"That's how it works. You leave everything on the water." Peter looked back to the field at the cracking sound of the bat hitting the ball.

"Is that how you felt on the water? When you were rowing?" After finishing *Blood over Water* Emelia felt like she had a small understanding of what might drive him to risk everything to get to the top again. But she wanted to hear it from him.

"Yeah." He looked back to her, his face contemplative. "Those guys, they were closer to me than my own brother. You'd do anything not to let the team down. All of us would. When I came to in hospital that night in Italy, one of my first thoughts was, *At least it didn't happen in the boat*. If I had to get injured, at least I didn't fail the team."

"How old were you when you started?" This was safe territory. She could talk to Peter about rowing all day without worrying about her secrets trying to escape.

"Fourteen." He laughed. "Poor Mum. If she'd had a clue how bad I was going to get the bug, she never would have promised to be there to cheer me on at every race."

"Your mom was at every race?" But if he'd become an elite athlete, surely that must have been . . . hundreds?

"Every one in England. Rain, sleet, or sun. I let her off the hook for the overseas ones. Though my parents did manage to make it to a couple of world champs." He shook his head. "I can still see her like it was yesterday. Every race. There she was with her blanket and thermos of tea."

"That's so—" Without warning, Emelia found herself choking up. She coughed and tried to finish her sentence like a normal human being but found herself unable to speak past the boulder in her throat.

She didn't even get why this mattered so much. She'd been fine without a mom. Sort of fine. Managed to pave her own way in the world. Then suddenly she'd gotten exposed to a stupid ordinary Peter story about his mother and all she wanted to do was curl up and cry for years.

"Are you okay?" He leaned a little closer but not enough to touch. She wasn't sure whether to be relieved or disappointed.

"I'm fine. I'm sorry. I feel like such a dork." Emelia swiped at her cheeks, mortified to find them damp. The poor guy must have been wondering what kind of drama queen she was.

"There's nothing to be sorry for."

"It's so stupid. That story about your mom. I guess I just suddenly really missed mine." She picked up a couple of blades of grass and rolled them together between her fingers. "Most of the time I don't even think about it. And then sometimes, like today, it just kind of sneaks up on me that I don't have one. I just wonder what she would have been like."

"Can you tell me about her?"

Emelia sneaked a glance sideways to find him looking right at her. She didn't know what to say. Most of the time when people found out she was motherless, they hurried to change the subject, move the conversation along, as if somehow her bad familial luck might rub off on them. No one, not ever, had asked about her.

And now that someone had, it was like a balloon had blown up in her chest, ready to burst if she tried to squash it. "She was very beautiful. But then I guess all six-year-old girls think their mom is the most beautiful woman they've ever seen. She loved Narnia more than anything in the world." More than the world itself, in the end.

Emelia drew in a breath. "I used to come home from

school and we'd play our favorite parts in the books. We would pretend that the dining room table was the *Dawn Treader* and we were sailing for the Eastern Islands. Or that our garden was the woods in between and we'd jump in the puddles and move between the worlds." Where play ended and the mental illness began, Emelia would never know. She hadn't even realized until she was a teenager that most kids didn't have mothers who forgot about things like dinner and homework because they were too busy living in a land of make-believe.

"So you got your love of Narnia from her."

"I did." She cracked a smile. "She's also to blame for why I can't even microwave popcorn. She was a terrible cook. Couldn't even boil an egg. But for some weird reason, she could make the best waffles in the world. That was it. We probably would have lived on waffles if it wasn't for cereal and takeout. And she had a heart as big as the Atlantic. She hated to see anyone in need."

"She sounds like a great woman."

Peter was close enough that she could smell his musky scent. It was an act of will not to reach up and run her hand along his jaw, which hadn't seen a razor in a few days. She forced her gaze to go over his shoulder. "She wasn't perfect, but she was mine."

"What about your father?"

The perfect topic to ruin the moment. Emelia huffed out a breath of air as she tore up some more grass. "He might as well be dead."

He might as well be dead. A gust of wind caught Emelia's caustic words and threw them back in her face. It wasn't true.

A live, but uninterested, parent was definitely better than two dead ones.

"I'm sorry, that's a horrible thing to say." Emelia dropped her decimated blades of grass onto the ground between her feet and kept her focus there, not wanting to see the judgment that she was sure had to be written across his face. "I'm sure he did his best."

"But it wasn't enough?"

She chanced a look up. Searched his gaze for condemnation but found only concern. Emelia shrugged her shoulders. "We'd been close. At least I feel like we had. Then, when my mom died, it was like he couldn't be around me. I look a lot like her. Maybe I reminded him of too much. So, I became the ward of after-school programs and summer camps. The occasional trips to see his parents, who had no idea what to do with me either. They'd had children quite late, and so they were already older by the time I was born. My aunt did her best to help but she had her own family and didn't live close."

"What about your mother's family?"

She tucked a piece of wayward hair behind her ear and looked anywhere except at him. "My mom was an only child. My grandfather died of a heart attack when I was a baby and then my grandmother died not long after my mom from cancer." She laughed mirthlessly. "Great set of genes I've got."

Peter didn't say anything for a few seconds, no rushing to fill the void with pointless platitudes. It made her like him even more.

She forced her gaze away again. Focused on his gray flip-flops, which showcased feet so white today had to be the first time they'd been let out in public this summer. His second toes were longer than his big toes. She'd finally discovered a part of him that wasn't attractive. If she could hold every conversation looking at those for the next few months she'd be fine.

The silence stretched until eventually she couldn't stand it anymore. "What are you thinking?"

He sighed. "I was thinking about how I felt like I'd been robbed when I had to give up my dream of rowing at Rio. But that doesn't even come close to being robbed of a parent. Feeling like you've lost two. Then I was thinking what a terrible human being I was that I could even compare rowing to what you've been through."

"You're not a horrible human being. Far from it." She should know. She'd crossed paths with more than a few of them. Become one herself.

Peter's fingers brushed against hers and she sucked in a breath. Let herself look up and be captured by his intent gaze. "I'm sorry your father doesn't realize what an amazing daughter he's missing out on."

How could he know that her fear was her father knew exactly what he was missing out on? Emelia swallowed. "Thanks." She just managed to get the word out. Time to get this conversation back onto neutral ground.

Peter nodded toward the field, like he knew what she was thinking. "So, this looks like it's all going pretty much perfectly. Hopefully we'll make a decent chunk of change off it."

The university had kindly donated the use of the grounds,

so SpringBoard's biggest expenses were in printing tickets, advertising, and hosting a reception after the event. That had been her idea after seeing at the ball how some girls totally lost their heads around Boat Race rowers. Host a reception for both teams and charge a hundred quid a head for a select number of groupies to get to be in the same room as their idols. Though she was going to hazard a guess, from the perfect hair, sultry gazes, and skimpy sundresses she'd seen around, that most of them would be gunning for far more than that.

Emelia stretched out her legs in front of her. "Well, I guess that's the upside of it being the most boring game in the world. The opportunities for it all to go badly are very limited. If all goes well we should make almost twenty thousand pounds off this."

Not even close to what they needed to save the charity, but it was still something. And since the row-off there had also been a slight uptick in potential donor interest, reversing the trend of the last six months.

"You're doing a great job."

"Thanks. I couldn't do it without you." Emelia smiled up at him, the late-afternoon summer sun setting a halo behind his hair. The green of his eyes seemed to darken as his gaze held hers. Emelia caught her bottom lip in her teeth. You couldn't deny the chemistry between them any more than you could deny gravity.

"So—"

"I—"

Whatever they were both about to say was cut short by shouts from the field. Jerking her head toward the commotion,

Emelia gasped as she registered what she was seeing. On the field the teams looked to be slugging it out, while spectators wearing the two universities' blues were streaming onto the pitch, some fists already flying.

A brawl. She was pretty sure this would count as going very badly.

Twenty-Eight

Emelia shrank back into the comfort of darkness. All the better to not see the papers she held in her hands, resting between her torso and wedged-up legs.

She pushed some clothes away from her face, the hangers scratching along the rail, and breathed in the smell of laundry detergent and her own fear.

Peter was right. She never should have taken this job. Because of her, SpringBoard was worse off than it had been six months ago. Not only wasn't she going to save it, she was going to be the final nail in the coffin.

A tear meandered down her cheek and she swiped it away. She deserved no one's pity. Not even her own.

Voices echoed from outside on the landing. Allie's New Zealand accent came first, then a deeper one. English. Her pulse kicked up a notch. She hadn't seen Peter since he'd bolted into the fray of the brawl. Hadn't responded to any of the messages he'd left in the ten days since.

It had all been over ten minutes later, the appearance of the police enough to calm even the most rabid of spectators down. But ten minutes was all it took to destroy everything she was trying to save.

"I don't think she's home from the office yet." Allie's voice. A knock at her door.

"I've tried the office. She's not there."

The click of her door opening. Them peering into her empty room with its perfectly made bed. "Well, she's not here either."

"I have an idea. Just give me a second."

Sure enough, a few moments later there came a tapping on the wardrobe door. Why couldn't he just leave her alone? Hadn't she already done enough damage? And that was just the stuff he knew about.

She shrank back into her corner, pressed her lips together, hoped he would just go away.

No such luck. The door creaked open and Peter, crouching down, stared right at her.

"Leave me alone." Her words whispered out. "Please. Just go away."

"I don't think so." He peered inside. "I'd ask if I could join you in there but I'm pretty sure there isn't enough room."

The thought of Peter trying to fold his huge frame into her small wardrobe was enough to cause one side of her mouth to lift.

"That's better." He stood, holding out his hand to help her out, and she pushed her way through her clothes to standing, the papers clutched tightly in her hands. Behind him Allie stood in the doorway.

Great. Now her roommate knew she was a weirdo who hid in wardrobes. She opened her mouth, trying to find some words to explain her particular brand of crazy.

Allie held a hand up to stop her and smiled. "You don't need to explain. Everyone needs a hiding place. I've got some engagement-party planning to do so I'll leave you guys to it." She disappeared, leaving Peter looking at her with concerned eyes.

"You didn't go to work today. Elizabeth is worried."

"Actually I did." Long enough to open what sent her scrambling for her hiding place. "I just had to leave. I left Elizabeth a message."

"This is not your fault, Emelia. This is not on you. No one blames you for the brawl."

The rational part of her knew that. In all the discussions about risk and contingencies not once had anyone raised the possibility of a bunch of tree-sized rowers turning the so-called gentlemen's game into a fistfight. The worst-case scenario had been the match getting rained out.

"Do you know who threw the first punch?"

She didn't know. She didn't even care. "Who?"

"Victor."

Of course he did. "Why?"

"Well, neither him nor the other guy are saying but best anyone can work out the Cambridge guy made some slur about Anita."

The whole debacle had been on the front page of the paper for the first three days. The reception had been canceled. All the tickets had to be refunded but all the associated bills still had to be paid.

She had failed. The only reason she was here was to save Anita's charity and after two events they were back to square one. She should just walk away now. Walk away from Spring-Board. Walk away from Peter. Walk away from all of it. Except she had nowhere else to go. All her eggs were in this one messed-up basket.

"This came today." She held out the sheaf of papers to Peter.

"What is it?"

"Estimated costs to repair the damage. Because the university didn't charge us to use the grounds, their insurer is saying the damage isn't covered by their rental insurance policy."

Peter scanned the document, turning the pages until he got to the figure on the final page. Then he let out a low whistle. "Eighteen thousand pounds?"

"Once we refund the reception tickets and pay all the costs, that's pretty much everything we've made from the row-off and the cricket match." Emelia felt tears building in the back of her eyes and blinked them away, but she didn't prevent one from spilling over.

Peter looked at her, pulled a pressed white handkerchief out of his pocket, and handed it to her. Only the English. "Why does this matter so much? I mean, I'm personally invested because Anita was my cousin. But this feels like this is much more than a job to you."

This was it. This was the moment when she should just tell him the truth, the whole sordid truth, and let the chips fall as they might. But the fear of the unknown clogged the words in her throat. "I just need to do something right."

Peter studied her, as if wanting to ask more. More than she was able to give. "Okay. Well then, I guess we're just going to have to put on the best charity ball that Oxfordshire has ever seen."

She had to give him points for sheer optimism but she just couldn't see it. "How are we ever going to put on a ball that will make a million pounds? With pretty much no money? Let's be honest. It's no more likely to happen than me getting to Narnia through my wardrobe."

Peter just looked at her, jaw sagging. "That's it!"

"What's it?"

"Narnia!"

"You've lost me."

"SpringBoard is a literature charity. It's December. Winter. Highbridge is a manor in the country. Just like in the book. I can't believe we haven't thought of this before. It'll be perfect."

"What?"

The next thing she knew Peter had picked her up and was spinning her around. Her heels skied across the side of her bed, through the air, then along the wall. "Narnia. We make it a Narnia-themed ball."

He dropped her to the floor, leaving her breathless and giddy. Images of Highbridge's ballroom decked out with tables of Turkish delight, a huge lantern post in the middle of it, custom-made wardrobe doors as the entry, spinning through her mind like whirling snowflakes.

"What do you think?" For a second he looked like he was doubting himself.

"I think . . ." Emelia said the words slowly, drawing them out. Then she grinned. "I think it is the craziest, most amazing idea I have ever heard."

They both stared at each other for a second, breathless with the sheer audacity of what they were going to try to pull off.

And suddenly it didn't seem so crazy when Peter leaned down and kissed her.

Twenty-Nine

Emelia walked tentatively into Peter's average-sized living area. "Hello?" No answer.

Such a bachelor pad. A couple of rowing posters and another poster for the games of the 2015 Rugby World Cup were the only wall decorations. One of the two mismatched couches had been inherited from the seventies. The money saved had apparently been invested in the huge TV that sat on the main wall. It was tidy though, which was more than she'd expected.

It had been four days since Peter's Narnia ball idea tipped Emelia over the brink of recklessness. They'd been saved from themselves only by Allie's coming to ask for opinions on something to do with the engagement party, the two of them both springing apart at her voice like a pair of teenagers busted by a parent. Emelia had spent the time telling herself it was better that way, that a little bit of distance was all it would take to get over this foolish infatuation that had somehow managed to sneak under her guard. The way her heart hammered at the sound of him on her voice mail called that out for the lie that it was.

He'd sounded stressed. Said he had to go out of town

unexpectedly and asked if she could top up Reepicheep's water in the morning. Told her where to find the spare key.

In one corner sat a scratching post, and cat bowls of water and food sat on a piece of newspaper. No sign of the world's ugliest cat.

Retrieving the water bowl, she made quick work of washing it out and refilling it. In the hour since she'd picked up his voice mail her mind had spun trying to think of one good reason he would need to leave so suddenly yet still remember to make sure his cat got fresh water. She'd come up with none.

She placed the bowl back on the newspaper, then turned to leave. She'd send Peter a text back in the car. Let him know his cat's hydration needs were met.

She froze midturn. The guy hadn't been joking. On the far side of the room, by the door, sat a glass case on the bookshelf.

She walked toward it, crouching down slightly to look at the model straight on. "Wow." The *Dawn Treader* sat inside. A beautiful model, meticulously assembled, maybe fifteen inches long by ten inches high. Even from behind the glass, she could see the tiny detailing and intricate construction of Lewis's famous boat.

On one side of it sat copies of all the books in *The Chronicles of Narnia*. On the other side sat a collection of Lewis's works. *The Great Divorce. Mere Christianity, The Screwtape Letters*, and others. She picked up *Mere Christianity* and flipped through its pages. She'd never read it. Never really been interested in what Clive had to say about religion, no matter how much she liked him. Not when his team included people who had never met her mother but took some kind of wacked-out pleasure in insisting she was burning in hell.

But she'd promised herself when she came to Oxford that she'd try to build this new self with an open mind. If Allie, Jackson, and Peter all thought there was something to be found here, maybe she should at least hear them out. Hear Clive out. He had, after all, even called himself the most dejected and reluctant convert in all of England.

Picking up a book titled *The Weight of Glory*, she flipped through the pages.

> *It would seem that Our Lord finds our desires not too strong, but too weak. We are half-hearted creatures, fooling about with drink and sex and ambition when infinite joy is offered us, like an ignorant child who wants to go on making mud pies in a slum because he cannot imagine what is meant by the offer of a holiday at the sea. We are far too easily pleased.*

His words struck something deep inside her. Infinite joy. What would that even look like?

Her pondering was interrupted by the sound of retching. Spinning around, Emelia saw Reep had not only appeared but was violently hacking on the carpet, his little head arching forward and back.

He was choking. Badly. Peter was going to return to a feline corpse. No matter what she thought of the squat furball, that wasn't an option.

Moving across the room, she picked him up under his rib cage, feeling the strength of his efforts as his abdomen sucked in and shuddered out. She'd never had a cat. She had no idea what to do. Smack him on the back like you did a person? She had no better idea. Lifting her hand, she tapped him on the back. He kept choking. Another whack. Firmer. This time his sound changed, like something had been dislodged.

Another cough and a hairball flew out and landed on the back of the couch. Ew.

"You all good, little guy?" Emelia held him up and rotated him to face her. He gave her squinty eyes. Then proceeded to latch both of his paws onto her bare arm and shred it like a piece of paper.

For a second, Emelia just stared into his triumphant face before softly dropping a word that should never be used in polite company.

Then her hands flew apart, and Reep fell to the ground before bounding up the back of the couch and out of her range of vision.

Her left forearm and hand featured thin red ribbons. She took a deep breath before she could give in to her desire to commit caticide, and then Emelia turned around to try to see where he'd gone.

Her spine stiffened. Where the Narnia books had been, Reep now sat. With one paw batting at the *Dawn Treader* case. She let out her breath as she saw it wasn't moving. Of course it wouldn't. He was just a little cat.

Staring straight at her, Reepicheep pushed his face between the back of the case and the wall. Slowly, the corner of the case shifted forward until it edged off the shelf. As he forced himself even farther forward, the corner moved another inch or so off.

"Here, Reep." Emelia stepped backward to his food bowl and picked it up. She tiptoed toward the bookshelf and shook the bowl, the dry cat food clinking against the metal sides. "Look, Reep. Are you hungry? Yummy food?" It smelled disgusting. Like fish and bones.

As if to tell her what he thought of her offer, Reep pushed the case so that almost a quarter of it was being held up by nothing but air.

Okay, enough was enough. She put the food down and reached out. If he scraped both arms up, so be it. The *Dawn Treader* was not going down on her watch. She grabbed the ends of the case, picked it up, and pulled it toward her.

Reepicheep leapt off the bookshelf, landed on top of the case, and gave her what could only be described as a "die, girl, die" glare before opening his mouth and sneezing in her face.

Emelia's eyes clamped shut, and she stumbled back, trying to get away from the evil spawn. Her foot went right into the food bowl and slipped, sending her sideways.

The next thing she knew, something struck her across the back, sending her flying forward. The case flew out of her hands and hit the window with a crack. A line appeared in the glass, but the case stayed intact. She held out a smidgeon of hope until it flipped and flipped again as it dove to the floor and landed upside down.

Crawling across the ugly carpet, she reached the case and tipped it over. Inside where the boat had once been sat a collection of matchsticks, string, and material.

Then, behind her, came the sound of spawn cat purring.

Peter stood in the doorway, bewildered by the scene spread out before him. Books on the floor, cat food strewn all over the place, and in the middle of it all, Emelia crouched over pieces of wood and glass. He blinked. Maybe he was hallucinating from no sleep.

Something rubbed against his leg, and he looked down to find Reepicheep. "Hey, little guy." He scooped him up and gave him a pat as he walked across the living room.

"Are you—" His words clogged his throat as he saw what it was that had gone flying from her grasp and hit the window. What she now held cradled in her arms. The case with his beloved model. The one thing he had left from his grandfather. Inside, the *Dawn Treader* lay in pieces. Not even pieces, more like shrapnel.

"What happened?" He breathed the words and blinked back unexpected moisture rising in his eyes.

It's just a boat, Peter. It's just a boat.

That didn't stop the lump in his throat.

Emelia's eyes were huge. "I'm so sorry."

Red lines ran down one of her arms. "What happened?" He repeated the question.

"I tripped and—"

"No, not to the boat. To you." He reached out and lightly touched her arm above one of the scratches.

She looked down at it as if it were the first time she'd seen it. "Let's just say it's been confirmed your cat isn't exactly an ardent fan of mine."

His pet purred and looked up at him innocently. But the lines down Emelia's arm were clearly from little claws.

What could he do? It wasn't like you could put a cat in time-out. "Stay right there, I'm going to find something for it."

Striding to the kitchen, he rummaged in the top cupboard until he found the box of assorted items that passed as his medical supplies and pulled out an almost empty tube of antiseptic cream. Better than nothing.

He took a couple of deep breaths, squashing down the well-worn memories of building the boat with his grandfather. If he dwelled on the fact that it was now in tiny pieces, he wouldn't be able to hide how gutted he was.

Returning to her side, he squeezed out a little cream and dabbed it on her arm, trying to gently spread it up and down the scratch. Emelia winced. "Sorry."

"Do I need a rabies shot?"

Good grief, he hoped not.

"I'm so sorry about the *Treader*."

"It's okay. It was just an accident. Mostly my fault. It was me opening the door that sent you flying." He kept his gaze on her wounds, refusing to look at her face.

"Reep was up there and I thought he was going to push it off, so I'd picked it up to put it somewhere safer and then—" She shrugged.

"Bad timing."

"I wish I could have seen it better. It looked beautiful. It must have taken you ages."

"Months." But it wasn't as beautiful as she was. He didn't know where the thought came from. All he knew was that after a late night drive to London, then spending the small hours trying to negotiate the release of his unapologetic brother out of the latest jail cell, there was nothing he would have rather found when he came home than her. Even if she was holding the remains of his most beloved possession.

"If I tell you something, can you try not to hate me?" She blinked up at him with long, damp eyelashes.

"I'll try."

She scrunched up her nose. "I don't really like cats. And I really, really don't like yours."

He ran his hand across her jawline, then slid it into her hair, running his fingers over its wavy edges. "Can't say I blame you after what he's done to you."

She looked at him. Properly. Her eyes traveled his face, no doubt taking in his rumpled clothes and haggard face. "Is everything okay?"

He ran a hand through his hair. Tried to remember what he'd said in the message he'd left on her voice mail. "It was a long night." He was going to stop there, but something compelled him to go on. "Victor got into a bit of trouble in London."

"Ah." Her expression revealed no surprise at his words. But then, why would she after her first meeting with him? "What kind of trouble was he in?"

"Got arrested for drunk-and-disorderly."

"So, you went to rescue him?" He couldn't tell from her tone if she disapproved or not.

Peter shrugged. "It's what brothers do." Though in this brotherhood it was very much a one-way street. Always had been. He ran his fingers across the cracked case. "To be honest, I'm surprised he didn't break this long ago. He was always jealous of how close Pop and I were."

"When you left the party and that time you ran out of my office. Were they both Victor too?"

For once he didn't mind talking about his brother. It was a good distraction. "Yes."

"So, you rescue him pretty often?"

"I guess." Peter tried to sort through his tired thoughts. "He's always had a bit of a thing for drinking and girls. But it's gotten out of control. This last year, I've spent more time getting him out of pubs, or parties, or police cells, absolutely wasted, than I care to think about. But then a few hours later, he's on the erg pulling the kind of times that some guys train years toward and never achieve." He shook his head. "Anyway, looks like his luck is about to run out. It's looking pretty certain he's going to get charged this time."

Emelia tucked back a piece of hair that had fallen across her face. "Maybe it will be good for him. It's not your job to save him from himself."

The angry scar down the side of his brother's face insisted otherwise. And he was done talking about Victor. At least he didn't have to worry about his getting kicked off the squad anymore.

Emelia's finger traced the crack along the glass. "I'm so sorry. I'll find a way to fix it."

"No." His thumb ran across her cheek, wiping another tear away. "It's okay. It's just a boat." This time he meant it.

She tilted her head and gave him the kind of smile that made him ignore all the warning sirens going off in his head insisting that if he didn't pull back, he would cross a point of no return. "It wasn't just a boat." Her finger now traced a line down his arm.

He was a goner. Lack of sleep and wanting to forget everything to do with Victor overrode all rational thought. Resting his forehead against hers, he closed his eyes for a second, breathing in the heady scent of jasmine. "I'm just glad you're here."

He felt her relax as she leaned into his hand, her breath wafting over his lips. "I'm glad I'm here too."

Opening his eyes, Peter pulled back for a second, allowing his gaze to drink her in—her big eyes, brown hair, and naturally rosy lips that made her look like Snow White in the cartoons he'd watched as a child. They could get him into big trouble if he let them. They already had. Just being around Emelia sent every logical reason he'd ever had about not falling for someone who didn't share his faith clear out of his head.

She smiled at him, tilting her face up. Peter may have been out of the game for a while, but even he could work out that if he went in for a kiss, she wasn't going to turn him down.

He had never been so tempted. He'd split up with Sabine because even though she shared his faith and what they had was good, he knew that somewhere out there was great. That a girl was out there who would make him feel all the crazy all-consuming things he was feeling right now.

Peter sucked in a tortured breath and summoned all his self-control. Removing his hand from her cheek, he pulled back slightly.

They had to talk. He never should have kissed her in her room. It had been a moment he'd replayed in his mind over and over in the few days since. It had felt so right, yet it had been wrong.

He couldn't have great with Emelia. No matter how much she made him feel like maybe life would be okay without rowing. No matter how much he wanted something more with her. He couldn't. And right now he was being dishonorable, flirting and enjoying the feeling of her in his arms when he couldn't give her what she deserved. He needed to tell her why. He needed to tell her now.

"I have to talk to you about something."

Something he couldn't interpret flickered across Emelia's face at his words. Whatever it was, it changed the air between them. Her expression tightened for a second, and she shifted away, as if she already knew what he was going to say.

Thirty

I HAVE TO TALK TO YOU ABOUT SOMETHING. EVERY FEMALE OVER the age of fourteen could tell you the something that followed was never good. The only question was how bad it would be. It didn't matter if you were in a restaurant or a car, or sitting on a living room floor staring at a shattered model ship.

People didn't preface good news. It just burst out.

I love you. We're pregnant. I got the job. The tests are clear.

Then there were the things that needed framing.

It's not you, it's me. I've met someone else. I cheated on you. We're letting you go. The test results are back.

The iterations were endless, but the lead-ins were limited.

We need to talk. I need to tell you something. There's something I have to say.

"I don't understand." After Peter's pronouncement, she'd stood up, moved to the couch. He'd followed. Situated himself a safe distance away. Then he had haltingly, awkwardly, told her that he liked her *a lot* but that there couldn't be anything more than friendship between them because he believed in God and she, well, didn't. At least, not like he did.

This from the guy who, only a few minutes ago, had been inches away from kissing her. Again. He couldn't deny it. She wasn't going to ask him to.

Emelia focused on a spot just over his shoulder. "I don't understand." Had she said that already? Well, she didn't. She truly didn't. What was the big deal? She'd known plenty of people who had married across religious boundaries. It had never seemed like much of an issue to them. As far as she could see, they both agreed to respect each other's beliefs, or lack thereof, and all was well.

"I'm not a guy who just goes to church on Sunday because it's a thing to do. Like . . ." He shrugged. "I don't know, grocery shopping."

"Okay." She still was no closer to getting it, but she took a shot at filling in the gaps. "So, you try to live your life with all of those kind of values?" She was mentally trying to catalog what that might include. Sex was out. She hadn't been in a relationship for years and she wasn't a casual sex kind of girl, so it wasn't like she was having any right now anyway. She'd seen him have a beer, so he wasn't a teetotaler. She had no clue where he stood on gambling, but she didn't care. Dancing? She'd no sooner have gone back into another nightclub than she would have drunk gasoline, so whatever.

"I do."

"Okay. I can respect that." What was she doing? This was the barrier she'd been hoping for, the one that would force her to get a grip on her growing feelings. She couldn't date a guy when she was responsible for the death of someone he loved. And this was the perfect excuse. God. If she'd believed in Him, she would've offered up a prayer of thanks. Or whatever it was one did.

But despite all her attempts to tell herself the million reasons why this was a good thing, her heart wasn't buying it.

Peter mumbled something that she couldn't quite make out.

"What was that?"

He sucked in a big enough breath to fill three people and looked her straight in the eye. "That's not enough."

She couldn't have been more taken aback if he'd slapped her. It wasn't enough? What more did he want? "Why?" The three letters leaked out of her. Small. Hurt.

She wasn't enough. Even though that wasn't what he'd said, that was what he meant.

He seemed to have read her thoughts because the next thing she knew, her hands were captured in his. "Emelia, look at me."

She tilted her chin a little, but not quite enough to be able to see into his eyes. That would be her undoing.

"I really like you. I would have asked you on a date weeks ago if it wasn't for this."

Well, that was a nice consolation prize.

"I know how this goes. My mum, she believes. My dad doesn't. My whole life I've watched what it looks like when two people love each other but don't agree on something that infiltrates your whole life. I would love nothing more than to throw caution to the wind and explore whatever this is between us. Hope that along the way you'll come to believe what I do. But that wouldn't be fair. I can't do that to you. I can't do that to me."

"You didn't think it might have been a good idea to mention all of this before you kissed me?" She couldn't keep the bitterness out of her voice. Why did she even have to go there? Bring it up?

"I'm so sorry." He did look genuinely stricken. "I acted dishonorably. It should never have happened. I just . . ." He sighed. "Sometimes when I'm with you everything feels so right. And the truth is there's not much that's right about my life right now. But that doesn't excuse what I did."

"Couldn't we just . . ." The words died on her lips before she could even say it. Peter wasn't that guy. He wasn't the guy who dated for some casual fun. He was the guy who went all in. He was the guy every mother wanted for her daughter because he was honorable. He wouldn't play around and carelessly break someone's heart.

And she couldn't deny that he was right. In the haze of blazing attraction, she might like to think that she could be all understanding and tolerant of his beliefs, but she knew that when it really mattered, she wouldn't. She'd get annoyed. She'd get frustrated. Resentful. Eventually it would poison everything.

And that was before the guilt got to be too much and she would be forced to look him in the eye and tell him that she used to be Mia Caldwell. That she was the reporter responsible for his cousin's death. And then he wouldn't just leave her. He would hate her for the rest of his life.

Outside of her friendship with Allie, knowing Peter was one of the best things about her life in Oxford. It was too important to sacrifice trying to pursue something that might feel good in the short term but ultimately would end in heartache.

"Couldn't we just . . . ?" He was waiting for her to finish her question. Thankfully, he seemed to have no idea what she was going to say next.

"Stay friends?" Emelia said.

There was nothing she wanted less. There was nothing she wanted more.

"Stay friends."

For the first time, Peter understood what Dickens meant

when he penned the line *It was the best of times, it was the worst of times.*

He could no more imagine his life without Emelia than he could imagine it without rowing. But the reality—that what he desperately wanted with her would never happen—was brutal. He was going to need some space. Despite all his lofty words, the truth was that when he was around her, most of his reasons flew out of his mind.

The fact that he'd managed to utter them coherently, that she'd seemed to understand what he was trying to say, was pretty much a miracle.

Emelia bit her bottom lip. "Just so we're clear. If I were . . . If I believed like you do . . ."

Peter's fingers curled around the edge of the couch cushion. "If there's one thing I've learned in my life, it's that no one can find God for someone else. They can only find Him for themselves. My biggest hope is that you do find Him. But you have to do it for you. Not for me. Not for anything we might have."

That was optimistic. There was such a lack of single Christian girls in this town that the minute Emelia came through the doors of any church, she'd find herself swarmed by guys.

A horrible, selfish part of him hoped it never happened for exactly that reason. If they ever shared the same faith, she'd soon discover her new dating pool held options far superior to a failed wannabe rower whose current best claim to greatness was *almost* being an Olympian. It would only be a matter of time before he lost her.

He felt like the world's biggest heel that the thought had even entered his consciousness. But there it was. A tiny part of him wanted things to stay the way they were because at least then he'd still have her in his life, even if it wasn't how he wanted. Because a voice inside him told him that the minute she found God, she'd also realize she was way out of his league.

Thirty-One

"Hi, Emelia speaking." Emelia wedged her phone against her ear as she mouthed *just a sec* to Allie, who had just entered her office. Clicking her mouse, she set her computer to shut down.

"Oh, thank goodness. I was beginning to think I was never going to get you!" Lacey's breathy tones came down the line, the words tumbling over each other. Her cousin spoke at the same speed she lived her life in general.

"Sorry. Have you been trying to get ahold of me?" Emelia glanced at the unfamiliar number on her screen before realizing that it wasn't going to show any missed calls while she had a call open. Knowing her luck, if she tried to play with the screen to see, she'd hang up on Lacey.

"Have I been trying to get ahold of you? Only for like the last week."

"Oh, was that you?" She'd had a few missed calls from a blocked number, but since no one had bothered to leave a message, she'd assumed it was a telemarketer or someone equally exciting. "Why didn't you leave a message?"

Her cousin blew out a blast of air. "You know I hate voice mail. So, what are you up to this weekend?"

"Not much. More ball stuff." She and Peter needed to take a trip out to his parents' to measure the entrance to the ballroom for the wardrobe. Their first decent amount of time together since the excruciating conversation in his living room.

"Fancy some company?"

"Um, what?" Something started dawning. "Hold on. Where are you?"

"Right now? London. I'm over for the week for work. But tonight I'm going to catch the train and come to Oxford for the weekend. Surprise! I've already looked at the timetable, and I can catch a six fifty from Paddington and get into Oxford at seven fifty."

"Oh, wow." Which were not the words going through her mind, but it was all irrelevant. Her date with destiny was coming for her.

"So, can you pick me up or should I catch a cab somewhere?"

"Um . . ." Emelia was left fumbling. "I'll have to check and get back to you. Is this the number you're using?"

"Yup. Okay, see you tonight! I'm *so* excited."

"Me too!" Emelia tried to imbue her voice with some enthusiasm. Her cousin knew she hated surprises. That was partly why Lacey loved springing them on her. She closed the call and dropped her phone into her bag.

"Is everything okay? You look a bit stunned."

Emelia startled. For a second she'd forgotten Allie was there.

"My cousin Lacey is in London. She's coming to stay for the weekend." Oh, heck. She hadn't even checked with Allie. "I mean, she doesn't need to stay with us. She can get a hotel or something."

"Don't be silly!" Allie tucked a stray piece of auburn hair behind her ear. "If she doesn't mind taking the couch tonight, she can have my bed tomorrow while I'm in Cambridge."

"Thanks. That would be great." As much as Emelia loved her cousin, she wasn't offering to share her bed. She needed her personal space while she slept.

"What's she doing in London?" Allie asked the question as they exited the offices, Emelia locking the door behind her as the last staff member leaving for the weekend.

"No idea. She's a publicist. Mainly books and movies. Does a lot of jet-setting." She should warn Allie what was coming at her. "She looks like Malibu Barbie and she plays on it, but she's one of the smartest people that I know. Any chance I can borrow your car to pick her up?"

Allie's face fell. "Oh, I'm sorry. It's in getting some work done. We were going to pick it up in the morning before dropping me at the station."

"Of course. Sorry, slipped my mind. I'll call Lacey and give her an address and she can just catch a cab."

"Well, if she's related to you, I'm sure I'll love her. I'm looking forward to learning all sorts of things about Emelia before Oxford."

Allie said the words lightheartedly, but they had the force of a brick. Lacey knew all about Mia, and she had no idea of the lengths to which Emelia had gone to cover her tracks in Oxford. All it would take was one wrong sentence over the next two days and everything she had worked so hard to leave behind would be undone.

She had to get to her before Allie did.

By the time seven thirty rolled around, Emelia was almost hyperventilating. She was sure she'd also developed a nervous twitch, not that Allie appeared to have noticed.

"I think I might grab a cab and go meet Lacey at the station. Just to make sure she doesn't get lost or anything."

Lacey would have laughed in her face if she'd overheard. For a start, someone mute and blind could still manage to find a cab at the train station and hand over Allie's address. Secondly, her cousin had once driven in Italy without a map and knowing no Italian and successfully navigated to find their destination. But it was the best Emelia could come up with since Allie's car was out of commission.

"Okay. By the time you're back, the brownie will be done." Allie didn't look remotely suspicious of Emelia's transparent ruse, which took some tension out of her shoulders. Her roommate added a handful of chocolate chunks to the mix, gave it a stir, and then started transferring the dark brown batter to a tin.

"Okay, great. I'll just give them a call now and get them to pick me up—" Emelia was interrupted by the sound of knocking on the door.

Emelia jammed her phone into her pocket, marched through the hall to the front door, prepared to tell whoever was selling or proselytizing on the other side she wasn't interested.

Unlocking the door, she pulled it open and promptly felt all the air leak from her lungs. There stood her cousin in all her blond, long-legged, trendy glory.

"Surprise!" Lacey flung her hands up in the air. "I caught an earlier train."

Emelia just stared at her, openmouthed, no sound coming out.

"Are you going to let me in?" Lacey pushed the door open wider with a perfectly manicured finger as she spoke and hefted a small travel case behind her. Her slender legs were encased in black leather boots up to her knees. Emelia could tell with one glance they probably cost more than she earned in a week. She closed the door behind Lacey with a thump.

"Is that your cousin?" Allie's voice came from the kitchen.

"Um, yes. She took an early train." Emelia tried to force her voice to come out normally, but she obviously didn't manage entirely because Lacey quirked an inquiring eyebrow at her.

Her palms were damp. She wiped them down the front of her jeans. All it would take was one sentence from her cousin and the life she'd built here would be over. She swallowed, her mouth dry.

"Lace, that's Allie, my roommate." She dropped her voice to a whisper. "She doesn't know anything about Mia."

Her cousin's brow wrinkled. "What are you talking about?"

"I'm Emelia here. They don't know about what I used to do. Who I used to be. Any of it."

Lacey's eyes boggled. "Are you telling me that you are working at Anita's charity and they have no idea who you are? Oh my gosh."

She had like five seconds before Allie came looking for them. "I'll fill you in later."

"What do they know?" Lacey whispered back.

"Um . . ." For a second, Emelia couldn't think of a single thing. "That I love Narnia." It was the first thing that came to mind. Her cousin gave her an incredulous look.

"Hi!" Allie's voice came from behind them. "I'm Allie. Emelia's flatmate." She approached the two of them, wiping her hands on a dish towel.

Lacey immediately pulled out her most charming smile. "Lacey, Emelia's cousin. So sorry to drop in on you unannounced like this. I was in London for work and tomorrow's engagement was canceled so I couldn't miss the opportunity to come and see M— Emelia."

Allie offered a friendly smile. "No worries. I'm afraid it will be the couch tonight, but I'm away tomorrow night so you're welcome to take my room. Come in, come in. I've just put a brownie in the oven."

"Yes, come in." Emelia realized that in her panic she was being rude. "Just leave your bag by the stairs if you want." She watched as Lacey parked her travel case and then led her to the living area. She gestured toward the couch. "Grab a seat. Do you want something to drink?"

"I'm good. I've got some water." Lacey grabbed a large bottle out of her purse, then leaned back and unzipped her boots. "Oh, that's so much better. Those shoes were not made for walking."

"So, you're a publicist?" Allie finished setting the timer on the oven and came over to the couches with a mug.

"Yes. I'm just over pitching some follow-up stories from London Fashion Week for a couple of clients." Lacey levered the boots off her feet using her toes.

"And which side are you cousins on? I'm very jealous. I only have male cousins and we're not particularly close. It wouldn't cross their mind to look me up if they were in the city, let alone the same country."

Lacey's eyes widened toward Emelia.

Emelia jumped in. "Lacey's mom is my father's sister."

She was saved from any further explanation by Allie's phone ringing. Allie glanced at the screen and her face softened. Jackson, apparently. "Excuse me for a few minutes. If the timer goes off, can you get the brownie out?"

Emelia almost sagged from relief. "Of course." The brownie had at least another twenty minutes, so Allie was going to be away for a while. Enough time for Emelia to bring Lacey up to speed.

Allie was already halfway out of the room, phone to her ear. The door closed behind her.

"So, you're Emelia Mason and you love Narnia." Lacey took a slug from her water bottle.

"What? I am and I do."

Her cousin's gaze flicked over her jeans and cheap sweater. "And why are you dressed like a hobo?"

Emelia checked out her outfit. So it wasn't exactly the designer fare she used to wear, but it wasn't that bad. "I gave most of it away."

Her cousin gagged, a trickle of water dribbling out of her mouth. "You did not."

"I did."

"Louis? Jimmy? Valentino? You kept some, right?" Her cousin said their names like they were orphaned children. Not handbags and shoes and gowns.

"Nope." They were the second thing to go. After her job. After she'd quit—or been fired, depending on who was telling the story—and cleared out her desk, the next stop had been clearing out her wardrobe.

"Not the Birkin." Her cousin's tone was almost begging.

"Yup." That one had been the first to go. The beloved Birkin handbag had been her reward for a year where she'd broken scandals at a ridiculous pace. It was her loudest accuser when the pile of cards she'd constructed her life with came tumbling down.

"You sold them, right? At least made some decent money."

"I didn't. But hopefully Goodwill did." Or not. She didn't actually care. Sometimes she liked to think they had no idea what she'd left on their doorstep in four huge trash bags. It made her smile to imagine a single mom struggling to make ends meet wandering around Walmart with a Birkin worth ten grand that she'd bought for five bucks.

Her cousin let out a strangled cry, then spent a few seconds breathing deeply, blond head in her hands. No doubt trying to find her Zen, or center her chakras, or whatever was the latest fad in such things.

Eventually Lacey lifted her head. "So, you're dressed like you shop at Target and your new friends know nothing about Mia Caldwell. Nothing about your life before you got here. That's how you got the charity job. By hiding your entire past."

Emelia let the first part of her comment slide. "No. And only little bits and pieces."

"I get wanting distance from everything that happened, Meels." Her cousin switched to her childhood nickname. "But divorcing yourself completely? That seems a bit unnecessary. And, dare I say, unhealthy. Not to mention it has the potential to blow back on you so bad if someone discovers the truth."

She had to make her cousin understand. Get through how critical it was that Lacey didn't blow this for her. "It was totally necessary. They wouldn't have hired me if they knew. And I need to do this, I need to try and make something right. It's only for a few more months. I'm not Mia anymore. I don't want to be related to her. If I could wipe my brain of her existence entirely, I would. She's finished. Over." She didn't even try to keep the desperation out of her voice.

Her cousin contemplated her with a troubled gaze. "You can't just delete years of your life."

"Maybe not. But I sure can try."

Thirty-Two

Peter stared at his phone as he pulled up in front of Allie and Emelia's house. The text had just arrived a few seconds earlier.

Surprise visit from cousin. She's coming with. Try not to ogle.

What on earth was that supposed to mean?

Jogging up the front path, he rapped on the door. Within a few seconds, he heard footsteps and the door was thrown open.

He held up his phone. "Wh—" The words froze in his mouth as he realized it wasn't Emelia standing in front of him but a tall, willowy blonde. A very attractive one.

She peered at his screen. " 'Try not to ogle.' Oh, isn't she classy." She thrust out a hand. "You must be Peter. I'm Lacey. Said cousin and gatecrasher. I would say I've heard all about you, but I'll be honest, all I know is that you and she are involved in planning this high-society ball."

Peter managed to find his voice. "Peter Carlisle. And that pretty much covers all the basics."

Lacey studied him. "I feel like I know you from somewhere."

"I used to do some rowing." Just saying it felt like something jammed in his throat.

"Hmmmm." She appeared unconvinced. "Maybe."

Well, she certainly couldn't be mistaking him for Victor and his paparazzi-attention-seeking ways. One of the many benefits of looking nothing like his brother.

"I wish I could say I know more about you too, but, honestly . . ." He pocketed the incriminating screen. "That message is all I've got." It reinforced how little he knew about Emelia's background. Had she ever mentioned a cousin before?

"So, what's the plan for the day?" Lacey asked just as Emelia appeared at the top of the stairs.

"We're heading to my family's estate to take some measurements for somc of the fit-out for the ball. We're planning to hold it there."

Lacey raised an eyebrow. "Gosh, that sounds very fancy. Are you like a duke or something?"

Might as well tell her. It would be obvious as soon as they got to the house anyway. "I'm not. But my—"

"Okay, we're good. Let's go." His sentence was cut off by Emelia, who was almost tripping down the stairs in her haste to get to the bottom. Tension radiated off her whole body, a sharp contrast to Lacey's relaxed demeanor. Odd. And he wasn't the only one who noticed. Lacey gave Emelia a scrutinizing look as she picked up a bottle of water from the hall table.

Emelia didn't seem to notice as she picked her bag up off the floor and pulled some keys out. They all stepped outside as Emelia closed the door.

Lacey turned to him. "Did you say your surname is Carlisle?"

"I did." Was it his imagination or did Emelia freeze for a second mid–key turn?

"Not related to Victor Carlisle at all?"

Peter tensed. "He's my brother."

Something crossed Lacey's face. Like pieces of a jigsaw were falling into place. *Don't tell me she somehow had the misfortune to meet Victor when he was in the States last year.*

"Do you know him?" If she was another of Victor's conquests, what could he do? Take her back to the estate? Introduce her to the parents of the guy who'd no doubt gotten whatever he wanted and then tossed her aside like a toy?

Lacey fiddled with the lid of her water bottle before raising her chin. "Not personally, no. So, Anita Van Rees was your cousin?"

Anita's name appearing out of nowhere took him by as much surprise as if she'd suddenly punched him. Maybe more. "She was."

Sympathy shadowed Lacey's eyes. "I'm so sorry for your loss. Anita had great potential."

"Did you know her?" It felt like his feet were glued to the porch. He couldn't have moved if he tried.

"I'm a publicist. Our paths crossed a few times back in the US. Charity events, things like that." Lacey looked at Emelia. "You never mentioned you were working with Anita's cousin on this ball."

"Didn't I?" Emelia's words were nonchalant, but not her big round eyes. Her face was ashen. Weirdly, Lacey's resembled a rolling thunderstorm. Something told him he was chauffeuring an impending storm. He just didn't know why.

"Have you lost your mind!" Lacey added an expletive at the end of her sentence. Then a couple more in case Emelia had missed the first one. Her cousin had her hands on her hips and was unafraid to get in her face. She was so close, she was almost on Emelia's toes.

Emelia had spent a car ride, a tour of the estate, and a couple of hours working through ball details with Peter's mom trying to pretend her cousin wasn't lasering her with her eyes. But her luck had run out when Lacey had sweetly asked if there was somewhere they could freshen up before lunch and practically frog-marched Emelia to the fancy bathroom they'd been directed to.

Emelia leaned back against the porcelain sink to try to regain some personal space. She wrapped her fingers around the cool rim. "I didn't know who Peter was. I only found out when he brought me here when we were location hunting."

Her cousin huffed a breath of incredulity in her face. "C'mon, Meels. You're smarter than that. You used to be a freaking award-winning reporter. It never crossed your mind to think that Peter Carlisle might be related to the Honorable Victor Carlisle?"

"No. Because I never thought of Victor by his last name. I thought of him as Victor, heir to the Viscount Downley. That's the title he threw around all over town."

Lacey ran her hands through her hair, leaving it all tousled, and not in a trendy, sexy way. "I cannot believe this. I cannot believe *you*."

"You were fine with me leaving Mia behind last night. You got it!"

"That was before I knew you were having some kind of *thing* with Anita's cousin under your new nom de plume!"

"We're not having a *thing*."

"Oh, c'mon. The national grid is about to call and ask for

its electricity back. Are you seriously trying to tell me you two haven't even kissed?" Emelia's silence had her cousin just staring at her. "Seriously?"

"Just once! And it was a mistake. And we've talked about it and it won't happen again. There's no thing and there won't be a thing. That's all been well established."

"Why not?" Her cousin finally took a step back, giving Emelia a little room to breathe.

"Because he's religious."

Lacey scrunched up her face. "So what? I've dated a few religious types. Remember Aaron? He was Jewish. Then Brad. He was a Scientologist. That was a bad move though. Don't ever date a guy who believes in a drug-free, silent birth."

"It's more than just a set of rules for him. Like, it's a real thing. He won't date someone who doesn't believe the same as he does."

"And you don't think that's something you might want to consider?" This from a girl who considered a new Prada bag a spiritual experience.

"Lacey. I'm not getting religion for a guy." Emelia had done some underhanded things in her life, but she certainly wasn't going to add faking a belief in God to it. Though she had a sense that even if she tried, Peter would see right through it. It would have to be real or not at all. And, even if she'd wanted to believe, real wasn't an option. If God even existed, it was for people like Allie and Jackson and Peter. Not people like her.

"I didn't suggest you do. I'm just saying that, you know, there might be something in it worth considering if it's that important to him. He's a great guy. Which brings me back full circle to, have you lost your mind?"

"What do you want me to say to him, Lace? 'Oh, hey, Peter. Remember that cousin of yours who died? I'm the reporter who drove her to kill herself.'"

Lacey paced the small room from one floral wall to the other. "He will find out one day. Karma kind of bites you like that."

"He's it, Lace. He and Allie and Jackson are the best friends I have here. They're the best friends I've had in years. If I tell them that, I've got nothing. I won't even have a house to live in." Even Allie, the nicest person on earth, wouldn't want anything to do with her if the truth came out.

"What about Victor? Surely you'll run into him sooner or later. Doesn't he live around here? He's Peter's *brother*. I need a Xanax or something." Lacey started digging through her purse.

"I already have."

Her cousin froze mid-dig. "And?"

"He recognized me but we've come to an agreement." Only because they both held weapons of mutually assured destruction.

Lacey let out a breath with a whoosh. "I've seen you play with fire, but this isn't that. This is a nuclear power plant. How can you do it? How can you be planning all this fund-raising together, with that chemistry the two of you have, and not feel sick keeping this from him?" She pulled a tube of mints from her purse, unraveled it, and shoved one in her mouth.

"It's not like I made her drink. It's not like I put the cocaine up her nose. She did all of those things herself. She made her choices, I just exposed them." It was a line Emelia had used many times to justify her work, and it still rang as hollow as all the others.

Her cousin's steely face told her she wasn't buying it either.

The crack as she chomped down hard on her mint said all she needed to.

Emelia pushed herself off the basin. "Of course I hate it. I feel horrible about it. Sometimes it swells up inside me until I feel like I might just vomit it out all over him. But I can't. If I do, he will walk away. Just like everyone else. And then I'm left with nothing. Just like I always am."

Lacey's eyes widened as the ugly, honest words hit the air.

Turning around, Emelia twisted the cold tap on full blast. Putting her hands under the water, she splashed some up on her face, trying to gain herself a few seconds.

Pull it together, Emelia.

She leaned against the sink and watched the water swirl down the drain. Grabbing the hand towel, she pressed it against her face.

"What if he's different?" Lacey's voice was soft and tentative.

Emelia dropped the towel back on the counter and turned around. "You know how I met him, Lace?"

"How?"

"I fell out of a wardrobe in an antiques shop and he caught me. Then he asked me if I was a Susan or a Lucy. How am I supposed to tell that guy I'm the person he probably hates most in the world?" She could already see the loathing in his eyes if she told him.

"I don't know. But you have to. Because if you don't, then someway, somehow, he will find out. And there's no coming back from that."

"Is that a Dr. Donna thing?" Dr. Donna was a relationship expert and one of Lacey's most famous clients. Her cousin was a walking record of the woman's sound bites.

Something flickered in her cousin's eyes. "No. It's a Lacey

O'Connor thing." Lacey closed the two-step gap between them and took Emelia's shoulders, forcing her to look her in the eye. "I may not be into the whole God thing, but even I know the truth always comes out eventually. And that guy out there, he deserves to know the truth. From you."

Thirty-Three

She was responsible for Anita's death. And saving her charity was the closest thing she could think of to atonement. If it weren't for those two facts, Emelia would have been out. Done. Gone.

Emelia stabbed a piece of cake with her fork. Mashed it between the prongs. She'd tried to convince herself it didn't matter. That her life as Mia Caldwell was behind her. That Emelia Mason was all that mattered. And Emelia Mason hadn't done anything wrong. But there wasn't a single cell in her body that was letting her believe it. Especially since Lacey had called her out.

It was good they had the religion thing between them. She could hide behind that without any difficulty. Her gaze lingered on Peter's broad back as he stood at the counter of the boutique bakery, ordering another dessert.

His Olympic dreams and decency and faith were far too good for her. She'd been foolish to ever hope there might be a possibility of anything different. But now she'd had a cold dose of reality.

Not even Peter would be able to forgive her for what she'd done. What she'd cost him. His family. There was no God big enough to conquer that.

Every time she saw him, a loud, insistent voice nagged at her, telling her she needed to tell him the truth. No matter how much she tried to muffle it, it refused to stay silent. It felt like she had a tumor inside her, growing and growing.

She just had to get through the next four months of planning this ball, and then it would be over. Her job would be done. She'd resign. Probably leave Oxford.

"So, are you going to tell me what's going on?" Peter returned to their table as she stabbed the cake again.

Emelia dragged her attention back to what they were supposed to be doing: choosing the two desserts for the sit-down dinner. They should have done it weeks ago, but somehow it had fallen off her color-coded, cross-referenced spreadsheet. "What? Nothing's going on."

"Sure. And you and Reepicheep are best friends."

"Ha. Very funny."

"Is it the cake?" Peter pointed his fork to the sample of black forest layer cake that sat practically untouched on her plate.

"It's a bit dry." Emelia poked at it with her fork and a few crumbs toppled off. She tried to focus on the task at hand. The sooner they got through it, the sooner she could go home, get in her pajamas, and read some Narnia. Maybe *The Voyage of the Dawn Treader*. Right now she could do with sailing off to the ends of the earth.

Speaking of which, hopefully she'd get home to find Jackson had accomplished his mission of finding and retrieving his broken model from wherever Peter had stashed it. She'd found someone who thought they might be able to fix it for her. She just needed to get the thing without Peter's knowing. Just in case it couldn't be done.

She made a show of dipping her fork into a piece of chocolate torte. "This one is better." And it was chocolate. Who wouldn't want a chocolate torte at a ball? In the background the refrigerated cabinets hummed.

She flipped through the folder that sat on the table in front of her. It held pages of all the different desserts the bakery did. The torte and crème brûlée both looked fine. And right now fine was good enough. "I think we go with these two." She pushed the folder toward Peter.

He didn't even look at it. "Have I done something?" The guy wouldn't let it go. Clearly she wasn't as good at pretending as she'd given herself credit for.

"We should split the rest of the list." The words fell out of her mouth. "There's not much left. Divide and conquer and all that." The only things left were confirming arrangements already made and getting Elizabeth to approve the deposits on anything that wouldn't accept credit cards. They didn't need to see each other to work on promotional details.

"No." Peter's voice was firm.

"Excuse me?"

"No. I'm not splitting the list unless you tell me what I've done. I must have done something." He leaned forward on his elbows, pale blue T-shirt stretching across his chest.

"You haven't done anything. It's me, okay? I'm the one who's done everything." The words burst out of her.

"What are you talking about?"

"I'm never going to believe like you do."

"What?" Peter looked at her like he didn't know what the drama was. He forked another piece of torte and popped it in his mouth, not looking the least bit perturbed.

"You keep looking at me with these hopeful eyes, like maybe one day I'm going to wake up miraculously converted, and it's just not going to happen. I'm so glad it works for you, but it's just never going to be my thing. I have too much stuff to believe in a good God. I can get a disinterested one. A vengeful one. An ambivalent one. But not a good one. So what's the point?" She gestured like an insane woman with her fork, not even caring that a piece of cake got flung across the room.

"Of?"

"Of this." Emelia gestured to the two of them. "Of just being 'friends.'" She stuck up her fingers to do the air quotes and almost stabbed herself in the side of the head. "We can't pretend we don't have chemistry. Well, maybe you can, but I can't. I like you and it is *killing* me. I'm planning a ball with the one guy I want and can't have. But at the same time I think he is *insane* for wanting a piece of metal so bad he's willing to spend the rest of his life disabled for a shot at it. If there is a God, I've got to give Him points for the irony of it all."

Peter just stared at her, fork halfway to his mouth.

"You don't know me. If you knew the things I'd done, you'd want nothing to do with me." Emelia's fork smashed into a piece of pastry, grinding it into the plate.

Peter had put his fork down, but his mouth still hung half open.

"What?"

"You're right. There is a lot I don't know about you. And a lot you don't know about me. I wish you trusted me enough to tell me. But there is nothing that you could have done that would make me want to have nothing to do with you." His eyes shone with certainty and conviction.

"You have no idea what you're talking about." Emelia pushed out her chair and fled.

The chaotic scene played back in Peter's mind as he drove and tried to work out where it had gone so horribly wrong. Emelia had been off since he'd picked her up. Wooden. Stilted. Going through the motions. The dying world of Charn in *The Magician's Nephew* had more life.

It didn't take a psychologist to see the hurt that she was hiding. And he'd stupidly decided to push it, instead of just leaving her be. What she'd said had sliced through him. It didn't matter. It didn't matter how much they liked each other or what chemistry they had. She was right. If she never had a faith of her own it was all for naught.

He forced out a breath and reminded himself of everything. Emelia falling out of the wardrobe. The teacup. All the ways their paths had been forced to cross.

He didn't believe in coincidence. Not at this level. Coincidence was finding a free parking spot. Not this. This was God making a move. Even if Emelia didn't see it that way.

The question was, what was he meant to do? Was he meant to step back and let it all go? Or was he meant to help show her the God who never gives up?

He parked the car and half jogged up the steps to Highbridge. Opening the front door, he strode down the hallways toward the kitchen. He pushed the door open to see his mum standing with her back to him, spooning flour into a rotating bowl. It dusted the air as the beaters caught it and threw some back up.

She jumped at the sound of his entering the room. "Peter. You gave me a fright. Did I forget you were coming today?"

"Would you do it again?"

His mother turned the beaters off. "Would I do what again?"

"Marry Dad."

"That's like asking me to wish my life away. If I hadn't married your father I wouldn't have you. Or Victor." Not exactly an emphatic statement that she wouldn't change anything.

"But what if you could go back in time. What if there was no me or Victor? Would you marry him again?"

She studied him, her gray eyes processing whatever it was she was reading in his face. "No." The two letters hit him like a pipe bomb. "And the truth is he wouldn't marry me either."

Peter sank into one of the chairs at the small table in the corner of the kitchen.

His mother wiped her hands on a towel, then walked over and pulled out the chair beside him. "Emelia?"

"Yeah." There was no point in pretending.

"Do you love her?"

"I don't know. She just has so much stuff. And she won't let me in to . . ." His words trailed off. To what? To help? To make it better somehow when he didn't even know what it was?

"It's not your job to fix her." His mother's soft words interrupted Peter's train of thought.

"I know that."

"Do you? You have a habit of shouldering the burden of things that aren't yours to carry. Victor's face. My health. Anita's addictions. Whatever it is that is going on in Emelia's life. Don't get me wrong. I really like her, but you can't fix whatever the wounds are that she bears. There's only one who can do that. And she has to want to let Him."

Peter rubbed his forehead. "I keep trying to distance myself, I do. I know we can't be anything more than friends unless she's a Christian. But, I don't know, it doesn't make sense. I just feel like God has me in her life for a reason."

"I'm sure He does. The question is, are you okay if it's not the reason that you want it to be? Then what?"

"I don't know." He hadn't let himself go there.

"It is the toughest thing in the world to spend your whole life battling with the person you love most on the one thing neither of you can compromise on. I wouldn't wish it on anyone."

"Is it really that bad?" Maybe he'd been kidding himself that his parents had a good marriage.

His mother sighed. "Your father is a good man. And he loves me the best he can. Of course it's not that bad. It's just not as great as it could be. And, for you, I want so much more than what we have. I want the girl you can share your whole life with, not just compartments of it." She gave him a wobbly smile. "Plus, I'm your mum. I don't want to see you get hurt. And Emelia has the potential to break your heart. I've known that since the first day you brought her here."

"And Sabine didn't?" Sabine was the smart choice. She was great. She loved God. She would be the first person to cheer on his comeback. It wouldn't be feckless or selfish to her. Maybe he should just give what they had another chance instead of getting tangled up in something that all the signs suggested had the hallmarks of a disaster.

Emelia didn't believe in God and thought his Olympic desires were crazy. There was no chemistry or fierce hoping in the world that could paper over those canyon-sized cracks.

His mother stared out the window to where, just a couple of weeks before, Emelia had paced out steps to work out how many outdoor lights they would need for the ball. "You never looked at Sabine the way you look at Emelia."

Over his mother's shoulder, he could see the large family sideboard. Inside the glass-fronted top cupboard sat her collection of Aynsley teacups. The latest addition sat front and center.

He felt the desperate need to grab on to something, anything. "The teacup was in the wardrobe."

"Pardon?" His mother's brow wrinkled.

"The teacup I gave you. The one that completed your set. I looked for it for ten years. It was in the same wardrobe that Emelia fell out of when we met. The day before your birthday. Surely that means something."

"I suspect it means that God is pursuing her." She fixed him with a long look. "Make sure you don't get in the way."

Thirty-Four

Going to church with Peter and his mom, followed by lunch with his parents. So much for keeping her distance. All she'd wanted was to cross a few final things off her list that could only be done on location.

"Emelia?" Peter spoke from across the lunch table. "Can you pass the butter?" He gave her a questioning look. It obviously wasn't the first time he'd asked.

"Sorry. In my own world." She picked up the cream ceramic tray beside her plate and handed it to him, holding it at the end so there was no chance of their fingers touching.

Pushing her chair back, she took her and Maggie's plates to the sink. On the way back she paused at the cupboard, looking at the teacups lined up inside it. The one at the front was familiar. "Those are beautiful teacups."

"Peter gave that front one to me for my birthday. He'd been looking for it for years."

"Years?"

Maggie came over from where she'd been serving dessert at the counter and opened the cupboard, pointing to the familiar one with pink roses. "It was the last one I needed to complete my collection. He looked for it for years, then finally found it in an antiques shop the night before my birthday."

Suddenly Emelia remembered where she had seen it. It looked just like the teacup that had been in the wardrobe. She'd forgotten all about it. He'd been looking for it for years? What was going on? She turned to see Peter studying her. "Is that the—"

Somewhere behind her there was a huge thump, followed by a crash.

She glanced around the table, but no one else seemed to have noticed. Then a man yelled, "Over there! No, not there, there."

"Um, do you have guests staying?"

Peter's mother had returned to serving up dessert. Another thump and yell pulled her attention toward the doorway leading to the main parts of the house. "Oh, sorry. We're so used to them, these days we hardly really notice."

Them?

Peter paused buttering his last piece of bread. The guy must have packed away almost half a loaf. "Film crews. Quite a few use the house as a location for period dramas."

Huh. Now it made sense that Highbridge had seemed familiar back when she'd done some cursory research on Victor. She'd probably seen it on TV once.

Maggie scooped a huge spoonful of pudding into a bowl. "A very handy income stream to have. God bless *Downton Abbey*, and not just for being one of the best shows ever. Since that screened, we've had more business than we could accommodate."

"What's filming today?" Even though she'd spent a decent chunk of her career reporting on movie stars and their scandals, she'd never been on a set. She'd tried to sneak into a few but never quite managed to make it.

Peter's mom thought for a second, her brow rumpling. "Honestly, I couldn't tell you. I'll have it in the booking schedule somewhere. I can go find it if you—"

"Oh, no." Emelia returned to her seat. "Don't go to any trouble."

"Why don't we go have a look after lunch?" Peter suggested.

"Can we?" The two little words somehow managed to betray her excitement.

He shrugged. "Sure. It's our house."

"Thanks, darling," Bill said as Maggie put a huge bowl of apple pudding in front of him. Emelia had completely forgotten he was beside her.

Then an equally huge bowl landed in front of her. The scent of cinnamon and mixed spices warming the air. Oh, wow. She wouldn't need to eat for a week after this.

"Cream." Peter's mom placed an enormous bowl of whipped cream in front of her, the slight tremor of her hand the only sign of the degenerative disease infiltrating her nervous system. Emelia ladled a spoonful into her bowl and waited for Maggie to rejoin the table with her own dish and Peter's.

"Eat while it's hot." Peter gestured to her bowl.

She didn't need to be told twice. Within a second her mouth was filled with sweetness and spice, warmth and cool cream. It was so good she closed her eyes for a second in bliss. "This is possibly the best thing I've ever tasted in my whole life."

"So I see."

She opened her eyes to find Peter staring at her like she was dessert. His expression threatened her resolve to keep her emotional distance.

"Think I might go eat this while I watch the cricket." His

father suddenly pushed back his chair and reached his spoon across her, scooping up some cream and dumping it over his pudding in one smooth motion.

"I'll join you." Maggie hadn't even put Peter's bowl on the table yet but followed her husband out of the room, carrying her own.

She had never seen two middle-aged people move so fast. Was it something she'd said?

Peter pushed back his chair and went to claim his dessert as if nothing out of the ordinary had just happened. "Would you like anything else to drink while I'm up?" He asked the question while helping himself to a few more generous spoonfuls from the serving dish.

"No. Thanks."

Peter put his bowl down opposite her and sat back down. It was piled so high, she was sure anything he added would slide down the slopes and onto the table.

"What did you think of the service today?" He asked the question cautiously, as if half expecting to find himself on another emotional landmine.

She moved her spoon through her bowl. She'd only gone because every time she saw him she felt so riddled with guilt that suffering through a church service seemed like a small penance to pay. "It was different from what I expected."

"How so?"

"Quieter. More . . . peaceful." She'd been braced for some kind of long thundering sermon that made her feel even more condemned than she already did. Instead, a soft-spoken woman with blond hair had talked for all of fifteen minutes about the Good Samaritan. She still felt off balance from the experience.

Church not being what she'd expected, braced herself for, created more questions than answers.

She'd sat next to Peter's mother and spent half the service wondering what Maggie would do if she had any idea she was sitting next to the girl who had a role in the death of her niece. A sermon featuring a vengeful God would have been welcome. That was what she deserved. She knew what box to put Him in.

"Julianne is a great vicar. Maybe I should go to her for advice on handling career change since she's managed it so well." Peter poured himself some orange juice.

"What did she used to be?"

"A trader in the city. Hedge funds. Crazy money stuff I don't even understand. Really good at it too, from what I hear. One of their biggest earners. Then one day she resigned to go to seminary."

Emelia almost choked on her first mouthful of pudding. "No way."

"Yes way. This is her first vicarage posting."

"How do you go from being a London trader to a vicar? How does that even happen?"

"God." He said the word easily. Like it was a simple explanation. Rather than the three most complicated letters in the universe.

Emelia had been as prickly as a hedgehog when they'd gone to church. Like she was expecting to be set upon at any moment from all directions. But as the service had continued, she'd seemed to relax. Unless it was optimism clouding his perception.

Peter cobbled together a mangled prayer as he loaded the dishwasher, not sure how to phrase what he wanted to say. He knew Emelia couldn't find God to make him happy. People had to do it for themselves. He could point her in the right direction, light the path with flashing runway lights, but he couldn't walk the path for her, no matter how much he wanted to.

Make sure you don't get in the way.

His mother's words rang in his ears. If only he knew what they meant. This was why he was good at rowing. You made a plan. You executed the plan. He wasn't good without a plan.

"Okay, I'm good." Emelia came back into the kitchen. She'd gone to wash her face after practically licking her pudding bowl clean. The woman could inhale food at both a quantity and a speed that would make her fit in perfectly with any rowing team.

"Great. I'm almost done." He rinsed the last remaining plates under warm water and added them to the appliance. Tried to relax. Which was impossible around her. "Did I tell you I ordered the chocolate torte and crème brûlée?"

"Good choice."

"Yup." He closed the dishwasher and turned the wash cycle on. "Okay." He grabbed a tea towel and wiped his hands. "Shall we go and see what the interlopers are up to?"

Emelia laughed. "Interlopers?"

He shrugged. "Having your home as a set loses its appeal after the first few times. Especially when they're filming at all hours of the day and night."

Peter opened the door to the hall leading to the main wing and ushered her through.

"Such a hard life you lead." She grinned up at him, and

he longed to run his fingers through her hair. He settled instead for a playful tug on the end of her ponytail, like he was twelve.

Opening the door at the end of the hall, they stepped into a world of bustle. Cameras and lights were being moved all over the place. People traversed the space with purpose. A few director chairs lay scattered around. Peter took a quick glance. From the look of things, they were preparing to film in the main entryway and the parlor. In both rooms, people were busily arranging furniture, setting out props, and taking light readings.

There were no actors to be seen—they were still in makeup or costuming—meaning Peter and Emelia had a little time to look around before they'd be in the way.

They stood for a few seconds watching the swarm.

"What do you think they're filming?" Emelia's gaze followed a middle-aged woman cutting through the room holding a stack of papers.

"Looks like something set in the twenties." He gestured at a set of fringed flapper dresses being wheeled past.

"Do you think we might be able to watch some filming?"

"Maybe. If we stay out of their way." He almost added "and if it's soon" because he wanted to get home at a decent time, but one look at her shining eyes sealed his mouth. He'd be here all afternoon if being able to watch a few minutes of filming would keep the excitement on her face.

"Let's go see what's happening in the parlor." Grabbing her hand, he weaved them between people into the other room. It was more set up in here—cameras and screens placed, the space where they were all focused immaculate.

Someone rushed past them, bumping Emelia, so that she

was thrown against his chest. He grabbed her under her elbows to steady her. "You okay?"

"Fine, thanks." But she kept standing there, gazing up at him.

Peter couldn't stop himself. His fingers ran lightly down her arms. When they reached her hands, her fingers curled around his.

He tried to drag in a breath, find a rational thought, but everything dimmed in comparison to the girl standing in front of him staring at him like he was her whole world.

Something flickered in her eyes as he reached a hand up and ran his thumb across her cheek.

"So, we should, um . . ." She stepped back and started to turn away. He felt himself sag with disappointment.

The next thing he knew, she'd spun back again, wrapped her arms around his neck, and pulled him down, leaning against him as her lips found his.

For a split second he didn't move, then his arms slid around her waist, his hands running up and down her back as he leaned into the kiss. All reason fled his brain. All that remained was the feeling of Emelia cradled against his chest.

"Wow." After a few seconds, she pulled back, both of them breathless.

He didn't say anything. Just stood there.

Emelia peered over her shoulder. He looked too. In all the hustle of the room, no one seemed to have noticed them.

She grabbed his hand. "Let's go."

He blinked. "You don't want to stay and watch some filming?"

"Nah. I'm good." She shot him the kind of smile that almost had him pulling her into his arms for an encore performance.

But she tugged at his hand and started striding toward the door that would take them back into the hallway.

He tried to catch his breath as he followed her. He knew he should be sorry. Except he wasn't. Not at all.

What had she done? Emelia tried to keep the thought at bay as she dragged Peter back through the main foyer, past the safety of the door they'd entered from.

Once again, her need to poke her nose into things had screwed up everything. She and Peter had managed to find their way to some kind of even keel and she'd gone and ruined it all again.

The whole morning she'd held herself together, managed to resist the pull of his appeal. She had been turning around to walk away.

And then it had all collapsed like a sandcastle hit by a rogue wave.

Her stomach still felt curdled from the moment she'd turned around and seen Jude using his trademark smile on a simpering production assistant.

In that second, she'd forgotten that she wasn't Mia. That she didn't look anything like her. That Jude wouldn't even glance her way for a moment because he was all about blondes, and he'd never in a million years have had any reason to think his most-hated reporter would be here. Especially when she was a wavy-haired brunette in the middle of the English countryside on his movie set.

But in that moment when she thought Jude would see her, and destroy everything, she'd done the only thing she could think of. She'd turned around and laid one on Peter like she meant it. Which she did. Every single part of her.

And now she was in the world's stupidest mess, all because she hadn't kept her wits about her. She'd lost her ability to keep her cool under pressure, something she'd been known for in LA.

"Emelia." She barely heard Peter as she kept barreling down the hall, not wanting to stop or deal with what had just happened. "Emelia!"

"What?" She dared to look up at him.

Peter smiled and it almost undid her. "Is there a fire somewhere I should know about?"

Emelia sucked in a breath, forcing herself to slow down. "No. Sorry."

"Was it that bad?"

"What?"

"Was the kiss so bad that you need to flee?"

"No." The kiss was . . . perfect. But it wasn't like she could exactly tell him why it had happened. That she'd seen a movie star who'd had a target on her head ever since she'd flirted with him in a nightclub and gotten him on record propositioning her while his wife was two blocks away in the hospital with their one-day-old daughter.

She wasn't one bit sorry his marriage had subsequently broken up and his ex-wife had taken him to the cleaners in the divorce. The guy was a grade-A creep.

"Thanks. Your fulsome denial was very reassuring."

"It was fine."

"Fine." Peter's eyebrows ratcheted up a notch. "You've got real skills in making a guy feel good. Has anyone ever told you that?" He stepped closer, a dangerous glint in his eye. "It was much better than fine and you know it."

Emelia stepped back, bumping against the wall at the end of the hallway. Trapped between the wall and the guy she had a huge crush on, who was advancing on her with intent written all over his face. In any other situation it would have been the best thing ever.

"Now you've got two choices." Peter leaned his arms on the wall, a hand on either side of her head.

"Yes?" She hated that her voice was all breathy, like some damsel in a soap opera.

"You can either admit that it was more than fine, or . . ."

"Or?"

"I can refresh your memory."

Oh.

"Which will it be?" He moved one hand down to loop a strand of her hair around his finger, twirling it like he had all the time in the world.

She couldn't breathe. His green eyes drilled into hers. Her knees felt like they were melting. She was a cliché, every female stereotype she'd ever mocked.

You're never going to be good enough for him. Even if he never finds out the truth, one day he will still leave you. Just like everyone else.

The thought ripped through her head with the power of a nuclear bomb.

Before she could rethink it, give in to what she really wanted to do, she planted both hands on his chest and shoved. Hard.

Peter stumbled back, almost falling.

"What do you think you're doing?" Emelia pushed herself off the wall.

"I . . ." He stared at her, speechless.

"Is this some kind of game to you?"

"No." He grabbed a breath. "Of course not."

She summoned up her death stare. "You've told me that I'm not good enough for you. That I never will be as long as I don't believe in the big guy in the sky. You know how I feel about you. You know that every time I'm around you it's torture. So, what are you doing? Do you like messing with me? Get some kind of kick out of taunting me with what I can't have?" She ignored that she had kissed him first. That had been by accident. Sort of. But this, his tormenting her with what she couldn't have, was on purpose.

His face had whitened, the freckles standing out. He reached out toward her arm, then stopped. "I'm so sorry. I never . . . I would never . . . You're right. That wasn't right. You deserve better. Will you forgive me?"

He deserved better. He just had no idea how much. "We're done here. Take me home."

Thirty-Five

What had gotten into him, pulling a stunt like that? Frustration bubbled up inside him as he stormed down the hall of his flat. And Emelia had called him on it. Rightly so. Peter felt sick remembering the stricken look on her face as she'd pushed him away.

The drive back to Oxford had been an hour of strained silence.

He checked the time. A couple of hours left of daylight. Maybe enough time to get out for a row if he moved fast. After this afternoon, he needed some punishment in the boat—body screaming, lungs burning, hands bleeding. It didn't matter whether his shoulder could take it or not. There was no time to ponder all the ways your life was stuffed when you were trying to suck in enough air to stay conscious.

He pushed open the living-area door with enough force that it hit the wall with a crack.

"Nice to see you too." Jackson sat on one of the couches, a plate of food in his lap and sports blaring on TV.

"Sorry. Didn't think you'd be here."

Jackson shrugged. "Allie had a baby shower for a girl from church." He shoveled some crisps into his mouth and kept speaking around them. The guy had the physique of a professional athlete and the eating habits of a three-hundred-pounder. "Missed you at the service this morning."

Peter headed for the kitchen and pulled a bottle of water out of the fridge. "Went home for lunch. I went to church with Mum."

"And Emelia." It was a statement, not a question.

"We had some ball stuff to do."

Jackson nodded. "So, how's that working out?"

"What?"

Jackson picked up the remote and turned down the volume. "Playing with fire."

"It's not. We're not. She's not . . ." Peter stopped talking. He didn't even know what he was trying to say.

"Not what? Attracted to each other? Because you'd have to be as thick as the Great Wall to expect anyone to believe that."

"It's complicated."

"It always is." Jackson shoveled some crisps into his mouth.

"What's that supposed to mean?"

"Just tread carefully, buddy. I don't want to see either of you getting hurt."

It was a bit late for that. The pain in Emelia's face as she'd shoved him away was etched in his mind.

"Sometimes you have to do the hard thing to do the right thing. If it's meant to be, God will work it out. Remember, I walked away from Allie. Then I let her walk away from me. Almost killed me both times."

"I'm going for a row." He knew that Jackson was right, but he didn't want to hear it. He'd already been forced to let go of one dream in the last year. Surely that was enough.

Peter strode down the hall, grabbing his already prepared kit bag off the floor. Pulling open the door, he halted, not entirely sure he should believe what he was seeing. Emelia stood on his front porch, a purple cardigan pulled around her and hair blowing in the wind.

"Hi." It had been three hours since they'd kissed.

"Hi." She shifted on her feet. "Have you got a minute?"

"Um, sure." He dropped his kit bag back on the floor, gestured toward the porch. "Want to sit?" After their conversation he didn't particularly want Jackson to hear this. He stepped out, closed the door behind him.

"Sure."

They both lowered themselves down onto the top step, leaving a good couple of feet between them.

"I'm really sorry about today."

"It's okay." She turned toward him; a sad smile crossed her face as she wrapped her arms around her torso. "It's my fault. I was the one who kissed you."

Like that was going to make him feel better about being such a cad. "It's killing me too. But the other way? It would just kill both of us slowly."

"I know." Emelia said the words with quiet resignation as she craned her neck up at him. "I never asked you how your latest scans went."

Peter ran his fingers along the banister beside him. "My shoulder's healing, but not as fast as we'd hoped."

"What does that mean for you?"

"A return to competitive rowing is possible, but it will be a long road." He tried to push the specialist's other warning out of his head. That if he tore his shoulder up again, it wouldn't be a question of rowing, it would be a question of whether he would just have normal function.

"Guess it's a good thing you're the type of guy who believes in miracles, then."

Did he? He didn't know anymore. His miracle was supposed to be a podium finish. It had been his goal since he was a teenager. Instead, he was a barely employed coach. Sean didn't really need him for the Boat Race next year. He'd call any day now to confirm it.

Everything in him had been focused on the Olympics . . . yet he couldn't see his way clear to try again. The early mornings, the soul-destroying agony, not knowing if this time it would be enough. Or if he'd fail, again. Just like he'd failed Anita. "What if I'm not good enough? Or I totally ruin my shoulder like you said?"

"But what if you are? I know that I haven't exactly been falling over myself with enthusiasm for you trying to make a comeback, but you love rowing. I see it in your eyes whenever you talk about it."

"I do love rowing. But to get to the Olympics, it has to be more than love. It has to be an obsession. I know plenty of rowers with more talent, more ability, more everything than I've ever had. The only thing they lacked was the overwhelming desire."

"What do you mean?"

Peter studied the blue, cloudless sky, the warm, late July air seeping into his skin. "When it's five in the morning and you're rowing in the sleet and your hands are bleeding and blue, that's the only thing that matters. How much you want it. Whether your hunger is deep enough and strong enough to push you past everything else. I don't know if I still have that. What if it's more about wanting to try and do right by Anita?" Which was crazy. The same way that he knew Emelia couldn't find God for him, he knew he couldn't risk destroying his shoulder to attempt to keep a promise to his dead cousin.

"What do you mean?" Emelia's voice cracked a little as she wrapped her arms around her knees. How could she be cold? It was a perfect summer's day.

"She was my biggest supporter. She could've been an amazing rower. She *was* an amazing rower. But then she fell in with the wrong crowd at university. Started drinking. Doing drugs. As much as she tried, she couldn't seem to dig herself out. Not that you'd ever have known if you'd met her. She always said that I would win the gold for both of us." That was the last thing she had ever said to him. That she knew he could still do it.

"I'm sorry."

He stared across the street. A blue Nissan was pulling out of the driveway opposite. Somewhere a child laughed. "The night she died, she called. But I didn't pick up. I was feeling sorry for myself. I'd had a couple of scans that week and the results weren't good. And it seemed like she had finally gotten it together. Found a great guy. Gotten clean. Started Spring-Board. I didn't want to play along with her positivity about me making some great comeback. So I just let it go to voice mail. I was going to call her back in the morning. But by then it was too late."

Emelia had tears in her eyes. "Peter, it's not your fault. You are not responsible for what happened to her."

Easy for her to say. He might have been able to save his

cousin and he didn't. No one was ever going to convince him otherwise.

Emelia had to tell him. She'd felt guilty enough as it was but now, knowing he blamed himself? She couldn't walk away from this without saying anything.

Maybe he'd understand. He obviously knew what it felt like to live under the cloud of self-condemnation. The slump of his shoulders and the strain on his face said more than words ever could.

He'd still be angry, upset, need some time to calm down. But for the first time she felt a glimmer of hope that maybe, once the initial shock wore off, he might not hate her. He understood what it was to live under the blame for something horrible.

So maybe somehow, when the dust had settled, he'd find a way to forgive her. Or maybe he'd hate her even more. Maybe he'd take all the condemnation he'd been carrying around and heap it on her. Maybe tomorrow she'd be without a job, a place to live, and some of the best people who had ever happened to her.

"Peter, there's something I need to tell you." She curled her fingers around the rim of the step, pressed her palms into the wood of the porch. *You can do this, Emelia. He has to know the truth.*

Peter looked into the distance, didn't give any sign that he'd even heard her.

Memories overcame her. The strength of his arms when she fell out of the wardrobe. Dancing with him in the pub.

Kissing him. Spinning around with his crazy cat attached to her head.

In a few seconds none of those things would be what he thought of when he thought of her. Emelia would be gone.

"Peter?"

He turned to her with a fierce expression. "How do those people live with themselves?"

"Who?"

"The bottom-feeding lowlifes who call themselves reporters. I'm the first to admit that Anita wasn't perfect, that she'd made some mistakes, but destroying her life? Just for a scoop? Who does that?"

Emelia opened her mouth. But nothing came out. Instead tears formed behind her eyes. She did. She had.

"She was only twenty-four." Peter's jaw clenched. "Lost. What is wrong with people that we take such pleasure in witnessing other people's downfalls? That entire industries exist to exploit someone else's pain and publicly humiliate them?"

"I'm sure the reporter had no idea what Anita would do. I'm sure she would give anything she had for it all to be different."

"No she doesn't." He said the words with complete certainty.

"How do you know that?"

Peter ran his hand through his hair. "Because she's still there. Still bar-crawling. Still preying on people. Still breaking the same sleazy stories."

Emelia just stared at him, mouth hanging open.

She was what?

Thirty-Six

EMELIA PULLED HER COAT AROUND HER AS SHE WALKED OUT OF the Eagle and Child. Peter's revelation on his porch had been the thing that had finally broken her nine-month Google fast.

All it had taken was a few seconds to work out what he was talking about. She was no longer reporting, but Mia Caldwell still was. Her ex-boss was still using her byline. There was a different photo, but it was of a blond girl who looked similar enough that the average person probably wouldn't notice any difference.

Though discovering the truth had taken only a few clicks, finding the courage for her second attempt at telling him had taken weeks. Finally, she'd told Peter they needed to go over some final ball details. And as she was the pedantic spreadsheet queen, he hadn't questioned it.

The smart move would be to wait. Tell him after the ball. After she'd handed in her notice. But that was months away, and since the moment on the porch where he'd confessed the weight of blame he'd been carrying around and she had failed to give him the honesty he deserved, she hadn't been able to live with herself.

So she'd sat, in the Eagle and Child for two hours, waiting for him to show up. Checked her phone obsessively. Called him, only for it to go to voice mail. One vodka and soda for courage had turned into two as she'd tried to ignore the pitying gaze of the waitress.

And now she was a little tipsy and vacillating between angry and worried as she paid her bill and stepped outside. She closed the door to the pub behind her and leaned against the stone wall, sucking in a couple breaths of late-summer air. She should've stayed home and helped Allie with the final details of the engagement party that was only a couple of weeks away.

Squaring her shoulders, she pulled out her phone to call a cab. All the anxiety and fear she'd brought into the evening still rolled around inside her with nowhere to go. She began dialing, then turned her phone off and started down the street. It was a nice night. Home was only fifteen minutes away, and it wouldn't get really dark for another half hour or so. Even after a couple of drinks, she could still easily take down anyone stupid enough to try accosting her.

She'd thought the worst that could happen would be if Peter heard what she had to say and said he never wanted to see her again. It had never occurred to her he might not even come.

Emelia walked down the cobbled streets, the warm evening air swirling around her. Up ahead a couple sauntered, arms wrapped around each other, heads close together. They stopped and the woman wrapped her arms around the man's neck.

Emelia crossed the street. She was not in the mood for navigating around a couple making out in the middle of the sidewalk. When she looked up, she realized her feet had taken her to Turl Street, landing her right outside the antiques shop where they'd first met. She leaned against the glass of the second large window, pressing her palms against the cool surface as she peered into the adjacent room. Her wardrobe still stood majestic in the far corner.

Would she have crawled into it if she'd known everything that would follow that one impulsive decision?

Are you a Susan or a Lucy?

His first words to her rang in her ears. She'd flicked the piercing question off with a quick retort. From the first time she'd met him, she'd been deflecting the truth. She was a Susan. She'd always known it, and life had only confirmed it. She would end up alone. Just like Susan had.

"Emelia!" Her head jerked up as Peter's voice cut through the dusk. He was running up the street to her left. What was he doing here? He almost slammed into her as he came to a stop. "Please tell me you didn't wait for me the whole time." His hair stuck up at all angles off his head. His eyes red rimmed. His navy T-shirt wrinkled. If she hadn't known better she'd have thought he'd been on a bender.

"Of course I did." She huffed out a breath. Waited for his excuse. *Please let it be a good one.*

Peter closed his eyes. "I'm sorry."

"Where were you?" Now that he was clearly okay, anger was gaining dominance over the worry.

"Victor—"

He didn't even get the rest of his words out because she put her hand up and shoved him in the chest.

"On second thought, I don't even want to hear it. I could not be less interested in your compulsive need to rescue your drunken lout of a brother."

"He totaled his car. Wrapped it around a tree. This afternoon."

That paused her for a second. "Did he hurt anyone else?"

"No. Not even himself, really. He was so blotto they reckon he was saved by the fact he was probably floppy at impact." Peter's expression was half of relief, half of consternation.

"Good to know I rank so highly I didn't even warrant a call or a text. Despite the fact that I left you so many it's humiliating." She heard her whiny voice, her self-centered words, and immediately wanted to shove them all back inside her mouth.

Peter pulled his phone out of his pocket and swiped down the screen. Even from where she stood, she could see her name appearing multiple times. "I'm so sorry. I've been so busy trying to work out what to tell Mum and Dad."

Whaaaat? His brother had wrapped his car around a tree and Peter was concerned with doing parental damage control? "What does he have on you?"

"What do you mean?" The streetlights around them started to flicker on, showing the stress written across his face in better detail.

"I get sibling loyalty. I do. But from everything I've ever seen, he treats you like his little lapdog. And you just take it." In the distance a siren wailed.

He shoved his phone back into his pocket. "It's all my fault, okay!"

"All what is your fault?"

"His face."

"Are you talking about his scar?" Anita's death was his fault. His brother's face was his fault. His shoulder was his fault. Was anything not his fault?

"Yes, his scar. The angry, jagged welt that disfigures one side of his face." His legs gave way, and Peter sagged against the window next to her. "We got into a fight when I was thirteen. A heated one. He came at me. I grabbed the poker from beside the fire. I only meant to fend him off with it, but at the last moment, he dived and it slashed his cheek. It needed thirty-two stitches. Then it got infected. He's hated me for it ever since."

"And turned you into his servant as a result."

"Something like that. It would break my parents' hearts to find out what he was really up to. He's the heir. The future Viscount Downley."

As far as Emelia was concerned, Victor was old enough to look after himself. "You aren't responsible for him. Or his choices. And you always rescuing him just makes it worse. He never has to face up to his consequences. What if one day he plows into someone? Hurts them? Kills them?" She half yelled the last two questions, just as a middle-aged woman was coming down the sidewalk toward them. She quickly crossed the street to avoid them.

"I don't know how to let it go, Em. Don't know how not to show up. Then he'll really hate me."

"I hate to say it, Peter, but after all this time, I'm not sure whether your showing up or not is going to make any difference."

He ran a hand through his hair, leaving another tuft sticking up from his head. "You're probably right. I guess I just thought if I showed up enough, was always there, one day he might forgive me. That we might find a way to get past the enmity that has always been there. But you're right. It just keeps getting worse. Now he'll have a drunk-driving charge to add to the others." His shoulders slumped in the shadows.

Emelia blinked back the tears that were forming. This guy who carried the weight of the world on his shoulders. She knew too well what that felt like. She pressed her lips together for a second. Could she do it? Tell him what she'd never told anyone? Her fingers tapped the window beside them. "Why do you think I hide in wardrobes?"

He glanced around, as if only just realizing where they were. "Because you're trying to find Narnia?"

"My mom loved Narnia."

"I remember."

Emelia sucked in a deep breath. "What I didn't tell you is that my mom wasn't well. She . . ." Her voice trailed off.

"You don't have to tell me, if you don't want to."

She forced herself to look him in the eyes. Sometime soon she'd tell him the whole truth. He'd hate her. But at least tonight she could give him this. "No. I want to. I want to explain that I know what it's like to carry the weight of responsibility for something horrible.

"My mom loved Narnia, it's true. While other moms cleaned houses and made dinners, mine made up complicated stories of us in Narnia. She was Queen Isabelle. I was Princess Emelia. When you're six, it's a pretty blurry line between a fun mom and one who doesn't operate in reality. You don't know that a person you see as someone who builds the most exciting and complicated fantasy worlds isn't a great storyteller but someone who suffers from psychosis."

Peter's hand found Emelia's, and he wrapped his fingers around hers. She held on to them as if they were a lifeline.

With a deep breath, she forced herself to focus on what she needed to tell him. "But what I was slowly realizing was that we were different. I didn't get invited to other girls' houses on playdates. The other moms came to help at school. But mine didn't. My mom didn't like having other kids over to play. She said that I saw them all day at school and that she wanted me for herself after. One day, there was a new girl at school. She lived a few doors down from us. I got invited to her house to play and Mom said no. Sulked. She said that I didn't need any other friends as long as I had her. I got mad. Told her I was tired of her stupid Narnia games. That I didn't want to play them anymore."

She could still see her mom's face as she spat out her defiant, childish words, wanting to hurt her. Not realizing how much power her words had.

"I ran to Claire's house and told her mom that it was okay. That I was allowed to play. I had the best afternoon in the world. Until the sirens started. They got closer and closer. And I knew, I just knew that something had happened to her. And that it was my fault."

Tears dripped down her cheeks. "There were police and paramedics everywhere. Claire's mom held me as I kicked and screamed and scratched and tried to get to her. She'd taken a huge overdose. She left a note that said she had to find Narnia and this was the only way."

Emelia didn't even know until years later that the police were there hunting for her. That when her dad had found her mom and hadn't been able to find Emelia, he thought she'd done something to her as well.

"You want to know why I hide in wardrobes? The truth is I don't know. She always told me that if I was ever afraid, the wardrobe would keep me safe. That one day we would find Narnia. And she's right. Every time I crawl into one of those wooden boxes, even as my fingers scrape the back and I know there's no Narnia today, for a few seconds I still feel peaceful. I feel like I'm home. And I'm so scared but I can't stop. Peter, what if I'm just as crazy as she was?"

Peter sucked in a breath. Prayed for the right words. Fast. "Emelia, you are not crazy. You are about the least crazy person that I've ever met." She looked up at him. Even in the fading light he could see her eyes were riddled with fear. If only he could reach in and pull it out. "You're not crazy." The words came out as a whisper but seemed to have more impact than his adamant ones.

She peered up, cute freckles smattered over her tanned face. "You really think so?"

"I know so. You are the most beautiful, smartest, most organized ninja I've ever met. But you are definitely not crazy." He cleared his throat. He was a guy. An English one at that. He was not good at this kind of stuff. "C'mon. Let me walk you home."

She wobbled a smile. "That would be nice. Thanks."

They walked in silence for a little while. Both deep in their own thoughts. Emelia's hand tucked into his elbow.

"At least now you know the answer to your original question." She spoke softly.

His original question?

Emelia tugged at the edge of her long-sleeved top and studied the ground. "About whether I'm a Susan or a Lucy."

Why was she saying it like it was a bad thing? Lucy was great. She never stopped believing. She had the potion that healed people. She could be fierce and compassionate. Just like

Emelia. Susan was great too. She had the magic horn and was an awesome archer. She was brave and resilient. Just like Emelia. Neither option was bad.

"Oh, wow." Emelia was staring at him like she'd just had a revelation. "You haven't read it, have you?"

Peter attempted to laugh. "What are you talking about?"

Emelia stepped closer, studying him. "It's why you never know what I'm talking about when I refer to Susan. You don't know."

Peter swallowed.

Emelia's eyes had narrowed. He could practically see the cogs turning in her head. "You've read some of *The Last Battle* though, haven't you? Or have you just heard about it?"

"I've read some of it." The words seeped out of him. They'd just turned into Emelia's street. Were closing in on her house.

"How far have you read?"

"*If Aslan gave me my choice I would choose no other life than the life I have had and no other death than the one we go to.*" Peter quoted the words of Jewel the unicorn in chapter nine. They were burned into his mind as surely as if they'd been inked into his flesh. The sentence he could never get past.

"The great meeting on Stable Hill." Emelia said the words quietly, as if to herself. Then she directed a piercing gaze at him. "What happened?"

"What happened?"

"What happened?" She repeated the words again, softly. "You are the only person I've ever met who knows Narnia like I do. That's why none of this made sense. Why I couldn't reconcile you asking me if I was a Susan or a Lucy when we first met. It didn't make any sense. Except now it does. Something happened and you don't know how it all ended."

Peter ran his hand through his hair. "My grandfather died."

"When?"

"When I was nine. Dad was in the army and posted in the Middle East. So my grandparents moved in to help Mum. Every night, he would read me a chapter of Narnia before I went to sleep. That night he stopped on that sentence. Said he needed to get a glass of water. A few minutes later, he had a heart attack. He died on the way to the hospital. I've never been able to read past it."

"I'm sorry." Emelia nibbled her bottom lip.

"I know it's crazy. It's just a book. He would have wanted me to keep going. I can't even tell you how many times I've tried. Sat there and tried to force myself to read the next sentence, to keep going. But I just . . ." He shrugged his shoulders. How could he explain that his eyes just refused to read any farther when even he didn't understand it?

Emelia was silent as they walked up the path leading to her front door. No doubt thinking it was one of the stupidest things she'd ever heard. Almost twenty years had gone under the bridge and still he couldn't get past it.

"Do you think he knew?"

"Who?"

"Your grandfather."

"I don't know."

"I think he knew. How else would he have left you at such a perfect place? A sentence on either side would have meant little. It's like a message for you."

"I'd never thought of it like that."

"There aren't many people who can say that. *I would choose no other life than the life I have had.*"

"Can you?"

Emelia shook her head. "Most of the time I feel like I would choose any other life than this one. You?"

"If I had any other life but this one, I wouldn't have met you." The words kind of fell out of his mouth before he'd had a chance to think them through.

"Peter, we—" Whatever Emelia was about to say, she cut herself off. "It's been a big day. For both of us. I should go."

Thirty-Seven

"Morning." Emelia opened her eyes to find Allie perched on the end of her bed, a steaming mug in her hand. She was still in her pajamas, her hair mussed from sleeping.

"Hi." What time was it? What day was it? Emelia's eyes felt puffy, her throat scratchy. After she'd revealed her twisted past on a street corner, Peter had held her, told her she wasn't crazy, walked her home, and handed her over to Allie. Who had taken one look at her face and given Peter a fierce glare that would have frozen lava. Poor guy. Emelia had tried to explain her state wasn't his fault. Well, not in the way Allie clearly thought it was. Then she'd taken herself to bed and given in to exhaustion. She'd probably have stayed in it all day if not for her roommate perched at her feet like a bird.

"Want to come to church?" It was the first time Allie had straight-out asked her.

Emelia pulled herself up to sitting and rubbed her eyes. "I don't do church."

"Can I ask why not?" Allie sounded more curious than judgy.

Emelia sighed. Since she was apparently on an honesty streak, she might as well keep going. "The last time I voluntarily went to church, I was sixteen. A friend took me. I thought I'd give it a shot. Why not? It wasn't like I had anything to lose.

Then the preacher got up and thundered about how people who commit suicide go straight to hell. I've avoided them as much as possible ever since."

Allie peered at her across the top of her cup. Her eyes were troubled, full of questions.

"My mom killed herself when I was six." It had been years since Emelia had said it out loud. Now she'd said it twice in twelve hours.

Allie closed her eyes for a second and drew in a deep breath. "I'm sorry."

"Me too."

Allie didn't say anything. Emelia grew disconcerted. Shouldn't she have been jumping in with some kind of theological discourse? But then, that wasn't Allie's style.

Up until six months ago, Emelia had thought she needed religion about as much as she needed to ride a three-legged camel through the Sahara. It had been easy to jam Christians into the fundamentalist, judgmental box and close the lid.

Then she'd met Allie, Jackson, and Peter. And they'd refused to fit into her nice box of stereotypes. Now a tiny part of her wondered if she might be missing out on something real. If maybe there was a God who could transcend everything the worst of His believers made you think of Him. And then she wondered if maybe she was just grasping at straws because of how she felt about Peter.

"Where do you think my mom is?"

Allie lifted one shoulder. "I don't know."

Emelia blinked. She hadn't been expecting that. Wasn't the point of being religious that you had all the answers? And then you painted them on placards and marched around DC waving them?

"That man had no idea what he was talking about. The only one who knows what happens when someone dies is God. He knows every single one of us. Everything we've done, everything we haven't. Every good and bad decision we've made. What happened in our last moments. He makes the call. Not some guy in a flashy suit."

"You really believe that? That He cares about you? Me?"

"I know it."

"How?"

Allie took a sip of her drink, traced a pattern with her finger on Emelia's comforter, actually looked like she was thinking about the question. It made Emelia feel she could trust whatever she was about to say more than if she'd just launched into a prepared spiel. "Do you remember the day you asked me about my spare room?"

"Sure."

"Did you notice that I looked a little startled when I walked into the office and you had that card in your hand?"

"Sort of." Emelia remembered thinking something at the time, but it obviously hadn't made a huge impression.

Allie pulled her knees up to her chest and wrapped her arms around them. "I never put that card up on the notice board."

"I don't understand." Emelia blinked at her, trying to process what she was saying. "But it's in your handwriting."

"I made the card. A couple of them. I had meant to put one up there. But I never got 'round to it. To be honest, I was a bit uncertain if I wanted a flatmate, so I'd procrastinated. Left them in my bag."

Emelia's eyes felt like they were about to pop out of her head. "But if you didn't put it up, how did it get there?"

Allie shrugged. "No idea. Maybe it fell out of my bag and

someone saw it and put it up? All I know is that to me you can't explain it away as coincidence. It has to be more. It has to be bigger."

Emelia sucked in a breath. Well, she could see that. But then, if there was a God, of course He'd be interested in Allie. She was sweet, and kind, and funny. A much better person than she was.

"It wasn't about me."

Emelia didn't know if she'd spoken her thoughts out loud or if Allie had read her mind.

"It wasn't about me." Allie leaned forward as she repeated herself. "It was about you."

Emelia shook her head. Her fingers twisted around themselves as she tried to process what Allie was saying. Claiming. It sounded too much like a fairy tale, from a land where the story started with "Once upon a time" . . . That had never been her story.

"That first time we met? Over the photocopier? Didn't that ever strike you as strange? That someone you'd never met would invite you to a house party?"

It had. A little. But she'd been so desperate to get out of the horrid B and B, she hadn't wanted to question it too much. "I just thought you were one of those super-friendly people who invites everyone you meet to things like that."

Allie laughed and fished a half-dissolved marshmallow out of her mug, popping it in her mouth. "I wasn't even meant to be in that morning but my first lecture got canceled because of the weather. And I was only photocopying because my first set had landed in a puddle. And I really don't randomly invite strangers 'round. But for some reason I invited you.

"You know, the truth is that sometimes when people ask

how you *know* that God exists, it's hard to come up with one compelling reason. It's often such a conglomeration of so many things that, put together, create the proof that you need. But watching all the things He's put in play the last few months around you, that's all the proof I need."

Emelia shook her head, trying to absorb it all. It was all too big. Too crazy. Too overwhelming. To even consider for a second there might be an omniscient being who had made so many things happen for her. Because of her.

And if it was true, why now? Why didn't He step in and save her mom? Or Anita? Had she finally had enough bad stuff happen to her to get His attention?

"Know what else?" Allie grinned at her.

"What?" Emelia wasn't sure she could take any more.

"You need to ask Peter about the teacup."

Emelia just looked at Allie. "The one he got his mom for her birthday?"

"You say it like it's so ordinary. Have you ever sat down and really thought about what the odds are of you and the teacup that Peter has been looking for for years being in the same wardrobe? The same night he just happens to be at that exact antiques shop and find both of you?"

No. She hadn't. If she started thinking too deeply about that, then everything might change.

Thirty-Eight

Where on earth had Allie disappeared to? One minute she'd been the life of the engagement party, the next she seemed to have disappeared. And it wasn't on some lovers' escapade, since Emelia had just seen Jackson talking to a group of people.

"Emelia." She turned around, trying to spot who had called her name while she restacked the mountain of presents into something that didn't look like it might topple at any second. Judging by the large pile, she'd been the only one who hadn't ignored the "absolutely no presents" instructions on the invitation.

Kat, Allie's best friend, who had flown in the night before, was crossing the small lobby. Her entire appearance screamed exactly what she was: a hair-and-makeup guru in hot demand for movies all over the world. Just being within a few meters of Kat made Emelia feel frumpy. And this was the best she'd looked in months. "Hey. Have you seen Allie?"

"Yup. I'm just doing some touch-ups upstairs before the formalities start. Can you give us a hand with something?"

"Sure." She turned and followed Kat up the grand staircase of what once had been a country manor house for one of the aristocracy before it had been converted into a small boutique hotel.

Kat didn't waste any time and was soon tapping on a door.

"Come in," Allie called from inside.

Kat opened the door and gestured Emelia in ahead of her. Emelia's heels sank into the carpet as she walked into an opulent bedroom. The door clicked behind them.

Allie stood in front of her, like something out of a Botticelli painting. Gone was the jade cocktail dress she'd been wearing half an hour ago. In its place was a long, figure-fitting but classy cream-colored dress, V-neck, flared out at her knees. Her auburn hair was caught in an elegant knot that sat at the nape of her neck. Tall sparkly shoes completed the ensemble. "Surprise!" Allie grinned at her. Radiant.

No. They hadn't. They weren't. Oh, they were. Emelia opened her mouth, but no words came out. "Wow." A couple of seconds later it kind of croaked out. "Holy moly." Then she started laughing as she shook her head, undone by the crazy, giddy girl standing in front of her.

Allie laughed so hard the neckline had a hard time containing her cleavage. "I take it that's a good thing?"

"You look . . ." Emelia's voice trailed off. "Beautiful" didn't cut it. Nor did almost any other adjective she could conjure up. "Wow. Just wow."

"Good. That's what Kat was apparently going for. She brought it. Saved me from scary dress shopping." Allie did a slow spin. The gown hugged her in all the right places. Closely. Jackson would probably swallow his tongue.

"Jackson knows, right?" How had she lived with Allie for over six months and had no idea she was planning a surprise wedding?

Allie laughed. "That he's getting married today? Yes, he definitely knows. We decided to do it that night we had the fight about the prenup."

"Hold it right there." Allie paused midturn at Kat's command, facing the floor-length mirror set against the opposite wall. On the table beside Allie was an extensive assortment of hair and makeup tools that Kat had turned her attention to.

"Hold still." Kat stood back and peered at Allie, then picked up the world's smallest makeup brush from her kit and started doing precise strokes along Allie's jawline like an artist painting a canvas.

"How do you feel?" Emelia sagged down into an upholstered chair by the door. Jackson and Allie were getting married. Today. She'd somehow found herself in the middle of a surprise wedding. Of all the crazy things.

"Happy." Allie paused. She scrunched her nose at herself in the mirror, then looked at Emelia in the reflection. "A little weird."

"About?"

"Getting married again. I kind of expected to be scared or something after it went so badly wrong last time."

"And you're not?"

Allie grinned radiantly as Kat stepped back again and put the brush down. "Not even a little. I want to kick myself for planning an evening wedding. What was I thinking? I could have been married by now!"

"Easy, tiger, you'll be Mrs. Gregory soon enough." Kat shook her head as she dabbed something across Allie's forehead. She stepped back and studied her charge. "And we're done. Now it's your turn." Kat turned her gaze on Emelia.

"Me?" What was she talking about? Her makeup was done. Her hair wasn't perfect, but it was passable.

"Look, no offense, because you're really quite good for a makeup Muggle, but I just can't let you go to the wedding like that. It's against my moral code."

"But, I'm not anyone."

"Quite the opposite. Plus it's really your public duty."

"Huh?"

"We still have twenty minutes, and look at her." Kat gestured at Allie, who was spinning around in her dress. Bubbly as a bottle of champagne and as giddy as if she'd drunk one when, as far as Emelia knew, all she'd had to drink was some sparkling water. "If you don't give us a reason to stay here, then she'll be the first bride in history to be standing at the altar before the groom or the guests."

"Are you going to do her up?" Allie had just clicked into the conversation. "Oh, you have to. Peter will be taken out at the knees when he sees you." Allie grimaced at her words. "Sorry, I know it's complicated. Not helping, am I?"

Well, she wasn't exactly going to turn down being made up by the magician in front of her. And if Peter got taken out at the knees . . . Emelia clamped down on a smile, but not before Kat saw it and let out a low whistle. "I'm always happy to give a fledgling romance a shove. Just ask Allie."

"We're just friends."

Kat grinned. "Well, that's a bonus. Jackson and Allie couldn't stand each other when they met." She pulled out a cloth and poured something from a large bottle onto it. "Sit down." She gestured to the end of the bed. "Let me work my magic."

Fifteen minutes later, Emelia stared at herself in the mirror Kat held up to her face with a flourish.

"Wow." She could barely get the word out; she was too entranced with the girl staring back at her with big eyes, pouty lips, and a flawless complexion. It was like an airbrushed version of herself.

Her hair had been pinned loosely up and tendrils floated

around her face. Her natural waves, which never took instruction or direction, had somehow been tamed into something elegant yet sexy. Her eyes and lips combined to look classy but alluring.

At least she would get to enjoy today at her best. Peter had promised her a dance and she intended to savor every last moment in his arms. She was going to remember every look, every word, every moment of magic. No regrets. She'd probably kiss him again if she got the opportunity. Call her crazy. Or stupid. Or naïve. Or foolish. But soon enough she'd have to tell Peter the truth about who she was, and it would all be over.

She was on death row. It was just that no one else knew.

"Emelia?" From the way Allie said it, it wasn't the first time she'd said her name. "I've just realized we've left the bouquets downstairs. In the kitchen. Can you grab them and bring them up? You can take the back stairs at the end of the hall down to the kitchen."

"Okay." Following Allie's instructions, Emelia made short work of navigating down what must have been the old servants' stairs to the main kitchen. Dodging caterers bustling around with trays, she made her way to a sideboard where two bouquets of peonies sat. She nestled the two bunches in the crook of her arm and inhaled in their light floral scent.

Making it back to the second floor, she breathed a sigh of relief as she started down the hallway toward Allie's room.

"Please tell me I'm wrong about what I fear I'm seeing." The haughty voice came from a small alcove to the right.

Emelia flinched, then turned. Allie's mother. How could she have missed seeing the sparkles? She'd only met her at the beginning of the party and it had taken all of thirty seconds to work out what Allie meant when she said her family situation was complicated. The woman had all the warmth of an iceberg. "Mrs. Shire? Are you looking for something?"

"I prefer some privacy when I go to the bathroom, so I came up to our suite." Veronica took a step toward Emelia, her eyes narrow. Her silver dress glittered as she moved. All that Emelia could think was that somewhere a nightclub needed its disco ball back. "Don't try to change the subject."

"I'm afraid I don't know what you're talking about."

"I think you do." Veronica stepped forward and rested a perfectly manicured nail on the blooms. "Let's start with the fact that peonies are Allison's favorite flowers. Add in that they are predominantly a spring and early summer flower and we are into autumn. Factor in that those look extraordinarily like the kind of bouquets a person might carry at, say . . . a wedding?" Veronica tapped her elongated nail against her perfectly painted lip. "But I'm being very foolish, aren't I? Because there is absolutely no way my daughter is getting married today. Not before her latest fiancé has signed the prenup. I assume you've heard of Allison's propensity to fall in love with gold diggers."

Jackson? A gold digger? Emelia would have laughed aloud at the ridiculousness of it all if it wasn't for the fact that the woman's face told her that Jackson and Allie's almost perfectly executed plan was about to go up in smoke.

Peter rounded the top of the stairs, his mind still reeling from the news Jackson had just landed on him. A surprise wedding. He had to hand it to them. It was going to be a surprise all right. At least it was a much better one than seeing his brother here, the plus-one to a brunette who looked at him with adoring eyes. The girl had to be a friend of Allie's, but Peter didn't know her from Eve.

Emelia and Allie's mother stood in the hallway. Emelia held two large bunches of flowers and her face suggested she was trying not to panic. Emelia was in on this too? He couldn't see Veronica's face but from the ramrod set of her back and the pointed finger she was waving around, he guessed they weren't talking about the nice autumn weather.

"Is everything okay, ladies?"

Emelia gave him a look of relief that almost melted him. "Mrs. Shire is, um . . ."

"Going to put a stop to this nonsense."

Peter tried not to squint. The woman's blinged-out dress could have made a blind man see. "I'm sorry?"

"Don't play dumb with me, young man. I know you're in cahoots on this travesty too."

Peter felt his protective instincts rise. "If by 'travesty' you mean a beautiful wedding where two of my friends get to pledge their lives to each other, then yes, proudly so."

"I demand to be taken to my daughter." The woman spat out the words like nails.

Peter glanced at Emelia, who mouthed the words "no way" at him. He thought quickly. He knew the house well. Before it had been sold and converted it belonged to the parents of an old school friend.

One possible solution came to mind. If he had the nerve to do it. He let his shoulders slump, as if defeated. "Of course. I'll take you to her right now."

Emelia just gaped for a second, which Veronica seemed to take as a sign of victory.

He gestured. "After you."

Veronica started stalking down the hall. Peter followed close behind, scanning the doors to the right for the one he was looking for. It had been a coat closet that led to a large windowless linen cupboard back in the day. He couldn't imagine the hotel would have found another use for the space. He searched his memory for whether there was a lock on it but came up blank. If not, well, he'd have to stand there and hold it shut. Jackson and Allie had not spent months planning a surprise wedding for it all to be ruined now. Not on his watch.

He found the door and almost gaped in disbelief at a gold key glinting from the lock. "In here. There's a short hallway first." He gave a quick knock, then turned the knob and pushed open the door.

Veronica stepped through the doorway. "Allison Marie Shire." Her voice was sharp enough to cut glass. As soon as she stepped past the door, Peter slammed it back into the doorframe and turned the key.

Peter pocketed the key as Veronica Shire thumped on the door from the other side. Yelling words that were thankfully muffled by the thick oak door.

Emelia stared up at him, eyeballs goggling like something out of a cartoon. "Did you just . . just . . . lock the mother of the bride in a closet?"

"Of course not!" He patted his pocket just to double-check the key was still in there. "It's a bit larger than that. She'll be perfectly comfortable for the next fifteen minutes or so until the ceremony."

Laughter burst out of Emelia. Her face was transformed by her grin as her shoulders jumped up and down with the force of her mirth, bouquets bouncing along with them. "Oh, I love you."

The words dropped between them. Peter froze as Emelia blushed. "I mean, I love that you did that."

"I think I liked the first one better." His voice was husky, his heart feeling like it was about to break out of the jail his ribs were holding it in.

They stared at each other, the air between them charged. He wouldn't have been surprised if he'd lifted his hand and received an electric shock.

He'd done it. He'd gone and fallen in love with the one girl he shouldn't. Every direction from here just held hurt. But when she stood in front of him and looked at him like that, he wanted to ignore everything and be one of those crazy fools who hoped their fundamental differences would just magically sort themselves out.

"I just . . ."

"I thought . . ."

"We should . . ."

Their words clashed together, neither of them quite able to get out anything coherent.

"There you are, Emelia." A voice came from beyond them. Kat stopped a few feet away, and her head turned from one of them to the other. "Oops, sorry. I've clearly interrupted a moment. That's kind of my specialty. Just ask Allie." Striding up, she grabbed Emelia's wrist and tugged. "Don't worry. I'm sure you two will be able to pick it up again later. This is a wedding after all. Can you go let Jackson know we're ready? He's in room two oh eight." Kat looked at Peter.

"Um, sure." The words were barely out of Peter's mouth before the girls had disappeared into a room just a few doors down.

Peter shook his head as he turned to find Jackson's room. At least two people would be getting their happy ending today. Emelia's "I love you" changed everything. Except the one thing that really mattered.

Thirty-Nine

"Ladies and gentlemen, please welcome Mr. and Mrs. Gregory for their first dance."

Peter forced his eyes up from his dessert plate and onto the married couple. He had to at least pretend to be interested, even though the thought of watching Jackson and Allie all wrapped around each other in their little love cocoon was more than he could stand.

Jackson led his bride onto the floor, unable to keep his eyes off her as the band opened with a Michael Bublé song.

Peter pinched the bridge of his nose as Jackson took Allie in his arms. He'd had it all under control. Had managed to force all his feelings for Emelia into a box. Then she'd said she loved him. Followed by Jackson's springing a reading on him; he'd found himself standing in front of two hundred people reading the Song of Solomon, staring right at her.

> *Place me like a seal over your heart, like a seal on your arm, for love is as strong as death, its jealousy unyielding as the grave. It burns like blazing fire, like a mighty flame. Many waters cannot quench love; rivers cannot sweep it away.*

The verses were branded in his mind. Emelia had been shanghaied into a reading too. A haunting poem by Tolkien. They had been allocated seats next to each other for the ceremony. The whole time his hand itching with his wanting to take hers.

Not fair, God.

The only good thing about their sitting next to each other was that it had prevented him from spending the entire time ogling her like a thirteen-year-old boy at his first mixed dance.

He'd managed to avoid her for the rest of the evening. During the mingling after the service, the canapés and cocktails, he was aware of where she was at every moment.

Like right now. She was standing on the other side of the room, talking to an elegant blonde. He couldn't have stopped himself from noticing the way Emelia's red gown hugged her curves in all the right places if his life depended on it.

His avoidance was all well and good, but he owed her a dance. Had claimed one earlier in the day. And he might have been many things, but someone who went back on his word wasn't one of them. The only way he was going to manage a dance without his defenses crumbling would be major divine intervention.

"Seriously, go talk to her already."

"Excuse me?" He turned toward the voice and saw Kat dropping into the chair beside him. Her full skirt billowed around her like she'd parachuted in.

Kat pointed a well-manicured nail across the room. "Emelia. For the sake of all of us in this room, stop looking at her like a bereft puppy and go talk to her."

"That bad, huh?"

Kat rolled her eyes. "Dude, you read the Song of Solomon

to her. The entire congregation would have had to be blind not to have noticed. So, yeah, that bad."

"It's . . . complicated."

"Why? Are you already married?"

"What? No."

"Excellent. I'm pretty sure she isn't, which makes you streets ahead of where Allie and Jackson started. Don't make me tip you out of your chair."

"Anyone ever told you you're bossy?"

She smiled serenely. "All the time."

Peter ran his hand through his hair. What was he even nervous about? This was Emelia. The girl who had fallen out of a wardrobe on him. Who'd snotted all over his favorite T-shirt. Who'd curtsied to his mother. Whom he'd drawn very clear lines with. Though that line kept getting more than a little blurred. And he was to blame.

He forced himself out of his chair. Wiping his palms on his trousers, he checked around for something, anything that he could use as an excuse to talk to her. Except the dance. That required music that was upbeat and partyish. Definitely not the slow and sultry stuff that was currently crooning out of the speakers.

Emelia didn't have a drink. Grabbing a couple of flutes off a passing tray, he headed in her direction. He had to go now, before his courage failed him.

Emelia caught his eye when he was just a few feet away and gave him the kind of smile that almost made him drop the glassware.

"Hi. Um, you looked like you could use a refill." He held out one of the glasses.

"Thanks." She took it and gestured to the woman next to

her. It had to be Allie's sister. Blond, perfectly coiffed. She was the younger version of Veronica. Except she actually looked happy to be here. Unlike her mother, who had spent the entire ceremony with the face of the funeral goer.

"Peter, this is Allie's sister, Susannah."

"Pleasure to meet you."

"You too." Susannah's gaze flickered between the two of them, and she gave a knowing smile. "Sorry to be rude, but I need to go and track down my children."

Apparently Kat was right. His mooning over Emelia from a distance had all the subtlety of a bathing suit at a black-tie ball.

Emelia looked around the room at people laughing and dancing. "I can't believe they pulled it off."

"I'm sorry I haven't spoken to you since the ceremony. I just . . . you look so beautiful, I wasn't sure I'd be able to string a sentence together."

So much for playing it cool.

"Thanks." Emelia tilted her head, a wavy lock of hair dangling across her collarbone. "I think."

She smelled good too. Like citrus and flowers and fresh sheets. He slammed the door shut in his mind before it could go there.

"So—" They both spoke at once.

"You go." Both of them again.

A moment of silence followed. Her all big eyes and open face. "It was for you."

"What was?"

"I wanted to look beautiful for you. Which is crazy, because there can't be anything between us, but . . . wow, I can't believe I said that. I feel so stupid."

He had never wanted to kiss someone so badly in his entire life. But all that would do was make everything worse. She loved him. You didn't kiss girls who loved you when you couldn't love them back. "Well, it worked."

She looked around them. "You know, sometimes, on nights like tonight, I think it might even be true."

"What?"

"The whole God thing." She gestured to where Jackson and Allie were wrapped around each other on the dance floor. "When you think about their story. Could it really just be coincidence? It all just feels too perfect, too impossible, for there not to be someone bigger behind it all."

"I know they believe that."

"But then I can't believe in a God. Because if there's a God, then He also made my mom sick and let her die. What kind of God leaves a six-year-old girl without her mother? Leaves any children without their mothers?"

Clearly not the moment to launch into a treatise on the original sin and fallen creation.

"I want to believe it all. I really do. But I don't know if I can. And I can't fake it for you."

Without his permission, his hand reached out and tucked a strand of hair behind her ear, lingering on her face. "I know. Come with me for a minute . . ."

Without allowing himself to think through what he was doing, he grabbed her hand and started walking toward the ballroom exit. He had the overwhelming urge to show her the stars, to ask her if she thought they stood there as the result of a cosmic accident.

He whisked her out a set of French doors, and they found

themselves on a side patio. The still night was broken by the sound of her heels clattering across the cobblestones beside him.

"Peter, can you slo— Oh!" A sudden jerk pulled at his arm, and he reached out instinctively as Emelia stumbled. Grabbing her around the waist, he managed to take a step to anchor himself and stop her from hitting the ground.

Her fingers grasped his upper arms. Anyone watching from inside would've thought he was doing some kind of extra-low dip.

She blinked up at him, hair dislodged and tumbling behind her. "Sorry."

"You're welcome." You're welcome? This girl was causing him to lose his grasp on his faculties. There was no recovering. He couldn't even try.

Straightening, he pulled her back to her feet. "You okay?"

"Fine. Just embarrassed. I'm really not a klutz." She peeked up from where she had ended up cradled against his chest. The stilettos that had been responsible for her fall now placed her at the perfect kissable height.

The electricity between them could have lit up Times Square. He groaned and burrowed his fingers in her wavy hair. "Em—"

"Sorry for interrupting, little brother." From out of the shadows, Victor stumbled. Peter hadn't seen him since the ceremony. Had forgotten he was even there. Emelia stepped back and turned toward the intruder. "Hi, Mia." Victor had his drunken gaze on Emelia.

The hairs on the back of Peter's neck prickled. "Her name's Emelia."

Victor shook his head in the slow, deliberate way that drunks did when they were trying to pretend they were sober. "Maybe to you, Bunny. Not to the rest of the world." Beside Peter, Emelia's whole body tensed, as if waiting for a blow. "You going to tell him, Mia, or should I?"

"I—"

Victor cut her off with a smirk. "She's Mia Caldwell, little bro. You've been duped."

His brother really was drunk. The photo Peter had seen of the tabloid reporter looked nothing like Emelia. Mia Caldwell was blond, with a know-it-all smirk.

"You're out of your mind." Just like any other Saturday night. Not even the raft of charges he had pending against him had curbed his drinking.

He turned to Emelia to apologize. But the expression on her face stopped him cold. It wasn't confusion. Or pity. Or even repulsion. But one of someone who had been cornered. Found out. Her gaze locked on his.

"I'm so sorry." The words whispered from her lips. The same ones that just a few seconds before he'd been considering kissing.

"No." He shook his head. "You can't be. It's not possible."

He must have misunderstood. She was apologizing for something else. He waited for her denial, for her to say she had no idea what Victor was talking about.

"I-I . . . ," Emelia sputtered, her beautiful eyes glowing with tears that betrayed the truth. She straightened her shoulders and looked at him unblinking. "He's right. But you have to know that I—"

"That you're a tabloid fop." Victor slurred his accusation with a drunken grin, as if the whole scenario were funny.

"But Mia Caldwell is in LA. Still working for that paper. I get the newsfeeds." His stilted sentences splintered in the cool evening air.

Emelia closed her eyes for a second. "It's a different reporter using my old byline. Has been since I left. I had no idea until that day on your porch."

Peter stepped away from her. From Victor. The cold truth set like a block of ice in his stomach.

"You killed Anita. She's dead because of you."

She flinched but didn't deny it. "I'm sorry."

That was it. Two lone words. No explanation. No real apology. "How dare you." Repulsion surged through him, wiping away whatever he'd felt a few seconds before. "Is anything about you true? Or is it all just a cover? What do you want? Get close to Anita's grieving family? Do some kind of exposé on them?" Had all of it been a lie? Had he spent the last seven months being played for a fool?

"No." Her face was panicked. Her hands gripped the front of her dress, scrunching it in between her fingers. "I'm not a reporter. I quit right after her death. I swear someone else has been using my byline. Just look at the photos. It's not me."

Peter stepped back. Put even more distance between them. "Like I'm going to believe anything you say. You make me sick."

"I'm so, so sorry." A sheen slicked her eyes. No doubt that was fake too.

"'Sorry' doesn't raise someone from the dead. 'Sorry' doesn't give my aunt and uncle their daughter back." He said the last few words so violently, they flew out and splattered across her face. She flinched.

"Sorry" didn't take away the guilt he'd been carrying for the last ten months.

"Steady on." A hand clamped over his shoulder. He saw Jackson out of the corner of his eye. Allie stood just behind him, her eyes wide. At some point in the last few minutes, they'd gained an audience.

"She killed Anita."

"Anita killed herself." Allie's words were soft and did nothing to pierce through his fury.

"Because of her." Peter stabbed a finger at Emelia, Mia, whatever her name was, before storming away into the darkness.

Three strikes and she was out. Three seconds to go from possibility to devastation.

"You okay?" Allie stood beside her but didn't touch her. As if knowing that if she did, Emelia might shatter like a crystal vase hitting a concrete floor. Of all the places, it had to happen here. Lacey was right. Karma finally got her.

"I ruined your wedding. I'm so sorry."

"Don't be crazy. Here. Sit." Allie gestured to a nearby set of patio furniture that Emelia hadn't even noticed. She'd been too busy being wrapped up in Peter's arms. Now hers were cold, bare, exposed. Just like her.

Allie pulled out a chair with a scrape and tugged Emelia's elbow until she sat down.

They were the only ones left on the patio. Victor had disappeared back into the shadows. Where he belonged. Jackson had obviously had the good sense to make himself scarce.

Emelia's back collapsed into the chair's canvas covering.

She was so stupid. Stupid to think that, even here, her mistakes wouldn't find her. Stupid to hope she'd be able to escape her past. But, most of all, stupid, stupid, stupid to let herself wish for one second for what she could never have with Peter. Like a fool, she'd even said she loved him.

Her hands plucked at her red dress, bunching it up between her fingers, the fabric running like blood when she let it go. Deep scarlet, like a wound. How appropriate.

Her hair had come loose at some point, and now the wind flung it around her face as if trying to hide her shame for her. She grabbed a handful with one hand and used the other to feel for some bobby pins in the mess to pin it back. Her fingers grasped at a couple, and she pinned enough hair off her face that she could see.

Allie sat across from her, but where she expected to see judgment and condemnation reflected in her green eyes, Emelia only saw concern.

"I'm so sorry about your wedding."

Allie batted her words away with one hand. "What are you even talking about? We're married. The reception is almost finished. The only thing you ruined was the inappropriate-in-front-of-children kiss Jackson was spiriting me outside for. And there will be plenty of those in his future."

The girl was either the most serene bride Emelia had ever met, or she was seriously hopped up on the love drug, sitting with the girl accused of killing her friend's cousin like they were talking about the weather.

"So are you Mia or Emelia?"

Emelia let out a wry smile. "Both. Emelia is my name. Mia was what I wrote under as a reporter."

"Caldwell?"

"My mother's maiden name."

"Huh." Allie didn't say anything more. Just sat there, staring at the stars as if she had all the time in the world. Or was a Michelangelo statue. The only thing that gave her away was a slight shiver in the moonlight.

"Want to tell me what just happened?" Allie's tone was casual. Anyone else would have been burning up with curiosity, already pumping her for all the details.

"How do you do that? Make it sound like you really don't care one way or the other?"

"Oh, I care. I also know what it's like to have a hurt so deep that just talking about it feels like ripping open the wound again. When Victor called you Mia, I could see on your face that you do too."

"I never, ever meant to hurt her. If I'd had any idea . . ." Emelia's voice trailed off. It wasn't entirely true. She may not have meant to hurt Anita, but no one could become the kind of reporter she'd been without knowing the impact they could have on people's lives.

"Anita had been unwell for a long time." Allie shifted in her seat.

"Did you know her?"

"I met her once when she was back here visiting. In passing. I'd just arrived in England. It was a month or so before she died." Allie drummed her fingers on the table for a few seconds, thinking. "She came to a quiz night at the pub. She'd had too much to drink. One second she was flying high, the next crying her heart out. Peter mentioned later on she'd had addiction issues since she was a teenager. Had been in and out of rehab for years, but the family had managed to keep it quiet. Protected her wholesome image. I remember thinking that you could have all the beauty, brains, and money in the world, but it really didn't matter if you were hooked on booze, or drugs, or whatever your vice might be."

"I wasn't even there that night because of her. It was just pure chance that she was there. I'd heard a rumor that CeCe McCall might be there." But the A-list starlet was nowhere to be seen when Emelia had arrived.

She took a deep breath. "Anita was in the VIP room."

The scene she would never forget. She could still close her eyes and hear the thump of the bass in the song that was playing, the darkness splintered by the strobe light, the crush of bodies, alcohol on people's breath, guys getting closer to her than required as they squeezed past. And then there Anita was, snorting up a line of cocaine that was being cut for her by Victor. No different from half the room. Almost everyone snorted, swallowed, or shot something in those rich party-circles.

"It wouldn't have been a story if she was anyone else. But when you're engaged to an heir to billions who's a famous anti-drug campaigner and you've been sold as his straitlaced fiancée who's committed to clean living and yoga? That's a story." Especially when you were in possession of a high-tech camera that could take a photo in the dreariest of nightclubs and turn it as clear as day.

"Two days later, the front page of the *Star Tribune* was my photo of her snorting cocaine through a hundred-dollar bill. The day after that, Logan announced the end of their engagement, and the morning after that she was dead." The girl had enough booze and pills in her system to take out an NFL linebacker. The speed at which everything had unfolded still, almost a year later, left Emelia dizzy.

"No one knew whether to call it a tragic accident or suicide. I didn't go in to work for three days. When I returned, there was an email from Anita from hours before she died. All it said was, 'This should make you happy. See you on the other side.'"

Against her boss's wishes, Emelia had turned it over to the police. Then she'd quit. Then she'd decided to come here, figuring she might as well use the one thing her mother had left her—British citizenship—to run away, to try reinventing herself.

"So. There you have it. She's dead because of me."

Allie propped her elbows on the table between them and leaned forward. "No. She's dead because she had a lot of issues. She's dead because she decided to make some poor decisions. You can't take her choices onto you. Sure, your story didn't help, but she was heading for disaster when I met her. If it wasn't your story, it would've been something else."

"Or it might not have been. She might've gotten some help. Sorted herself out. She was only twenty-four. Plenty of people make bad decisions in their twenties and turn out to be fine."

"Or she might've walked out of another nightclub one night smashed out of her mind, gotten into her car, and plowed into an innocent family. Ever think about that? Ever wonder who might be alive right now because you did expose her?"

Emelia stared at Allie, struck dumb. The thought had never crossed her mind, the idea that the horrible events that had led to Anita's taking her life might have preempted something even worse. It bounced around her brain, trying to find a place to settle, but it was too crazy.

Allie ran a hand through her hair, grimacing as she hit a bobby pin. "Here's the thing. You'll never know which it would've been.

Probably neither. Probably something completely different. But you can't carry Anita around with you for the rest of your life. You have to forgive yourself for your part. As brutal as it sounds, she is dead. But you are not. If you carry this around with you your whole life, this takes out two people, not one."

"How did you get so wise?"

Allie smiled wryly. "By making some really, really bad choices. But here's the thing, Em. God can find a way to redeem even the worst of choices, if you let Him. If I hadn't made mine, I never would have met Jackson. If Jackson hadn't made his, he never would have met me."

"You really think God cares about you that much?"

"I know He does."

Emelia turned the concept over in her mind, trying to reconcile this idea of a God who could take the worst things in your life and use them to lead you to something good. But she couldn't. It clashed so deeply with the God she thought existed. If there was one at all. The one who'd left her abandoned as a little girl. Who'd let her get cheated out of her dream career. Who'd never done anything for her. Everything she had was something she'd achieved for herself. "Peter hates me."

"He sure might think he does right now. But he doesn't. He will be deeply hurt. Anita was like the little sister he never had. He was distraught when she died. It hasn't even been a year."

"I don't know how to fix it."

"You probably can't."

Truer words were never stated. Emelia glanced to her right and saw Jackson standing just inside the patio doors, waiting for his bride. She tilted her head in his direction. "You need to go."

Allie looked over her shoulder, and her face lit up even as she said, "It's okay, he can wait."

"No! Go!"

Allie gave her a long look. "You going to be okay? Call me if you need anything. Anything."

Emelia managed a half-convincing laugh. "I'll be fine. I am not going to call you on your honeymoon!"

Allie got to her feet, silk rustling around her. "I love my husband, but three weeks of talking to just each other will drive us both batty. I give us three days before one of us is annoyed about the other squeezing the toothpaste wrong." She leaned down to give Emelia a brief hug as she passed by. "I'll see you when I get back. Hang in there. You never know what might happen." And then she was gone in a whirl of cream and a hint of floral perfume.

You never know what might happen. Well, it would take a miracle to make things right with Peter. And miracles never happened. Especially not for her.

Forty

Emelia walked into the office, everything aching from a sleepless night. In her purse sat her resignation letter. Neatly typed and dated. It was over.

Entering her office for the last time, she strode around her desk and put her bag down. She hadn't even bothered to bring a box. For the most part the room was as bare and impersonal as it had been the day she arrived. Opening the bottom desk drawer, she fished out a spare pair of heels and pantyhose she'd kept there for emergencies. Moving to the middle drawer, she grabbed a couple cans of tuna. Finally the top drawer. Two packs of gum and a couple of her own pens.

That was it. All she had to show for the entirety of the seven months she'd worked at SpringBoard. Reaching into her purse, she pulled out a fat folder that she'd spent all of Sunday working on. Inside it, sheets of A4 detailed everything anyone would need to know about the ball.

The hard stuff was done. Anyone with half a brain could follow her checklist over the next two months for the tasks that remained.

It would probably be Peter. Flipping open the cover, she uncapped a black pen, poised it over the page, and paused. Sighing. She put the cap back on. There was nothing she could say that would change anything. Everything she needed to know had been written across his face on Saturday night.

"Write a novel over the weekend?" Elizabeth leaned against the doorway.

One look at her steady, knowing eyes was all the confirmation she required. "I need to give you this." Emelia plucked the envelope out of her purse and walked around the desk, holding it in front of her.

Elizabeth looked at it but didn't take it. "Why don't we talk first. In my office." It wasn't a suggestion.

Emelia followed her heels as they clicked down the corridor. Walking into Elizabeth's office, she saw they weren't alone. John Simons, the chair of the board, sat in a second chair that had been brought in.

The door closed behind Elizabeth like a jail cell.

"So." The older man leaned back in his chair, hands folded over his stomach. "Would you prefer to be called Mia or Emelia?"

"Emelia, sir."

She looked to where Elizabeth had settled herself behind her desk. Emelia still held the envelope in her hand. She offered it to Mr. Simons.

He also just looked at it. "What's that?"

"My resignation, sir. Effective immediately."

"We don't want it."

He could not have shocked Emelia more if he'd taken a cattle prod to her. "You don't?"

"We don't," Elizabeth confirmed.

"But I lied and I . . ." She trailed off.

"Did you actually lie? Or did you just not tell us the whole truth?"

"I didn't tell you the whole truth. I knew you wouldn't hire me if I did."

John nodded. "And you're right." He leaned forward, his chair creaking. "Peter called me yesterday morning. I'll be honest, when I heard what he had to say, my first instinct was to sack you on the spot. But Elizabeth and I had a long conversation last night and there was one question that we kept coming back to."

"Yes?"

"Why are you here?"

"I read that SpringBoard was hemorrhaging donors. I just . . . I had to help."

"And we decided we want you to finish what you started."

"I can't."

"Emelia." Elizabeth spoke the words softly. "Anita would want you to do it."

Emelia looked at her kind eyes. "Really?"

"She, more than anyone else, believed in second chances. She had her struggles but she was kind and generous. She would want you to have your second chance."

A tear tripped over Emelia's cheek.

"But you need to know something. Even if the ball is a huge success, even if you achieve what you came here to do, I don't think you're going to find the atonement you're looking for here."

Forty-One

Emelia fingered the ship in her hands, holding it carefully as she examined it from all angles. It seemed perfect. Apart from the hairline crack running around the middle of the boat that couldn't be completely hidden, you'd never have known it was the same one that had shattered on Peter's floor.

She nestled it back into the padded box that sat on the passenger seat of Allie's car and drew in a deep breath. This wasn't a big deal. She was just going to leave it on Peter's doorstep. She'd checked the schedule, and he would still be at the rowing club for a couple of hours teaching. There was no chance he'd be home. She'd never met his roommate, so if he happened to be there, she could just give him the box and run.

She climbed out of the car and crossed to the passenger side. Reaching in, she picked up the box and closed the door with a swing of her hip.

Up the path, put it down, and get back to the car. The whole thing should take less than thirty seconds. She strode up the path, climbed the six steps to the front door, and paused.

She'd decided not to leave a note with it because, really, what was there left to say?

She rested her head for a second on the front door, only for it to swing open at her touch. "Argh!" She stumbled forward over the stoop, the box crushed to her chest.

Hands grabbed her elbows, steadying her.

Please let it be anyone but him. Please let it be anyone but him.

The fingers released her arms like they were hot coals. "What are you doing here?"

Of course it was. She chanced a glance up. "You look horrible." It was true. He was even whiter than usual, never good for a redhead, with glazed eyes and a sheen across his forehead. "Are you okay?"

"Thanks." Even though he'd let go of her arms, the box was still wedged between them. "I have the flu. I heard footsteps and thought you were my Panadol and Gatorade delivery.

"What are you—" His words ended as he saw into the box. "Is that my . . ." He trailed off as he studied the boat, then leaned down to look more closely.

"I didn't think you'd be home. I was just planning to leave it on your doorstep." She pushed the box toward his torso so he was forced to take it, then stepped back.

"I . . . don't know what to say." Placing the box on the hallway table beside them, he carefully lifted out the model and studied it. "How did you do this?"

"I didn't. But I found someone who could. It was precious to you, so I . . ." She trailed off too, unable to find words to bridge the distance her deceit had created.

"Thank you." His gaze softened for a second. "Um, I should probably put it back. My hands aren't too steady at the moment." He placed the boat back into its packaging before turning to face her again.

"I'm sorry I ruined everything. I'm sorry I lied. I'm sorry about Anita. More sorry than you could know." The words tumbled out of her.

He didn't say anything.

"I should go." She took a backward step toward the threshold.

Feet pounded behind her. "Sorry I took so long. I ran into Brett in town—" An expletive. "What are you doing here?"

Emelia closed her eyes for a moment. Seriously? Could she not catch a break? Not even when she was trying to do a good thing?

Victor shouldered past her, pushing her into the door. Turning, he stood between her and Peter. "You've got some nerve coming here after what you did."

She was not taking this. She would silently take whatever Peter dished out, but she was not taking anything from Victor.

"After what *I* did? That's a bit rich coming from you, of all people."

Victor flinched and turned a lighter shade. "You wrote the story. That's what drove her to the edge."

"I didn't know she had addiction issues. No clue about her being in and out of rehab. Unlike you. Great *cousin* you are." She spat the word into his face.

Over his shoulder she saw Peter's face. Confused. Bewildered.

Oh. Understanding hit. "He doesn't know, does he?" She nodded her head at Peter.

"What is she talking about?"

"Nothing. You know you can't trust a word Mia says." Victor threw her name in with a sneer, but it was impossible to miss the desperation in his eyes.

"It's Emelia." She said the words through gritted teeth.

"What. Is. She. Talking. About." Peter's words came out staccato. Individual verbal bullets aimed at his brother.

Emelia turned toward him. Poor guy. But since she had nothing to lose, she might as well tell him the whole ugly truth. "You want to hold me responsible for Anita's death, I don't blame you. I blame myself. But you might want to ask your brother who she was with that night. Who's the owner of the hand in the photo that cut her line?"

Who's the owner of the hand in the photo that cut her line? Emelia's words shot through Peter's ears and into his heart like a laser.

Worse. For everything she hadn't told the truth about, he could tell by the look on her face that on this one thing—this one, life-changing thing—she was.

Which meant . . . He grabbed Victor by his shoulder and swung him around. "You. Were. There." He could barely get the words out through his clenched jaw.

All the holes he had dug his brother out of. All the times he had taken the blame for him to try to keep his name in the clear. The lifetime's worth of guilt Victor had heaped on him and he'd accepted, for the accident that had marred his brother's face forever.

"Hey." Victor held his hands up in an attempted gesture of innocence. "Look, all I did was slice it up for her. She already had it when I got there. If I didn't, someone else would've."

Peter stared at his brother. Of everything he'd thought Victor capable of, something like this had never crossed his mind. He'd believed him without question when he'd said he wasn't even there that evening. That the last he'd seen of her had been a couple of days before and she'd been fine.

"She'd been out of rehab for five days. Five!"

His brother rolled his eyes. "I hate to break it to you, Bunny, but Neets wasn't our cute little cousin in pigtails anymore. She was a big girl." There was something about Victor's words that made Peter think he was trying to convince himself as much as anyone else. Maybe it would have been okay if Victor had stopped there, but he had to keep talking. "I wasn't her chaperone, or her conscience. At least I got her out of there before she landed herself in a stranger's bed. She got around, did our—*oof!*"

Peter's first punch was a direct hit to his brother's torso. As Victor instinctively doubled over, Peter brought his fist up into his nose. Blood spurted, drops hitting the wooden floor and splattering like violent starbursts.

"Stop it!" Emelia's scream reached his ears about the same time his brother barreled into him. They both went down, Peter's head cracking the floor, his vision shattering for a second. Which was all it took for Victor to take his second strike, a well-aimed knee to the groin. This time it was like the entire galaxy exploded in his head.

"About time, little bro. Not the good guy anymore, are we?" Victor's grunted words cut through the haze as Peter grabbed him by the front of his T-shirt and threw him backward. The hall table flipped over and landed with a crash by the door.

"Stop it! *Stop it!*" Emelia's screaming was loud enough to wake a coma patient.

In the seconds it took for the two brothers to get back to

their feet, puffing, Victor swearing a blue streak, she had managed to dart between the two of them.

"Get out of the way, Em."

There was no way they could get at each other in the narrow hallway without involving her. He certainly didn't trust his brother to let that stop him. Not after what the last few minutes had revealed.

"Why? So you two can beat each other to death? Not a chance." She shook her head with the determination that had drawn him to her in the first place.

"Em, get out of the way. Please." Desperation tinged his words.

"I'd listen to what Bunny says. You really don't want to be in the middle of this."

Emelia didn't even look at Victor. Her eyes stayed fixed on Peter. Bad move. Because of the two of them, only one played dirty. He saw Victor's foot start moving, aimed at her ankles.

"E—" He didn't even manage to get a single syllable out of his mouth before she had spun around, grabbed his brother by one arm, and flipped him over her back. A guy at least twice her weight and almost totally muscle. Victor landed on the floor with a smack, opening his eyes to find her heel poised above his groin.

"Try that again, clever guy, and you will never have children. Not that that would be such a great loss to the world."

Victor was silent, staring at her with a vicious glare. But he didn't move so much as a finger.

"No? I didn't think so." She took a couple of steps back toward Peter. "Now get out."

Victor clambered to his feet. For a split second, Peter caught something that might have been remorse or regret flashing across his face. But it was gone in an instant, replaced with his usual haughty expression. He didn't say a word as he backed across the threshold, slamming the door behind him.

"That's going to need some ice." Emelia put a light finger to his cheek. Peter just stared at her, still dazed. "How many fingers can you see?" She held up three fingers and moved them from left to right.

"What . . . how did you do that?" It was like something from a movie. Except in his hallway. Was any of this real? Or had he just fallen asleep on his couch and this was all a dream?

She gave a sad smile. "Occupational hazard. Martial arts training comes in handy when you have a job that makes you enemies by the week. How many fingers?" She did the same again. This time with four.

"Four."

"Any double vision?"

"No, I'm fine." The truth was the feeling of a thousand knives slicing through his groin was making him want to curl up in the fetal position and weep like a little boy, but he was hardly going to tell her that.

He looked at the ground and saw it was covered with splinters of wood. The hall table he'd flipped was intact, so what was . . . oh. He slid down the wall until he sat on the floor amid the ruins of the *Dawn Treader*. He picked up two tiny pieces of mast. For some crazy reason, he tried to piece them together, like the rest of the ship hadn't been blown to smithereens all over the floor.

They didn't fit. So he tried again, stabbing the two tiny segments together like he could make them connect through sheer force of will.

What had he done? What had Victor done?

"They won't fit." His words echoed in the hall.

Emelia's fingers wrapped around his as she knelt in front of him. She took the two pieces from his hands, studied them for a second, then folded them into her fist. "I guess some things are just meant to be broken."

Forty-Two

Well, that went well. She'd caused a brawl between brothers and the *Treader* was back in a million pieces. No one could say she did things by halves.

Emelia's phone rang as she drove up to her house. She pulled up at the curb and answered the call. "Aren't you supposed to be on your honeymoon?"

"I am." Allie laughed. "Italy. I've sent Jackson to go find some sports to watch. Told you we'd only last three days before we got sick of each other."

"It's been over two weeks."

"Has it?" Allie sounded genuinely surprised.

Emelia leaned her head against the headrest. The two weeks may have felt like two minutes to Allie but they had felt like two years to her.

"I guess we'll see you soon then."

"I've started packing." If worst came to worst she could just go stay at a backpackers' hostel until the ball was over. She didn't have much.

"Why?"

"I just . . . assumed you and Jackson would want the house to yourselves when you get back." Allie's contract at Oxford had been extended for another year and she definitely wouldn't want to be sharing four walls with the besotted newlyweds.

"Don't be silly. We're going to base ourselves out of Cambridge while we work out what Jackson is going to do with himself. We've got his apartment there and I'll just commute for the first term. Stay a few nights a week at our house when it doesn't make sense to go home."

Allie's blithe tone made it sound like it was no big deal when it was. Emelia couldn't have been more wrong about one thing. Allie hadn't abandoned her when she found out the truth. "Why would you do that for me?"

"Because you deserve good things. No matter how much you struggle to believe it."

"Peter doesn't want anything to do with me." Emelia's voice betrayed her with a wobble.

"Peter needs a bullet." At least that was what it sounded like Allie muttered under her breath.

"Sorry?"

"Nothing. Just an expression from home."

"I just took the *Treader* over to his house. I never should have gone. He and Victor got in a fight. It got smashed again. Everything I touch goes bad."

"That's not true. That fight has been waiting to happen for years. Just give him time. He has a lot to get his head around."

Emelia sighed. "Not that it matters anyway. Even if he could somehow get beyond all of that, I still don't believe the same as he does. That's the dealbreaker. I've gotta be honest, Al. Between you and Jackson and Peter I was beginning to wonder if there might be something there. I know it's not fair but if Peter can't forgive me, then it's kind of impossible to believe in the

God he says does. At this point, I'm going to need an unmistakable sign. I'm talking like writing-on-the-wall, booming-voice kind of stuff."

Allie sighed. "Don't equate Peter with God. Believing in God doesn't make a person perfect. We're still just as prone to messing up and doing the wrong thing as everyone else."

"It doesn't really matter anyway. Lacey called this morning. She thinks she can get me some freelancing work with her firm. After the ball."

"Are you going to take it?"

"I don't know. It's not like I have anything keeping me here once the ball is over." That was what she'd come for. She'd never actually thought about what would happen after.

She asked a question that had been bugging her. She wasn't going to get an answer from the one person she really wanted to hear it from. "That teacup. In his mom's collection. Was it really the same one that was in the wardrobe that night?"

"What do you think?"

What did she think? The truth was she'd been trying not to think about it. Because if she thought too much, connected the wardrobe with the teacup, with Peter's being there, with the mysterious notice that Allie never put up, it all started pointing to a rather uncomfortable reality. "I've gotta go, Al. I'll see you when you get back."

Getting out of the car, she set the alarm and headed up the path. "You heard that, right? Writing on the wall, big booming voice, something really unmissable." She directed her words to the sky. Nothing came back except the sounds of birds and the cool fall wind rustling leaves.

Well, that was that, then.

Sitting on the porch was a square cardboard box.

Getting closer, she saw that her name was on it, written in cursive script. No address. No postage. It had obviously been hand-delivered.

Sitting on the porch, Emelia picked it up and turned it around. No return address. No sign of who or where it had come from.

She put it down, then reached her fingers inside the gap and released the tape. Lifting the lid, she peered inside to see a small, rectangular card with bunches of cream-colored tissue paper underneath.

She picked up the envelope, slid her finger under the seal, and tried not to hold her breath as she pulled the card out. She didn't even know what she was hoping for, but she prepared herself for disappointment.

The same cursive writing was inside the card. *Emelia, This will probably sound really strange to you, but God told me this was meant to be yours, not mine. Love, Maggie.*

Lifting the tissue paper, Emelia peered inside the box, already knowing what she would find. And there it sat. The pink rose teacup.

The one that had been in the wardrobe the night she met Peter. The one that he'd been trying to find for years for his mom. The one that said more than any booming voice from the sky or writing on the wall.

"Okay." She breathed out the words. "You're real. Now what?"

Forty-Three

"*You're a hypocrite.*" The morning's wake-up phone call from Allie echoed in Peter's mind as the rising sun bounced off Highbridge.

"Have you ever thought that maybe she was exactly who she said she was? Maybe you were one of the few people she let in to see the real her? She is Emelia Mason, Peter. There's a reason that she wrote as Mia Caldwell. There's a reason she came here."

The more he let Allie's words sink in, the more he knew she was right. He had been left a trail of clues. Emelia had told him she had been called Mia back home. That she'd wanted to be an investigative journalist. Had told him multiple times she had a past he would hold against her. But, like a fool, he'd just bowled on through her assertions.

"Why on earth would she believe in a God who forgives her when you won't?"

It was Allie's final words that had propelled him out of bed and out onto the water. She was right. About all of it. Peter was a hypocrite. Anita had been playing fast and loose with life long before Emelia, Mia, whoever she was, had written that article.

His oars had cut through the water with power. About the only good thing he had going was that his rowing was the best it had been since the accident. His shoulder felt smooth and stable when he went for a big reach. But not even a good row had managed to wipe away the storm whirling inside him. So he'd gotten in the car and started driving. Found himself almost home before he even realized that was where he was going.

His feet crunched on the gravel as he let himself into the back entrance. A pot of coffee sat, still hot, on the counter, so he poured himself a large mug and took it with him on the trek to the library. His mother would be there, reading the Saturday paper, as was her habit. He could only hope she had the words he needed to help bring clarity to this whole mess. He was certainly getting nowhere on his own.

He walked down the hall, averting his eyes from the spot where he'd trapped Emelia against the wall, almost kissed her. Even his parents' house wasn't safe.

As much as Allie's telling-off from Italy had knocked the air out of him, he still didn't know how to forgive Emelia. Didn't know even where to start. She hadn't told him. That was what burned deepest of all. All their time together and she'd let him think the biggest thing between them was faith, when there'd been another canyon equally wide. And then she'd sat there and just listened as he'd told her how he blamed himself.

She'd let herself get outed by Victor, of all people. He supposed he should be grateful to his brother for shattering the moment before Peter had done something that would have had him wallowing in even more regret, but he couldn't. Especially not now that he knew Victor had been there that night.

He was almost to the door to the parlor when footsteps came from his right, along with a dragging sound. He turned and sucked in his breath.

Emelia. The ball was still weeks away. It hadn't occurred to him for a split second she might be here.

She wore an old T-shirt and yoga pants. Hair pulled back in a haphazard bun with a pencil stuck through the center. A long roll of shimmery silver material was tucked under one arm and dragging beside her. Her attention was focused on that. She had no idea he was standing only a few meters away.

He gripped his mug so tightly, he wouldn't have been surprised if it shattered. There was nowhere to run, nowhere to hide. In a few seconds she'd be right on top of him. "Hi." It was brusque. He didn't know how else to do this.

Emelia started and dropped the roll of material. It unraveled across the wooden floor, spilling a shimmery silver lake in its wake. They both just looked at it until the wooden tube came to a stop.

Emelia spoke. "It's going to be puddles. For between the worlds."

"I'm sorry?"

Emelia gestured at the material. "We're going to put Astroturf down in the entranceway. Then this will be big puddles over the top."

From *The Magician's Nephew*. The woods and pools that transported people between Earth and Lewis's magical worlds. Narnia nerds would love it. "It's a great idea."

He looked up to see she'd come a couple of steps closer. Was looking straight at him. She looked tired. She looked beautiful.

He searched for something neutral to say. If she kept standing there just looking at him like that his heart might crack open. "Is everything going okay? With the planning?"

She looked at him, big blue eyes filled with questions. "Do you hate me?"

He flinched. "I don't hate you. And I owe you an apology."

He tried to loosen his grip on the poor mug he was strangling. "I told you there was nothing you could have done that would make me walk away and then I did. I spent months lecturing you about God, and then when it really mattered, I didn't even live what I said I believed."

"I believe now." Something like surprise flitted across Emelia's face. Like she hadn't meant to say it.

Peter stared at her. "Believe what?"

"'Yes,' said Queen Lucy. 'In our world too, a stable once had something inside it that was bigger than our whole world.'"

It was a Narnia quote she had spoken, no doubt, but he didn't know it. Which meant it had to be from *The Last Battle*. The part he hadn't gotten to.

Emelia seemed to realize it too. "He sent me a teacup. God."

"What?" Was this a really weird dream? He bit the inside of his cheek, the pain confirming it was reality.

"Via your mom. The one in the wardrobe. When we met. She left it on my porch. You didn't know?" She sounded surprised.

He shook his head. Not that it surprised him. His mother was frequently carrying out mysterious errands of kindness that she didn't want anyone else to know about.

"Why did you never tell me the full story? That the teacup in the wardrobe that night was the same one you'd been looking for for years."

"I didn't know if you'd even seen it. And if you had it just sounded too . . ." Something caught in his voice.

"Crazy?"

He gave up a half smile. "Wouldn't you have thought so? We don't exactly live in a world where magical teacups spring up by the dozen."

She shrugged. "True. I don't pretend to even begin to understand any of it now. Least of all why God went to so much effort to get through to a girl like me. But I'm glad He did."

"Me too." He meant it.

"Are you ever going to forgive me?"

His sigh was ragged as he poked at the shimmery ocean with his toe. "I'm trying. You have no idea how much I wish that I could get past this. I just don't know how. Even when I forgive I don't know how to move from there."

Emelia gave him a quivering smile. "It's okay. I get it." She dropped to her knees, started rolling up the material. "I need to get on with this. I'll see you at the ball. Maybe both of us will manage to get at least one thing we're hoping for."

He wanted to be the bigger man. To crouch down beside her and help her cut out magical puddles or whatever it was she was about to do. But there was no wishing on make-believe magic in the world that could fix this. So he turned and walked away.

Forty-Four

By any measure, the ball was a success. The huge wardrobe doors providing the entryway into the ballroom. The garlands hanging from the ceiling. The statues positioned around the perimeters of rooms and in unexpected corners. The huge lamppost that oversaw everything from the center of the dance floor.

Outside, pairs of horses took people on sleigh rides around the estate, complete with cups of hot chocolate and boxes of Turkish delight. A dusting of snow had fallen during the day, giving the countryside a newly whitewashed look.

Since she'd been given the chance to finish what she'd come to England to do, Emelia had spent the last two months eating, sleeping, and breathing the ball. Hadn't given herself any time or energy to think about anything else.

The result? A sellout event featuring some of London's wealthiest Americans. Emelia had never been more right about anything in her life than about targeting the moneyed American wives living in London and pricing the tickets at an amount that screamed "exclusive." Once Lacey had used a few of her London contacts to plant the seed that it was the winter event to be seen at, there was a virtual stampede for tickets.

She had achieved exactly what she had come to Oxford for. She'd saved Anita's charity. And yet it felt meaningless. Flat.

Emelia didn't know what she'd expected when the money was tallied and the outcome known. Relief? A small sense of satisfaction? But all she felt was hollow. Deep down she'd always known this ball was never going to give her the absolution she was looking for. But working out how to forgive herself . . . she didn't even know where to start with that.

There was nothing to keep her in Oxford now. No matter how much she wanted there to be. It wasn't like she'd expected God to sprinkle some magical fairy dust and conjure up a happy ending. Except that was exactly what she had hoped for. If He could land a teacup on her porch, surely He could fix things between her and Peter. Instead all there had been since the day they ran into each other at the house was silence.

Then he'd walked in tonight with Sabine on his arm and Emelia had let go of her final hope. The one that had held out that maybe, maybe, if he knew that she believed what he did, they could still find a way through. But she'd been kidding herself. She'd hurt him too deeply, betrayed him too fully, for that to be enough to glue their relationship back together. She'd tried to summon up a glimmer of gladness for them that they'd worked things out. Sabine was nice. They had history. She'd be the best aspiring Olympian's girlfriend in the world.

Allie was right. Believing in God didn't mean she didn't have to own her stuff and the fallout of her own decisions. Which included losing the best guy she'd ever known.

Focus, Emelia. She almost tripped as a couple pushed past her on their way to the Turkish delight bar. The man offered her a quick "Are you okay?" and at her nod, kept moving. Everyone had places to be, people to be with, except her.

What next, God? Lacey had called that morning, needing an answer on whether Emelia was going to accept the work for her firm. Emelia had managed to hedge a few more days instead of answering. She didn't even know why she was hesitating. It was just freelancing. Hardly a lifetime commitment.

In the corner of the ballroom a string quartet played. Two of the four sat in the thrones that had been created to look like the ones from Cair Paravel in Narnia. The other ground-floor rooms had been equally transformed. The library had turned into Uncle Andrew's study from *The Magician's Nephew*. The entranceway was the wooded area between the worlds. The parlor, the underground land from *The Silver Chair*. Even if you weren't a Narnia fan it was still pretty spectacular.

Speeches were half an hour away. She should do one final circuit of everything. There was no room for complacency just because everything seemed to be going perfectly. Cutting through the crowd, she took the hallway to the kitchen. The same hallway where only a few months ago Peter had threatened to kiss her and she'd thrown it in his face. Her stride was constrained by her red gown. The last time she'd worn it had been the second-worst night of her life. But she couldn't afford a new one.

"Emelia! Just the girl I was hoping to see. The caterers were asking about whether you want the petit fours right at midnight or a little after."

Emelia massaged her temples. There was a run sheet. Why could no one check her beautiful color-coded run sheet?

Breathe in through the nose, out through the mouth, Emelia.

She certainly wasn't going to be rude to Peter's mom, who had given up her house and had insisted on taking charge of running the catering for the evening so that Emelia could focus on everything else.

"Right at midnight is fine." Honestly? She had lost the care factor.

"Got it."

Emelia fished into the folder she was carrying. "Here's an extra run sheet. It should have everything on it." The thing was eighteen pages long. Every detail was covered.

Maggie took it. "Thanks."

"Why are you so nice to me?" The question slipped out before Emelia could even think about it. But she wasn't sorry that she'd asked. In all the time she'd spent at the house in the lead-up to tonight, Maggie hadn't said a single negative word or given her the slightest scathing look, even though she had to know the reason her son had suddenly quit having anything to do with the ball. "Your niece would still be alive if it wasn't for me."

"You know, a lot of people seem to be taking responsibility for that." Maggie made the observation as she arranged some chocolate truffles in a large crystal bowl.

Emelia looked at her.

"Peter blames himself. You blame yourself. Victor blames himself. You're all very determined to condemn yourselves and yet not one of you was there in her last moments. Anita was the one who made the choice that she did. None of you made it for her."

"But I took the photo. I wrote the article."

"And if it wasn't that, it may have been something else."

But it wasn't.

Maggie placed the last truffle on the pyramid she'd constructed. "What the three of you are all looking for isn't going to be found in saving a charity, or winning an Olympic medal, or in the bottom of a whiskey bottle." She quirked up a sad smile. "Emelia, even if you wanted to, you and Peter can't fix each other. Only God can do that."

Peter thought he'd known heartbreak after his rotator cuff had been shredded and he'd lost his shot at Olympic gold. But it didn't come close to comparing with the last two and a bit months.

Sabine looked gorgeous. Blond hair piled in some sort of fancy updo. Shimmering fitted gown. Any guy in the room would have been lucky to have her.

He felt sick. She probably thought there was a chance of their reconciling, but every second with her was proving to him that it didn't matter that she ticked all the boxes; she didn't tick the only one that really mattered.

She wasn't Emelia.

"You don't need to tell me, I already know."

"What?" He looked down to see Sabine surveying him with knowing eyes.

"You were trying to work out a way to tell me that it's not going to be me. But I've known that for months. You've never looked at me the way you look at her." She cast a glance across the room; he followed it to see Emelia weaving her way through the crowd in the same red dress she'd worn to Jackson and Allie's wedding. His breath caught just looking at her.

He turned back to his ex. "I'm sorry, Bine. I wish it was you. I really do."

She shrugged. "Me too. But it's okay. I'm okay."

He didn't know what he'd done to deserve such graciousness.

"I heard about her connection with Anita." He couldn't quite see her eyes at the angle her head was tilted, but he didn't detect any satisfaction in her voice.

Peter couldn't find anything to say. He just stared at the dance floor traveling by under their feet.

"I'm sorry."

"Me too."

"Is it true that Victor checked himself into rehab?"

"That's what my mum said." He hadn't spoken to his brother since the fight but he could only guess it had shaken Victor up as much as it had Peter. What had happened to him? He wasn't a guy who swung fists, no matter how good the reason.

"What happened to us, Seven?" Her change in conversation should have caught him by surprise, but not much did these days. "I know it's all in the past but I still need to know. I feel like one second we had this great relationship, then the next it was over. And I've been telling myself that it was because you were hurting and it was just too hard to see me still living your dream. But that's not it. Well, it's not all of it."

Peter let his gaze travel down to her set jaw. She tipped her head up and her eyes blinked rapidly, a sure sign that she was trying to hold back tears. He'd seen it many times. After disappointing races, when she'd missed out on something she'd had her heart set on.

He didn't want to hurt Sabine anymore. But he couldn't give her what she wanted. "Bine, do you remember our last six months? We weren't good."

"But . . ." Sabine opened her mouth, then closed it. She knew it was true as much as he did.

"I know we had crazy training schedules, but we used that as an excuse not to deal with us. I knew it before I got hurt, but I realized how much we weren't working after. It wasn't because I couldn't deal with you still living the dream. Without rowing we had little to say to each other." They'd tried to fill the gap with watching TV shows and seeing friends. But it didn't change the fact that when the TV was off and the friends had left, there was just awkward silence. "I didn't even know your dad had had a cancer scare."

"I said I was sorry."

"It's not about being sorry. I love you. I will always love you. That means I want you to be happy. I want you to be with a guy who is the first person you want to tell when you have big news. The good, the bad, and the scary. I haven't been that guy in a long time. We just didn't want to see it. Maybe we bought too much into the whole rowing-golden-couple thing. Neither of us likes to let people down."

That was what it came to. When he was with Emelia, she had made him feel like there was more to him than rowing. That there was a life for him beyond it. Now that he'd met Emelia, there was no going back. Even if there was no going forward with her.

Sabine blew out a long breath, the resignation on her face revealing she knew it was true. "So, are the two of you going to get together?"

Peter bit back a bark of laughter. "Not hardly."

Sabine stared across the room for a long few moments, thinking so hard he could practically see the wheels turning in her head. Finally, she spoke again. "I want you to be happy too. I know how much you loved Anita, but you can't hold what happened against Emelia. She was just doing her job."

"I told her about Anita, Bine. About how I blamed myself. And she just sat there. Didn't say a word."

"What did you want her to say, Peter? 'Oh, by the way, that reporter was me'? I don't know anyone who would have been brave enough to do that. Especially if she feels about you the way you do about her."

Peter rubbed his hand across his brow. "Even if we manage to find a way past all that, I don't think she's okay with me wanting to make a comeback." That was one thing he'd learned in the last couple of months. The rowing bug was still in his blood. He couldn't give the dream up without one more try.

Sabine stepped toward him so another couple could pass behind her. "But that can be worked through. You talk about it. Work it out. Like every couple does when someone has been injured. You take too much responsibility for things that don't belong on your shoulders. Always have. Your responsibility is to forgive her. Tell her. You don't just give up on the person who might be the love of your life. The rest is in God's hands."

"You make it sound so simple."

"It is. Doesn't mean it's not hard, but it isn't complicated. And, Peter? If it's not me and it's not Emelia, there will be somebody else. And she'll be even better for you than either of us."

"You don't know that." He wasn't sure where the words

came from, but they struck even him. They sounded bitter. Resentful.

"Except I do. You're a catch, Peter Carlisle. Even if you don't know it." She got up on her tiptoes and dropped a kiss on his cheek. "Now I'm going to go find myself someone to dance with, because it's not a whole lot of fun dancing with someone who wishes I was someone else."

And with that she let go of his hand and stepped away.

"Bine?"

She paused.

"Thanks."

She tilted her head. "You can thank me by winning gold in Tokyo."

Forty-Five

" 'YES,' " SAID QUEEN LUCY. 'IN OUR WORLD TOO, A STABLE ONCE *had something inside it that was bigger than our whole world.'"* Emelia's words had come back to Peter as he watched Sabine walk away. They'd tormented him as he'd tried to play the role of board member. He couldn't remember a single conversation he'd had in the last hour of the event. Hadn't even asked how much money they'd raised. Whether they'd achieved their goal.

He hadn't even stopped to get himself out of his tux when he'd gotten home. He immediately went to a book that had sat in his bedside drawer for over a decade, with a bookmark that had never moved from the last time his grandfather had placed it there.

Peter rested his head against his headboard, closed *The Last Battle*, and placed it beside him on the bed cover. Everything had clicked into place. He had been such a fool. If only he'd read it sooner, realized earlier, things might have been different.

"A true Narnia fan would never ask a girl if they were a Susan or a Lucy." Emelia's words from the first time they'd met circled around his head.

I'm a Susan. And he hadn't understood what she was saying. How she viewed herself. Until now. Emelia saw herself through a distorted looking glass, condemning herself for who she thought she was.

He picked up the book again. Flicking back through its pages to the crucial scene, he read the critical line again.

"'My sister Susan,'" answered Peter gravely, "'is no longer a friend of Narnia.'"

Susan had grown up and called Narnia just a silly game from their childhood. Ultimately, the rest of her family had been summoned back to Narnia and she'd ended up alone.

A six-year-old Emelia had told her mother she didn't want to play her silly Narnia games anymore and her mother had died. Emelia's father had abdicated responsibility and she'd ended up alone. That's why she believed she was a Susan.

He might not have been able to change everything that had happened, but maybe he could change that, figure out a way to show her the truth.

There were now only two things on his to-do list. Win Emelia back. And row his way to Tokyo in 2020. One was hopeful. One was nonnegotiable.

He picked up his phone, selected the required name on his contacts, and let it ring. "Allie, it's Peter. I need your help."

Forty-Six

"This is the place." Of course it was. Of all the places in Oxford, Allie had to want to buy her chair from this one. Two days before she and Jackson flew to Iowa for Christmas. What was she planning to do? Take it back on the train? Did they not have decent antiques shops in Cambridge?

She'd never told Allie which shop she'd met Peter in.

They opened the door. The grizzled proprietor was sitting in the exact same position as the first time Emelia had come into the store. She was pretty sure he was even wearing the same shirt and knitted vest. If not for the absence of cobwebs, she might have suspected he hadn't moved in the last ten months.

Allie pointed toward the archway. "It was in this next room."

Why was she not surprised? Emelia stepped under the archway, preparing herself for whatever it was she might feel when she saw it again. Everything had changed since then.

She stopped. Turning around, she found that Allie had disappeared, the sound of the bell tinkling giving away her rapid exit.

Spinning back around, Emelia tried to take in what was

there. The room had been totally cleared out. The hodgepodge of furniture was all gone. In the middle of the room sat a lamppost—a large wrought-iron one, its head grazing the ceiling as it leaned toward her, beckoning. The one she'd commissioned for the ball. The wardrobe was where it had always been, except it had been moved so it sat against the corner at an angle.

She laughed. A row of mismatched artificial Christmas trees fanned out from either side of the wardrobe. Some looked like the evergreens they were pretending to be, others were outrageously loud versions in silver and gold, like they'd been dragged back from the eighties for the occasion.

Fairy lights crisscrossed the ceiling, their tiny bulbs flashing and dancing to something unheard and magical.

From nowhere, snow started falling. In an antiques shop in Oxford. Wisps of fake snow settled on her nose. Her hair. What in the world? She walked in farther.

On the other wall, a life-sized picture of a fireplace was taped. In front of it sat two armchairs and a small table set with plates and food. Emelia tiptoed forward and peered down. Boiled eggs, sardines on toast, cakes. Just like Mr. Tumnus the fawn had laid out for Lucy when they had afternoon tea.

Something in the room changed. She knew without even turning around that Peter had entered.

She turned slowly, biting back a nervous giggle. Peter was wearing the same ugly sweater that he had at Allie's party. "Hi."

"Hi."

"Hi." Again. She didn't know what else to say.

He smiled. "I think you already said that."

"Then it must be your line. No one gave me the script."

"I need to clear something up first. Actually a few things."

"What?" Emelia batted some fake snow away from her face so she could see Peter more clearly. Whatever this was, she didn't want to miss a moment of it.

"I'm not with Sabine. I forgive you and I'm sorry."

"You're not? You do?" The words came out all breathy. She struggled to hold in the ridiculous grin that was threatening to take over her face; the invisible weight that had been on her had disappeared the moment he said it.

He crossed the room in two strides. "No. Yes. And you are not a Susan."

"You read it?" Fake snow wafted onto Peter's hair and her fingers itched to brush it away.

"For you, I would do almost anything."

She blinked, completely unprepared for the knowledge that he'd finally finished Narnia. For her. Something warm settled in her chest and flowed out into her limbs.

"But I am a Susan. Don't you see? I let myself get distracted and I lost everything. Just like Susan did. Everyone left me." Including him. Or so she'd thought until right this minute.

"You're a Lucy." His words were definite, no doubt in them.

She shook her head, unable to find the words of rebuttal in the face of his insistence.

"Lucy never stopped looking for Narnia. Yearning for Narnia. I met you right here, in this wardrobe, when you fell on top of me. And what were you doing in there?"

"Looking for Narnia." Her words were soft, tentative.

"And then, in Allie's wardrobe, you were . . . ?"

"Looking for Narnia." This time her words were a little more certain, matching the growing hope in her chest.

"And what is the one thing that you can't stop yourself from doing, no matter how hard you try?"

"Climbing into wardrobes and looking for Narnia." Maybe, just maybe, what she'd thought of as the crazy gene inherited from her mom was actually something more.

Peter reached out and grabbed one of her hands, entwining his fingers around hers. "Susan never looks for Narnia. She follows Lucy there through the wardrobe. She gets summoned there by her own horn. Then she grows up and says it was all just a childish game. Susan is cautious and content with positions of ease and comfort. You're one of the bravest people I've ever met."

"I . . ." She wasn't brave. That was the last thing she thought she was.

Peter reached for her other hand and tugged her closer to him. She peered up into his deep green eyes. "Remember the dwarves, in the end, when they're in the true Narnia, but they think they're still in the stable? No matter how much Lucy and Tirian and the others try to tell them the truth. Not even Aslan can convince them otherwise."

Emelia nodded. Not quite able to find words.

"Like the dwarves, you've so convinced yourself as to who you think you are, what you think your life is destined to be, that you can't see the truth even when it's standing right in front of you."

"And what's that?" She could barely force the words out. Terror and anticipation warred inside her.

"That you're a Lucy, who always hopes, always seeks, who

never stops believing, no matter who tells her that she's wrong. That you're an Edmund who made some bad decisions but doesn't let that define you. That you're a Peter who stands up for what is right and just. That, of all the Pevensies, the one that you aren't is Susan. And you're not alone."

It sure didn't feel that way. "Who do I have? My mother is dead, my father is one in name only, I have no real brothers or sisters."

"Me. If you'll have me."

She stared at him. "What are you saying?"

He drew in a shaky breath. "I don't know what I'm saying. I kind of hoped these words would show up and now I'm left with white space."

Wow. That wasn't an anticlimax at all.

Then he reached forward and pulled her to him, tipping her chin up with the pad of his finger. Fake snow flurried around them. Out of the corner of her eye, a garish silver Christmas tree glittered.

"I'm saying that I'm crazy about you, Em. I'm saying that I started falling in love with you the day you fell out of that wardrobe, I've been falling ever since, and I never want to stop. I'm saying that I don't know what this could be, but I will regret it the rest of my life if I don't give it everything I have to find out. And it seems to me that God has gone to some pretty crazy lengths to bring us together, so we should at least try to see what this could be. Oh, and I should tell you I've decided I want to try to make a comeback. A proper one. To get to Tokyo. For me. Not for Anita. I know it isn't exactly—"

Emelia stood on her tiptoes, bunched his sweater between

her fingers, and pulled him down until their noses touched. "Peter. Seriously. Just kiss me."

He gave her the kind of languid smile that stripped away her breath. "With pleasure."

As he buried his hands in her hair, she wrapped her arms around his neck and let her eyes drift closed. For the first time in her life, she allowed herself to begin to believe that maybe she was a Lucy after all.

Author's Note

As a reader living in New Zealand, there is nothing that annoys me more than a character in a book who is supposedly in New Zealand or who is supposedly from New Zealand, and they just *aren't*.

And so it was with much trepidation that I wrote a book set in Oxford (where I've never been) with a hero whose sport is rowing (which I knew nothing about, beyond screaming myself hoarse at the TV every four years during the Olympics). Since, alas, I'm not in the echelon of authors with bank balances that facilitate gallivanting to the other side of the world to research their books, I've had to work with the next best things. But, let's be honest, there's only so much that the combined powers of Google Street View, YouTube, books, and the knowledge of those who actually know what you don't can do before you inevitably get something wrong.

So to those of you (odds are you're either English, a real rower, or in my worst nightmares both) who have caught some kind of error that has made you want to throw the book across the room, my apologies.

First up, thanks to Cambridge for going and winning the Boat Race in March 2016 when I turned this book in in January.

The underdog-cheering part of me was thrilled for you. Not so much the author part of me that had Oxford winning. But good news! It's a novel and, like it says on the copyright page, "any references to historical events, real people, or real places are used fictitiously." Which is great when you forecast an event that will be a historical one by the time your book comes out and get it wrong.

Second up, an ode to the British government for forbidding reading from sacred religious texts during a civil wedding ceremony (that is, a ceremony not held in a church). So, no, in real life Peter couldn't have done a reading from the Song of Solomon at Jackson and Allie's wedding because it would have been illegal. But since I was writing a romance novel, not a how-to guide on getting married in England, I chose cute over bureaucratic correctness.

Thirdly, my apologies to those advisers in the many aspects of this story that I knew nothing about who provided their experience and knowledge, and yet I still managed to get something wrong. I give you the gift of anonymity so you are not tainted with my mistakes.

Finally, my eternal gratitude to YouTube for the many wasted hours when I started off watching rowing tutorials and somehow found myself following that evil sidebar and ending up in some weird corner of the Internet, watching dancing rabbits set to Japanese pop songs.

Acknowledgments

If *Close to You* is the dream-comes-true story, *Can't Help Falling* is the dream-gets-real story. Every book requires a village, but this one felt like it required an entire tri-state area. As always, there are no words that are adequate enough to describe how grateful I am to the team that makes this author life possible.

Jesus: I still can't believe I get to live this writing dream. Thank you for showing your faithfulness in this story. For showing up in all the moments when I was out of my depth and somehow weaving it together when I had no idea how all the pieces fit.

To my husband, Josh: Thank you for being my biggest supporter and my superhero when I had to abandon our Christmas holiday to hibernate in the library for a week and rewrite this book. This living the writing dream wouldn't be possible if it weren't for you.

To the Buddy, the Buzz, and the (ever-growing) Bump: You're still too young to really understand this whole crazy book thing, but I hope one day it inspires you to chase whatever your crazy dreams are (unless they involve risking life and limb, such as being a professional base jumper or rodeo rider, in which case I encourage you watch as many videos on YouTube of said dream as you like and find great fulfillment in pottery or origami).

My amazing SisterChucks: Laurie Tomlinson, Halee Matthews, Jaime Jo Wright, Sarah Varland, and Anne Love. This book would not exist if not for the five of you. Thank you for the brainstorming, the not laughing when I confessed I had 80,000 words but no real plot, assuring me it wasn't as bad as I thought it was (even though it really was), for putting your own writing to the side to read terrible drafts and slightly better rewrites on crazy timelines, and for believing that I had it in me to get it done in the times when it was just a really tough write. But most of all, thank you for your incredible friendship.

My editor extraordinaire: Beth Adams. There had to be moments that you were holding your head in your hands wondering how on earth this story was ever going to come together, but you never showed it. Instead, you made me believe that I had what it took to turn it into something great. You could probably have a lucrative second career as a poker player, if you so desired.

Katie Sandell, Ami McConnell, Bruce Gore, and the rest of the team at Howard Books: for believing in my writing, yet another gorgeous cover, and all the hard work that you do to connect my stories with the right readers. I am so grateful that I get to be on your team.

To my family and family-in-love: Thank you for being so excited about this adventure and for doing your part to help the sales numbers. I'm pretty sure there are people all over the world who have received *Close to You* and who didn't even know we were related!

Elizabeth Norman: for not only agreeing to make sure

Peter could pass as an Englishman but for the stream-of-consciousness messages that you sent as you were reading. You loving this story was when I first started believing that maybe, just maybe, it might not be terrible.

Ann-Maree Beard, Olivia Williams, Fiona Conway, Anna Holmes, Bec Bonnevie, Tina Robilliard, Jen Gibbs, Ally Davey, Steph Mowat, Myra Russell, Nikki Parlane, Elise Teves, and so many other friends who have prayed for this story and stepped into the gap for my family when I have been on deadline and completely overwhelmed with all the balls I'm trying to keep in the air. Thank you.

To Team Harper and Team Benson: for the best dinner parties in the world, where religion, politics, and money are not only perfectly acceptable topics of fierce debate but are actually encouraged. The world would be a better place if everyone had friends like you.

To those wonderful readers out there who loved *Close to You* and took the time to somehow let me know how much you enjoyed it: In the moments when this writing gig has felt beyond me, it's hearing from people like you that makes the hours wrestling to get words on the page worth it. Thank you.